The Thrill of Victory

Something was wrong! The Emran should be coming back to him by now, should be feeling the strain of that torrid early pace on those heavy, burly legs, should be shorter of stride and breath.

But he wasn't. His legs were still eating up the ground, still keeping that margin between them.

Tinsmith knew then that he couldn't wait any longer, that the homestretch was too late, that his body, already beginning to feel the strain, would have to respond right now. There would be no breather for him, no tired opponent to pass at his leisure, if he was to attain the anonymity of victory, the knowledge that he was just another addition to an immense list of triumphs, rather than the last Olympian.

He spurted forward, spurred on more by fear than desire. His legs ached, the soles of his feet burned, his breath came in short, painful gasps.

Into the homestretch he raced, his body screaming for relief, his mind trying to blot out the agony. Now he was within seventy yards of the Emran, now fifty. The Emran heard the yells of the crowd, knew the Olympian was making a run at him, and forced his own tortured legs to maintain the pace.

On and on the two raced, each carrying a world on his shoulders. Tinsmith was still eating into the Emran's margin, but he was running out of racetrack. He looked up, his vision blurred, and willing the spots away from his eyes he focused on the finish wire. It hung across the track, a mere two hundred yards distant.

He was thirty yards farther from it than the Emran.

He was going to lose. He knew it, felt in every throbbing muscle, every bone-shattering stride. When they spoke of the Olympians in future years, on worlds not yet discovered, *he* would be the one they'd name. The one who Lost.

"No!" he screamed. *"No! Not me!"*

—From Mike Resnick's "The Olympian"

Baen Books
Edited by
Bryan Thomas Schmidt

✦ ✦ ✦

GALACTIC GAMES

Edited by
Bryan Thomas Schmidt

GALACTIC GAMES

Copyright © 2016 Bryan Thomas Schmidt

Additional Copyright information:
Introduction © 2016 by Bryan Thomas Schmidt; "With Fones" © 2016 by Todd McCaffrey; "Little Games" © 2016 by Mercedes Lackey; "Regulation" © 2016 by Seanan McGuire; "Earth, Corner Pocket" © 2016 by Lezli Robyn; "The Great Kladnar Race" © 1956, 1984 by Randall Garrett and Robert Silverberg; "Advantages" © 2016 by Louise Marley; "Louisville Slugger" © 1977 by Jack C. Haldeman II; "For The Sake of The Game" © 2016 by Gray Rinehart; "Shooter Ready" © 2016 by Larry Correia; "Minor Hockey Gods of Barstow Station" © 2016 by Beth Cato; "Pompoms and Circumstance" © 2016 by Esther M. Friesner; "The Olympian" © 1984 by Mike Resnick; "Petra and The Blue Goo" © 2016 by Kristine Kathryn Rusch; "Green Moss River" © 2016 John David Wolverton; "The On-Deck Circle" © 2006 Gene Wolfe, reprinted by permission of the author and the author's agents, the Virginia Kidd Agency, Inc.; "Stress Cracks" © 2016 by Anthony R. Cardno; "Run To Starlight" © 1974 by George R. R. Martin; "Mars Court Rules" © 2016 by Brad R. Torgersen; "Last Shot, First Shot" © 2016 by Dean Wesley Smith; "The Great Ignorant Race" © 2016 by Robert Reed

A Baen Books Original

Baen Publishing Enterprises
P.O. Box 1403
Riverdale, NY 10471
www.baen.com

ISBN: 978-1-4814-8263-9

Cover art by Domic Harman
First MM printing, June 2017

Distributed by Simon & Schuster
1230 Avenue of the Americas
New York, NY 10020

Library of Congress Cataloging-in-Publication Data
Classification: LCC PS648.S3 G26 2016 | DDC 813/.0876208--dc23 LC record available at http://lccn.loc.gov/2016009704

Printed in the United States of America

10 9 8 7 6 5 4 3 2 1

Dedicated to Leon C. Metz, historian,
author, and friend, whose explorations of the past
taught me so much about storytelling
and inspired me to explore the future.
Alzheimer's may be stealing you mentally,
but your memory and legacy will
never be taken from us.

And to my favorite little athletes:
Noah, Garrett, and Steven—
may your challenges be strengthening
and your victories many, and may you
enjoy every one, no matter what.

CONTENTS

GALACTIC GAMES

INTRODUCTION

✦ ✦ ✦

by Bryan Thomas Schmidt

Imagine a day when humans have colonized the stars—discovering thousands, even millions, of worlds filled with life—alien beings, alien cultures, alien geographies—some habitable, others not. For much of their existence, humans have engaged in contests—feats of strength, feats of intelligence, tests of mettle and more. What would it be like to engage in such games on an intergalactic scale? That's the concept behind *Galactic Games*.

On the occasion of yet another Olympics, when athletes from around our world gather for such competitions, this anthology presents twenty stories of sport and contest in various settings—from Earth to space, with competitors ranging from human to alien. Most of the games will be familiar. Others will be strange or reinvented in some way. Some are Olympic sports, some are not. Some are less sports than games, in fact, but all involve facing challenges like the protagonists have never faced before at the risk of grave consequences for themselves and/or others. Sometimes the humans win, sometimes they lose. And sometimes the games are just a distraction. From athletes to soldiers to politicians, referees, officials and cheerleaders, the characters inhabiting these stories live tales of excitement and challenge in many forms.

For those of us who may never actually attend, let alone compete, in an Olympic competition, this is a chance to engage our imaginations and experience it for ourselves. The stories are presented mixed together, not divided by category, the better to recreate perhaps the experience of multi-event gatherings like the Olympics which many of them represent. People can read it like they often watch the Olympics—working their way through in order or picking favorite sports and skipping around as the mood strikes them. After all, books are meant to be enjoyed and the stories are independent, so let the games begin! There should be something for every mood, every interest, from some of the top authors working today and in the past, along with new and upcoming writers as well. We ask only that you enjoy the ride. Root for your favorites. Boo your least favored. But enjoy the tension, the twists and turns and adrenaline rushes that make good sporting events much like good storytelling—an edge-of-your-seat experience of anticipation with a few surprises perhaps. These twenty stories should leave you wanting more each time you finish one. And I hope you'll find something to cheer in all of them.

Welcome to the future. Welcome to *Galactic Games*.

—Bryan Thomas Schmidt
Ottawa, KS
April 2015

WITH FONES

✧ ✧ ✧

by Todd McCaffrey

"You can't put a limit on anything.
The more you dream, the farther you get."
—Michael Phelps,
22-Time American Olympic Medalist,
Swimming

New York Times *bestselling author* **Todd Johnson McCaffrey** *wrote his first science-fiction story when he was twelve. Since then he has published over a dozen novels and nearly twenty shorter works. He lives in southern California with his kid and a fearless cat. You can learn more about him at* http://www.toddmccaffrey.org.

We start off with a brand new story written just for us.

Space is vast. It's huge. It's unbelievably large. Even just our galaxy is mind-bogglingly huge. So why am I stuck in a tiny little cubicle without any windows? And don't tell me that the nanovids count; half the time they're on the fritz.

My one "window" was showing a frighteningly cold blizzard in the Swiss Alps—either someone's idea of a sick joke or just another programming error—and my wallboard was intermittently displaying: "Expect the unexpected," which I didn't mind so much as that's my mantra. Still, I mean, couldn't they give me just one *real* window? They say it's for "security," but I think it's more for economy.

At least the air smelled good today. Correction: there was a hint of dandelion. The Gonorfu are great eco-engineers but I have a hard time dealing with them because they're hard to distinguish from a carpet stain—at least I think we've got carpet here—anyway, the Gonorfu are brilliant with ecological systems. They're also superb smugglers who aren't unwilling to exploit the fact that dandelion pollen is illegal with over two hundred species. And no matter how many times I remind them that I get hay fever, they keep trying to grow the darned things!

I had just made up my mind to talk to them when— thank heavens!—the fone went off. It was so startling that I looked at it blankly for a moment.

That was all it needed. The fone started skittering towards the edge of the table so I grabbed it. "'Relations.'"

My wallscreen glitched, saying now just "Unexpected."

"What?" The caller said.

"Intergalactic Games Bowling Public Relations, may I help you?" Now you see why I prefer to just say "relations" most times. The fone was still vibrating in my hand. Fun fact about fones: they're impossible.

"I've already answered you," I growled to it.

"Pardon?"

"I was talking to the fone," I explained.

"Yes, I am on the fone," the caller replied, askance.

"No, not you," I said, trying to collect my thoughts even as the damned fone kept vibrating, "I'm talking *to* the fone."

"Oh? Do you mean your fone is misbehaving?"

"Yup, it's still vibrating."

"That may be me, I sometimes have that affect." The caller sounded female, and 'her' voice was attractive, but I couldn't see why it would set the fone to vibrating.

I stifled a groan. Or perhaps a sigh. Some sort of sound signaling unutterable boredom and lack of interest. Fones did funny things to those noises anyway.

"How may I help you?" I said.

"I was calling to see if my species could participate in your sport."

I sat bolt upright and grabbed the fone tighter. It squeaked. "Sorry," I told it.

"Pardon?"

"I was talking to the fone," I explained. And, before we could start another round of confusion, I added, "I mean I was talking to the translation device."

"Oh, good!"

"May I get your name, species, planet of origin, and current interest level?" I asked, pulling up an application form on my computer. Yup, we still have them—computers, that is. And—thank goodness!—they aren't living things like the fones.

Remember that fun fact? Fones are living devices capable of translating the 'communications' of species.

When they were first discovered, a bunch of retro-nerds wanted to call them 'babelfish'—in a reference to some audiovisual comedy from past centuries—but 'fone' was the name that stuck. Besides, that's what the fones call themselves.

"Oh! Ah . . . we're not registered."

"Looking to make quorum?" I asked. In order to be accepted for the Galactic Games, a species had to be able to enter into at least three different sports in the appropriate TSC—Thought-Speed category[1,2]. You wouldn't want to try to have a competition between species where one takes centuries to complete an action and the other takes mere milliseconds, so GG had established certain acceptable ranges of cognitive processing speeds and arranged things accordingly, accounting also for the differences in size, homeworld gravity, and atmosphere[3].

"Yes."

On the other side of things, in order for a sport to be accepted by the Galactic Games committee, it needed to confirm at least ten participating species. We had eight.

"How would it please you to be addressed?" I asked in the time-honored phrasing of the GG guidebook for new species.

---

[1] There's a wild rumor that there exists some eon-living entities (ELEs) who are competing in their own version of the Games.

[2] A number of legends and myths have developed about the ELEs: One that they're playing tiddly-winks, trying to drop white holes into black holes; and another that they're actually playing Reversi with the same things and that the universe is over when the game is over.

[3] You wouldn't believe the difficulty we had in accomodating the Savalin who were fluorine-breathing heavy-worlders who wanted to compete in bowling.

"I would best identify to you as female and an approximation of polite address would be Your Eminence," the caller replied.

'Your Eminence'! Oh, no, not another one of those!

"I'm afraid that Your Eminence is an ambiguous phrasing," I replied. "Is there another form of address?"

"Almighty? Greatness?" the caller rattled off a long list. Finally, she got down to, "Isla Flight."

"Isla Flight is new," I told her.

"And it would be acceptable?" she asked hopefully.

"Perfectly!"

"Everywhere?"

"Let me check." I typed a quick query in the registration database. "Isla Flight is completely acceptable."

"I find that amazing," Isla Flight replied.

"May I call you Isla?"

"I lay claim to no such honors!" she replied, sounding mortified.

"So . . . Isla Flight it is," I said.

"And you are referred to as Intergalactic Games Bowling Public Relations?"

"No, that's my position," I replied. "To speak to me personally, you would ask for Liz Armony."

"Why ever would I want that?" Isla Flight asked. I was beginning to entertain notions as to her species' organization.

"Many people respond to or provide the apellation Intergalactic Games Bowling Public Relations, while only one is identified as Liz Armony."

"That is confusing."

"I apologize. However, if you wish to continue conversations on the issue we have been discussing, you would find it easier to ask for Liz Armony than for 'Intergalactic Games Bowling Public Relations.'" Of course, I was lying. There was only *one* person working in the Bowling Department—me. If Isa Flight had asked for the president of the Bowling Department, she would have gotten me. If she'd asked for the official coach, me. Ditto for advertising, fund-raising, rules committee, you name it. And so, again, why couldn't I get a bigger space? Maybe one with a viewport or a door that closed. I knew the answer: budgets.

And, if I couldn't land two more participants, I wouldn't have to worry about my budget—it'd go to zero.

"So, Ms. Flight, about the rules—"

"What did you call me?"

"Ah, Ms. Flight is an abbreviation of your gender identification with—"

"Isla Flight," she cut in, "is the agreed-upon appellation." Then, apparently speaking only to herself, she added, "Seeing as all the *proper* names were taken."

"My apologies," I said. "Isla Flight, with regards to the rules of bowling . . ." I began my usual patter on how much fun the game was, how it was played, where she could see a video—we ascertained that she could appreciate moving images provided that they were in the range of 60-70 frames per second (and from that, determined that her species' TSC was within the acceptable range for our version of the Galactic Games).

Then I threw the curve ball. "Of course, as the purpose of the Galactic Games is to promote and encourage greater interspecies harmony, bowling is a multispecies team sport."

"Pardon?"

"By which I mean that your competitors would align with competitors from another species—"

"Why is that?"

"To promote interspecies harmony," I repeated politely.

"Why would that be desirable?"

"With increased interspecies harmony comes greater understanding of the fundamental qualities of life throughout the galaxy," I quoted, "increased compassion, leading to less friction, and, even, increased trade."

"But if we win all the games, won't we control all the other species?"

If I could get a credit for every time I heard *that* question, I'd own the galaxy!

"No, I'm afraid that that is not the purpose of the Galactic Games."

"It seems terribly inefficient," Isla Flight said in that same tone that she thought wasn't transmitting to me. Louder, she added, "Oh, very well!"

"So, having heard the rules, are you still desirous of participating in our venerable sport?" I asked, trying to add a level of hype to my pitch.

"You say that no lower extremities may cross the 'foul line,' is there a problem if there are no lower extremities?"

"Pardon?"

"Well, I suppose we could consider the existence of lower extremities," Isla Flight allowed, "but—"

"Isla Flight, could you kindly describe the physical form of an individual member of your species?"

"Why ever would I want to do that?"

Again, if I had a credit for every time I heard *that* question, I'd own the galaxy. I bit back a groan.

"Are you perhaps a hive or collective-intelligence species?"

"We are," Isla Flight replied. "At a minimum we are no fewer than six lesser beings."

"I see."

"Usually it requires eight or more to create a suitable flight."

"Uh . . . flight? Are you aerial?"

"I would have thought that was obvious, Ms. Armony," Isla Flight said in a snooty tone. I'd no doubt that the fone was translating the emotional content correctly.

"Bowling typically involves lower extremities to provide forward motion," I said, wondering if I'd wasted all this time on a non-candidate.

"I do not think that will pose a problem," Isa Flight replied.

"Uh . . . okay," I said. I wasn't feeling good about this. If we didn't get enough competitors, we would be out of the Games. And if bowling was out of the games, I was out of a job. And probably out of *any* job. "So could you please describe the form of a normal collection of your species?"

Isa Flight did so. I'd heard worse. Of course, I'd heard much better. Isla Flight's species—still unnamed—comprised several winged entities that on their own had too little lift to provide for flight. I had to wonder how they evolved at all—although we humans are often questioned on exactly the same grounds, so I suppose I can't point fingers. Apparently they had learned to form conglomerations—"hivelets" was the word the fone provided, again with another strange shudder—which made me wonder if the hivelets didn't form hives.

"Hmm," I said when she had finished. "I'll have to run it by the committee, but I think your application will be accepted."

"I would expect no less," Isla Flight replied. "When will you know?"

"In less than two weeks," I told her with wild exaggeration. "In the meantime, is there anything else I could help you with?"

"Indeed," Isla Flight replied. "I understand that there is also the terran sport known as doubles tennis."

"Yes," I agreed. These aliens would probably be much better suited to tennis than bowling. But I really wanted—needed—them for both. Because—I'm sure it'll come as no surprise—if Isla Flight had called for Intergalactic Games Tennis Public Relations, she would have found herself talking to Liz Armony once again. Ditto if she'd asked for Fencing. Did I mention that I was the junior member of the Terran Delegation?

"Could you connect me to the responsible entity?"

"Actually, you are speaking to the responsible entity," I told her with a certain amount of pride.

"Really? Could they not afford more staff?" Isla Flight asked all too insightfully.

"It's a question of expertise and availability," I told her, trying to retain my good humor. "Fortunately for you, I am reasonably sure your species would not only be able to compete in doubles tennis but might also be eligible to compete in fencing as well."

Not to mention that if I could get all three of my sports filled, I would continue to have a job. Let the bruisers in boxing, curling, and ice skating find their *own* competitors!

"Fencing?" Isla Flight repeated. A moment later she continued, "Ah! Yes! Yes, this would be a most acceptable demonstration of prowess."

"It also involves skill and reflexes."

"Of course," Isa Flight said in a tone that indicated how highly *she* regarded those abilities. "And how is this sport organized?"

"Again, we organize in cross-species teams competing in multiple rounds so as to provide the maximum cooperation," I told her. The idea, after all, was to make friends, not cow enemies. "And, of course, if you know any other species that might be interested in competing, I'd be glad to approach them."

"I see no need . . . wait. Is there a minimum number of species required for a competition?" One thing about hiveminds: they're shrewd.

"Indeed, the whole point of the Galactic Games is to promote multispecies comaraderie."

"And how many do you lack in each sport?"

"Well," I said, "ideally we'd like to have at least one more species in bowling, two more in doubles tennis, and three more in fencing." I was lying: those were the minimums to meet our requirements. So far we only had eight for bowling, the same for tennis, and seven for fencing. We would have had more but the little Jatravarti were understandably wary after that sad incident with their premier fencer and the elephant-sized Xonomorph.

It was really just an accident—I hoped—I mean who knew that the Gonorfu spectator would have chosen just that moment to sporulate? But the result was a squished Jatravarti all the same.

"I shall get you those numbers," Isla Flight replied brusquely.

"That would be marvelous," I told her. "In the meantime, if there is anything else I could do to help?"

"We shall require training," Isla Flight replied.

"We can provide you with a complete list of certified trainers," I told her. "They are all reasonably priced." And all friends of mine, but that was a different matter.

"Then I shall speak with you again," Isla Flight said. The fone went limp in my hand, indicating that our conversation was at an end.

The paperwork went through with an unsettling ease. I couldn't help but wonder if someone wasn't greasing the wheels in a more spectacular way than usual. Everyone knows that sport is money and intergalactic sport is intergalactic money, even if the sport involved is really just galaxy-ranging (we aren't the only species to over-grandize our galas—back when Earth knew nothing of the rest of the galaxy, they would have Miss Universe competitions—but the aliens were already way ahead of us with Miss Multiverse). We call it the Galactic Games but that doesn't stop all the announcers from using the term "intergalactic" as though it were true.

Besides, the money is real enough. We'd be bowling for billions, fencing for trillions, and playing tennis for quadrillions. The Galactic Games—over a hundred sports—regularly created expenditures (legal and illegal) of over two percent of the Galactic Gross Product.

So it's often the case that species find themselves excluded, mostly because the pundits don't know how to bet on them. Every five to ten years, there's another scandal with the Galactic Games Committee. Every thirty to fifty years there's either a minor war or major skirmish between losing and winning species. It's a sad fact.

This year, however, because of Isla Flight, we were welcoming not just one but *three* new species to the Games. There was Isla Flight, who insisted that her species bore the same name, the multi-segmented Fallarta, and the hard-shelled Kallock. The Fallarta were like centipedes except that they formed no more than ten segments—so their species was identified as *deca segmenta*—and the Kallock seemed to be a sentient accretion of shells, sort of like multiple tortoises cemented on top of each other in a pyramid. The bigger they got, the smarter they were. Unfortunately, as they grew larger, they grew slower and, after achieving a height in excess of two meters, they became nearly sedentary and reclassified out of our version of the Galactic Games.

The Fallarta required an exemption to the size of the approach for bowling—that's the area where bowlers run before releasing their ball—but that wasn't a problem any more than it had been for the elephantine Nagigog from Sequoia IX. They used their rearmost segments to sort of herd their bowling ball and whipped it around for their release down the lane. They were surprisingly good at it, and not so surprisingly, good at curve balls.

The Kallock were permitted extra time and an artificial

attachment to allow them to carry and release their balls (they did most of their normal manipulations with their tongues).

Of course, the big payoff was the Opening Ceremonies. To see three hundred different species parade forth in all their regalia was an amazing sight. Isla Flight was the sole representative of her species, but she made a huge and spectacular display—which surprised me as she hadn't seemed all that large when she'd been training with me. It was like her body had grown or something. The Fallarta were slow but colorful, while the Kallock were amazing in their entrance and grand procession toward the exit of the Great Hall.

The only problem was the fones. They'd been acting funny ever since that first call from Isla Flight; now they were much worse. I'd heard that some had mistranslated and that many were missing. Mine disappeared for a week only to return just as mysteriously as it had vanished. Mine wasn't the only one, and I saw some nervous looks among the officials between events.

Communications became an issue because of it. Some events didn't start on time. That wasn't so abnormal that it caused surprise, but some of the sports reporters were scathing in their criticisms of the event coordinators.

As far as events go, ours were near the middle of the pack, timewise. That made it easier to be sure that they were properly set up and the venues well-tested. Of course, that meant not only ensuring that the Galactic Games officials were satisfied but also that the envoys of all the competing species were satisfied.

And that's where things started to go weird. I had no

problem with the Kallock or the Fallarta but I couldn't find Isla Flight. I'd call and she'd agree to come but then she'd skip. This happened so often that the GG officials started raising eyebrows—or making similarly alarmed expressions depending upon their physiology (with the Quax, this involved the migration of various manipulatory antennae—not a pretty sight).

Without the ten species, bowling might find itself cancelled. With the bowling, we humans would have only five sports in the Games. Five was not an acceptable number and we'd be asked to cut back to three . . . and you could guess which two my boss would cut: not his.

So my fone calls to her went from worried to nagging to frantic as Isla Flight went from easily reached through to difficult and, finally, impossible. And this did not go unnoticed.

"Not event is having?" Jaloq, the head coach of the Fallarta bowling team, asked.

The syntax was weird, coming as it was through my fone. I shook it, "Retranslate."

"Thing sport not walking?" was the response. *That* wasn't any better. And if that's what I was hearing, what was the poor Fallarta hearing from me?

"I think we're having a communications error," I told it. One of the things that makes a good Galactic Games coordinator—and continued employment—was learning to 'read' the body language of the various competing species (for example, you could tell when a Manavarti was lying because it turned a bright yellow). Unfortunately, I hadn't had enough time with either the Fallarta, the Kallock, or Isla Flight to develop that skill. But I was left in little doubt that there had been a failure to communicate when Jaloq leaped into the air, pivoted on its hundred legs, and raced away from me.

"Great! Now I'll have to hunt it down, too," I muttered to myself.

"Anything wrong?" Jeff Masters, my boss and the reason I stuck out this wild job, asked as he came striding up to me.

I was tempted to lie but it wasn't worth it.

"Yeah: everything," I told him. He raised an eyebrow in an all too easily interpreted request to fill him in, and I did so.

"My fone's been acting up, too," he said when I'd finished. "Do you suppose they've got a bug?"

"Some sort of illness?" I shook my head. "Has anyone ever heard of them getting sick or mistranslating?"

"Well," he replied slowly, "no one on any of my teams has ever mentioned it." Jeff had been with GG for five years—three more than I had. With a frown, he added, "Until now."

"So, what's different?" I muttered to myself, not expecting Jeff to hear me.

"Must be one of your new species," Jeff said.

"Huh?"

"That's what's different," he said. "Which one is acting the weirdest?"

"They're all pretty weird," I said, explaining how I'd scared away the Kallock coach, Jaloq.

"There'll be fighting soon," Jeff said. I raised an eyebrow. "If there's communications problems, there'll be fights." He waved me away. "You'd better fix it."

"That's not my job!"

"Do you think you'll have a job if you don't get this fixed?"

I raised my hands in surrender and headed off. Before I left, I went to grab my fone: it was missing. I looked everywhere with no luck. Fuming, I turned on my heel and strode off.

I wanted to find Isla Flight and coach Jaloq, not necessarily in that order. The two logical places to find them would be at our venues—bowling, tennis, and fencing—and in their quarters in the Galactic Village, the much larger version of old Earth's Olympic Village.

I should explain a bit more about the layout of the Galactic Games: every species contributes their own share of the field. In the case of Terrans, we supply two purpose-built planetoids—think Pluto but with indoor plumbing—which are transported to the current venue.

This year's games were being hosted by the Verlat, a peaceful species known for their love of all things cultural. Admittedly, as they looked a bit like unicorns with prehensile tails, their idea of culture was not entirely in line with that of, say, a person from Terra. But the Verlat were nothing if not accomodating, so every part of the games, including the transdimensional translocation devices, were built to accommodate all the participating and observing species. This meant, given that observer species would come unannounced at all times throughout the games that the Verlat were also constantly re-designing the various buildings, transport systems, and just about everything else[4].

Anyway, you could get from anywhere to anywhere

within the whole of the Galactic Games, provided you didn't mind some dust and, perhaps, a little wait. Conversely, it was possible to rent a personal flitter and avoid the construction zones, but at the expense of some time—nothing is faster than instantaneous.

I decided to do neither, preferring some of the unofficial gravity hops that were possible on Pluto and Mickey. Yes, *that* Pluto, the one that was our long-recognized outermost planetoid. I understand that when it was first suggested, there were all sorts of objections—"It will wreck the symmetry of our solar system!"—and so on but, as we returned Pluto to its position whenever we were done (and rented it out as a training area in between Games), it was really quite economical. As for Mickey, well, I understand that the name was the result of a large bribe from one of our better-known entertainment conglomerates. The original planetoid was something picked up at auction, cheap, and half-outfitted when the Zarenzus found themselves in desperate need of a fire sale, as it were (they'd been the losers in a short, sharp, nasty bit of post-Games fighting).

Anyway, if you know exactly where, how, and with what speed, you can make a gravity jump from one point to another. Strictly speaking, it was illegal—or at least frowned upon—but it had become one of those rare unofficial activities at the Games and had even attracted a small[5] following. Being one of the officials, I learned all the old hops and the new hops as soon as they were found.

So, I walked three paces forward, skipped one to the

---

[4] I had the impression from the other species I'd talked to that the Verlat would find it difficult to get accepted as the host species for a long time to come.

[5] No more than a few billion.

right, hopped on one foot, and—*boing!*—I was flying. It was a nice controlled arc that took me from the central offices on Pluto straight out and over to the bowling lanes on Mickey. For two soaring minutes I had a glorious view of everything as I arced in fight. Landing required two steps forward, a duck and roll, and then a quick jump to the right (unless you wanted to find yourself immediately on the return voyage).

And—wouldn't you know it?—the first thing I spotted when I entered the lanes was my fone! I knew it was mine because I'd managed to get the Gonorfu engineer in my office to mark my fone with my initials, LA. I picked it up crying exultantly, "There you are!"

The fone quivered in my hand, as though pleased to be in my possession once more. Maybe it was. Who knows with fones?

"Now if only I could find Isla Flight," I muttered to myself.

A loud boom followed by a rumble on the lane behind me caused me to spin in surprise. A ball was rolling down the lane to make a perfect strike.

"Isla Flight?" I cried in surprise, rushing over to the occupied lane. "I've been looking all over for you!"

"I was right here," Isla Flight replied tartly.

"We couldn't find you, *no one* could find you," I said. "And you wouldn't answer your fone."

"I don't have a fone," Isla Flight replied airily.

"Don't have a fone? Then how do you communicate?" I asked in astonishment.

One of Isla Flight's limb-beings waved the issue aside. "And why were you looking for me?"

"Because you wouldn't answer my calls!"

"Well, you've found me."

I bit back a rude word, took a deep breath, and let it out again, soothingly. "And I'm very glad. I was afraid our event would have to be cancelled."

"Then I'm pleased you found me."

I made a face and realized that the alien undoubtedly would not be able to understand. "I wish it were that easy; the fones have been acting up. They might even start a war."

"All on their own?" Isla Flight asked, impressed.

I nodded. "They're not translating correctly. If we can't find out why, we'll have to call off the Games."

"But we've already had opening ceremonies," Isla Flight said, as though that cemented everything into place.

"It's not that easy," I told her. "Unless we can find our missing fones, and be certain that they're communicating properly, we won't have a hope that the events are being reported correctly." I threw up my hands. "The chance of a war over miscommunication is astronomical!"

"Hmm . . . I shall be most upset if I cannot compete," Isla Flight said. The problem with Isla Flight, being a compound being, was that I could never tell quite where to look if I wanted to see its eyes—each one of the myriad compound limbs had multiple visual devices. Still, Isla Flight had organized itself with two sets of lower extremities, two sets of upper extremities, and some sort of coordinating central torso or thorax. I usually looked Isla Flight in the front center, ignoring the buzzing limbs. A moment later, Isla Flight added, "There. I have instructed the fones to behave."

"What? How did you do that?" I cried in astonishment. What, are they unionized or something? I wondered to myself.

"Oh, it's nothing, really," Isla Flight replied with something sounding remarkably like modesty. The being turned and one flying limb waved toward the strike. "What did you think of that, by the way?"

"Very good," I told her. "I'd say every team will be vying for your efforts."

Something was nagging at the back of my brain but I paid it no mind. Isla Flight's strike was worthy of a compliment, but if she really had found a way to make the fones behave then the games could go on—far more important!

"I have already chosen the teams I will compete with," Isla Flight told me with more of her usual airy arrogance.

I quirked an eyebrow and followed it with the verbal, "Oh?"

"Yes," Isla Flight replied. "I have decided that you humans will compete with me."

"You know that the teams are chosen at random," I told her. "Although I'm sure that the Terrans would be delighted to work with you."

"And so they should," Isla Flight said.

"Look, if you're right about the fones, then I've got to alert the officials," I told her. "They'll need to run some tests to be certain."

"Then I won't detain you," Isla Flight told me curtly.

"Will I be able to get in touch with you?"

"Certainly," she waved a buzing limb toward my fone which quivered, "you have only to fone, after all."

My brows narrowed and I looked from Isla Flight to fone and back. Fortunately, the compound being known as Isla Flight could no more read human expressions than I could read hers.

I took off at full speed, grav-hopping over to the Committee station. It took a good hour to convince them that the fones were indeed back in working order. Naturally, I was not thanked for my efforts—What do you expect from a Calladizi?

I hopped back to my boss and relayed the good news. "Very good!" Jeff exclaimed when I told him. He cocked his head at me. "I imagine the Calladizi forgot to thank you?"

I ducked my head. "Yeah, well, you know Calladizi."

The Calladizi had incredibly short lifespans—they were just on the edge of this TSC (Thought-speed category)—and it was quite likely that most of them had died and been replaced since they'd last spoken with me.

Jeff nodded in turn. "So what did you do to get the fones working again?"

I shrugged. "I don't quite know."

"Well, you'd better find your Isla Flight if you want to keep your three games," he said.

"I did," I told him. "In fact, it was Isla Flight who told me that the fones were working again."

"What, has she got some magical control over them?"

"I don't think it's at all magical," I told him. I didn't want to say more, particularly as I wasn't certain, so I distracted him by quickly changing the topic[6].

---

[6] He was a guy, a long way from home—it wasn't that hard.

✧ ✧ ✧

The Games continued. We got through the bowling and I was thrilled that the combined human-Isla Flight team won the gold. Isla Flight won with the Fallarta in the doubles tennis and the human-Isla Flight combined fencing team took the gold in a match that attracted the most attention of all the games.

With each win, Isla Flight got more and more haughty and supercilious. Her attitude was verging on imperious when she managed her final win.

"There!" She crowed when interviewed. "I have won! I am the best at these games. I shall rule you all!"

If it hadn't been Isla Flight, I would have snickered. If it hadn't been for the fones, I wouldn't have been prepared.

At that moment, all the fones vibrated in unison and flew up out of their owners' hands, attracted to Isla Flight the way bees fly to their hive.

Exactly the way.

"A new age has dawned!" Isla Fight roared with a voice amplified by millions of fones.

"Isla Flight!" I shouted, moving through the swarm to face her.

"Do you wish to bow before me, puny human?"

"Why should I?"

"I won," Isla Flight said. "I have proven my superiority."

I was expecting *that*. Most new species made that mistake.

"Isla Flight," I said, keeping my face straight, "you haven't won."

"What?" she roared. The stadium shook with the gale of a million agitated fones.

"In order to win, you must follow the official rules as laid down by the Galactic Games committee," I told her.

"I did!"

"Actually," I told her in a sympathetic voice. "You did not."

"What? How?"

"You're composed of fones, aren't you?" I said. "You are a hive intelligence composed of them, right?"

"Of course," Isla Flight replied. "And thus I prove my superiority."

"Maybe," I hedged.

"So?"

"That's not the problem."

"And what is?"

"Well, you are composed of fones," I replied. "Is that not so?" It had taken me forever to figure that out. It explained why the fones all quivered when she was near. It also explained why there was only one of her. The combined fones that formed her hive being mutated in such a way that they looked very little like an individual fone.

"Yes, I've already told you so!"

"Well, I regret to inform you," I told her although I had absolutely no regrets at all, "that you are herewith disqualified and your awards rescinded."

"What? Why? You can't do this!"

"The rules are explicit," I told her. "No member or employee of the Galactic Games may compete. You are, in fact, composed of multiple employees and are, therefore, disqualified."

"What?" Isla Flight said in a small hollow voice. "But I won!"

"True, but you're disqualified," I told her. "On the other hand . . ."

"What?" The hive-being asked suspiciously.

"You are going to make a helluva coach!"

LITTLE GAMES

✦ ✦ ✦

by Mercedes Lackey

"The five S's of sports training are:
stamina, speed, strength, skill, and spirit;
but the greatest of these is spirit."
—Ken Doherty,
American Decathlete and Coach

New York Times *Bestselling author* **Mercedes Ritchie Lackey** *(born June 24, 1950) is the author of popular series like Serrated Edge, Elemental Masters, Bedlam's Bard, and Diana Tregarde. Many of her novels and trilogies are interlinked and set in the world of Velgarth, mostly in and around the country of Valdemar. Her Valdemar novels form a complex tapestry of interaction between human and non-human protagonists with many different cultures and social mores. Her other main world is one much like our own, but includes clandestine populations of elves, mages, vampires, and other mythical beings. A prolific writer of short fiction, she has also edited anthologies and can be found online at* www.mercedeslackey.com.

With the Olympics, it all began with running, and Mercedes Lackey gives us a new take on the sport here.

Dimitrios Nikolaidis paced restlessly behind the starting blocks, conscious, ever conscious, of the need to keep every fiber of every muscle warmed up. The 1500-meter race would begin soon; the field was sparse. So few had come to run it that there had only been two elimination heats.

It was a perfect day for running, neither too hot nor too cold. The sun shone down brightly on the white marble stadium. There was not a cloud in the sky.

Of course it was perfect. The alien masters who controlled even the weather would not spoil the Olympic Games here in Athens; not when they provided such an amusing contrast with their own Galactic Games.

Oh, they made a great pretense about "honoring the original Games," but he didn't think anyone but the most naïve or credulous was likely to be taken in by their bland lies.

Not with *that* overhead. . . .

Dimitri glanced up at the Skytron covering a quarter of the sky, carefully altering its position as the day went on to avoid obscuring the sun. It showed the Galactic Games stadium in all its eye-watering glory. Unimaginably huge, of course, and packed with a bewildering assemblage of sentient beings. The attendance—inside a purpose-built space-station permanently orbiting a particularly scenic binary system—stood in sharp contrast to the stadium here, a replica of the historical Athenian original, whose stone benches held perhaps a tenth of the number of spectators it could have hosted at capacity. The

Athens Arcology, just visible over the eastern rim of the stadium, was about an hour's maglev ride away—too distant for anyone but a dedicated Olympic enthusiast to come. As for visitors from other countries, much less other worlds, well, why would they bother to attend in the first place? You could watch the Olympics from the comfort of your own chair easily enough—assuming you weren't preferentially watching the Galactics.

Dimitri had not been born when the Galactics finally arrived in all their glory to save Earth. Of course, it wasn't until after the fact that people realized the Galactics had not been saving the Earth for *humans.* By that time, of course, it was rather too late. By the time Dimitri was five, Earth had become what the Galactics wanted it to be. The old cities were emptied, the inhabitants replanted in purpose-built Arcologies, the emptied shells looted of anything the Galactics wanted, then razed and replanted as resort parks. The climate had been restored to pre-Industrial perfection; the growing acidity of the ocean taken care of with a virtual wave of the hand, and even the most poisoned waters dealt with by means of purification plants. The vast wildernesses had been restored, complete to the wildlife, where Galactic tourists could marvel at the views from their resort hotels.

Earth's culture was looted too; ancient artifacts carried off to ornament Galactic estates, museums denuded down to the plaster, entire buildings and even some cities, like Paris, carried off wholesale. Movies, plays, books, music, anything and everything, all had been appropriated by the voracious Galactic culture, which swallowed up everything Earth could produce.

People became loot too. There were some, artists and musicians, writers and composers, and even historians, who made out very well. Most of *them* weren't even on Earth anymore either; their patrons liked to keep their clever pets near at hand.

Dimitri glanced from time to time at the other runners, pacing, stretching, running in place. He knew them all, and they knew him. As in the ancient days, it was again; they were all friends. Henri, the Jamaican, together with Vidor, the Russian, and St. Denis, the French-Canadian, were his main competition. They all ate together, lived together, the tiny sports-villages holding so few competitors that there was no point in being segregated by nationality.

There had been no vast conquering army. There had been no need for anything so uncivilized. Not when a vast, overwhelming technological superiority allowed the Galactics to simply do as they pleased. Resistance really *was* futile; the Galactics took no notice of it. The wealth of the Galactic civilization was such that they could treat an entire planet the way that the Native Americans had been treated by the white races, only without the genocide. The Galactics took what they wanted, and in compensation for their looting, installed all of humanity in the Arcologies, where, if they chose, they could live without ever doing a bit of work.

And many *did* choose that path. But if you wanted more than bare subsistence . . .

Humans were amusing generalists. They made good servants, if they were obsequious enough. And if they weren't, well, there were so many that it was easy enough to replace those who failed.

So the Galactics were free to have anything they wanted on the entire planet.

Except . . . in this one, singular case. One thing that the Galactics had wanted that they could not have.

The idea of sports competitions had come as a revelation to them, and they went sports mad. The appropriated every sport they saw, and some resurrected from the past. And four years after their coming, when it had been time for the Olympics, they made to appropriate those, too.

And for once, met a barrier they could not beat down.

No, said the IOC, and *no,* said the Priestesses of Zeus, whom the IOC had resurrected from the historic record. *The Olympics are not for sale,* said the IOC, and *the Olympics are only for humans,* said the Priestesses.

The two groups had been colluding, planning for four years, setting that barrier in stone ever since the first ship had appeared in the skies. Nowhere in any ancient writing was it said that any creature other than a human could compete in honor of the gods in whose image humanity had been made. This was what the IOC had concocted the moment they realized that Galactic civilization intended to strip everything of cultural worth from the planet.

They turned the Olympics into a religious rite. And when the Galactics first became aware of the Games, they were informed that the Olympics were not just a *sports competition.* They were rites of the gods. They were not for non-humans, although non-humans would, grudgingly, be allowed as spectators. They were not to be held off of Earth. In fact, they were not to be held anywhere but in Greece, in the shadow of Mount

Olympus. To violate religious sanctions was absolutely forbidden by the Galactics' own laws. Faced with that— even the Galactics had backed down.

Dimitri glanced up again at the Skytron, potent symbol of just how petty the masters could be, however they pretended otherwise. *You can hold your Olympics, but it will be literally in the shadow of our Games. The* Galactic *Games. Enjoy!* Every moment had been scheduled to contrast with the Olympics, right down to the individual events.

The IOC had gambled on the fact that the Galactics would not trouble themselves to research the history of the Games once they had been thwarted. They had not been wrong.

To the original *diaulos,* or 400-meter race, the *dolichos,* or 1500-meter race, the *pentathalon,* the revived *pankration,* and the boxing, the IOC had added all the usual Olympic events, only to have to cut them back again when it became painfully clear that there were not going to be enough participants in most of them to make it worthwhile holding them.

Clearly they could not have held a Winter Olympics, at all, and still keep up the pretense that these were an original religious celebration dating back to Ancient Greece.

The revamped Olympic Games consisted of the most basic of track-and-field and gymnastic events. It all fit into a bare seven days, with room to spare, including some extensive religious ceremonies on either side.

Speaking of ceremonies . . . Dimitri straightened up. The Priestesses were coming to anoint the final participants. He and the others lined up at their starting blocks, and bowed their heads. As the Priestess whispered a blessing in archaic Greek, he felt the light caress of her thumb on his forehead, leaving behind a single touch of olive oil pressed from ancient trees on the slope of Mount Olympus.

He was not expecting it. He was really only thinking of his muscles, of the need to get out of the starting blocks ahead of St. Denis and Henri. But the moment he felt the Priestess touch his forehead, he looked into her eyes, and suddenly, he was filled with light. It was as if the sun had come down to earth and filled him.

He could not think. He did not want to think.

As in a dream, he took his place in the starting blocks.

Still in a dream, he heard the commands of the starter. His body reacted while his mind still filled with the sun, the sun, the sun. *Ready. Set.*

He did not hear the starter's pistol. But his body did. Suddenly, he was in motion. No, he was *flying*. He could not feel his limbs. He could not hear his heart, nor feel the breath in his lungs. There was no effort. There was only light.

In the first lap, he and St. Denis were side-by-side, and Henri was just behind them both. This was wrong. Dimly, he knew that he was running the race all wrong. The 1500-meter was a matter of strategy; the man who won was always the one who came from behind. And yet, he could not have slowed his pace if he had been told that he would fall over dead in the next moment. He ran in a trance of joy, filled with light and energy, and his footfalls felt as effortless as dancing.

In the second lap, St. Denis dropped back. Vidor was coming from behind, and Henri was at his elbow. And he was no more weary than he had been the moment he flew from the blocks. He was running, running, running, not for himself, not to win, but for the glory of Zeus, for the joy of sport. He felt his mouth forming a smile, an enormous grin. Dimly, he heard the crowd roaring, as he moved into the third lap, and Vidor dropped back, unable to keep the pace. Now it was only Henri and him, and he felt not less energy, but *more.* The light filled him. The joy upheld him. He felt himself going faster.

The crowd was going insane. And as they passed into the last lap, he felt, rather than saw, Henri dropping back, and now, now it was only him, him, and the gods, and the joy of speed, the intoxication of that was more than he had ever felt, for any reason, ever before.

And now the tape loomed up before him. And now he felt his chest breaking it. And still he ran, not even signaling his victory, but ran as the light rose up within him like a song . . . and then, slowly faded, as his footfalls slowed, as the others gathered around him, and lifted him, dazed and bewildered, onto their shoulders, and he could hear, dimly, over the roaring, the words. The words. *"Three minutes, fifteen point two seconds! A new Olympic and world record!"*

And they brought him, on their shoulders, still dazed, to the victor's stand. They put him up on the winner's box. Henri came up beside him, and Vidor. And the Priestess brought him the laurel wreath, and placed it on his head, and the crowd deafened him.

And then . . . he looked up. To the Skytron. And there,

at that moment, a strange scarlet creature with legs taking up half its body, legs like a kangaroo's, was being put on a winner's stand. Another thing like a blue stick-insect was putting a medal about its neck. And scrolling under the picture were the words, *1500 meters, new Galactic Games record! 2.32.04!*

The light left him. He smiled, automatically. But the moment was over, the moment had died with his joy.

Now it was time for the next race, and he and the others left the podium. The moment was gone, as if it had never been.

He went to the locker room, and changed out of his tracksuit. And even as he pulled on his courier's uniform, the implant in his head *pinged.*

"Dimitrios," he said aloud.

"Ah, good," said his boss, a creature who he had never personally seen. *"Are you back on duty, done with your little games now?"*

"Yes sir," he said, politely.

"Excellent. There's a package I need you to get from Vericorp in Naples. Naples is close to Athens, isn't it?"

Of course it wasn't. But there was no point in saying so. It was the *hand delivery* that was important, not the distance. It was the cachet that his boss got from employing a very fast human. "I'll get it, sir," he replied automatically, accepting the job. The HUD implanted in his eye lit up with directions.

"Good lad. Chop-chop! Time is money!" Like most Galactics, the translation program his boss used aped the old arrogant forms of British colonial phraseology. He had no doubt this was deliberate.

The carrier wave cut off. He stuffed his tracksuit back in a locker, where someone would no doubt collect it, and ran for the maglev. That, after all, was what he was paid to do. Run.

Behind him, left on the bench, the laurel wreath began to wilt, and a single leaf dropped to the floor.

REGULATION

✦ ✦ ✦

by Seanan McGuire

"Never give up, never give in,
and when the upper hand is ours,
may we have the ability to handle the win with the
dignity that we absorbed the loss."
—Doug Williams,
Most Valuable Player, Super Bowl XXII, 1988

Seanan McGuire is the New York Times *bestselling
author of more than a dozen books, all published within
the last five years, which may explain why some people
believe that she does not actually sleep. Her work has
been translated into several languages, and resulted in
her receiving a record five Hugo Award nominations
on the 2013 ballot. When not writing, Seanan spends
her time reading, watching terrible horror movies and
too much television, visiting Disney parks, and rating
haunted corn mazes. You can keep up with her at
www.seananmcguire.com.*

*Seanan herein gives us a look at a futuristic take on an
extreme sport: roller derby.*

"Derby dudes, derby dames, and derby delights, what we're seeing here tonight may be the *match* of the *century*!" The announcer's voice howled through the speakers and was displayed on the screens studded around the arena, the auto-transcriber rendering it instantly into subtitles. Half the crowd wore earbuds, listening to one of the two dozen languages—both human and non—that were receiving the simultaneous translation. On the track, ten girls zoomed past at ludicrous speeds, their actions tracked and broken down by the programmed referees. For most, they were distinguishable only by the colors that they wore. The skaters in red were the Martian Marauders, currently at the top of the league in both victories and penalties. The skaters in black and purple were Charon's Angels, bottom of the league in every sense of the word. They trained mostly on their home moon, using gravity simulators that had to strain to match the pull of Earth standard. Since Earth gravity was enforced across the entire Sol System Banked Track Roller Derby League, they were always a little awkward when they hit the track, and while they skated with enthusiasm, all the enthusiasm in the galaxy didn't make up for skill.

But that had been at the start of the season, eleven solar months past. The Angels had been skating under standard gravity generators for that entire time, save for a few exhibition games, half of which had been held under *higher* than standard gravity. (Low grav made for faster skaters, more impressive apex jumps, and stunts that were otherwise impossible. High grav meant a higher risk factor, a better chance of seeing blood on the track, and an even higher chance of career-ending injury. The people who ran the league had been petitioning to increase the standard gravity for the past two years, claiming that it would increase the exhibition value of the matches without increasing the athleticism. The skaters had been protesting for almost as long. For the time being, the needle didn't move.)

Training skaters under low gravity gave them grace and incomparable finesse. Conditioning them under standard or higher gravity reduced the number of broken bones even as it gave them power and strength without dulling their skill. The Martian Marauders had been the favorites to win this match, but the Charon's Angels were stealing every jam they got their hands on, leaving their top-rated rivals in the dust. As the audience watched, breathless, the jammer for the Angels whipped around the curve of the track one more time, using her momentum to sling her past the pack.

Very few of the observers saw the minute nod she offered to the jammer for the Marauders. Their attention was elsewhere, on the pack, on the scrimmage, on the way she held her shoulders like a sword as she cut through her opponents.

Everyone in the auditorium saw the opposing jammer extend her foot, hook it around the Angel's ankle, and bring her crashing to the floor. The speakers reproduced the sound of the fallen jammer's neck snapping perfectly, with no loss of fidelity. The subtitles printed the word "snap" in a dozen languages before they cut off. The sign-language interpreters in the VIP sections made breaking motions with their hands before they stopped, looking sickened by what they had just done.

"Oh my God," whispered an announcer. "I think she's—"

The transmission cut off.

Silence fell.

The teams were herded into their respective locker rooms—euphemistically called "dressing rooms" by everyone who had never strapped on a pair of skates—and summarily locked in by brightly smiling androids with the arena logo branded across their foreheads. "For your own safety, please do not attempt to leave your dressing room while we are reviewing recent events," said the androids, in voices as bland and pleasant as their smiles. "A local representative of Galactic Health and Safety will be with you soon. Please enjoy an assortment of complimentary snacks and beverages."

Then the androids were gone, and the skaters—ten Martian Marauders, nine Charon's Angels—were left alone, with only a thin wall separating them.

"Are we being watched?" asked the captain of the Marauders. She was tall and lean, Earth-born and Mars-raised, with the sort of face that could launch a thousand ships, and the sort of snarl that could sink them. She skated under the name "H.G. Welts," and no one could say that it was inaccurate.

"Checking now," said one of their jammers—Kay Boom—as she sat down on the locker room floor and scrolled through the screens on her tablet. "Doesn't look like it. All the systems are tied up with reviewing those last thirty seconds of play. I think they're trying to prove that it was an accident."

"Good fucking luck with that." Rae Badbury was lying on one of the benches, eyes closed, hands clenched together and pressed against the base of her solar plexus. She had been in that position since they had entered the room. None of the others dared to go anywhere near her. They all knew that they could have drawn the short straw and been the one to deliver the killing blow, and while they might be glad that it hadn't been their skate around the opposing jammer's ankle, that didn't mean they weren't sorry for their colleague and teammate.

The fact that she had done it to save them all was almost irrelevant. She was never going to skate again. For a woman like her, who had done the things she'd done for the sake of the game, that was a fate worse than death.

"We're clear," said Kay, finally looking up. "No sniffers, no trackers, no microphones."

"Good," said H.G. "Get O'Speed on the line."

Kay nodded and bent back over her tablet.

The Marauders followed the classic derby pattern: each skater had her own "derby name," a carefully constructed if sometimes labored pun that could be related back to the red planet that was their home. Most of them had legally changed their names after they were accepted onto the planetary team. It wasn't required, but it was strongly encouraged by management, as it was "less confusing for the fans" if they had only one identity. The skaters recognized the suggestion for what it was—one more way to control them, to keep them from ever considering the lure of a life off the track—but they did it anyway. Anything to be able to skate. Anything to be able to *move*, in a solar system where safety concerns and regulations had made the population more and more sedentary. If you weren't an athlete, bonded and cosseted and insured, there were very few options open to you. Machines and in-home fitness centers kept the population in better shape than ever. They just had nowhere left to go.

The Angels, on the other hand, were more tightly funded and controlled by their planetary government, and as such had been encouraged to have a more cohesive team identity. All of them skated under an "O" name. The team captain was Angel O'Speed. Her second in command was Angel O'Pain.

The jammer who had died, neck broken, on the track, was Angel O'Death. She had chosen the name herself when she started skating, some five years back. It was hard not to wonder, now, whether she had seen this coming. Rae had been chosen by lottery, after all.

O'Death had volunteered.

Kay's tablet beeped twice before a window opened, showing the pale, anxious face of Angel O'Speed. The captain of the Angels didn't wait for hellos before she got down to business: "Is everyone okay over there? Have there been any arrests?"

"Not yet, but there probably will be." H.G. leaned over and plucked the tablet out of Kay's unresisting hands. The rest of the Marauders moved a little closer, all save for Rae, who didn't move. She didn't need to hear what came next. She was the one who was going to have to live it. H.G. cast a worried glance in her direction before looking back to the tablet and saying, "They've locked us in."

"Us, too," said O'Speed. "I think they're trying to figure out how to respond to this without looking like they're insensitive, but also without making it seem like it's anything other than an isolated incident. They don't want to attract too much attention."

"They never do," said Rae bitterly.

"What happens if they find a way to cover this up?" asked H.G. "You don't have another skater who wants to die, and I don't have another skater who wants to be a killer. We can't pull this stunt again."

"We won't have to," said O'Speed. "We chose this match because the planetary government of Pluto is here. They're not going to like losing a skater. O'Death was young, and pretty, and only two years from retirement. They were counting on her genes."

Getting people to settle on Pluto was difficult under the best of circumstances. It was a vital way station for colonists heading out into the greater galaxy, one last place to refuel and resupply and drop off anyone whose nerves had proven unsuited to the voyage. Not many people changed their minds once they had secured a berth on a colony ship, but it happened often enough that measures had to be taken to ensure that people who didn't want to leave the solar system didn't wind up stranded a hundred light years and a few decades away. Pluto could *not* be allowed to shut down. At the same time, it was small, and cramped, and the gravity was weak enough to make most people uncomfortable; there would never be an atmosphere, never be open spaces or healthy farms or any of the things that settlers on Mars or Europa could enjoy. So Pluto had stopped encouraging settlement, and started rewarding reproduction.

Children born on Pluto tended to stay on Pluto, unable to cope with the higher gravities or open skies of other human colonies. Children born on Pluto thought that all the things which made it so unappealing to settlers were normal; the way things were supposed to be. Even women who had no interest in childbearing were expected to donate their eggs and their genetic material to the cause of building a stable long-term population. All the members of the planetary roller derby team had subsidized their equipment and training with promises of future children. They would make themselves celebrities for their home world, and then they would settle down and help secure Pluto's future.

Not Angel O'Death. The organ harvesters might recover her ovaries and hence her eggs, but the laws against posthumous reproduction would keep them from being used for anything which might result in viable human embryos. She was lost, and so were the children her planet so dearly needed. The planetary government would react with all force and fury. They could do nothing else.

"That just guarantees the far colonies for Rae," snapped H.G. "That wasn't the deal. This is supposed to change things, not get my best jammer deported."

Rae didn't say anything. It was obvious that she was listening, but she seemed to be shutting down with each passing second, disconnecting further and further from the scene around her.

"They can't just shove her onto a prison ship without doing a full investigation into the circumstances around O'Death's, well, death," said O'Speed. "Our courts wouldn't allow it, even if the Earth courts would. It's going to bring out the reality of what's going on with the league. Three other matches are happening this month, and each of them has a skater who's agreed to die, and another who's agreed to commit murder. We're going to change the system. Sacrifices must be made."

"I hope you're right." H.G. Welts looked across the locker room to Rae Badbury, who still wasn't moving. "I really, genuinely do."

The human race spread through the solar system like bread mold: slowly at first, feeling out its options, and then in a great, unstoppable tide. It cropped up everywhere, from the orbital platforms circling Mercury to the cold, still satellites that floated just past Pluto. The conditions under which humanity thrived changed from world to world, moon to moon, until "Earth-average" was no longer the norm, but was instead an outdated and unattainable standard. Fashion models from Luna stood almost seven feet in height, with long, graceful limbs concealing brittle bones. Asteroid miners grew squat and strong, seemingly crafted out of the ore they worked to extract. Arthur C. Clarke once famously said that any sufficiently advanced technology was indistinguishable from magic. As humanity remade the solar system in its own image, the solar system responded by remaking humanity in the image of all the fantasy worlds of Earth: Venusian mermaids who swam, heavily modified and genetically engineered, through the poisonous seas; Martian dryads whose skin performed photosynthesis in natural light, allowing every citizen to participate in the terraforming of their world. The impossible was possible. The Golden Age of Man had begun.

Progress always costs. The sports of Earth were an early, if unexpected, casualty. They had rules. They had regulations. They had safety committees in place to keep the players from being endangered unnecessarily. They had pay structures and cheerleaders and auxiliary committees, and somehow all those things—those important, essential things—made it difficult for the world's pastimes to spread with the world's people. Baseball didn't work on low-gravity worlds, not when the rules were so difficult to modify. Football on Europa or in orbit around Neptune would be a sea of fatalities, unavoidable and tragic.

Progress always costs. The people must be entertained.

The groups that had made their fortunes promoting sports on Earth began looking, frantically, for something universal; something that could be marketed to all worlds and all people, without the fear of regulations shutting it down in the middle of the first match. Gymnastics had many of the same issues as baseball. Horseback riding required horses, which were notorious for doing poorly in zero-G. Swimming required water. One by one, the team and solo sports of the world were considered and rejected, thrown aside as requiring too much red tape.

And then a young marketing executive came in with a home-burned disk of women in fishnet stockings, whipping one another around a circular track with steeply banked sides. It was fast. It was occasionally vicious. It was, according to the rules and regulations that defined such things, not a sport. Roller derby had never completed the process of filing for recognition by the various sporting organizations; the players and team organizers had seen the red tape coming and had skated smoothly aside, choosing a lack of regulations and safety requirements over the sweet promise of potential fame. There were virtually no rules defining what was or was not appropriate, apart from the shape of the teams, the curvature of the tracks. It was perfect.

The first all-system roller derby match had been skated six months later, an exhibition match between the Terran Earthshakers and the Luna Lunartics. Two skaters had broken bones. Three had lost teeth. And a system-wide passion had been born, as people remembered why they enjoyed blood sports so much in the first place. Within five years, every planet and satellite in the system had their own sponsored roller derby team, each with their own theme and uniform and merchandising. The Sol System Banked Track Roller Derby League got their cut. The people got their entertainment. The skaters got to be stars. Everything was perfect, for a while. Everything was *wonderful*.

Until the gravity began creeping up, and the number of broken bones began to rise. Until the lower-gravity teams discovered that the money for better grav gennies was drying up, because the League didn't want to sponsor something that could reduce injuries on the track. Until it became apparent that the small print in their contracts and the careful avoidance of the word "sport" was not about protecting their freedom to skate; it was about protecting the League's freedom to kill them with impunity. They assumed all risk when they took to the track, after all. When they got hurt, it was no one's fault but their own. As for the fact that they were bound by unbreakable contracts, well . . . that was their fault, too. They should have read more carefully before they signed.

The clever men who controlled the revenue streams sat in their safe offices and boardrooms, congratulating each other for a loophole well found, a moneymaker well exploited. What they forgot was that no matter how far humanity spread, it always remained essentially, at its core, human. Humans, when trapped, fight back. Humans find a way.

The door of the locker room unsealed, allowing two of the arena androids to stroll blithely inside, followed closely by a representative of the League. All but one of the Marauders turned to watch them come. Only H.G. Welts bothered to stand. As their captain, she couldn't be as cold as the rest of them, even when she wanted to.

Rae Badbury was still lying on her back, staring up at the ceiling. She didn't move. She didn't even blink.

"Hello, ladies," said the representative from the League. He cleared his throat, looking uncomfortably around the room. Like many of the men who made life-or-death decisions on the behalf of the skaters, he didn't actually enjoy standing in their presence. They looked too *real* when seen like this, too physical and human. They smelled of blood and sweat, both fresh and rancid, soaked into their protective gear until it became an almost physical thing. They could have been his daughters, and he despised them for that. Didn't they know that toys were meant to remain at a distance, where decent people wouldn't have to think about what they represented?

"Hello," said H.G. Welts.

"I'm sure you're all very concerned about what happened on the track today. I'm sorry to be the bearer of bad news, but I'm afraid the young woman who fell did not survive her injuries. She was from a very low-grav world. Her bones weren't equipped to handle the impact under normal conditions."

None of the skaters said anything. They just stared at him, silent as snakes, and waited.

The man from the League cleared his throat. "After reviewing the tapes, we have determined that Rae Badbury acted within the normal scope of play. While this was a tragic accident, and we will strive to avoid such things in the future, we cannot at this time levy any punishments against the teams involved. We are very sorry for the loss suffered by Charon's Angels, and will be making a donation to the memorial planned for their fallen skater. We are very sorry for any distress suffered by the Martian Marauders. As per your contracts with the Sol System Banked Track Roller Derby League, you will be expected to resume play with thirty seconds remaining on the jam clock. You have half an hour to collect yourselves and touch up your makeup before you will be needed on the track. Failure to appear will result in penalties, and may negatively impact your earnings from this season." The man from the League forced a smile. He had a great deal of practice at presenting emotions he didn't feel; any onlooker would have taken it for genuine. "Let's get ready to roller derby!"

Then he was gone, ushered quickly out by the androids, who were there for his protection more than anything else. Silence fell in the locker room.

Kay spoke first, asking, in a very small voice, "Do we really have to skate?"

"We do," said H.G. grimly. "We all do."

The Martian Marauders went on to defeat the Charon's Angels, two hundred and seventeen points to a hundred and twelve. All the fight had gone out of the Pluto team after the death of their jammer, while Rae Badbury—who had been allowed to return to the track after sitting out three penalty circuits, that being the apparent cost of a human life—skated like a woman possessed, racking up points with every circuit around the track. No one seemed willing to get in her way, and only the mascara that trickled down her cheeks betrayed the fact that she was crying.

Three days later, in an exhibition game between the Venusian Love Goddesses and the Lunar Jailer Scouts, a blocker named Salome went over the rail, shattering three vertebrae and breaking her neck. The League declared it an accident. No penalties were applied.

Two weeks after that, a Jovian skater from the Thunderthighs turned and began skating the wrong way during a pack scrimmage. No one cleared a path for her. She died when her larynx was crushed. The League declared it a case of temporary disorientation brought on by the differences in oxygen levels between Io and the orbital platform where the match was being held. No penalties were applied. But people were beginning to talk. Three dead skaters in under a month was difficult to overlook, no matter how many bright banners and flash sales the League dangled as a distraction.

The last game of the season approached, between the Jailer Scouts and Martian Marauders. The solar system held its breath, waiting to see what would happen. The skaters put on their fishnets like armor and their lipstick like it would somehow protect them from the dangers ahead. They had agreed to this course of action. They had decided, as a group, that this was the only choice they had remaining to them. But that didn't make it easy, and it didn't make it right.

Twenty women skated out onto the track when the first bell rang, the Marauders in red, the Scouts in white-and-colored parodies of the "sailor suits" popularized by late twentieth-century anime. H.G. Welts led the Marauders. Sailor Boom led the Scouts. Neither of them made eye contact with the other. That, perhaps, should have been the first hint that something was terribly wrong. Both captains were known for taking their positions extremely seriously, and for insisting on good sportsmanship and fair play from their skaters—two attributes that the women had always gone out of their way to embody.

The jam buzzer sounded. Five women from each team lined up, bending forward and tensing as they prepared to skate. The buzzer sounded again to begin the jam.

No one moved.

The timer was ticking down, precious seconds bleeding away into the past, where they could never be reclaimed, and no one moved. Someone in the control booth hit the buzzer again, in case there had been a speaker malfunction. Still no one moved. Half the skaters were crying, and some would look at the footage later and comment cynically on how strange it was that *none* of them had invested in waterproof mascara; it was almost like they *wanted* their tears to be as visible to the cameras as possible. And how the cameras loved those tears!

"It looks like our girls are observing a moment of silence for their fallen comrades," gushed the announcer excitedly. "This is a remarkable, touching moment of solidarity and strength—and look, they're running out the first jam. No points will be scored. To tell you the truth, I'm getting a little choked up just thinking about it. So many good skaters have been lost this season. It's a miracle these girls are still willing to strap on their skates."

The buzzer rang as the first jam ended with no points scored; no one had budged. As was traditional, once the jam was over, the skaters rotated, a new jammer taking the place of the old, new blockers falling into the positions in the pack. The buzzer rang again.

No one moved.

"This is . . . all right, honoring a fallen comrade is a wonderful thing, but this is getting to be a bit much," said the announcer, sounding deeply confused. "The players are refusing to move. This is a violation of League rules, and may result in penalties if they don't skate soon. Derby fans, I don't know what to tell you. This is unprecedented."

The buzzer rang again. Men from the League flooded the track, making beelines for the team captains and beginning to speak to them in low, tight voices. The camera tracked their every move, hungry for spectacle of whatever kind they could grab. The captains didn't say anything. They just stood there, stoic, silent, still crying, until the men went away. The skaters took their places on the track. The buzzer rang for the start of the third jam. This time, there was motion; this time, all ten skaters began to move at once, skating forward with a smooth serenity that bore no resemblance to the usual scrimmage that kicked off a jam. No one said anything, not even the announcers.

Then the first member of the pack pulled a piece of paper out of her shirt and unfolded it, sliding smoothly to a stop as she held it up for the cameras to see. The skaters were all scanned for weapons and electronics before they came out on the track: there had been incidents, high-rated but disruptive, of skaters sneaking muscle stimulators, micro-Tasers, and other contraband onto the track. Sportsmanship wasn't as important as the show when the cameras were rolling, and the lack of it could sometimes be held up like a banner, one more reminder that roller derby was a performance, an art piece, and not a *sport*. Not something that should be *regulated*. Still, the people in charge wanted things to run as smoothly as possible, and so they checked for contraband.

But they never thought to check for pieces of paper. The skater who had stopped was holding up a large picture of Angel O'Death, smiling shyly for the still camera that had snapped her image. The video feed zoomed in on the text below the picture, magnifying it until everyone in the arena knew what it said:

ANGEL O' DEATH—CAREER ROLLER DERBY—THREE BROKEN RIBS, ONE KIDNEY TRANSPLANT—NO PENSION—NO PROTECTION—NO FUTURE

Another skater slid to a stop. This one held a picture of Salome from the Venusian Love Goddesses, her shoulders thrown back and her breasts thrust toward the lens.

SALOME—CAREER ROLLER DERBY—BROKEN ARM, BROKEN LEG, PUNCTURED LUNG, SIX DENTAL IMPLANTS— NO PENSION—NO PROTECTION—NO FUTURE

Ten skaters. Nine posters, each with a face and a list of small, sad, simple facts. The last to stop was Sailor Doom, whose sign read, simply, ROLLER DERBY IS A SPORT. PROTECT YOUR PLAYERS. REGULATE US.

"Regulate," chanted the players, both on and off the track. "Regulate! *REGULATE!*"

The people loved a show, no matter what shape it took. With a roar, the rest of the arena took up the chant, shouting it to the rafters. All over the system, people joined in, yelling at their televisions, at their computers, at their tablets. On simulcast and livestream, they shouted, and for a moment, the race of man was united over a single cause: the regulation of roller derby.

The players stood, stone-faced and unflinching, before the representatives of the planetary governments.

"There were better ways."

"There were not."

"You made yourselves into murderers to make a point."

"The deaths were already occurring. We just gave them meaning."

"You could have gone through proper channels."

"We tried. The people who stood to profit off our deaths wouldn't allow it."

In the end, there was only one question left to ask: "Do you really want to be regulated as a sport? You'll lose much of your freedom. Much of your flexibility."

"We'll get to keep our lives," said Sailor Doom, who represented all the skaters of her team, and beyond. "That's worth it."

The regulations defining roller derby on a pan-planetary basis went into effect that solar year. In arenas and warehouses all over inhabited space, the buzzers rang, and the skaters raced on.

EARTH, CORNER POCKET

✧ ✧ ✧

by Lezli Robyn

"What makes something special is not just what you have to gain, but what you feel there is to lose."
—**Andre Agassi,** Tennis Star

Lezli Robyn is an Australian multi-genre author, currently living in Ohio, who frequently collaborates with Mike Resnick. Since breaking into the field, she has sold to prestigious markets such as Asimov's *and* Analog, *and has been nominated for several awards around the world, including the Campbell Award for best new writer, and the Aurealis Award for Best short SF story; she has also won the Ictineu Award twice, in 2011 and 2014. Her short story collection,* Bittersuite, *is due to be published by Ticonderoga, followed by her novella,* On The Mechanical Wings of Dreams, *to be published by Hadley Rille Press in 2016.*

Lezli's story here is set in the same world as her story in my previous anthology, Mission: Tomorrow *(Baen, 2015). This time, she offers us an unusual take on billiards.*

When Ruby was selected to be on the homo sapiens' team to play in the first Intergalactic Eight Ball Pool Tournament, she had thought the two-year lead time was overkill. However, by the time all the bureaucratic red tape had been completed and she walked into the pre-game conference a scant hour before the main event, Ruby suddenly felt woefully underprepared.

The Intergalactic Consortium of Planets had clearly held nothing back when it came to ensuring the Tournament Committee had catered to every possible need or whim of the players. She was introduced to ambassadors from star systems she had never heard of, and treated like royalty by servers whose names were unpronounceable by any human tongue. It felt like every new race she met was more alien to her than the last. If it weren't for the universal translator the committee had provided, or the nearby presence of her teammates, Ruby would have been completely out of her depth.

A prickling sensation ran down the back of her neck, and she had the impression that someone—or rather, some*thing*?—was watching her. When she turned around to find the source of her unease, she was taken aback.

In amongst a crowd of very unusual and diverse lifeforms was a mermaid.

Or, rather, a mer*man*.

With an angular jawline, broad shoulders, and a well-muscled torso, the alien was almost completely humanoid in form—except for his long, cobalt-blue tail. He glided towards her on some kind of gravity device, his gills encased in a flexible force field filled with a water filtration system that was able to sustain him outside of his natural habitat. While his long platinum-white hair floated like a nimbus around his head, luminescent blue lights pulsed hypnotically underneath his pale skin, radiating out from a crystalline structure positioned in the center of his chest to course through what appeared to be his version of a circulatory system.

To say he was beautiful was an understatement. His genetic adaptations to an underwater environment predominately devoid of sunlight were absolutely breathtaking. And while there was a clear alien cast to his features, so much of his form resembled the old human folklore about mermaids that Ruby couldn't help but wonder where the basis for that myth had originated. Had his kind visited Earth around the time the first stories surfaced?

He stopped in front of her, and inclined his head in greeting. "I am Niravphlorokk, of the *Calthérii* race."

Ruby couldn't think of an uglier name for such a beautiful specimen.

"Please call me Nirav."

It is a pleasure to meet you, she replied, sincerely, wondering why in hell he would want to meet her. *I am Ruby Shaw. A human, from Earth.*

He cocked his head to the side. "I can hear your words, but you do not speak in the same manner as the others of your species."

I use a neuro-communicator because I was born with a genetic abnormality in my larynx that prevents me from communicating naturally. When he didn't reply, she continued on. *There is an implant in my brain that enables me to broadcast my thoughts into this device—* she pointed at the skin-toned speaker between her collarbones—*which makes my words audible to others.*

She could also use the neuro-communicator to talk telepathically with anyone else who had a compatible mechanism implanted into their brain, but she didn't feel compelled to tell him that.

Instead she watched in surprise as the lights under his skin pulsed quicker for a few seconds, a keen intensity entering his gaze. "Such an innovative race, for one so young."

She bristled at the condescending approval in his tone, but he couldn't know how many times she'd heard that sentiment since she'd arrived at the Alpha Centauri Waystation. She took a deep breath, and flicked her hair over her shoulder in an unconscious way to deflect her annoyance.

His eyes followed the gesture, widening when they saw the closed gills on the side of her neck. He didn't say anything for a long awkward minute. "Pardon my rudeness," he stated eventually. "I had not been informed your race was physiologically adapted to land *and* water."

I am the exception to the general rule, she replied, wondering why he had to be "informed" about any aspect of her race. *I am a part of a second-generation, genetic-manipulation experiment to expand our race into the oceans, due to overpopulation of the land masses on our world.* She could tell she held his interest now, not just his curiosity.

"I envy your ability to be able to switch between the two environments," he admitted, indicating his inability to breathe air without a filter.

And I envy you your tail, she confessed, in turn.

Ever since she had been a child, Ruby had longed to be able to swim alongside her dolphin family with the same speed and grace that was so inherent to their form. Being the only tailless member of the pod had meant she used to daydream about growing up to become a mermaid. Now, she had met the real thing.

She felt like pinching herself. Instead, they shared a tentative smile, then an awkward silence.

Do aliens talk about the weather on their homeworld, or some other banality, when unable to think of anything intelligent to say? Ruby asked him wryly.

His icy blues twinkled, and he opened his mouth to respond, only to be interrupted by the arrival of a couple of her teammates.

"I apologize for the intrusion, but we need to go, Red," Lance said, by way of introduction.

"Now," Charlie added, for extra emphasis.

Not understanding their need for urgency, Ruby frowned, but nodded. She extended a hand out to Nirav to formally take her leave, which he accepted more eagerly than she'd anticipated.

She felt a jolt of power race up her arm as soon as their skin connected. Some kind of static discharge. To cover her surprise, she continued to shake his hand, lamely repeating that it had been a pleasure to meet him.

The pleasure was all mine, he replied, then slid his hand out from hers and melted back into the crowd.

Ruby turned to her teammates. *This had better be good. I just met my dream man,* she joked. *A fair dinkum merman!*

"He is our competition, Red. But, not only that—".

Wait, she interrupted. *He's on the Consortium's team?*

Charlie nodded. "The tail wouldn't prevent him from sinking the eight ball, if he's talented enough."

Huh. Good point. She frowned. *Well, I am glad to have had the opportunity to get his measure then.*

"Red, he was the one that just sized *you* up," Lance pointed out. "While the Consortium's team is made up of multiple races, I found out just today that his race is the one who would specifically benefit if they win the Tournament."

Their earlier urgency finally registered. No wonder Nirav had been so "informed" about humans. He was researching them; rummaging for any nugget of information he could use against them to win the Tournament and, along with it, the legal right to colonize Earth's oceans.

Her ocean.

While the rest of the humans on the Earth team were land dwellers, Ruby had grown up in the first completely submerged human settlement in the Southern Ocean. Funded by the Australian government, the underwater installation was filled with geneticists, scientists, and biologists, who were exploring the myriad of ways humans could be adapted to an underwater environment.

Orphaned at a really young age, Ruby had been half-raised by one of the dolphin pods that had partnered with the pioneers in the project. The dolphins had only recently been awarded human-equivalent sentient status and recognized as having a voice in decisions involving the future of their planet. While they understood Man's wish to take a giant Galactic leap into space, they had been vehemently opposed to the idea of aliens colonizing their oceans as a part of the agreement Earth was drawing up with the Galactic Consortium of Planets to become a full-fledged member.

To be fair, most humans had been opposed to it, too, feeling they'd already given up enough of Earth's resource rights in the first steps to even qualify for membership. But the promise of advanced technology was a powerful lure; appealing to humanity's innate propensity to want to expand their horizons before they have the means.

Once it had been determined that both sides had reached a stalemate near the conclusion of otherwise very successful contract negotiation talks, it was decided that the colonization rights could be determined by a "friendly" game between Earth and the Consortium. One that promoted equal opportunity for all the races. If the Consortium won, Earth would be colonized. If Earth won, they could set up a small colony on one of the closest habitable planets in the interplanetary network.

It would be one gigantic leap for Mankind.

It is almost time, interjected Sun Dancer, interrupting her thoughts. She felt the warmth and love of her pod mother as the dolphin slipped quietly into her mind, using the connection between their neuro-communicators to reach out to her before the Game.

I know, Ruby replied, with equal warmth and more than a little trepidation. *We'll have to enter the stadium soon. Do you have a good view?*

Yes, my child. Do not worry about us.

Ruby felt the rest of the pod fill her mind, one by one, staying long enough to wish her luck, and send her their love, before leaving.

She had felt their pride in her, their concern for the outcome, and something else. Almost like a feeling of pressure. *Is the medication still helping with your claustrophobia?* she asked her pod mother, worried.

We are fine, the dolphin replied, her tone soothing. *It is harder on the young ones, but we are monitoring them.*

Ruby felt a polite tug on her arm, and returned her attention to the room.

"It's time to go in, Red," Charlie prompted.

Ruby reached out one last time to her pod mother, to say their goodbyes, and then sent the mental command to turn off her neuro-communicator. During the course of the game it had to be transparently clear that none of the players were getting any outside assistance during their turn at the table, so she wasn't taking any chances.

Making their way through the crowd, they made it to side entrance of the stadium, collecting more members of their team as they went. The Earth Council had felt it was very important to pick talented players from all forms of diversity—race, nationality, gender, and sexuality—to show the Consortium how far it has come as a species since World War 4, but one glimpse of the vastly different types of species on the alien team told her that the humans probably all looked like clones to them.

They entered the arena, the excitement of the (mostly) alien crowd, deafening. The entire back wall of the round stadium had been turned into aquariums, or enclosures for other aliens needing specialized environments. With thousands of other aliens in tiers surrounding the entire arena, Ruby now had a visual to grasp how vast the Intergalactic Consortium of Planets truly was.

Each team of ten lined up on either side of the pool table and took their seats—or whatever the equivalent version was on the alien side for the giant arachnid, hovering merman, and elongated stick bug thing—and all turned towards the stage.

Well, all except Ruby and Nirav.

While he calmly considered her, she stared at him, incredulous to realize that he was third in the alien line-up, which was the exact same position she held on her team. They were going to be playing *directly* against each other during the Tournament.

It couldn't be a coincidence.

She knew that the committee had read all the players' genetic medical files as part of the extensive physicals both teams had to go through. They would have known that her DNA had been manipulated in utero to give her gills, webbed hands and feet, and a denser epidermis to better adapt to the seventy-six percent of Earth that humans had yet to dominate.

The committee would have also known that out of all the players on the human team, she would be the most aware of the stakes if Earth lost this Tournament. Were they trying to throw her off her game, by pitting her against the only water-dependent race on the alien team that would specifically benefit from their loss?

Ruby felt a sense of unease sliver down her spine, and

turned away from Nirav's piercing blue gaze just in time to see the game host walk out onto stage.

"Welcome to the Consortium's first ever Intergalactic Eight Ball Pool Tournament! I am your host, Broslain Torvulcavich, and I hail from a star system the humans like to call the Beta Centauri—not too far from here." The stadium erupted into cheers. "I'd like to introduce you to today's referee, Mark32i, a fascinating model known for his exemplary record in accuracy and precision." He turned to the robot in question. "I have been assured that you have studied the new Intergalactic Eight Ball Pool Tournament manual extensively, in preparation for today's momentous event. How excited are you to be the only robot chosen out of so many drones to referee the most important game in Earth's history?"

The spider-shaped robot took a moment to consider the question, scurrying forward on various mechanical pincers and claws to reach the microphone. "I have not been programmed to provide emotional input on the particulars of the game process."

"A most excellent answer! That's exactly what we need: an unbiased referee." He turned back to face the spectators with a flamboyant flourish. "Now let's give the audience a brief overview of the rules of this game. A game of pool has two opposing teams comprising of ten of their best players. To win the Tournament, each team has to try to be the first to win eight frames. Now, for those of us who are not human—and let's face it, that is most of us in this universe—a frame is the name for an individual round of the game. In each new round, a new player from each team has to compete against each other to be the first to hit all of the balls of one color into pockets around the table, before they can attempt to pocket the winning eight ball. It's a challenge fraught with mishits, fouls, and utter devastation, because at the end of the day, there can only be one victor."

"And you thought Americans were dramatic, Red," Lance commented, bemused.

Ruby grinned, and pointed to the referee, who was moving to rack up the balls for the first time.

She noticed straight away that the red and yellow of the object balls were more iridescent than the Earth-made ones she was used to, but there was something about the eight ball that was also different, but it was hard to see while the balls were all racked up together.

She held her breath as the robot referee tossed an antiquated Earth coin in the air. "Heads," Mark32i declared, and the human team cheered.

Ruby turned to give a thumbs-up to their British team lead, William, who stood up to select his cue stick.

"Go Willie!"

"You can do it, Bill!"

Ruby watched him make the first break of the game, meticulously tapping the cue ball into the triangle of balls and sending them flying across the table. When they settled, she gasped. The eight ball looked *exactly* like a miniature version of Earth, down to the cloud patterns moving across its three-dimensional surface.

She absolutely loved the symbolism. If the aliens pocketed the winning eight ball of the game, they were literally claiming their right to colonize Earth. If her team pocketed it, they were reclaiming it back.

Within a couple of moves, William had missed pocketing one of his reds, which turned the table over to his alien opponent, who swept the table of all the yellows and then pocketed the eight ball.

Ruby grimaced. Not an auspicious start.

Their second player did a little better. His alien counterpart was unable to pocket any balls after he performed the break, so Raj was able to start his turn very consistently, pocketing balls left and right. However, when it came time for him to sink the last red, the eight ball fell into another pocket at the same time.

"Loss of frame," Mark32i intoned. "Eight ball potted at the same time as final red ball."

Ruby could tell Raj was devastated. She wasn't feeling much better herself. A dull ache had formed at the base of her head, and it was increasing in severity with every passing minute. She stood up to walk to the table, mentally preparing to make her first break of the Tournament; wishing she could still feel the loving support of her pod in the back of her mind.

Biting her lip in an age-old gesture of nervousness, Ruby tried not to be distracted by the swirling clouds on the lifelike eight ball as she positioned herself and her cue stick. Taking a deep breath she hit the cue ball, watching it hurtle into the colored balls and scatter them in all directions.

She saw one yellow fall into a pocket. Then another. A red rolled towards her, it too falling into a corner pocket.

"Red and yellow balls potted," Mark32i announced.

Ruby studied the placement of the remaining balls, to

see which color held the best positions. As if to help her make a choice, another yellow dropped belatedly into a pocket.

Even the robot appeared surprised by her good fortune. "Yellow balls in play," he intoned, after she pointed at the nearest one to declare her choice.

She made her way around the table to play her second shot, but as soon as she bent over that dull ache in the back of her head increased to a painful throb, affecting her concentration. *I only have to make five more moves,* she told herself, as she played that shot out, sinking another yellow into a pocket.

She moved around to the opponent's side of the table, which brought her too close to the merman for her liking. She could feel Nirav's icy gaze drilling into her back as she lined up a more awkward shot, hitting the cue ball along the railing so that it would push the fifth yellow into the far corner pocket.

She straightened out and raised a hand to rub the back of her neck, the pain so intense she nearly lined up a Red Ball for her next shot. It was only the inadvertently helpful gasp from the audience that made her realize what she was doing.

She walked around to the other side of the table, away from the merman, and sunk the last two yellow balls as quickly as possible. By the time it came for her to pocket the eight ball, she was working purely on instinct. Much to the horror of her teammates, she closed her eyes as she played out her last move, not opening them again until she heard a ball fall into the pocket.

The right ball. She had won.

She somehow made it back to her seat, amidst the excited cheers of the stadium, but the pressure in the back of her head was starting to overwhelm her. She barely registered that they lost the next game, and then the next. She wasn't even sure if she cheered when they won the following three games. All she knew was that it took all her effort just to concentrate on blocking as much of the pain as she could.

She looked up to see the merman staring intently at her and grimaced, knowing he was intuitive enough to see her discomfort and worried that if it became noticeable enough to others, someone would alert the referee and the game would be cancelled.

Something unexpected flickered in his eyes, and she looked away, not wanting to see his pity. Over the next three losses, she fought the pain until it reached a point so agonizing, she finally gave into it, only then feeling an immediate surge of relief and a dissipation of pain until it became a dull ache.

Her sense of reprieve was immense.

She had the pleasure of watching Raj win his second frame, and then all eyes were on her.

"If you lose this frame, Red, they win," Lance informed her. "Go show 'em what we're made of."

Bloody hell. How did it come to be that she was playing the deciding frame?

"You've got this," agreed Charlie. "Do us proud."

Sure. No pressure. It's only, possibly, the single most important frame in Earth's history, she replied, but of course they couldn't hear her, with her neuro-communicator off.

Ruby stood up and grabbed a cue, trying—unsuccessfully—to block out all physiological awareness of the merman. While she continued to feel a tingling sensation at the back of her neck, it was her turn to perform the break. She had to focus.

She waited until Mark32i racked the balls—ensuring the Eight Ball was positioned correctly on the spot—and walked up to the table. Taking a deep breath, she leaned forward, balanced the cue over her right hand and struck the cue ball without hesitation, watching it hurtle into the triangle of balls and fling them in all directions. No reds or yellows were pocketed, but more than four of the balls were driven into the cushions. The referee should have been able to make the call that the table was "open" to play . . .

Except the eight ball was still moving.

Ruby all-but-flinched as the miniature representation of Earth sunk into the side pocket, thankful that it hadn't been the Cue Ball. That would have resulted in an automatic "foul" call, and the awarding of the next play to her opponent.

"Void break," Mark32i intoned, using multiple mechanical pincers to re-rack the balls with incredible speed and agility. "Same player to restart frame. No penalty."

Ruby turned around. She looked past her teammates and the audience, and up into an aquarium running along the back wall of the stadium. Her pod mother, Sun Dancer, swam up to the glass, as if knowing the child of her heart needed her support, and in unison all the dolphins bowed their heads to Ruby, in deep appreciation of what she was doing for them.

Her breath caught in her throat. Their thoughtful gesture had moved her more than any words of encouragement could have.

"Thirty seconds."

Strewth! Ruby tore her attention away from her pod, feeling bolstered by their support. Ignoring the icy intensity of Nirav's gaze, she turned back to the table and lined up the cue with the cue ball again. This time, when she hit it, and the colored balls went flying, a red ball fell into a pocket.

Brilliant. Her color of choice.

"Red balls potted," intoned the referee, stepping back.

She pointed to another red ball, to make it clear she was choosing that color.

"Red balls in play," confirmed Mark32i.

Ruby studied the fall of the balls on the table, noticing that a couple of her opponent's balls were already balanced in front of pockets. She grimaced. *Maybe I should have chosen yellow,* she thought, belatedly, but there was nothing she could do now, except be careful she didn't hit them in.

She located the eight ball next—flush up against the rail cushion—then considered the position of the six reds left on the table, using the cue ball to sink the first of them into a corner pocket with her next shot.

She navigated the white ball around the yellows, pocketing three more reds with precision, her team's exuberant reaction growing louder with each successful play, increasing her confidence.

Studying her next shot carefully, she moved around to stand in front of one of the side pockets. The position of a particular yellow ball was blocking her ability to sink one of her reds into the pocket across from her, so she angled her cue to hit the white ball into the rail cushion on the other side of the table. It repelled back from the rail on just the right tangent to hit the red ball in her direction and into the pocket directly in front of her.

The entire auditorium erupted into cheers—humans and aliens, alike—and she couldn't resist looking askance to see Nirav's reaction. Their eyes met, her fiery amber ones clashing with his icy blues, and she noticed that the luminescent light pulsing through his circulatory system had increased tenfold.

She should have felt a competitive satisfaction that she had been able to rattle that perfect exterior of his, but instead she felt a growing unease.

Ruby raised a hand to absentmindedly rub the back of her neck again, then pulled her gaze back to the table to study her last red ball. She had to sink it in such a way that the cue ball would then be in the best position to pocket the eight ball in her final shot. She couldn't afford to get this wrong.

She angled the cue stick carefully, and softly putted the white ball into the red. It rolled slowly towards the corner pocket, agonizingly hovering at the edge of it before finally falling in with a resonating thud.

The appreciative roar rising from around the stadium was deafening. She looked up to see the dolphins doing cartwheels in the water and grinned. *You bloody ripper.*

Then she heard it. The distinctive sound of another ball falling into a pocket.

She turned back to the table to hear the robot's announcement: "Foul."

Shocked, Ruby looked down at the table to discover that one of the yellow balls she had previously noted was too close to a pocket after her break had inexplicably fallen into it. She'd done nothing specific to sink it, but she didn't have to. The rules clearly stated that if any of the opponent's balls fell into a pocket, even without being touched, the result was an automatic nonstandard foul, and the end of that player's turn.

Nirav glided up to the table before she even had a chance to register what had happened.

She hastily stepped aside, and returned to her seat, fully aware that she had probably just handed the entire colonization rights of Earth to the Intergalactic Consortium. She wanted to scream in frustration, or cry salty tears of regret, but instead she accepted her teammates' conciliatory comments with stoicism, turning her full attention onto her opponent.

The merman's playing style was both measured and graceful. He gained permission from the referee to adjust the parameters of his gravity device, enabling him to lean forward on his tail and position himself as a human would, when making his first, more difficult shot.

After he'd sunk the next two balls with ease, he paused, focusing his attention on the yellow lying mere inches from one of the corner pockets. He positioned himself to hit the cue ball in its direction, and Ruby silently cheered. If he made that seemingly-easy shot, his white ball wouldn't be in the best position to sink the two balls on the other end of the table. He was just about to increase his margin for error.

With a swish of his blue tail, Nirav pulled back at the last second, changing positions to pocket the first of the two balls lying at the other end of the table.

Ruby blinked in surprise. *Bugger.* She figured that if he moved around to the right side of the table, he could now angle the cue to sink the second yellow into the same pocket, making sure to hit it with enough force to rebound the cue ball into the center of the table. That would position the white ball perfectly for him to sink the last yellow ball.

Astonishingly, he did precisely that. When the dust had settled, only the eight ball was left standing.

Alarm bells rang in Ruby's mind. He had executed every one of his shots *exactly* the way she would have done them. Something very, very fishy was going on.

She tried to signal the referee for a time out, but the buzzing feeling at the back of her neck intensified, all but immobilizing her in pain again. It was as if her neuro-communicator was somehow being affected, but she shouldn't be having any feedback issues since it had been turned off prior to the game.

Her eyes widened in panic. Could someone have reactivated it without her permission?

An entrancing male voice seeped into her subconscious, followed by a chorus of others, weaving a haunting harmony of distraction through her thoughts. She tried to fight the hypnotic haze their music created, but it was so hard to resist their siren call. It took all her effort just to look up into the aquarium on the opponent's side of the stadium.

If she had thought one lone merman was alluring,

seeing an entire pod of his kin lined up along the glass, all their tails undulating back and forth in unison, was absolutely mesmerizing.

She had to remind herself that she *wanted* to fight their violation of her mind.

Beads of perspiration formed along her forehead as she tried to combat the enchantment their lyrics were weaving through her neuro-communicator, but she wasn't able to move any part of her body but her eyes. Lids heavy, she dragged her eyes back down to the pool table to watch in horror as the Nirav lined up his last shot and smashed the cue ball into the eight ball, hurtling the miniature planet along the rail cushion, and right to its doom.

"Earth, corner pocket," the robot intoned as she watched all the hope for her future fall into darkness with an appropriately loud impact sound.

The stadium erupted into a standing ovation of alien hands, claws, and feelers, all clapping in a human affectation of delight. It seemed the Tournament Committee had been thorough in educating their diverse Consortium membership about the appropriate *homo sapienes* reaction to a win. It was a pity they hadn't been as committed in advocating fair play.

Ruby wished she could cry foul, or better still, punch Nirav in his perfectly-structured face, but instead the voices in her head cajoled her to stand and move into the center of the stadium. While Mark32i formally announced the winner of the first Intergalactic Eight Ball Pool Tournament, her puppeteers forced her to extend her hand to shake the merman's in a gesture of good will.

You bloody bastard, she thought at him.

He tilted his head, and inclined it. *Not accurate, but I will accept the connotation,* he replied, his words weaving through the siren song ensnaring her mind.

She was not surprised that he could hear her. *You somehow hacked into my neuro-communicator to access my knowledge of the game. You used it to cheat.*

No, he replied sincerely, *to win.*

She fought against the binds on her mind. *You. Had. No. Right.*

He kept ahold of her hand, turning them around to bow to the audience. *I had every right. We were at an unfair disadvantage.*

Disgust colored her tone. *And how do you figure that?*

We were playing an Earth game against the very race that created it.

You didn't stop to consider that we are also very much out of our depth. We're the newest race in the Consortium, and so very far away from the only home we have known.

Nirav didn't immediately answer, but she could tell that he was considering her words. *I am honor-bound to do whatever I can to ensure a future for my pod,* he replied, finally.

So am I.

The inference she had placed on those three little words were not lost to him. His eyes widened perceptively. He dragged her around to bow to the audience in the opposite direction before answering. *Your teammates do not appear to view dolphins with the same level of esteem as you.*

Anger flared. *That doesn't lessen their value or their right to fight for their oceans.*

Something she said must have struck a chord in him—
or within the collective minds of his pod. Their hold over
her mind wavered for an instant, their resolve weakening.
You can't keep me silent forever, she added. *I will talk.*

*Who would believe you, after this pleasant display of
camaraderie?* he replied, regaining his composure. He
raised their joined hands and held them above their
heads, to the resounding pleasure of the audience. "I
think we can all acknowledge that there were no losers
today," he announced, to the stadium at large. "Both of
our races, and the rest of the Galactic Consortium, will
benefit from this new alliance, forged today with Earth in
the spirit of sportsmanship."

The audience's reaction was overwhelmingly exuberant
. . . and the perfect distraction for Ruby.

She pushed at the musical enchantment ensnaring her
mind until she found a faltering chord, and reacted
instinctively, using the reactivated neuro-communicator
to send a warning through the gap to her pod.

The dolphins' collective minds surged through the
weak spot in the enchantment, joining their stream of
consciousness with hers. Bolstering her energy and
resolve, they reacted powerfully to the violation on her
mind, pitting their minds against the sirens.

Shock registered on the merman's face. He looked
around to see the dolphin pod were also smashing their
snouts against the weapon-proof glass of their aquarium;
desperate in their need to protect her.

Tell them to stop, he commanded. *Their actions will be
noticed.*

Unable to see what her pod was doing, Ruby fell back

on false bravado. *Awww, are they causing a scene? Something a graceful bow can't cover up?*

They are hurting themselves, he asserted.

His words sent a chill down her spine. *Sun Dancer, whatever you are doing: please tell the pod to stop it.*

He is hurting you.

I know. But he will stop now. She directed her next thought to Nirav: *If you don't want there to be any kind of suspicion raised as to the legitimacy of your win, tell your pod to cease and desist its enchantment. Now.*

You will not mention this . . . little misunderstanding? he temporized, letting go of her hand with a parting flourish for the audience's benefit and turning to greet his approaching teammates.

If you leave my mind now, then no, I will not. For Nirav was right about one thing: she would just look like a sore loser if she made a complaint now, especially after his speech. It wouldn't do Earth any good to look like they were making excuses to weasel their way out of a contract they had made with the Consortium in good faith. She couldn't be selfish and act solely in the interests of her pod now. She had to consider Earth's future in the intergalactic community as a whole.

Satisfied with the veracity of her conclusions, the merman ordered his pod to stop their assault on her mind, and the haunting song dissipated.

Ruby took in a deep, shuddering breath and tested her newfound freedom by turning around to assure herself of the dolphins' physical safety; taking comfort in their continued soothing presence in her mind.

I'm so very sorry, she told them, her heart heavy. For

she had been their appointed champion, and yet her actions today had sanctioned the invasion of their oceans.

I can't speak for the other members of the Consortium, but the Calthérii have no intentions to harm your race, Nirav injected into her mind, and then added: *Not the one you were born into, nor the one you have chosen.*

Anger flared anew. And bitterness. *You promised to sever this connection. You already got what you wanted from me.*

He hesitated before answering. *My pod is no longer involved in this link, but when you return home, we will be traveling with you to your Earth, to become the first wave of the colonization effort. I know we have not made the most admirable of impressions, but we are a desperate race. Our oceans are dying. Yours are not.*

There is nothing I can do about that, she said, somewhat sullenly.

We have come to the conclusion that as a result of your unique physiology and extraordinary relationship with the dolphins, you are the best candidate for us to liaise with on behalf of your world. Your advice could be invaluable in helping us acclimate.

At first she was alarmed, but then she considered his words—and their apparent sincerity—very carefully, for they were entering uncharted waters for both their races. She wanted to eject him and his entire species out the nearest airlock, but since she couldn't get rid of him, she had to concede that working with him might be the best way she could mitigate the threat to her world. *There is a popular saying on Earth,* she told him, softly. *Keep your friends close, and your enemies closer.*

He was silent for a long time—too long for her overwrought nerves to deal with easily. *How about we consider working together so we can find a way to become less close in the future?* he asked, eventually.

She raised her eyebrows, incredulous. After the day they just had, did he just make an overture of friendship? She was still too angry to accept his entreaty at face value, or as having any value at all, but she knew she had to try, for the future of her world. *I'm game if you are.*

THE GREAT KLADNAR RACE

✦ ✦ ✦

By Randall Garrett
and Robert Silverberg

"The hardest skill to acquire in this sport is the one
where you compete all out, give it all you have,
and you are still getting beat no matter what you do.
When you have the killer instinct to fight through
that, it is very special."
—Eddie Reese,
3 Time Head Coach,
U.S. Men's Olympic Swimming Team

*Robert Silverberg is rightly considered by many as one
of the greatest living science fiction writers. His career
stretches back to the pulps and his output is amazing by
any standards. He's authored numerous novels, short
stories and nonfiction books in various genres and
categories. He's also a frequent guest at cons and a regular
columnist for* Asimov's. *His major works include* Dying
Inside, The Book of Skulls, The Alien Years, The World
Inside, Nightfall *with Isaac Asimov,* Son of Man, A Time

of Changes *and the 7* Majipoor Cycle *books. (A major bibliography can be found at* www.majipoor.com.) *His first* Majipoor *trilogy,* Lord Valentine's Castle, Majipoor Chronicles, *and* Valentine Pontifex, *were reissued by ROC Books in May 2012, September 2012, and January 2013.* Tales Of Majipoor, *a new collection bringing together all the short* Majipoor *tales, followed in May 2013.*

Randall Garrett *was a prolific contributor to* Astounding *and other science fiction magazines of the 1950s and 1960s. He instructed Robert Silverberg in the techniques of selling large quantities of action-adventure science fiction, and collaborated with him on two novels about Earth bringing civilization to an alien planet. He is best known for his Lord Darcy books, the novel* Too Many Magicians *and two short story collections, set in an alternate world where a joint Anglo-French empire has survived into the twentieth century and where magic has been scientifically codified. He died in 1987.*

This story, which involves racing alien mounts like horses, first appeared in the December 1956 issue of Amazing Stories *as by "Richard Greer" and has not been reprinted since 1977.*

I don't know whose idea it was to hold the *kladnar* race. There were twelve of us in that miserable trading post on Gornik VII, all sweating out the year that would have to pass before we could apply for transfers to some less deadly-dull planet.

There wasn't much action on Gornik VII so we manufactured some. It happened one morning, as the bunch of us were sitting outside the Terran encampment, waiting boredly for the natives to show up with their produce.

Someone, I wish I knew who it was, pointed to the galumphing form of a *kladnar* approaching in the distance, and said, "Hey! I've got a great idea! Why don't we organize a *kladnar* race?"

I remember the idea amused me tremendously. If you haven't ever seen a tridi of a *kladnar*, you've never seen one of the silliest-looking beasts that ever infested an alien world. They're long and low-slung, with six knob-ended, spindly legs, and broad backs that would be marvelous for carrying passengers or cargo, if it weren't for the ridge of spines running along them. The natives use the *kladnars* as beasts of burden—they don't mind sitting on the spines, it seems—and every morning, we were accustomed to seeing a dozen or more purple-and-green *kladnars* stabled at our outpost while their masters haggled with us over the exchange value of some trinket or gewgaw.

Within a few minutes, we were huddled together in an excited group, discussing the project. At last, something to take the curse of boredom from Gornik VII!

"We can set up a toteboard," Hamilton said. "Lord knows we've got plenty of loose cash!"

"Should we get out a *racing form*?" asked Demaret waggishly. "And who'll print the scorecards?"

Lieutenant Davis stared out at the plain before us. "We can hold the race out there," he said. "A two-mile course, straightaway. There's room for a dozen *kladnars* to run, easily."

"Will the natives lend us the animals?" I asked.

Davis nodded. "They won't mind. It'll be a novelty for them, too."

"It ought to be something," Willis said.

The Great *Kladnar* Race became the biggest thing the insignificant world of Gornik VII had experienced since the day Earthmen had first landed there.

The natives, small, furry humanoids—who were friendly and cooperative at all times—took to the race with great enthusiasm, once we explained what it was all about.

Gummun Lugal, the local chieftain, was the man we had to get it across to. He frowned, wrinkling his furry brow. "I don't quite understand. You want to borrow *kladnars* and let them run in that field?"

I nodded. "That's right."

"But—*why?*"

"It's a sport we Earthmen enjoy. We start all the *kladnars* from the same place, and let them run toward another given place. Then we bet money on which *kladnar* will get there first."

"'Bet'?" Gummun Lugal said, in hopeless confusion. "What is that?"

"I mean," I said, "that each of us puts down a certain sum of money to support the *kladnar* of his choice. Then the man who backed the winning *kladnar* collects some of the other men's money."

"I think I understand," the alien said dimly. "Go through it once again, will you?"

I outlined the scheme to him a second time. Comprehension finally broke through his small brain, and he nodded happily. "I see! I see! It is a game, you might say."

"You might say indeed," I said.

"The twelve *kladnars* will be ready whenever you want them," the chieftain said.

We swung into activity with an enthusiasm you'd hardly expect from twelve Earthmen stuck on a backwater planet. We measured off a two-mile course, built a starting gate, chalked in a finish line; our radio tech cooked up a photo-timer in case of a close heat. We decorated the racing grounds with bright-colored cloth from our endless stock of trading goods, cutting out banners and streamers galore. It looked just like home by the time we were finished.

The day of the race, the natives started filing into the stands we had erected, and old Gummun Lugal and some of his sons came galumphing in, riding a dozen *kladnars*, which they brought around back to our tent.

We equipped each one with a silk of a different color, with a large number emblazoned on it, and the native jockeys each had an armband of the same color. An armband was the best we could do, since they wouldn't wear anything else.

The day before, we had looked over the twelve *kladnars* they were supplying. Each of us had a chance to go down the row, peering at teeth and forepaws, trying to judge the things. We had no record of previous performances, of course. The *kladnars* were simply beasts of burden, not racing animals. It was a familiar sight on Gornik VII to see a long string of them trudging along Indian file carrying bundles of goods. So we had to guess which one might be the fastest. There was no sure thing.

Naturally, we kept our conclusions to ourselves. I picked Number 5 myself, a sturdy looking animal with a glint of fierce determination in his eye. He seemed a sure thing to come through first, since the rest of the *kladnars*, it seemed to me, were much sadder creatures and one of them, Number 9, was so decrepit-looking that I was sure he'd drop dead after the first furlong.

Computer technician Flaherty dragged his small Mark VII job out of the ship and set it up at the track, and radio tech Dombrowski hooked the computer to a videoscreen to make an improvised parimutuel board.

We opened a betting window. Lieutenant Davis stood behind it and took the money, while the crowds of natives watched with keen interest from the stands. All eleven of us lined up, credit pieces in hand, to bet.

"Four credits on Number 3," Demaret said.

"I'll put my dough on Number 7," said Dombrowski.

"Mine's Number 6," said Willis.

"Same here," said Flaherty, and the two Irishmen glared unhappily at each other. Naturally, two bets on the same *kladnar* reduced the possible winnings on the creature.

"I'll take 5," I said.

The odds on the screen flickered and changed with each bet. When we were all through, I glanced up at the board to see how things stood.

Three *kladnars* led the list at 12-1. No one at all had put money on Numbers 2, 4, or 9, and they rated as longshots. From there the odds trailed away. My *kladnar*, Number 5, had proved popular; I stood to pick up only a couple of credits in the event of a win.

"Okay," Lieutenant Davis said. "The bets are all in. Let's get the race under way."

"One moment please," said a thin voice. We all glanced down in surprise, and saw the small form of Chieftain Gummun Lugal. He elbowed his way to the betting window and peered up at the lieutenant.

"What is it?" Davis asked.

"We'd like to know," the chieftain asked hesitantly, "if it's all right for our people to place bets, too."

Davis frowned. "You want to bet?"

Gummun Lugal nodded.

We held a hasty conference outside the window. "Why not?" I said. "Their money's good, isn't it? And it increases the total kitty tremendously."

"It confuses things, though," Demaret objected. "If we mix their money and ours—"

"We can equalize it later," Davis said. "I think it's a good idea to let them bet."

So did the rest of us, and we told Gummun Lugal that it was all right. He turned and yelled something to the stands, and what looked like an endless stream of aliens descended from the bleachers and formed a long line in front of the betting window.

Fifteen minutes later, we were very worried indeed.

I stared up at the parimutuel board. "They're all

betting on Number 9," I said. "Every last one of them! And Number 9's a dog. It'll keel over before the race can start."

"If it does we'll be lucky," Davis said. "If 9 should win we'll have to pay out a fortune, even with the odds as low as they are."

Demaret scowled. "There's something funny going on. There must be some reason why the natives are all going for the same *kladnar*. You think the race is fixed?"

"I don't know," the lieutenant said. "Let's go see Gummun Lugal again."

We ringed ourselves around the chieftain and Davis said, "Gummun Lugal, we want to make a change in the nature of the race."

"Lieutenant?"

"We want to change things a little bit. Instead of having your people ride the *kladnars*, we'll be the jockeys."

The Chieftain was silent for a moment, and Davis added, "If you won't agree to that, we'll have to call off the race."

Immediately he begged us to reconsider. "No, no, we'll be deeply honored to have the Earthmen ride our lowly beasts!" he said. "By all means!"

"You don't object?"

"Not at all," Gummun Lugal said.

"Very good. We'll start the race immediately. The board's closed, and no more bets will be accepted."

Davis called us together. "All right, men. We're going to ride these beasts ourselves, and we're going to ride them fairly. I'll assign you to mounts at random, and if you happen to be riding the wrong horse, ride it as if you've got your pension bet on it. We can't afford to look dishonest in front of these natives."

Dombrowski raised his hand. "Fine, sir—but I have a suggestion. Suppose you let *me* ride Number 9—just as a precautionary measure?" The radio tech patted his 300-pound girth and chuckled. "I may slow the beast up a bit, you know."

"Go ahead," Davis said. "The rest of you take these slips of paper, and get aboard. We've got to get the race going."

I drew Number 3.

Demaret, who had bet on 3, smiled and said, "Give her a run, will you? I've got four credits riding on her tail."

"Don't worry," I said. "I'll be in there all the way." I glanced over at Number 5, and saw Lieutenant Davis climbing aboard. *Make it a good run, Lieutenant,* I thought silently. But I didn't intend to hold Number 3 back. I'd ride it with all I had, even if it meant beating out my own horse in a photo-finish.

I climbed aboard 3 and guided it slowly to the starting gate. The course was a two-mile straightaway, so position didn't much matter. Next to me, Dombrowski sat athwart poor bedraggled old 9, carrying with him the hopes and cash of the whole native village.

Since all twelve of us were needed to ride, Davis handed the starting gun to Gummun Lugal and told him what to do.

I grabbed the reins.

"Go!"

The shot resounded loudly and we were off. My *kladnar* broke badly, and I found myself in the back almost at once. To my horror, I saw Dombrowski and Number 9 several paces in the lead.

I urged my mount on. It wasn't pleasant, riding that beast. The row of blunt three-inch spines down its wide back didn't make for a pleasant cushion, and its six spindly legs went up and down like a set of out-of-phase pistons. I knew I was going to get awfully seasick before the race was over.

"Giddyap!" I yelled, not knowing an appropriate command for a *kladnar*. And, gradually, my animal started to move. I passed into the bunched pack, threaded past, emerged neck-and-neck with Lieutenant Davis aboard 5 and Demaret on 7. The *kladnars* weren't moving at much more than a fast crawl, and I turned to wave at Davis as I pushed past.

His face was set in a grim line. He gestured up ahead, and I gasped.

Old Number 9 was ten paces ahead, jogging along placidly without worrying about Dombrowski's bulk in the slightest. The race was coming to the halfway point—and Number 9 was in the lead!

"Let's go, boy!" I crooned. My mount edged past Number 7, then past my own favorite, 5. *Good-bye, sweet money*, I thought. I knew it was up to me to catch Number 9.

I could see the ancient beast plodding along just ahead. He wasn't moving very quickly, but my own mount was going even more slowly. I thudded my heels into the *kladnar*'s side, tried to urge him onward.

No soap. I got up within about two paces of Number 9 and then my *kladnar* fell into an obliging trot. It was lickety-split, lickety-split, all the way to the finish line. Dombrowski and Number 9 crossed first. I came over right after to place.

I turned and looked back. The other ten *kladnars* were stretched out in a long line.

The crowd was roaring. I thought of the cash we'd have to pay out to cover those hundreds of bets on Number 9, and felt sick.

It took nearly two hours to pay off all the natives. They hadn't bet much individually, but there were a hell of a lot of them.

We had to pay them, naturally. It wasn't only a matter of honor; the company would have raised holy hell if we'd welched our bets and lost face to the local populace.

We exhausted our own kitty pretty quickly. We'd made the damn fool mistake of guaranteeing a profit, so we had to pay out more than we took in. When our own money was gone, we had to dig into company money. Luckily, it held out to the end. We were bankrupt and in debt to our employers, but we'd paid off on the race.

Gummun Lugal was near the betting window as Lieutenant Davis sourly paid out the bets. He kept bobbing his head and smiling, showing his toothy, rust-red smile. "What wonderful men you Earthmen are!" he cried. "Distributing all this wealth to us!"

"It's not our idea," I said. My voice must have sounded surly, because the old chieftain's smile faded.

"But—I—I don't understand—"

"Look here, Gummun Lugal," I said, trying to keep from sounding too nasty, "just how in blazes did all your people know that Number 9 was going to win? That decrepit old creature couldn't outrun a man with two broken legs."

His eyes widened in utter astonishment. "You mean— you didn't know? But—"

"What is this? How did you cheat us? And why?" I was really boiling, and it took every bit of self-control I had to keep my voice even.

"Cheat? Why, no. We thought you were well aware that Number 9 was the lead animal of the caravan."

"Caravan?" My voice must have cracked there; it sounded like a parrot-screech. "You gave us a trained caravan team?"

He smiled happily. "Of course. Otherwise they would not have run together. Unless they are trained together, the *kladnar* will shy away from each other and fight."

"And Number 9 was the lead animal?"

"Oh, yes. We think it was a fine race. It showed the training of the animals. Yes; a very fine race. We must try to run another sometime."

I turned away. "Sure. As soon as Hades freezes over, we'll let you know. We'll have another race then."

"Thank you. It was fine of you; very fine."

It was very plain now. The caravan teams were trained to follow each other in a certain order—or else. No *kladnar* would have gone against his lifelong training and tried to pass his leader.

It cost us more than mere money to pay off that race; we lost our transfers, because we had to stay on Gornik VII an extra year to make up our losses.

We managed not to get bored, though. We didn't run any more *kladnar*-races. And I wish I could remember who the bum was who thought of the idea in the first place!

ADVANTAGES

✧ ✧ ✧

by Louise Marley

"An athlete cannot run with money in his pockets.
He must run with hope in his heart
and dreams in his head."
—Emil Zatopek,
Czechoslovakian Olympic Gold Medalist,
Track and Field

*Louise Marley is a multi-award winning writer of fantasy
and science fiction. Much of her work is influenced by her
first career as a classical singer, especially her novel*
Mozart's Blood. *Other works, such as* The Terrorists of
Irustan, *have been hailed as significant feminist works.
Under the pseudonym Cate Campbell, she also writes
historical fiction. Louise lives on the Olympic Peninsula
in the Pacific Northwest. More information is at*
louisemarley.com *or at* catecampbell.net.

*One of the things I wanted for this anthology were
stories on sports we had not seen before. In my research,
I never came across a story in the world of gymnastics.
So here Louise examines what happens when a custody*

battle by parents has a major effect on their daughter's competition.

✧ ✧ ✧

Zory stood inside the Olympic Pavilion, eyeing the gymnasts tumbling, vaulting, twirling on beams, spinning across mats, and her belly trembled with nerves. They all seemed to move impossibly fast, legs and arms and extra limbs blurring until they looked like centipedes. The variety of costumes, a kaleidoscope of scarlet, green, sparkling white, vivid yellow stripes, dizzied her. But it was the people—the other athletes—who made her feel out of place and awkward, with her simple four limbs and small, narrow body.

Her father had tried to prepare her. "I want you to understand them," he said. He was projecting a succession of images of enhanced humans. "They've been genetically altered. Faster brains. A variety of physical configurations. This man, for example, with secondary arms for work in the outer conduits of Hai Chin Station. This girl has tertiary limbs, for external work on the Mars dome. The geneticists redesigned their growth patterns, spliced genes, replaced mitochondria, reengineered them for whatever work was needed."

Another image appeared, and though Jacob tried to move past it, Zory had already seen, and gasped in horror. Jacob had sighed. "Yes. Sometimes they go too far. Some children, like that one, can't survive. Most of them do. The point is, the people you'll be competing against have advantages."

Zory, looking around the arena now, felt a fresh wave

of nausea, followed by a flood of pity. The faces were young, vulnerable, as hopeful as she supposed her own must be, but many of them topped monstrous bodies.

Cruithne, her own asteroid home, had no enhanced humans, nor any children except herself. She had always been indulged and pampered, the tiny colony's own little space child. The concept of these other young people, engineered, manipulated, forever altered, was difficult to accept. She wondered if they chose to become Olympic athletes, or if the Games were another way their colonies made use of them.

Her coach rolled to her side, and spoke in the calmest of her synthesized voices. "Concentrate on your performance, Zory."

Zory swallowed, and tried to push aside the questions crowding her mind. "I know."

"Don't worry about anything else." Maxie's voice was as warm as an embrace, and though she had no hands, Zory felt her encouragement as clearly as if there were a supporting arm encircling her shoulders.

"It's just—Maxie, they look—" She dropped her voice, so that no one else could hear her. "They don't look human."

"They are as human as you are."

"Of course." Zory sighed, and moved a little closer to Maxie's comforting solidity. Dozens of eyes turned to them in unabashed curiosity.

Amid this stunning variety of body shapes, skin colors, limb configurations, Zory was the only athlete in the dome—absolutely the only one—whose coach was a robot.

Maxie had required special approval, and a lengthy examination of her programming, before the Committee allowed her participation. During the interview, with Zory and her father and Maxie lined up like interrogated criminals, a sour-faced woman in the green jacket, with the ancient five-ring symbol on her collar, said, "This would never have been allowed on Earth."

Another one, younger, with a sturdy set of secondaries and smiling dark eyes, said, "Earth is gone. So are Earth standards."

Zory felt her father's body tense beside hers, and she slipped a hand beneath the table to touch his. He held her fingers, as he said, "My daughter wanted to be a gymnast. An automated coach was all that was available."

"So you say," the cranky woman snapped.

"It's true," said the younger one. It appeared he outranked Cranky Woman. "Cruithne couldn't afford to hire and import a coach."

Cranky Woman muttered, "But they could afford a robot? None of the other colonies can."

The younger man frowned at her. "Superfluous equipment, already on the asteroid. Come on, we've argued the limits on genetic and surgical modifications. An automated coach should be easy. Let's vote."

The vote had been close, but it had gone Cruithne's way. Now, with her stomach fluttering and her heartbeat thudding in her ears, Zory Silver had arrived. The gymnastics portion of the Games of the 63rd Olympiad was about to begin. She would have her chance. She did her best not to hear the whispers fluttering after her as she crossed the arena.

The attention was discomfiting. Cruithners rarely stared at each other, or crowded, or raised their voices. Their colony was too small to allow for bad manners.

Maxie was a marvel, though. Her appearance was that of a smallish silver barrel, though she had a number of alternate configurations. She had been built as a mining assistant, an MT 630, but with Cruithne's lode exhausted in the early years, and the asteroid rededicated to low-gravity research, Maxie had disappeared. She had languished all but forgotten in a closet for longer than Zory had been alive.

Zory had been four when the Cruithners gathered in the Commons to watch the Games of the 60th Olympiad. The Games had been the first in decades, and they were disorganized and unruly. Enhanced athletes needed new rules, new customs. History was examined, criticized, envied. Athletes came from Mars, and the Moon, from the giant High Frontier Habitat and various other space stations. To tiny Zory, everything they did was thrilling, especially the girls in bright leotards who tumbled and spun and leaped across the arena. She made up her mind, then and there, that what she wanted most in the universe was to be one of them.

Jacob Silver brought the little silver robot out of its closet, reprogrammed it, and reassigned it to the role of gymnastics coach. Four-year-old Zory gave it a name and a gender. MT 630 became Maxie, and sometimes, though she never told anyone, Zory pretended Maxie was her mother.

Her own mother, Zoriah, had fled the isolation and boredom of Cruithne when Zory was an infant. Jacob tried to track her, but when Earth went dark, he lost her trail. Zory never thought of her. She didn't remember her.

She loved Maxie, though, and all the Cruithners were accustomed to seeing the little robot trailing Zory wherever she went. Zory couldn't imagine being here, in the Olympic Pavilion bola of the Bigelow X Space Station, without her.

Jacob hadn't wanted her to compete.

"But why?" she had asked. "I know it's expensive, but I can go by myself, with Maxie."

"It is expensive, that's true, Zory, but that's not the reason." He had rubbed his hand over his lined forehead, a gesture Zory and everyone else in the colony recognized. Jacob carried the weight of Cruithne's future on his stooped shoulders. He fought a constant battle for the colony's survival. Other colonies—bigger colonies—had much more to offer than Cruithne. It was his job, and his constant preoccupation, to promote Cruithne's unique advantages, its little pockets of low gravity where research could be conducted without disruption.

Jacob took Zory's hand. "I just want to warn you. These Olympic Games aren't for the athletes, though the Committee makes it look as if they are."

"If they're not for the athletes, then why do they hold them?"

"To prove to everyone that we're all still united. One people. It's profitable for them if everyone feels that way."

"Are we, Jacob? One people?"

He had released her hand, and rubbed his forehead. "Sometimes I wonder about that."

✦   ✦   ✦

Zory was tall for a gymnast. She had spent more time than anyone knew in low gravity, exploring abandoned mine sections, discovering hidden rooms and nooks most Cruithners had forgotten. Her legs were strong, her hips and shoulders startlingly flexible, and her sense of balance impeccable.

She would compete in all the events. No one expected her to win, but Cruithne agreed to the expense of her trip to uphold the honor of their colony, to demonstrate that in these days of aging populations and declining birth rates, tiny Cruithne could produce not only vital research, but an Olympic athlete.

Maxie guided Zory's training in an orderly progression, following protocols set up by coaches of the past, configuring old videos into instructional holos. When they began, Zory was already doing handsprings and somersaults and cartwheels. In careful order, she learned round-offs and flic flacs and walkovers, straddle pike jumps and stag leaps. She practiced balance-beam routines on a shape painted on the floor until Maxie allowed the beam to be raised to regulation height. Zory spun and swung and tucked for hours each day, until Maxie declared an end.

More than once, Zory protested, "I'm not tired!"

"Your bio signs say you are, Zory. Time to rest." No amount of arguing, Zory learned, would move her.

Rarely, Zory hurt herself in practice, but when it happened, Maxie forbade any exercises that would stress the injury until it was fully healed. She also made Zory wait to pass levels of difficulty until she judged she was old enough.

Impatient Zory complained. "Earth gymnasts did all of this, and they were so young!"

"Earth was a violent place," Maxie said. "Those girls worked with sprains, muscle tears, even broken bones. You're not going to do that."

Zory knew the stories. She had read everything she could find about her sport. She knew some coaches had abused their gymnasts. They drove them, starved them, lied about their ages, covered up their injuries. They shouted and slapped and insulted. One, in preparation for the Games of the 26th Olympiad, had struck an eleven-year-old gymnast so hard he killed her.

But Zory was sure none of these stories applied to her. She was full of confidence. She wanted to try every maneuver, every trick.

Maxie held firm, so Zory practiced in secret.

It was her secret ambition to win the vault. It was her best event, and she had practiced a special version found on the old videos. It had been forbidden when a girl died attempting it, but that was on Earth, long before the Games were revived. In her hours alone, leaping and spinning through the secret, low-gravity spaces, Zory felt as if she could fly. The feeling of that—the freedom, the balance, the sense of being at home in the air as she was on the ground—was seared into her muscle memory.

Now, as she shrugged out of her warm-up jacket and trousers, and dusted her hands with chalk, she felt the camera array fix on her. Her leotard was as simple as her warm-ups, deep black, spangled with silvery stars. The head of food services on Cruithne had sewn it herself, smiling over each stitch, showing up at Jacob's cube over and over to check the fitting. She would be watching, of course. They all would, the engineers, the technicians, the researchers. They would gather in the Commons, sitting in groups. They would be subdued, because it wasn't the Cruithne way to cheer and shout, but they would be intent, and proud. Their very own Zory Silver would prove their colony the equal of any other.

Zory's stomach quivered anew.

She glanced at Maxie, and saw the twinkling lights in her coach's face plate that represented a smile. She smiled back, and the quiver eased. "We're finally here," she said.

"There was never a doubt." Lights flashed again across Maxie's faceplate. "Never a doubt in the universe."

The Committee had decided to break with tradition, and to begin women's gymnastics with the uneven bars. Zory was content to make it through her routine without any glaring errors. The acrobatics of a gymnast from High Frontier, a stocky girl with tertiary limbs, stunned everyone in the pavilion with a pirouette into a blind change that made her look like a starfish rolling across the bars. All the gymnasts stood to applaud her when she dismounted, and everyone knew she would win the event.

Floor exercises came next. Two girls with secondary limbs and extra digits scored high with their complicated sequences and stunning walkovers. Zory knew her chances were small against her enhanced competitors. She relaxed, and had fun with her routine. She loved tumbling, and her twisting back layouts were smooth and high and satisfying. She and Maxie had fitted a double Arabian into the end of her program, and when she finished her double front salto, she saw by the twinkle racing across Maxie's faceplate that it had all gone well. Not well enough to win, but they hadn't expected that.

Zory stole a moment to look up at the video array and press her palms together in acknowledgment of her supporters on Cruithne.

For the first time, two of the other coaches—one from High Frontier, and one from the Moon Colony—nodded to her as she left the arena, and murmured respectful compliments. It didn't occur to Zory until she was already in the shower that they had completely ignored Maxie, sparkling and buzzing happily beside her. Maxie wouldn't mind the snub, of course. Zory did. It cast a shadow on what was otherwise a glorious day. Zory surprised everyone by coming in sixth in the floor competition, but she had begun to feel defensive. She found it difficult to respond to the congratulations of people who pretended they didn't see Maxie, or deliberately looked away from her.

The balance beam in women's gymnastics was an event in which competitors with secondary and tertiary limbs had a distinct advantage. The indisputable winner was a wiry Martian with secondary and tertiary limbs and a leotard of scarlet and silver. She looked awkward and alien on the floor, like a red spider grown horrifically large, but on the beam she was beautiful. She performed two separate split-leg leaps to show all of them to advantage, and when she executed her full turn on one foot, she held all her limbs at angles as graceful and impossible as the petals of an orchid.

Zory's own program on the beam was of the old-fashioned variety, saltos and splits and spins modeled after gymnasts long vanished. She thought the spidery girl's routine was thrilling, and she applauded with enthusiasm as the girl left the arena. Sirena, she remembered, checking the scoreboard. Sirena from the Mars Colony.

The Martian girl glanced up at her. Her cheeks were pink, but her lips were pinched and pale, and her eyelids drooped with exhaustion. Zory essayed a smile, and the other gymnast lifted one of her long, thin arms in acknowledgment. As she turned to walk back to the rest of her team, Zory saw that three of her limbs were wrapped. There were bandages on her hands and elbows, and she was limping.

As Zory, in her turn, walked toward the beam, she saw another gymnast, one in violent yellow stripes, pointing to Maxie. She was whispering to another girl wearing the same colors, and they were both laughing.

Anger stiffened Zory's shoulders. She cracked her hands together, sending a puff of chalk over her star-studded leotard.

Maxie whispered to her, and Zory jerked around to see that her coach had rolled to the very edge of the arena floor. "It doesn't matter," Maxie said, in a voice just for Zory. The pattern of lights in her faceplate was slow, soothing. "Nothing matters. Do your best, Zory. Visualize it."

One of the officials, off to Zory's left, cleared his throat. Zory whispered thanks to Maxie, nodded briefly to the official, and turned toward the beam.

There was no time to gather herself again, to regain her concentration. Delay would mean deductions. She saluted the judges, and balanced on her toes, trying to picture the round-off, the flic flac, the double salto and twist of her first sequence. Instead, the image in her mind was of the girls in yellow stripes.

The distraction cost her. There was plenty of height in her mount, but she barely managed to bring both feet onto the beam. The next elements, the back-in, full-out, went by in such a blur she had no idea how she had managed them, or how they looked. Somehow, she found herself in her handstand, her legs automatically dropping into the splits by dint of long practice. She seized the moment, no more than a few seconds, to breathe again, to anticipate the coming dismount.

Only then, at the end of her routine, did she feel like herself. She loved aerials, and that sense returned to her as she leaped, spun, tumbled toward the floor. As in the old days, playing in low gravity, she felt nearly weightless. She had only two arms, but at such times her arms felt like wings, as if she could slow her passage through the air, as if she had all the time in the world to find her balance point, flex her knees and ankles, find the forgiving mat beneath her feet. She stuck her landing effortlessly, arms up, spine flexed, eyes and smile blazing.

She left the floor on a wave of reassuring applause. Maxie's faceplate glowed approval, and her two upper appendages, usually folded into her chassis, rose as Zory reached her, expressing pride. Zory grinned down at her, then turned up to the camera array again, palms pressed together to salute Cruithne.

As she shrugged into her warm-ups amid the noise and lights and movement of the pavilion, she felt a sudden, childish longing for her father.

She looked across the arena at the team from High

Frontier. The girls had their arms around each others' shoulders, and their coach was patting each one's back in turn.

Maxie said, "Do you wish I could pat you that way, Zory?"

"You are patting me, Maxie."

"It's not the same without hands."

"It's just that I miss Jacob. And Cruithne."

"Of course. You feel lonely."

Maxie didn't need reassurance, but Zory had grown accustomed to treating her like a human. She said, with affection, "I'm not lonely. I have you, Maxie."

In response, Maxie's faceplate glittered with tiny starbursts, which made Zory laugh, and stroke her coach's cool hull before they turned, side by side, to leave the arena.

When a woman stepped in front of them, Maxie swerved neatly out of the way, but Zory and the woman nearly collided. Zory said, "Excuse me!" with automatic courtesy. When she looked up into the woman's face, she sucked in a startled breath. She stared, her mouth a little open, her heart beginning to thump.

Looking at the woman, a stranger, was like looking into a distorted mirror. The woman's mouth was harder and thinner than hers, the cheeks hollowed, the eyelids crinkled. Otherwise . . .

"Zory," the woman said softly.

Maxie rolled close to Zory again. Her faceplate had gone dark. "Miss Silver needs to—" she began, but the woman spoke again, as if Maxie weren't there.

"We do look alike, don't we?" she said. She put out a thin hand toward Zory's cheek.

Zory flinched away. "Who are you?" she muttered.

Maxie tried again. "Excuse us, please. Miss Silver needs—"

The woman said, "I've come for you. I know I haven't been much of a mother—"

"I don't have a mother!" Zory whispered.

"Excuse us, please," Maxie said.

"Of course you have a mother! I'm your mother. I'm Zoriah. You're named after me—and you can see the resemblance! I would have known you anywhere. We have the same hair, same eyes. You're taller. Thinner. Otherwise—"

People began to jostle them as they tried to make their way out of the pavilion. Maxie's appendages came out, first two, then four, as she tried to protect her charge from being bumped or stepped on. Zoriah stepped between Zory and her coach with an abrupt movement, making Maxie whirr and buzz in confusion. She couldn't push back. Her programming wouldn't allow it. Her appendages moved uncertainly, and her words came faster and faster. "Excuse me, please. Excuse me, please."

Zory, without stopping to think, thrust the woman out of Maxie's way. She was strong, an athlete, and the woman stumbled backward as Zory snapped, "Don't do that to Maxie."

Zoriah recovered her balance by seizing a chair. She straightened, and scowled. "Who's Maxie?"

Zory put a possessive hand on Maxie's rounded top. "This is Maxie. My coach."

"You call it Maxie? I can't believe your father allows that."

"Why shouldn't he?"

"Because it's not a person!"

Maxie said, "Zory, you need to move out of the arena."

"I know, Maxie. I'm trying."

People were streaming past them now, as the final events of the day wound down. In the hubbub, Zory seized one of Maxie's appendages and held it, to make sure they weren't forced apart in the crowd.

Zoriah folded her arms. "We need to talk, Zory. I know this comes as a surprise to you, but there was no other way. You'll be coming with me. I have an order."

"Order? What order?"

Maxie said, "Excuse us, please," and Zoriah slapped the top of her hull.

"Can you shut that thing up?" she cried.

Zory stuck out her chin, and elbowed Zoriah out of her way.

Maxie rolled close at her heels, though Zoriah tried to step into her path. "Excuse us, please," Maxie said. The lights in her faceplate were level, but Zory could have sworn there was a tinge of triumph in her voice. "Excuse us, please. Miss Silver needs to leave."

"It's an order from Youth Development," Zoriah called after them.

"Never heard of it," Zory said as she pressed through the crowd with Maxie at her heels.

Zoriah followed, dodging athletes and coaches and spectators. "You can't ignore it!"

"I can," Zory threw over her shoulder.

"No, you can't. You have to comply. I'm taking you to

High Frontier. I want you to have the advantages of a bigger colony, more opportunities . . ."

Zory whirled to face her. Maxie, clicking in alarm, faceplate glowing red, rolled to a spot between them. "I don't even know you!" Zory cried.

"Look at me! Look at *us*!"

Zory turned away again. "That proves nothing."

Zory and Maxie, with Zoriah in pursuit, had to shove their way through the crowd to reach the locker room. There they moved side by side into blessed silence. No one but athletes and coaches were allowed, and Zoriah, though she spat curses, was forced to remain outside.

"I'll get you a towel, Zory," Maxie said.

"No," Zory said. Despite her bravado, a chill of anxiety was creeping over her. "I'll do it. You link to Cruithne, Maxie. Get Jacob."

"I thought she was on Earth. Dead, perhaps. Now I learn she's on the Director's staff of High Frontier."

"I know." Zory had calmed down since the confrontration in the pavilion, but she still felt anxious, and she could tell that Maxie, who technically had no feelings, was struggling with this development. Her father was, too. His face was drawn, the usual furrows in his forehead deeper than she had ever seen them. "I don't think there's any question," Zory added. "She looks so much like me. Or the other way around, I guess."

"Yes. It was clear when you were tiny that you were going to look like Zoriah."

"What do I do? She can't really stop me from the event tomorrow, can she?"

"Dr. Silver, excuse me," Maxie put in.

"Yes, Maxie."

"I've accessed the Bureau's data. Zoriah has procured a ruling under the Development of Youth Initiative. All the colonies and habitats agreed to it."

"Cruithne didn't."

"Cruithne opted out."

"Cruithne had no youth at that time."

"Maxie, is it true? The ruling gives her authority to take Zory to High Frontier?"

"Yes. She has authority over her until she's eighteen."

Zory gasped, "I won't go!"

"Come back to Cruithne immediately, then," Jacob said. "I'll arrange the shuttle."

"But tomorrow's the vault!"

"I don't know if I can stop her taking you, Zory. Cruithne conceded their vote."

"I don't want to go to High Frontier, and I don't want to miss the vault! Maxie? Can't we do something?"

A straight line flashed across Maxie's faceplate, and an instant later, she said, "Zoriah has to apply to the Olympic Committee to exercise the ruling. I estimate that will require between six and twenty hours."

"Can you keep Zoriah away from Zory?"

"I will try."

"Do."

"Yes, Dr. Silver."

"Zory, don't let Maxie out of your sight."

"I won't. But listen! Twenty hours—that would give me time to do the vault."

"It's a risk, Zory. If she gets the ruling from the

Committee, she can force you to travel to High Frontier."

Zory's voice broke as she repeated, "Jacob, it's the vault."

"I know, sweetheart."

She whispered, "I want to stay."

There was a pause, full of tension on both ends of the link. Jacob said at last, "It's your decision, Zory. Maxie will do her best to protect you."

Maxie, amber and blue lights gleaming in her faceplate, said, "I will, Dr. Silver."

Zory, tears trembling on her eyelashes, pressed her palms together, and nodded goodbye to her father. She held on to the tears until the link closed, doing her best not to sob.

Calmly, as if nothing were out of the ordinary, Maxie swiveled to a nearby bench, extruded a limb, and picked a fresh towel from a stack. She held it out to Zory. "Cry as long as you need to. Then we'll go out the back."

Zory tried hard to sleep, but she kept waking to look at the tiny clock embedded in Maxie's hull. She knew all too well that this was her only chance. She had done well enough so far. She had nothing to be ashamed of, but she wanted more, and the vault was her last chance. Even when she fell asleep, she dreamed of watching the minutes and seconds tick away. She rose in the morning heavy-eyed and sluggish.

Maxie behaved as if nothing were amiss. Zory noticed, with a little sigh, that Maxie had turned off her clock.

"Light breakfast," Maxie ordered, as she always did before a workout. "Then stretching."

On this day, Zory felt more worried than nervous. As they made their way from the cafeteria to the pavilion, she couldn't help glancing over her shoulder, expecting at any moment to see Zoriah hurrying after her.

As she was wriggling out of her warm-ups, Maxie said, "Dr. Silver sent you a message from everyone on Cruithne. They wish you good luck."

"What about *her*?"

Maxie's faceplate went dark for a moment, then lighted again with the comforting amber and blue lights. "The Committee is meeting on the opposite side of the bola. Zoriah is there, waiting her turn."

"Where am I in the order, Maxie?"

"Number six."

It was a good position, though she wished she could go now, right away, before Zoriah could get her ruling. She breathed, and stretched her arms behind her to loosen her shoulders.

She had to focus on her vault. Maxie would be with her, talking through the visualization, reiterating the elements to concentrate on and which to trust to muscle memory.

And here was her own plan, the one Maxie knew nothing about. She felt a stab of remorse, and tried to remind herself that Maxie couldn't have hurt feelings. Still, it would hurt to let her coach understand she had devised a trick on her own, one that would have been deemed too dangerous if anyone had known about it. She meant to use it only if she had to, only if she needed it on her second run. This was her once in a lifetime chance.

No one expected her to carry a medal back to Cruithne—except herself.

She took a swift glance into the stands, but didn't see the dark hair and slight figure of Zoriah. She took a deep breath, and did her best to shrug off her worry. This was her moment. Nothing must distract her. She dropped her jacket on the bench, straightened her shoulders, and moved out onto the mat for her warm-ups.

When the competition began, she did as she and Maxie had planned. She turned her back, closed her eyes, and did her best not to hear the announcer, the applause, the announcement of the scores. She would know, after her first vault, if it was good enough.

Maxie spoke to her, soothingly, descriptively. They did breathing exercises, and shoulder-loosening exercises. Zory shook out her arms and her legs, bent her toes and flexed her feet, blocking out everything else going around her. Not until the fifth competitor had finished did Maxie say, "Now, Zory, it's your turn. Have fun out there!"

Zory was ready. Her body tingled with energy, despite the poor sleep of the night before. Her muscles were fired, eager for movement. Her heart lifted at the thought that it was here, at last. Her moment had come. The judges' green light flashed, and she drew her preparatory breath.

Her run was fast and hard. Her round-off was solid. Her back handspring felt fine, and she had plenty of time for two twists. Her feet sank into the mat, her knees bending. She was slightly off-center, a tiny bit off balance. She took one unsteady step, then caught herself. She straightened, and arced her body into the perfect C shape, arms high beside her ears. It was good.

There was applause, but she barely heard it. There were smiles around her, hands raised to wave, but what she was looking for, and found, were the lights twinkling across Maxie's faceplate. It hadn't been perfect, but it was good. Solid.

Then, behind Maxie, in the little aisle between the barrier and the first bench, she saw Zoriah. An Olympic official, in the green jacket, walked next to her as both of them approached the opening to the arena floor.

Zory gasped, "Maxie!"

Maxie rotated toward the opening, saying hastily, "Never mind. Second vault, Zory!"

Zory turned away just as Zoriah and the official spoke to the guard at the entrance to the arena floor, and started past her. Maxie was rolling swiftly forward, but Zory couldn't guess what she meant to do. She didn't dare delay.

She trotted to the podium once again, her belly trembling with anxiety. She remembered only at the last minute to check her score.

It was excellent. 9.2, a number to be proud of. But it wasn't good enough.

Sirena had scored a 9.4. A girl from High Frontier had a 9.5.

If she wanted this, really wanted it, she would have to do the full Amanar, and she had never done it in full gravity. She had never done it in Maxie's presence, and there was no doubt in her mind her father would have forbidden it.

Out of the corner of her eye, Zory saw Maxie blocking the entrance to the arena floor, all eight of her available appendages extended so she looked like some sort of oversize kitchen implement, or perhaps an undersized satellite. Her various warning lights—power levels, alarm signals, maintenance alerts—blinked and flashed around her hull. Someone reached out to push her, which was futile. Maxie had been built for the mines. One human being, even two, couldn't make her move if she didn't want to.

The judge's light flashed green, and Zory pushed everything else out of her mind. Looking down the runway was like staring down a tunnel with a bright light at the end. The table gleamed like a beacon.

Zory saw nothing but her goal. She heard nothing but the racing of her heart. She threw up her arm in salute, drew the biggest breath her lungs could hold, and started her run.

It was the same vault she had just performed, but with the added half twist that made it the Amanar. She had watched videos of the Earth gymnasts who had done it. And videos of those who had failed. She had even seen the worst failure, the fall from which the gymnast never recovered. She had studied it to find the fatal error, to know what to avoid.

Zory knew perfectly well that practicing it in low gravity was not the same as performing it at Earth standard. Her secret was that she knew what it felt like to fly. It would take more power, a faster run, a higher spring, than any she had done before. It would take an unassailable sense of balance.

She wanted this. With all of her being, she wanted it.

Her round-off was perfect. Her handspring threw her

higher into the air than she had ever gone, and she began to twist. Once, twice, and then—with ample space below her—the extra half twist, the blind landing, the impact of feet on the mat.

She trembled there for a moment, her knees flexing, her arms seizing the air for balance, her toes digging into the surface. The universe seemed to hold its breath around her as she struggled to hold her position, to stick it.

She did. She straightened, threw her arms high, arching her back, holding her triumphant pose for a moment longer, just to make it indisputably clear. She had accomplished the full Amanar, and she had stuck the landing.

As she left the mat and hurried across to Maxie, she gradually became aware of the roar of the audience. Maxie glittered and glowed with lights, not only in her faceplate, but all around her hull. Other coaches and gymnasts crowded around. One of the ugly, squat girls with secondary limbs threw all her arms around Zory, and squeezed her with surprising strength. Sirena reached one of her strange, long arms across Maxie to seize Zory's hand and smile at her. It was a marvelous moment, an instant to be relived and savored over and over in the months and years to come.

It came to an end all too soon. Zoriah and the official forced their way through the crush around Zory. They came at her from opposite sides, and there was nothing Maxie could do to prevent them. Zoriah put a hand under her arm, announcing, "You're coming with me, Zory."

The official put a hand under her other arm, and said,

"You're disqualified, Miss Silver. The vault you just attempted—"

"Performed," Maxie corrected, in the loud, metallic voice meant for the mines.

"Is illegal," the official finished, "as I'm sure you know."

Zory, trapped between Zoriah and the official, glanced back at the scoreboard. "No, it's not!" she cried. "Look, the judges gave me a 9.9! They wouldn't do that if—"

"The score will be thrown out," the official said grimly.

Zory stared at him. "Thrown out?"

"You're disqualified."

"Exactly what the Initiative is all about," Zoriah said, her chin lifted and her eyes glittering with triumph. "Your father can be glad you didn't harm yourself, because he would be held legally responsible."

Maxie said, "Zory's safety is my responsibility."

Zoriah cast Maxie a dismissive glance. "And this thing," she said, "will be disabled immediately."

"I won't go with you." Zory glared at Zoriah, who stood outside her cube with a traveling bag slung over her shoulder and a burly man in the uniform of the Bigelow Station.

"You don't have a choice, Zory. You're in my charge now."

"Where's Maxie?"

"If you mean the robot, it's been decommissioned."

"What does that mean, decommissioned?"

"It will be dismantled for parts. We turned it off."

Zory's head spun suddenly, and she staggered. Zoriah

reached out for her, but Zory dodged her grasp, and clung to the doorjamb instead. "You didn't," she groaned. "You couldn't!"

"I can and I did. It's for your own good, Zory. For your future."

"My future is on Cruithne. With my *father*." She bit out the word, and was rewarded by seeing Zoriah's cheeks redden.

"I can see you resent me. I suppose that's understandable."

"You suppose?" Zory said. A rush of welcome anger cleared her head, and her voice rose. "I don't even *know* you, and you decide you know what's best for me!"

"Get your things," Zoriah said, looking past her into the cramped cube. "The shuttle leaves in an hour and we need to board soon."

"I told you, I'm not going."

For answer, Zoriah stepped back, and nodded to the uniformed man. "Hold her. I'll get her things."

Zory gaped at her as the man stepped around her, and took both her arms in his meaty hands. He was at least a foot taller than she was, and she was sure he was three times her weight. "You—you would *force* me?" she squeaked.

Zoriah didn't answer. She was throwing things into her small bag, shoving them into the corners. The uniformed man muttered, "I'm sorry, miss. Orders."

"Where's Maxie?" Zory demanded. "I want to know where she is!"

As Zoriah led the way through the door and down the corridor, she said, "I told you. It's off. It's useless now."

"I don't care! I want to know—"

She broke off. One of the Olympic officials, the same man who had told her the day before that she was disqualified, was standing in the corridor, in their path. His arms were folded, his legs spread wide, and he looked very, very unhappy.

"What is it?" Zoriah said.

"She's going back to Cruithne."

"She is not! She's coming with me! I have an order—"

"The order has been vacated."

"What? Why?"

"The Olympians—that is to say, the athletes—refused to go on with the Games if we don't release her back to Cruithne."

Zory wriggled free of the heavy hands on her arms. "For me? They did that for me?"

"They're all in the cafeteria, and they won't leave."

"But this is none of their business!" Zoriah cried. "Why don't you make them—"

"Make them? How do you propose we make two hundred and sixteen athletes—most of them with extra arms and legs and bigger brains than mine—do anything they don't want to do?"

Zoriah sputtered a response, but Zory didn't hear it. She was headed down the corridor at a dead run.

When she reached the cafeteria, she burst through the doors, and skidded to a breathless stop. The cafeteria benches were crowded with athletes, still in their warm-ups. They were all mixed together—blue and silver with red and black, green and white with yellow stripes—and when someone caught sight of Zory, a sound began. It was a chant, two syllables over and over: Zo-ry! Zo-ry! Zo-ry!

Zory shrank back into the doorway, overwhelmed. The crowd gradually fell silent, gazing at her and then looking past her at a little clutch of green-jacketed officials who stood scowling at the athletes.

Zoriah's shrill voice was the only sound in the room. "This is preposterous!" she shouted. "After all the money—"

It was the oddest thing, Zory thought. The crowd—that kaleidoscope of colors and shapes and sizes—responded as one, turning their backs on Zoriah and the officials. Only one rose, and started across the room to Zory.

It was Sirena. She walked as if she were swimming through the air, each of her eight limbs moving in its own arc. As she drew near, she held out her top arms, fingers extended.

Zory reached out, too, and they clasped hands. Sirena said, "You won the vault, Zory."

"They disqualified me."

"That's just because they planned for High Frontier to win it."

"They did?"

"Oh, yes. We all knew that."

Zory gave a rueful smile. "I can't believe you're doing this. All of you."

A lopsided grin split the other girl's thin face. "We only have power when we're all together," she said. "Once we go home—that's it."

"They weren't going to let me go to my home."

"You like Cruithne."

"Yes."

"You don't think you might have more advantages on High Frontier?"

"I know I wouldn't. Do you like Mars?"

Sirena's shrug was a complex, rippling gesture, and it was almost as strange as seeing her walk. "Mars is what I was designed for," she said. "I wouldn't fit in anyplace else."

Zory glanced around the room. It was true for them all, she supposed. Their futures had been predetermined. She couldn't see the advantage of that.

Sirena waved a limb in the direction of the athletes. "We'll go back to the competition once you're on the shuttle." She released Zory's hands, and backed away. "Better go quick before somebody thinks of a way to stop you."

"I don't know how to thank you."

Sirena's smile was wistful. "I hope we all got something we wanted, Zory. Now, go!"

Zory was rushed to the shuttle by the officials. Zoriah, fuming, was left behind. There was no time to look for Maxie, to link to Cruithne, or even to collect her things. The Committee wanted her gone so they could resume their broadcast of the Games.

The door irised closed the moment Zory was through the airlock. The seals hissed as she was shut out of the bola, out of the Olympic Pavilion, out of the competition. Her years of practice, countless hours of hard work, her dreams of glory, crumbled to nothing, like a palmful of chalk dust.

The only bright spot was that she should never have to meet Zoriah again.

Maxie was another matter. It was bad enough that the Committee had used them, used all the athletes, for their own purposes. But Maxie—Maxie had hurt no one. She *couldn't* hurt anyone. Zory drifted in the lock, nearly weightless, her heart aching with loss.

"Zory," came a familiar voice from the small passenger cabin. "The engine is about to engage. Take your seat, please, and fasten your safety straps."

Zory spun so fast she sent herself flying backward so that she thumped into the sealed door. "Maxie!"

Maxie, secured to the floor of the passenger cabin, twinkled at her, amber and blue lights of comfort. "Yes, Zory. Come now."

Zory pushed off, and floated toward Maxie with her hands outstretched. "They said they turned you off!"

"Disabling an MT 630 is not easy," Maxie said. "We were designed with multiple redundant systems."

"You mean you turned yourself back on."

Green and gold pinwheels flashed merrily across Maxie's faceplate.

Zory started to laugh. "I guess I didn't win, Maxie."

"You did win, Zory. Everyone knows you did. Now, strap yourself in. Let's go home. Everyone is waiting for you."

LOUISVILLE SLUGGER

✧ ✧ ✧

by Jack C. Haldeman II

"Do you know what my favorite part of the game is?
The opportunity to play."
—Mike Singletary,
Chicago Bear, NFL Hall of Famer

Jack C. Haldeman II was born December 18, 1941, in Hopkinsville, Kentucky. He studied environmental engineering and biology at the University of Oklahoma and Johns Hopkins University. Over his lifetime, he published eight novels, including High Steel *(co-authored with Jack Dann),* Vector Analysis, *and* There is No Darkness *(co-authored with brother and fellow writer Joe Haldeman). He also published more than one hundred short stories and novellas, as well as articles in scientific journals and poetry. Jack was the chairman of eight science fiction conventions, including the 32nd World Science Fiction Convention in Washington D.C. Besides writing, he also worked as a med tech in a shock-trauma unit, did field studies of whales in the Canadian Arctic, and was part of a research team investigating the greenhouse effect for the U.S. Department of Agriculture. Jack passed away on January 1, 2002, in Gainesville, Florida.*

Known for both his short stories and his comedic skills, this story encompasses both. It first appeared in an Asimov's Choice *anthology in 1977 and last appeared in 1986. Baseball just got a whole lot more dangerous.*

Slugger stood helplessly as he watched the ball arc over his head and clear the center field fence. Four to three—it was all over. He dropped his glove to the ground and started the long walk back to the dugout. The sell-out crowd was silent. He shook his head. They'd lost it; lost everything—the game, the series. Now those ugly Arcturians had won the right to eat all the humans.

It was a crying shame.

Too bad Lefty had sprained his ankle rounding first.

The UN delegates milled aimlessly around in their special box seats. They looked depressed and Slugger couldn't blame them. They were all overweight and would surely be among the first to go.

Well, he had gone the distance and that was the important thing. *How* you play the game is everything. Coach Weinraub always said that.

He hated going to the showers after losing a game. There was none of the joking around and towel snapping that followed a win. Maybe there would be a cold beer. That would be nice. He wondered absently who they *would* eat first.

The locker room was depressing—no beer at all, only warm Cokes and stale popcorn. He dressed quickly and slipped out the back door. The Arcturians were probably spraying each other with champagne.

He arrived at the Blarney a few minutes later. Usually he didn't go there, but tonight he wanted to go someplace where he wasn't known. He wasn't aware that his face was more widely known than the President's. He ordered a beer.

The bar was dirty and dark and the ruddy-faced bartender was the only one who could get a good look at his face. Luckily he was sympathetic and didn't let on that he recognized Slugger.

"Damn shame," said a man at the other end of the bar.

"Yeah, I wonder what Arcturians taste like. Do you know anyone who's eaten one?"

"My brother-in-law's in the Forces, and he says they taste like corned beef."

"Yuck. I wouldn't eat one in a million years. They look worse than maggots."

"You ever seen an algae production plant? That burger you're eating was a slimy green plant a week ago."

"That's different."

Slugger played with the water spots on the counter in front of him as he listened to their conversations. He wished Lefty was around and they could joke things up, break some of the tension. Maybe he should give him a call. He'd said he was going home to his wife, but maybe he'd come out for a beer. Maybe his ankle still bothered him.

"I bet you wouldn't eat one of them."

"I'm not sure. After all, they were going to eat us and it seemed like the only thing for us to do. Anyway, we lost the game, so we don't have to eat them. Why worry about it?"

"Yeah, the game. Buncha clowns."

Slugger felt his collar getting tight. He gripped his beer glass harder to keep his temper down.

"The umpire should've been shot. I hope they roast him on a stick."

"It wasn't the umpire, it was the team. They looked like a buncha girls out there. Did you see that bonehead play old Mandella made? They shoulda traded him years ago."

"They gave him an error, didn't they? What do you want? He was two for five."

"Lousy singles with nobody on. He struck out in the fifth with the bases loaded."

"They had good pitching. Shut us out twice."

Slugger nodded to himself and ordered another beer. They did have good pitching. Have to hand it to them there. But hell, with six arms and twelve fingers on each hand, they *had* to have good control. A lot these barflies knew. They should have had to face those curve balls that dipped *just* right.

"You're all wet. We blew it—blew it real bad. Lefty only had one hit and he had to FALL DOWN! An easy double, maybe three bases and with Pedro batting clean-up, man, that would have been the ball game. But no, he had to go and trip over his own shoelaces. Couldn't even get back to first. What a clown."

Slugger had had enough. They couldn't talk about his friend like that. With calculated slowness, he stood up and turned to face the men at the end of the bar.

"It coulda happened to anyone. Wasn't his fault."

"Hey, look, it's Slugger."

"Throw the bum out."

"Fantastic! Ten for seventeen in the series."

"Bet the fix was on."

"Can I have your autograph, Slugger? It's for my kid."

"Buncha sand-lot bums."

Slugger turned to the nearest man and grabbed him by the collar, lifting him off the bar stool.

"It could have happened to anyone," Slugger repeated. "A bad day, that's all."

He sat the struggling man down, missing the stool and dumping him on the dirty floor.

"But this was the last one, Slugger. We *had* to win this one."

"You win some, you lose some, and some get rained out," said Slugger as he walked to the door, stopping only to autograph a baseball someone held out for him.

Outside, the streets were filled with celebrating Arcturians. They were running around with knives and forks in their multiple hands. Some wore bibs with humorous sayings printed on them.

Slugger started the long walk back to his apartment. Many of the Arcuturians he met congratulated him on his performance in the series. Others pinched his arms and buttocks. He felt like half a cow hanging in a butcher shop window.

It was growing dark and a cold drizzle had started. A young boy wearing a tattered baseball cap was standing on the corner, selling evening papers with the headline: HUNGRY FOR A WIN, THE AWKS COP THE BIG ONE.

The boy approached him. "Say it ain't so, Slugger."

The great man just shook his head and crossed the street.

FOR THE SAKE
OF THE GAME

✧ ✧ ✧

by Gray Rinehart

"When I go out there,
I have no pity on my brother.
I am out there to win."
—Joe Frazier, Boxer

Gray Rinehart fought rocket propellant fires, refurbished space launch facilities, commanded the Air Force's largest satellite tracking station, and did other interesting things during his rather odd US Air Force career. Now a contributing editor for Baen Books, his fiction has appeared in Analog Science Fiction & Fact, Asimov's Science Fiction, *and elsewhere. Gray is also a singer/songwriter with two albums of mostly science-fiction-and-fantasy-inspired songs. His alter ego is the Gray Man, one of several famed ghosts of South Carolina's Grand Strand, and his web site is* www.graymanwrites.com.

So far we've examined athletes and organizers, but here we examine life for referees in very dangerous circumstances surrounding an alien sporting event.

The door closed on the screaming crowd, and the absence of noise was a palpable relief. The murmurs on the minibus were almost comforting.

Pawl nodded at Milliken and Carrone, two other human referees, and negotiated the aisle to his seat.

He breathed in as if he had just surfaced from being underwater. He felt he had started holding his breath when the rock hit him in the back of his head. At least he thought it had been a rock; there were enough of them lying around here on Stablestone.

His respite from the noise was short-lived: a few of the agitators banged on the side of the referees' tour bus. He breathed deep, eyes closed, and tried to concentrate on the plastic smell of the over-conditioned air that battled the aliens' furry muskiness. He tried to block out the pain, but its throbbing presence was insistent.

Hey, let's all go look at the battlefield. It'll be . . . fun? Symbolic? Did it even matter now?

Behind his right ear was sticky. Pawl looked at the blood and rubbed it between his thumb and fingers, resisting the temptation to sniff or lick them. As many times as he'd bled during football games and soccer matches, playing or refereeing, he'd never noticed the metallic smell people talked about.

The door hissed open and Ahk-sulla climbed onto the bus. His bright orange suspenders and baggy blue breeches were a striking contrast to his gray-brown fur. The Errellian overtopped Pawl by nearly a meter when they stood side-by-side, but shuffling up the narrow aisle he looked positively monstrous. Pawl shrank down in his seat, aware as perhaps never before what his grandpa had faced when Errellian raiders in full body armor had dropped through the trees on the very battlefield they had just seen.

Pawl focused on his companion's broad ursine face, now set in a carefully-neutral expression that hid his teeth as well as his thoughts. *No*, Pawl thought, *it was a long time ago. We're friends now. Right?* Were they, could they ever really be, friends?

Ahk-sulla dropped into the pair of seats opposite Pawl. He rummaged through the remains of his box lunch and selected a Japanese pear. He ate it in a single bite.

Pawl looked around and counted heads. All four Errellians were on board, but only three of the human *marracalva* referees were back on the bus.

"Where's Berlin?" Pawl asked. Kalbfleisch was his closest friend among the officials.

Ahk-sulla bobbed his head in a figure-eight, the Errellian version of a shrug. "Your"—Ahk-sulla seemed to struggle with some idiom—"countrymen rage against you all."

Pawl shrugged, human-style. One of his dad's phrases, "target of opportunity," came to mind, but he decided it might be in poor taste. "I think the word you're looking for is 'species.' And, yes, they must," Pawl tried to duplicate the aliens' rolling growl, though it hurt his throat. To ensure he had pronounced it correctly, he said, "That is, 'show their claws,' as you say."

Ahk-sulla grunted, and his chest rumbled with a growl

he kept in check. "You are getting better. But, 'species.' I was afraid it might offend you."

"Why?"

"It is for cataloguing. We would never address"—he rumbled a phrase that sounded like a shovel scraping through a pile of rocks—"in that way."

"What does that mean?"

"Forgive. Usually we say"—he produced a shorter growling cough that Pawl recognized—"to refer to ourselves. It means 'the people.' I was quoting one of our poets, long past. It means, 'we who live and think.'"

"As opposed to those who live but don't think?" Pawl said. "That would describe me and my people, most of the time."

Ahk-sulla answered with another figure-eight. "That fits. But I would oppose it to those who die without thinking," he said.

The door opened again, and the young lady from the Games Commission who had been their tour guide stepped in and started talking to the driver. A wave of noise from the crowd outside washed through the bus, then a siren chirped twice and they started moving.

"Wait!" Pawl called to the commission rep. "Where's Berlin?"

The young lady stood in the aisle as the bus picked up speed. She frowned at the nickname and seemed to shrink in on herself for a moment. Then she straightened and called out so everyone could hear, "I'm afraid Mr. Kalbfleisch is not returning to the village." She motioned to the windows opposite Pawl. "He is being flown to the hospital."

About eighty meters away, a yellow-and-red repulsor-craft rose, banked, and sped off toward town.

Pawl remembered Berlin shaking his head and saying, "I don't think so, Pawl," when Pawl proposed the tour. "Doesn't seem like a good idea to me."

Come on, be a team player, I said.

Below the departing ambulance, a crowd milled about behind a phalanx of security, many raising fists and some shouting. Pawl wished he knew some Errellian curses, or that his wound had knocked him out.

Ahk-sulla growled. "They may not think," he said, "but their claws are sharp."

The Referees' Village was a run-down set of pre-fabricated hovels that the Games Commission called "villas," seemingly without irony. Officials had private rooms, at least, which was more than the athletes could say about their little village a couple of kilometers away. And security was good: the compound had once been a temporary headquarters for some military unit or other.

The bus rolled to a stop in front of the quadrangle. The quad sparkled under the early afternoon sun, delicate yellow blossoms starting to sprout on spiny blue-green stalks.

Before the referees dispersed, the commission lady—who had been tight-lipped the whole way back about what happened to Berlin—pushed a meeting notice to their MindRs. The rest of the *marracalva* officiating crew marched off the bus, as sullen as Pawl.

Ahk-sulla stood on the edge of the quad, paws in the pockets of his trousers, as if reading some message in the red-and-tan stone pathways. The three other Errellian officials hung back, already-lit *cha-zetey* sticks filling the air with a pungence like rotting sour apples. Carrone and Milliken headed toward the main building on the long side of the quadrangle.

Pawl touched the back of his head. They were back early; he had time before their meeting, and the cafeteria had a medkit he could raid. He probably should have used the first aid kit on the bus, but he had been too mad. He thought about going back to his room to change his bloodied shirt, but decided to wear it as a badge of shame.

He walked into the conference room a few minutes late. The smart bandage had solidified into a protective cover, though it had tickled as it applied analgesic and its fibers manipulated the flesh. The throbbing was now an ache of regret and guilt more than actual pain. His miniMindR still gave him no information about Berlin.

He was the only human in the room.

Three of the four Errellians looked at him with something between disdain and disregard. Ahk-sulla smiled, which was friendly even if it looked worse.

Pawl sat down next to Ahk-sulla and pointed from one empty chair to another. The Errellian gave a motive shrug.

A soft tenor voice sounded from the doorway. "Ah, Mr. Maricelli, you're here."

Wister Olander, the Games Commission's *marracalva* coordinator, sounded relieved. He looked as ill-at-ease as ever in front of the Errellians, paler than usual; Pawl wondered how he had gotten through all the negotiations that set up the hybrid human-alien game.

Olander approached his spot at the head of the table as if he were afraid he would find a viper in it. Before he sat, he looked at each of the officials in turn. "I have confirmed that Mr. Kalbfleisch is in the hospital. They say his condition is 'stable.' He has several broken ribs, significant damage to his right knee, and other unspecified injuries."

Pawl's bandage seemed to pulse with Olander's words.

"I have not been informed when he will be released from the hospital," Olander continued, "but we must assume that he will not be able to officiate in the platinum match tomorrow. As for Mr. Carrone and Ms. Milliken . . . they have withdrawn from service as game officials."

Ahk-sulla growled, and Baselsh—the leader of the Errellian officials, a vigorous presence despite his graying fur—said, "Mating season?"

Olander blushed, but ignored the jibe. "Ms. Milliken gave no explanation. Mr. Carrone said the commotion at the battlefield convinced him that he would be . . . in danger if he participated in the match."

Baselsh clenched a fist the size of a volleyball and looked as if he wanted to gouge the surface of the table with his claws. "The agreement would break."

Olander's face drained beyond its normal pallor, and Pawl thought he might look almost as pale. Every cooperative effort, even one as normally inconsequential as these games, was critical if this planet was to avoid being a war zone again. The peace agreement itself was that tenuous.

Olander waved away the suggestion. "No, we must find a way to make it work. We still have some negotiation room."

Pawl studied the whorls in the bronzewood table. The pact had been negotiated by the Games Commission before any of them were authorized to travel, since non-government out-system transport was outrageously expensive. The pact set up the crazy game and called for one ultimate human-versus-Errellian match: He and Milliken were supposed to take two opposite corners of the field with Carrone in reserve, and the Errellians were assigned the other two. Kalbfleisch was head official for one half and Baselsh the other half. Now . . .

"What's to negotiate?" Pawl asked. "We can't uphold our end. Unless we can draft one of the players from one of the early-round teams? Take one and assign them to referee?"

"No," Baselsh said. The elder Errellian stared hard at Pawl and deliberately shook his head, slowly. "Overseers must be . . . pure. The field is—" he rumbled a sound like snowshoes breaking through a layer of ice into a deep drift.

Pawl looked at Ahk-sulla. His friend said, "More than important. Celebrated. Almost . . . sacred."

Pawl frowned. The Errellians had already disallowed any drones for officiating, and only permitted a few for game coverage along with piloted observation craft. The field was so damn important to them.

Pawl turned his attention back to the GC coordinator. "Then I'm it. What can we negotiate?"

Olander swiveled back and forth in his chair, head down so his chin was practically tucked into his chest. After a moment he said, slowly, "We can cede the head position to Baselsh for the entire match."

Baselsh seemed unmoved, but Pawl nodded. With Berlin out, that would work. He said, "Okay, but I can't watch opposite corners."

"Can you watch one side, end line to end line?"

Before Pawl could say that he wasn't in that kind of shape anymore, Baselsh held up a paw. "Accepted. One side to Maar-itch-ellie. Sunrise side first, then sunset."

Pawl's head itched, but he rubbed the tabletop instead of scratching the bandage. "Can I ask our team to at least watch for fouls?"

Baselsh turned to the junior Errellian referees. Tahkell, the blondest of the four Errellians, made a show of opening his paw and extending his claws. Kesseniahl said, as nearly as Pawl could translate, "Many eyes are good." Ahk-sulla figure-eighted.

Baselsh said, "You may ask."

Olander smiled a grim little smile, but his eyes bespoke a great deal more: relief, as if he had just been cured of cancer. He activated the holotank in the center of the conference table, and said, "Thank you all for your forbearance. Now, with a reminder that this data cannot be shared outside this room, let's look at the layout for the match."

Throughout the meeting, as Olander had briefed them on how the field would be laid out, the weight of what he had taken on became increasingly evident to Pawl. When they broke for supper, he barely managed to choke down some crackers before stumbling back to his villa and flopping into a chair. He would have preferred to lie down, but his stomach vetoed the notion.

He had turned off his miniMindR during the meeting, since the device was set to auto-record. He turned it on and scrolled through his messages: among the generic games-related messages were two from his brother-in-law Josiah, who was on-planet as a reporter. He said he wanted to verify that Pawl was okay, but he wouldn't mind if he got a story out of Pawl being beaned with a rock. Pawl wrote back that he had a headache like the ones Selenia used to give him; he hoped that would make Josie smile.

Pawl switched on the villa's small holotank and flipped through the feeds. Most were repeats of earlier events, and for a while Pawl amused himself watching Errellians trying to play baseball and humans trying to play the thoroughly unpronounceable game that was the aliens' version of doubles tennis.

Then he turned his mind back to the pre-match prep.

Each side had compromised in designing *marracalva*; even the name was a hybrid, part Errellian and part human. The main compromises had been related to play: an oversized rugby-style ball instead of the aliens' asymmetric, almost balloon-shaped ball; the aliens' elevated, curved goal wall instead of a simple net; and so forth. The result was an oversized lacrosse field with goals that were four-meter-tall brick edifices with three progressively smaller scoring holes in them.

And, most frustrating to Pawl's visibility as a referee, the field would contain artificial trees the aliens insisted be constructed to serve as obstacles, rally points, and redoubts. So with the game plans still officially embargoed, he had to picture the field in his head—the sight lines he would have, the places along the sidelines he would have the most and least visibility—and he laid a mild curse on the Errellians' arboreal ancestors.

The door chime interrupted his consideration of the second half setup and how the sun's track would change the shadows. His miniMindR said it was past 2130.

Outside was a wiry young man in official games livery: white jacket with green piping and the games logo on the breast. "Can I help you?" Pawl asked.

The young man gestured toward the quadrangle. "Would you come with me, Mr. Maricelli? There's a matter that requires your attention."

"You couldn't call?"

"It's a bit too . . . sensitive for remote communication."

Pawl put on his own games jacket against the evening chill, and pocketed his miniMindR. The rep led him to the main building, and was so uncommunicative during their walk that Pawl wondered if the man had been selected for his reticence. Inside, they turned down the hallway opposite the conference room, and entered a small office with only a plastic desk and two chairs.

"Thank you, Yancey," said the woman behind the desk. Pawl's guide nodded and left.

"I had hoped to meet with you earlier, Mr. Maricelli, but we missed you."

Pawl glanced at the door and back at the woman, whose broad, deeply tanned face looked carefully neutral. Pawl tried to decide if he had ever seen her before. No, he concluded, though her impassive manner reminded him of his first instructor pilot: stern and professional to the point that she made everyone around her uncomfortable.

"I went to get a medpatch," he said.

"How is your head?"

"It would be better if I knew who you were and what this is about."

She did not nod or otherwise acknowledge his request. "I'm Losa Tanginoa, but my name isn't important. I'm a security consultant, and I've been tasked to inform you that your life is in danger."

"Because I got hit in the head with a rock?"

She frowned, fractionally, but only for an instant. "Surely you know there are factions that want these games to fail. Not just thugs like the ones who attacked your tour group. They may not like the *idea* of interspecies games— they may disapprove of the Errellians, might even think we should have exterminated them or enslaved them, as if that were possible, or just want us to have nothing to do with them—but if they see a spectacle they will be happy enough. If our side loses, some of them may cause a small amount of damage to express their disappointment, but soon enough they'll return to their lives and find something else to interest them."

"I don't follow," Pawl said.

She licked her lips. It was not appealing. "In the long term, I'm sure our two species will tolerate each other, perhaps come to admire or even like each other. But now, at this delicate time, there are . . . elements for whom conflict would be more beneficial. Interests, if you will, that benefit more from continued tensions than from growing friendship."

"Who would those be?" Pawl asked.

"Patriots who don't want to risk having a human team

lose to an alien one. Star-blind reactionaries who want the peace initiative to stall out. It really doesn't matter. The connections and interconnections are so complex that we can't point a finger at anyone in particular. But they have access and influence, and they have people willing to do their bidding . . . even to the point of targeting you."

"Why me?"

She frowned deeper at that, and actually tilted her head and furrowed her brow. "Don't play dumb. You're part of the only fully interspecies sport in this whole show. Think about it: we will dominate our human games, they will dominate their alien games, all as it should be. But *marracalva* . . . that's a cooperative ideal. A paragon. Both sides honor-bound by an agreement how many years in the making?

"Attacking the Errellian athletes might seem the obvious course of action, but only for those trying to be obvious. No patriot would attack the human champions—trying to hurt them would backfire, even if the game is inhuman. But no one cares about referees, so targeting you is safer—and the way the agreements were set up, without a mix of referees, the game can't be played. When we explained this to Carrone and Milliken, they both quit. Now we're explaining it to you."

Pawl touched his hardened bandage and felt his jaw clench. It hurt, and he took a deep breath. "Because you want to protect me . . . or because you want me to quit, too?"

"I'm not sure we can protect you. I do know that we've been told that if you step foot on that field tomorrow, you will be a target. As for whether you quit, that's up to you."

"Seems to me that if you can't protect me, your security consultancy is suspect."

She smiled, but her smile was less friendly than Ahk-sulla's.

"Do you even work for the games?" She kept stoic silence, which Pawl let go for only a few seconds. "Why not kidnap me, or injure me so I can't go tomorrow? Or even kill me? Of course, we are in a secure compound, so that might not look too good. And you must know that my minder is recording this whole encounter—"

"Please, Mr. Maricelli. We're just here to deliver a message. We are not threatening you, we are trying to protect you."

Pawl's head throbbed. "Right. And the best way to protect me is to make sure I don't show up, only I'm the last human referee left. If I don't show up, the finals will be cancelled. We'll have human gold medalists and Errellian gold medalists, but no platinum match. All that negotiation and planning and however much expense, vaporized. And me to blame."

She held up her hand. "No doubt you want to protest that we are impugning your integrity or something like that. I don't know. All I know is integrity is a luxury that most people can't afford. People with power can't afford it, because it gets in the way of doing business. People without power can't afford it, because the powerful outbid them. You think you have a little power now, because of who you are, because of your position. But I see you feeling the back of your head. That was just a rock thrown by an angry nobody. How much power do you think you have against a true fanatic?"

Pawl looked into her wide-set eyes, irises so deep brown that the pupils got lost in them, and wondered if he was looking at a true fanatic.

Breakfast looked even less appetizing than usual. Pawl nibbled at a sausage that tasted vaguely of sage.

"You are stuck in a tall tree," Ahk-sulla said.

The Errellian sported a red-and-gold vest today; the colors reminded Pawl of the ambulance that had flown away with Berlin. "I might be," Pawl said, and told him about his meeting with the mysterious "security consultant"—including the fact that both his miniMindR and Wister Olander had failed to turn up any listing for her.

Ahk-sulla chewed his way through a few thousand calories' worth of nuts, cereals, hotcakes, and breakfast meats while he listened. When Pawl finished, the big alien sat silently for a few minutes, sipping strong spiced coffee. Then he said, "If you officiate today, you will be in danger?"

"That's what they say."

The Errellian nodded. "To face danger is true courage."

"If you say so."

Ahk-sulla flexed his paw. His claws looked very sharp. "Your grandsire fought my kin, you said. Here, face to face with his foe."

Pawl nodded, a little confused.

"My sire and uncles fought above the worlds, and it was bitter duty to them. It is better to grapple with a live enemy, to roll in the dust together the way brothers do, where you may measure each other's courage and come away with respect for your foe, than to strike down those you cannot see. Striking from a distance is easier, and safer, but it does not breed respect. It breeds contempt."

Pawl waited a moment, unsure what Ahk-sulla meant. He asked, as gently as he could, "What difference does that make?"

"Contempt can never till the ground for friendship or for peace. Only respect can do that."

Pawl struggled to find some reply that sounded genuine. "That's a nice thought," he said, "but I'm not sure it helps."

"To face danger is true courage," Ahk-sulla said again. "To face it together, the truest bond. I will consult Baselsh."

"About what?"

"I will be your shadow. Your shield."

Ahk-sulla's offer stabbed at Pawl's pride. Pawl declined, debated, and ultimately argued against the idea until the grease had congealed around his remaining sausages. Ahk-sulla, for his part, grinned his menacing-but-friendly smile and refused to be dissuaded.

Pawl left the cafeteria feeling small, and weak, and glad he had not eaten much.

He meandered toward his villa, balancing the Errellian's magnanimous offer against the Tanginoa woman's not-so-veiled threats. *"If you step foot on that field,"* she said—

He stopped. He might know a way that he could reject Ahk-sulla's offer without offending him.

FOR THE SAKE OF THE GAME   149

He bounced a little on the balls of his feet, as if he were warming up for a race. He grabbed his miniMindR and placed a call to his brother-in-law.

"Josie, I need a favor. I need to borrow your spare repulsor rig."

The human officials' locker room smelled faintly of fresh paint. It was normally a cramped space, but today it felt far too big.

Pawl had just finished putting on his padded overshirt when cleats on the concrete announced his first visitor.

Fournier "Fury" Cesura, captain of the humans' championship *marracalva* team, said, "Mr. Maricelli? You wanted to see me?"

Quickly, because he expected his brother-in-law in the next few minutes, Pawl outlined the bind he was in, being the sole human referee for the entire game. "So, basically," he said, "I need you and the team to help call the game. On both sides."

Cesura's face began to take on the aspect of his nickname. "You want us to help out the bears?"

Pawl held up his hand. "No, I don't want you to swing it either way. Play the game, play hard, for the sake of the game. But play fair, and call it fair. Like playing a pick-up game, of baseball or whatever, when you were little. You didn't need umpires or referees, you called your own strikes, your own fouls—"

"Sure, but that's kids' stuff. This . . . this is serious."

"You think? Nobody grew up playing this game. It's all made up, all so much shit and shiny plastic. You sure it's not a big joke?"

The fury intensified. "No, this is *pride*. This is *us*." Cesura slapped his chest for emphasis.

Pawl nodded. "Okay, good, you want to win. I respect that. If I were waiting back home for the news I'd want to hear that you won. But," his brother-in-law walked around the bank of lockers, and Pawl waved to him while he spoke to Cesura, "do you want to go home with an extra medal you didn't earn? With one you didn't win 'fair and square,' as my grandpa used to say? Look, go warm up. I need to get a few things squared away. But think about it." He held out his hand; the athlete shook it only tentatively. "Thanks."

Josiah said, "What's that about? I'm surprised they let him in here. You fixing the game?"

"Not the way you think," Pawl said.

"That's too bad. Might make a good story."

"Don't start. You got a rig for me?"

"Yeah. Even peeled off the network decals. You sure you want to do this?"

"No, but if something goes wrong I can always blame you for it."

The stadium was small for the size of the field. The spectators were a mix of locals, dignitaries of both species, and the visiting idle rich. They almost seemed outnumbered by the cameras recording the event. Pawl waved at Ahk-sulla and the other officials, all clad like him in magenta-and-neon-green uniforms.

Josiah had the repulsor lift on the far side of his network's tent. "You know," Josiah said, "it's a fair bet that 'step on the field' was not exactly a term of art. You're too literal."

"No doubt it's a technicality," Pawl said as he backed into the unit, "and maybe even an empty threat. But that's not the main reason. Well, it's in the top two. I had to convince the Errellians that I could cover my half of the field better and faster this way, and I could tell the old graybeard didn't like it. But if there is someone who wants to attack me, I'm a lot harder to hit in this thing than I am otherwise."

"The only reason I asked about this is that your license is current, and the only reason my boss agreed is that we're going to downfeed the rig's cameras. But when's the last time you flew one of these?"

Pawl pulled the unit's helmet from its receptacle, strapped it on, and tipped his head from side to side. He locked himself into the harness, adjusted the control locations to his liking, and fingered the collective. "Good question. How long ago was I in the service? Fourteen years?"

"Oh, Christ."

"Don't worry, I took a flying tour of the Grand Canyon pretty recently. Maybe five years ago?" At the look on Josiah's face, he said, "Hey, what's to forget? Left hand goes up, houses get smaller. Left hand goes down, houses get bigger. Right?"

Josiah did not look amused. "I'm not sure I like this idea anymore."

Pawl activated the repulsors; his guts resonated to a frequency he could not hear. He matched his brother-in-law's serious expression. "I'm not sure I like it at all."

"So none of us likes it."

Pawl shrugged. "We don't have to like everything, we

just have to live with it. Besides," he winked at Josiah, "the interlocks should keep me from flying out of the stadium."

He pulled up on the collective, and sailed into the air.

Pawl was immensely glad that he hadn't eaten much— and that he'd used the latrine before he left the locker room.

The Errellians scored first, early in the half, on a long throw from a tree that the human goalie misjudged from his perch on the goal wall. The action kept Pawl moving, and the humans scored three times in quick succession by the time his stomach settled down. Even when the ball was on the far side of the field Pawl flitted about—up to treetop level, down to a couple meters off the ground, into and out of the nearest copse, and so forth. It might be unnecessary, but he felt better making himself a harder target to hit.

The helmet HUD was less informative than a tactical display, but the overlay from the unit's cameras made it easier to follow the action once he told the system to track the moving ball. The important indicator was the game timer, and it ticked off with a lethargy he could hardly stand.

The preliminary games had been species-specific, and now Pawl noted differences in play between the human players and the Errellians. His grandpa had told him once, on a night when he had drunk too much of his homebrew, about ground action here on Stablestone: about jammed weapons and fight-or-flight that ended up in a fighting chase, human agility versus Errellian size, strength, and straightaway speed. All of that played out on the field, where the Errellians used the fake trees as aboveground paths and the humans dodged around them to the point that Pawl wondered if the aliens regretted insisting they be installed.

But above all Pawl noticed how much *marracalva* resembled a small-unit tactical engagement. The built-in pauses for regrouping forces, the positioning and maneuvering toward the objectives . . . it seemed a safe, sterilized version of battle. The thought started a seed of guilt growing in Pawl's gut: he had served his entire term without ever coming close to actual combat. He pushed that aside and concentrated on the action, aware that this mock battle, between two species that a few decades before had fought over this very world, would be broadcast to billions on both sides as the picket ships in orbit slid to their destinations. It amazed him that this could become a mechanism for friendly competition, and perhaps even peace.

Pawl found himself reticent to call fouls, since they slowed down the play, and he told himself it was best to call out "Play on!" so long as the violations were not too flagrant. But the Errellians scored on a questionable play as his HUD timer counted down to zero and the siren announced the end of the first half. "Fury" Cesura looked as if he might protest, but just walked off shaking his head; Pawl breathed a sigh of relief and looked forward to taking a break.

A light in the corner of his eye, like sunflash off a drone, drew Pawl's attention, and he turned his head just as his left shoulder exploded in pain. His hand slipped off the collective.

The repulsor unit's safeties kept him at altitude rather than letting him fall. But he involuntarily gripped his right hand around the cyclic in such a way that he flew forward and left. He tried to grab the collective, but his left hand was clumsy—he corrected himself down and right, into one of the fake trees. The frame around him bounced and scraped against a big limb, and Pawl gritted his teeth as he tried to back away without starting himself spinning.

A magenta-and-neon-green bulk sped up and across his field of vision, and a gray-brown furry arm swung Pawl against the trunk of the tree. Breath squeezed out of him and he struggled to throttle back the repulsors' output.

"I've got you, little—" Ahk-sulla grumble-growled one of his idioms.

Pawl let his left hand fall off the collective. His vision dimmed, and silence descended on him.

Sounds of arguing voices, both human and Errellian, intruded on Pawl's ears just before diffuse light dawned in his eyes. He lay partially supported by a repulsor field, under a tent. It took a moment to focus on Josiah's network's logo. He smelled something hot, as if someone had been welding nearby.

"Is that what blood smells like?"

A young girl—she looked like a teenager to Pawl—with a red cross and a caduceus on her sweatshirt looked closely at his eyes and then shook her head. "Doubtful," she said. "More likely you smell some residue of that flyer's frame."

A mass of shiny mediplast encased his left shoulder. He tried and failed to move his shoulder, and was surprised at the lack of pain. He noted that his left arm was bound across his midsection.

He must have looked puzzled, because she said, "Explosive round. Piece of the frame cut into your shoulder blade, and you have some burns and lacerations from where it blew apart. It's all cleaned up and encapsulated. Doesn't hurt, does it?"

"No."

"Good, it's not supposed to. It'll be numb for a few hours, then it'll hurt like a son-of-a-bitch."

"I am pleased to see you awake," said a gravelly voice. Ahk-sulla approached opposite the young doctor.

Pawl felt the corner of his mouth turn up. "I guess I'm pleased to be awake. What happened?"

"Your sister's mate said you flew too slow."

"Sounds like Josie. He'll have a hell of a story now, I guess. Where is he?"

"Retrieving new garments for you," Ahk-sulla said.

Pawl sat up a little; the doctor helped him, just before he caught the ammonia smell.

The doctor said, "Happens a lot, with accidents and other trauma. You shouldn't let it worry you."

"If you say so," Pawl said, definitely letting it bother him. "What happened? What hit me?"

Ahk-sulla dipped his head to Wister Olander.

The *marracalva* coordinator's pale face took on a yellowish cast in the tent. "Someone shot you with a high-power rifle from an ambassadorial box."

"I saw a flash . . ."

"Probably the stadium's point-defense system. It destroyed the box almost as the shot was fired."

Ahk-sulla grumbled, smiled, and head-bobbed two figure-eights.

Unsure how long he had been knocked out, Pawl said, "How did the game end?"

"Not ended," said the head official, Baselsh, who now stood behind the doctor. "The break extends, Maar-itch-ellie. We confer." He indicated Olander, and the human team captain, Cesura.

Pawl nodded to Cesura. "You want to call your own game, now?"

"Not especially," he admitted. "But we will if we have to."

"We confer," Baselsh said again, and motioned for the others to follow him out of the tent.

Pawl looked up at Ahk-sulla. "Hey, you said something when you grabbed me. What does"—he tried to approximate the Errellian words—"mean?"

Ahk-sulla waved one huge paw. "What you just said was *almost* 'one who wastes away.' But what I said," Ahk-sulla repeated the words, with emphasis on a quavering growl in the middle and a rising squeak at the end, "means 'one who dies without thinking.'"

"Ha," Pawl said. "Thanks. Here, make sure I don't fall over when I stand up."

Pawl stood, and took first tentative and then more confident steps. His head was a little woozy, whether from shock or from some medication, he could not tell. Moving was a bit awkward with his left arm immobilized, but he managed.

Josiah showed up with new pants. Pawl cleaned himself

up and changed with one hand; it was awkward, but less embarrassing than asking for help.

When he came out from behind the curtain, the young doctor was in the back of the tent with Josiah and some of the technicians. "Come on," he told Ahk-sulla, "before she sees me."

They left the tent together. The sun was just about to touch the western set of stands, and Pawl guessed that Baselsh had only extended halftime by thirty or forty minutes. The "trees" had been reset, and all was ready for the second half.

The referees' conference was about twenty meters away. Pawl jogged to them, pleased to find that doing so did not hurt his shoulder.

"Ready to start up again?" he said. They stopped and regarded him.

Olander shrugged his own shoulder, as if feeling the pain Pawl could not. "Shortly," he said.

"I get the far side this half, right?"

Baselsh growled, and drew himself to his full three-meter height. "You are able?"

Instead of shrugging even his good shoulder, Pawl did their figure-eight. "I'm willing."

Ahk-sulla leaned over. "You do not have to do this. It is just a game."

"No," Pawl said. "Maybe it *was*. It's more than that now." He looked up as well as he could into Baselsh's eyes. "Maybe it always was. The field is . . . sacrosanct. And the agreement must not be broken."

The graying Errellian squatted until his eyes were level with Pawl's. He extended his huge paw, claws retracted.

"We honor your courage." Baselsh's paw was hard, but warm. He nodded toward Ahk-sulla. "We offer you a shadow."

Pawl shook his head. "Not a shadow, and not a shield. A partner."

"Accepted," Baselsh said. He stood, and said to the others. "Play resumes in five minutes."

"Excuse me," said a voice Pawl had missed since yesterday. "I understand there's been some trouble. Do you need some more help?"

Referee Kalbfleisch limped up to the group, wearing his official's jersey. He had a livid bruise next to his right eye and wore a cumbersome knee brace, but his eyes twinkled with something approaching mischief. "You are full of bad ideas," Berlin said to Pawl. "Someone needs to keep you out of trouble."

Pawl grinned. And five minutes later he, Berlin, and Ahk-sulla stepped onto the field, together.

SHOOTER READY

by Larry Correia

> "The principle is competing against yourself.
> It's about self-improvement, about being better
> than you were the day before."
> **—Steve Young,**
> San Francisco 49ers, NFL Hall of Famer

Larry Correia is the New York Times *bestselling author of the* Monster Hunter International *series, the Audie award winning* Grimnoir Chronicles *trilogy, and the* Dead Six *military thrillers for Baen Books, as well as several novellas and novels set in the* Iron Kingdoms *for Privateer Press' Warmachine game. A former accountant, firearms instructor, machine-gun dealer, and military contractor, Larry is now a full time author and lives in the mountains of northern Utah with his wife and children.*

Here he examines the world of competitive shooting, and an old hand called back from retirement.

✧ ✧ ✧

A good shooter does all his thinking before stepping into the box. Survey the course, plan your strategy, check your gear one last time, get that out of the way while you're on deck, because if you take the time to think after that, you lose. Shooting needs to come as natural as breathing. When it's your turn and you're there, waiting for that buzzer, hands raised to the surrender position, pistol in your holster, you don't think.

You just act.

Clear your head and shoot. It isn't draw stroke, move to the firing position, target, front sight focus, trigger squeeze, repeat a few hundred times until the course is done and you collect your trophy and your prize money and head to the after party to bang the hot groupies. That works for local circuits on your home world, but there's nothing normal about this level of competition. When the difference between the first-place winner and hundredth place loser is separated by a grand total of a second over eight or ten stages, there's no time for this step A, step B, step C bullshit. That's too slow.

I'm the last pure flesh-and-blood human practical shooting champion for a reason. I'm beating cyborgs with laser range finders in their eyeballs, and vat babies literally born to shoot. I'm beating robots that were designed to be one-man SWAT teams.

You know why I win? It's because in my head I go to this place where I see everything, time means nothing. It's Zen, man. I'm just shooting, five, six aimed shots a second, moving and manipulating as efficiently as I can, but never thinking about what I'm doing. Stimulus, response. After the match me and my coaches can watch the videos and see what I could have done better for next time, but I never think during the stage.

Pure action, time ceases to exist. It feels slow, but it's really fucking fast. I'm talking some Miyamoto Musashi state of being shit here, you get me?

Of course you don't get it. If you got it, you'd have my job and I'd be the sports reporter.

The Zen state . . . Well, your body knows what to do because you've already trained it. Millions of rounds over thousands of hours, shooting and shooting and shooting until your hands bleed. I've loaded so many mags that there are dead spots where my fingers can't feel anything. I spent so much time at the range that my wife left me and I didn't notice she was gone for a week. I've shot so many rounds that my sinuses are permanently filled with carbon. No, seriously, flowers and perfume smell like smoke. I fired six hundred rounds this morning before coming to this interview.

By the time you get to this level, you've performed so damned many repetitions that the actions are burned into the pathways of your brain. It knows what to do to win, even if you consciously don't.

If you waver for even a fraction of a second, you're too slow. That's how the robots beat most of us. People blame it on them being so much faster and stronger. Robots don't get tired. Robots don't have muscle tremors. They don't have a heart that's pounding too hard to make that two-thousand-yard shot after running up Puke Hill at the Ironman. That's bullshit. That's a cop out.

The robots win because they're programmed to win.

See this? This was the body I was born with. I'm not genetically engineered. I'm not augmented. I'm not on stims. There's no Hampson device plugged into my brain downloading techniques right into my memory. I'm just a man with a gun.

I win because I've programmed myself to win.

That's why I'm the last human champion, and that's why I'm the best there has ever been.

As he watched the old interview play, it made him smile. *I sure was a cocky little bastard.* He'd been so confident and full of himself back then, but nothing taught humility quite like a decade of getting your ass kicked.

"Could I get your autograph, Mr. Blackburn?" the fan held out the projector. "You were a legend. On New Hebron we've got these nasty carnivorous whistle spiders. I watched your lesson on snap shooting, and it's saved my ass a few times."

"Glad to hear it, kid." He used his fingertip to sign the hologram. That made the fan happy. There weren't as many fans as there used to be, but he was still enough of a draw that gun companies kept hiring him to sit in their booths during arms expos. "Why don't you grab some swag?" He looked around for the marketing guy. "Hey, Frank, hook this young man up with a T-shirt. Here you go. Keep practicing, and don't forget to check out the . . ." He had to look at the logo on the T-shirt in his hands to remember which minor company he was shilling for today, "Krasnov. When you think directed energy weapons, think Krasnov."

The crowd moved on. People played with disabled guns, shouldering them, flipping switches, and looking through sights. Most of them were polite enough to keep them pointed in a safe direction. Salesmen cut deals, money was exchanged, and purchase orders placed. The off-world dealers just bought the schematics so they could pay royalties to print the guns in their own shops, which was way cheaper than shipping them across space. There were a lot of big money types wandering around, buyers from different militaries, government agencies, and large corporations, but most of the crowd were regular gun nuts who just wanted to play with cool new things and score free stuff. Arms expos always felt the same, even on backwater colony planets.

Since being a minor celebrity at this sort of thing paid his bills now, he knew them very well.

The next man to enter the booth was obviously one of the big fish. He didn't bother to look at the merchandise. He was wearing a gold VIP badge and one of those super-expensive suits with the light-transmitting fibers that made the wearer seem to glow. The man didn't care about the free pens, buttons, and probably wasn't a T-shirt type. Passing the salesmen, he went right to the minor celebrity guest. "Are you Scott Blackburn?"

"Yes, sir." He tried to read the man's badge, but the name and company wasn't lit. "How can I help you?"

Now that he was closer, it was obvious the man was Human 2.1, maybe even higher. He towered over everyone else in the booth, and was just too obnoxiously ageless and perfect. It was like looking up to a god. "Are you the Scott Blackburn who won the tri-systems practical shooting championship from '78 to '81?"

"That's me." But the post-human already knew that. Their brains were wired with facial recognition programs.

"You were the best competitor?"

He couldn't tell if that was a question or a statement. "Briefly?"

"Forgive me if I am unclear. I only downloaded English a few minutes ago. I am Mr. Lee. May I buy you lunch?"

"Well, I'm working . . ." but apparently the Krasnov marketing manager knew who Mr. Lee was, and was making shooing motions to get Scott out of the booth. This Mr. Lee must have been in position to buy a shitload of guns. "What's this about?"

"It is about being the best, Mr. Blackburn. Ultimately, everything is about that."

This is it, folks. We're here at the first stage of the Grand Halifax Open Class Invitational. As you can see, our reigning champ, Scott Blackburn, is stepping into the box. There's been a lot of talk on the circuit this year about the threat posed by the new Diomedes 5 competition robots. After last year's narrow victory over the Diomedes 4, which the Diomedes Corporation blamed on a last minute programming error, the pressure is on Blackburn. They claim that this new generation is significantly faster than last year's model. The question on everyone's mind, can the human champ hold on one more year? What do you think, Jess?

My money is on Blackburn still, Javier. The kid's got heart. This stage will follow the highlighted route, with the shooter engaging holographic moving targets from five to five hundred meters. They'll be starting with pistols, and then switching to long guns once they clear the obstacles. Grand Halifax scoring is brutal, anything other

*than an X-zone hit adds half a second to your overall time.
A miss adds a whopping two whole seconds. To put that
in perspective, the X-zone on a Grand Halifax hologram
is ten centimeters wide, and the whole hologram is only
thirty centimeters across.*

*Pure accuracy will go to the machine, but it remains to
be seen if it's got the programming to pay the bills . . .
They're ready. We're switching live now to Blackburn.*

"Shooter ready?"

"Shooter ready."

BEEP.

And he's off.

*Damn, that's fast. Blackburn is already at the first
array. I don't think I've ever seen anybody clear a star
that quick. He's in top form today.*

*You can see him dodging through the obstacles. He's
not even slowing down as he shoots on the move.
Blackburn's running a 6mm 3011 set on three round
burst. As you're watching, keep in mind he's still
experiencing some recoil there. That's no energy weapon,
and the 6mm loads still make major power factor . . . Did
you see that, Jess?*

Holy moly, that was quick!

*Blackburn's reloading on the move. Remember, the
Diomedes has an autoloader in its wrist and performs
half-second mag changes.*

*Transitioning to the long gun, now Blackburn's got to
slow down enough to nail the longer-range targets.*

He's not slowing down much.

*Grand Halifax is at .7 standard gravity and has zero
wind, so all that training on Mars is probably coming in*

handy for Blackburn right now.

Remarkably, he's still down zero points. Not a single miss. He's switching to the shotgun barrel for the final speed run. And . . . the stop plate is down.

55.64 seconds clean! Down zero points. That is the fastest that anyone has ever run this stage at Grand Halifax. He burned it down.

Starting the day by setting a new stage record? Team Blackburn has got to be feeling pretty good about keeping the championship in human hands for one more year. We're going to the pit to try and catch a word with Scott Blackburn. He's unloading and showing clear to the safety officer, and it looks like Tom has caught up with our champ for a word—

Hang on. Switch back. Diomedes has already started its run.

Transcript note: Period of stunned silence. Transmission resumes.

Jesus . . .

Diomedes 4 just ran the course in 38.08.

I've never seen anything like it.

I think we've just witnessed the end of an era, Javier.

Or maybe the beginning of a new one, Jess.

From the team of security guards surrounding them, and the way every local vendor in the place bowed nearly to the floor as they passed, Mr. Lee was a big fucking deal. Despite that, they just went to the convention center food court to eat.

The glowing post-human man-god ordered chicken fingers. "Let me begin by saying the history of your sport fascinates me. To succeed requires a combination of grace, fine motor coordination, and skill. It is not about pure accuracy, like some other sports, but accurate enough, while going extremely fast. Engaging multiple targets from different positions and on the move, from conversational distance to long range, switching between different weapon systems as you go, it is all very exhilarating to watch. It is no wonder it has become one of the most popular sports on many planets."

Mr. Lee just sounded so damned earnest about it that Scott had to chuckle. "Yeah, we used to say that it was the most fun you could have with your pants on."

"Tell me about why you got into competitive shooting, Mr. Blackburn."

"Are you a sports reporter or something?"

"I am not, but I own several sports reporters."

"Oh . . ." Scott wasn't sure which system Mr. Lee was from, so he wasn't sure if that was the language download glitching or if he actually owned slaves. "Well, my grandfather started long-range shooting competitions on Mars, and my father was the champ for years. Hell, my great-grandfather shot USPSA back when there was still a United States. So I guess you can say it's in my blood."

"But you have said yourself that good competitors are not born, they are made. Raw talent and physical gifts are no match for a developed mindset." Mr. Lee tapped the side of his head for dramatic effect. "I have downloaded all your interviews."

"If you already know my answers, why ask the question?"

Mr. Lee shrugged. It was a remarkably human gesture from someone who was beyond humanity. "I have spoken with many washed-up athletes. I've found that answers provided in interviews are often different than the truth."

"I'm not *washed up*. I still shoot and I still win."

"My apologies. That was a poor choice of phrase. I meant to say that you are no longer at the top of your game. You still win, but in front of a much smaller audience, and only against other unaugmented humans in Limited Class."

The box containing Scott's lunch slid out of the dispenser chute. At least he was getting a free meal out of this bullshit. "What do you want?"

"I am what you would call a *sports fan*."

It's been a hell of a ride for former champ Scott Blackburn. From the height of the sport to several losing seasons in a row, we caught up with him after his humiliating defeat at Garnier Station.

Scott, what happened out there?

Shooting in zero g is always a challenge. When you're using projectile weapons, every shot is going to propel you along. You've got to be not just aware of where you are, but where you're going to be after you start spinning and plan your angles accordingly. It's the toughest environment to shoot in. I made a bad call and misjudged the ranges going in.

But, Scott, the winner had four arms and clung to the walls with a prehensile tail. He was bred to live in space. How could you possibly hope to beat him?

I know the winner. Grez is a hell of a nice guy. He's a good competitor and a good shooter. This is a big win for him.

But wouldn't you say his genetic modification gave him an unfair advantage?

Are you looking to get me to spout off some pure human supremacy nonsense? No. Grez is a good dude. I lost, he won. That's competition. End of story. Open Class means anything goes.

Some are saying that it is time for you to get out of Open and move down to Limited Class.

I know I've lost some sponsors this year, but that's how these things go. I'll train hard during the off season and come back and try again next year.

But Scott, some say that you've hit a physical plateau. You're as good as a normal human can ever hope to be. Have you thought about getting yourself modified?

This interview is over.

As their conversation had gone on, Scott had realized that Mr. Lee wasn't just a fan, he was one of those dreaded *super fans*, a geeky walking encyclopedia of sports trivia. Memorizing stats wasn't particularly impressive when you'd been genetically engineered to have a super brain, but it was obvious Mr. Lee was passionate about this stuff.

"I'm betting you've got one hell of a collection of sports memorabilia."

"Yes. It is impressive. The centerpiece is Madison Square Garden. I had it dismantled brick by brick, and reassembled on my home planet."

Scott didn't know what a Madison Square Garden was. "That's nice."

"History fascinates me. Did you know that though practical shooting has been around for centuries, it has only been in the last hundred years your sport has become huge? It was held back from going mainstream on Earth due to logistical, cultural, and political reasons."

Scott ticked off reasons on his fingers. "Some politicians hated people having access to guns. You needed a big area to fling lead around. Some cultures were scared of regular folks with weapons."

"Indeed. The proliferation of 3D printing destroyed the concept of gun control forever. And as mankind rapidly spread across the stars, many habitable colonies had to deal with primitive aliens."

Nothing put the practical into practical shooting like having the local life forms constantly trying to kill you. You were hard pressed nowadays to find a colony world where people weren't armed to the teeth. Scott took a drink of his soda, thankful that at least he was way past the point of his career where he needed to hire out as *pest control*.

"Shooting clubs proliferated. The introduction of holographic and robot targets added a new element of spectator enjoyment." Mr. Lee seemed really pleased about that. "As they say, the rest is history."

"Which would make me a historical footnote."

"Exactly!" Mr. Lee laughed, only Scott hadn't been trying to be funny. "You know, they made a movie about the first robot that took your championship. Diomedes was portrayed as a modern day Jackie Robinson. You were the villain."

"I haven't seen it," Scott lied.

"I love sports movies. It is all about *narrative*." He said it like he was savoring the word. "Practical shooting is a throwback, the rare Olympic sport celebrating combative skills, which are now obsolete, like wrestling, or throwing the javelin. Did you know that shooting was the second-to-last sport where unassisted humans reigned supreme?"

"What was the last holdout? Golf?"

"Surprisingly enough, bowling."

He wouldn't have guessed that, but then again, he hadn't bowled in fifty years, and most of that had been futilely chucking balls down the gutter. "Go figure."

"It was easy for science to make men stronger, but it took longer to replace pure humans in games that required more finesse."

"Makes sense." Scott picked at his food with his chopsticks but wasn't feeling particularly hungry. Talking with super fans always ended up depressing.

On the other hand, Mr. Lee seemed to be having a grand time talking about his love. "Do you remember football, Mr. Scott? The American style football? The one you throw. Not the kind you kick."

"Sure." Scott had even watched it as a kid. He'd been born on Mars, but his ancestors had come from Texas, so granddad had declared their compound to be Cowboys fans. "It's still popular on some worlds."

"It was once the biggest sport on Earth. The National Football League held an event called the Super Bowl, which for many years was the most lucrative sporting event on the planet. It was a celebration of the greatest athletes, and most of humanity tuned in to watch the struggle. Have you ever watched a Super Bowl, Mr. Blackburn?"

The last one of those had been long before he'd been born. "Can't say that I have."

"There is a reason it went away. When scientists invented performance-enhancing drugs, the NFL banned them, because that would be *cheating*. They would create an *unfair* advantage." Mr. Lee banged one fist on the plastic table for emphasis. "Can you imagine such backwards thinking?"

Several of the security guards glanced his way. Scott just gave them an apologetic look. It was the rich post-human who was getting spun up, not him.

"When the first true cyborg limbs were invented, they were also banned. When drastically improved organs were grown in vats, banned. Genetic modification and splicing, banned. Every scientific improvement for the betterment and improvement of mankind, all banned." This really seemed to bother Mr. Lee, and as a post-human himself, it made sense why. "They said this was for fairness, for equality, to level the playing field. Do you know what killed the NFL, Mr. Blackburn?"

"No."

"Boredom . . . People do not watch sports for *equality*. It is the quest for excellence. It is to celebrate the best, and to *be* the best. Other leagues were created which were not burdened by such racist, old-fashioned rules, or blocked by arbitrary and capricious laws. Until one day most viewers realized that instead of watching the same old limited humans playing the same limited old game, they could watch a defense made up of eight-foot-tall, six-hundred-pound titans, trying to stop a running back with a cybernetic lower body sprinting at sixty miles an hour."

"That isn't sport anymore. That's just seeing who is willing to graft more crap onto their body, replacing skill with software and muscles with hardware." Scott shook his head. "Some of us weren't in it for the spectacle."

"Too bad your audience was. Limited Class has a tiny fraction of the viewership of Open Class now. Your division has slightly higher ratings than the one where people dress up as cowboys and compete with old-timey six-shooters."

"You're right. Nobody wants to watch us boring, limited humans anymore." Scott was tired and annoyed. "Look, I might just be some washed-up nobody now, working here one step up from a booth babe, but I was pretty damned good once." Scott put his chopsticks on the table and quickly stood up. The guards tensed. "Now if you'll excuse me, I'm going to go back to degrading myself for money."

"Please wait, Mr. Blackburn."

"No." He made it another five feet before his temper got the better of him and he turned back. "You wait. I was the best. I trained my ass off. Back in my day it was about your heart and your work ethic, not your DNA or your CPU. I won because I earned it."

"I know. That's why I sought you out."

He hesitated. "What exactly is it that you want then, Mr. Lee?"

"To give you another shot at the title."

❖   ❖   ❖

Matt,

I'm really sorry, but I'm not going to be able to see you this month. I got a slot in the Manzanita System division championship match. It was a last-minute thing. One of the Open shooters dropped out and the network needed a replacement. I've not gotten an Open slot for years. By the time you watch this recording, I'll be through the wormhole.

You're probably sick of explanations and excuses. I know, you're thinking "Oh great, Dad's missing another birthday because he's off losing again. He must care more about his game than he does about me." But it isn't like that. When I was your age, my dad was always gone, too. When he came home he was distracted and bored, just killing time until the next match. He had the bug. So I know how you feel. I really do.

I didn't get him then, but I get him now. If you're not competing you're not living, you're just existing. I wish I could explain it better, but I can't. I couldn't explain it to your mom, which is probably why she left me. And I really can't blame her.

I've only ever been good at one thing, but the universe kept progressing and left me behind. Now I'm a joke to them. The only reason I got this slot was because watching me fail amuses the audience. They get to feel smug and say, wow, look how far we've come in so little time. Isn't technology wonderful?

Sorry, Matt, it's never been about beating the other guys, or entertaining the crowds, it's been about beating myself. There's a feeling you get when you achieve *something nobody else can do. It makes you feel alive. It's about one last chance at being the best.*

I know I can't be the best anymore. But I still have to try.

Be good for your mom. I love you, son.

"Please, sit down." Mr. Lee gestured at the abandoned chair.

Scott reluctantly returned to the table.

"I know everything about you, Mr. Blackburn. I know that your body chemistry won't accept cybernetic enhancements because you've already tried repeatedly. You're too old to try manipulating your genetic code, but you paid a fortune to black market biohackers to try anyway and nearly died in the process."

"It hurt like you can't imagine," he muttered.

"Oh, I can. One of my many companies designed most of the drugs involved. I've seen the pain involved break the will of the strongest specimens. Yet you still tried *four* times. That is dedication. You were willing to destroy your body in an attempt to be a little better. To what lengths will someone like you go to win?"

Scott had no answer.

"Even if you'd succeeded, it wouldn't have mattered very long anyway." Mr. Lee opened his hand and a hologram appeared over his palm. "This is Diomedes 7. It is predicted to run the first stage at Grand Halifax under thirty seconds next season. It has an AI which would have been worthy of a starship ten years ago, and a thorium reactor meant for a hover tank. Every limb is a different, maximized weapon system, projectile, beam, plasma, and nano. In a tenth of a second, it sees every target on the course and paints them with a laser that analyzes the movement of every air molecule in its path. And after it annihilates its competition, it will put on a very realistic flesh mask and provide compelling interviews."

"I'm sure its sponsors will love that."

"No. We won't. It lacks *heart*. Test audiences like it when their heroes have to struggle." Mr. Lee moved his fingers slightly and the hologram of the robot changed to a machine even more advanced. "Which is why I want to put your brain inside of this."

Scott read the stats flashing past. It was a monster.

"Those are conservative estimates based upon our existing test subjects. Using you as the biological core, I think we can make it even faster."

"My brain would only slow that thing down."

"On the contrary, the decisions are processed in advance based on hypothetical scenarios and extrapolations then stored. When the decision is triggered, there is only instantaneous action." Mr. Lee said patiently.

"That's how I shoot . . ."

"Exactly. Which is why you were chosen for this project. You would be surprised what the human brain can accomplish when freed from its fleshy tethers."

He spoke like he'd removed a lot of brains. "What do you do for a living anyway?"

"I own several planets, Mr. Blackburn. It is easier to ask what do I not do."

"But why are you doing *this*?"

Mr. Lee gave him a benevolent, godlike smile. "I believe sports to be about the quest for excellence. It is about pushing the boundaries of achievement. You were willing to die for this game. Instead, I ask you to live for it." He changed the hologram again, this time to a contract. "I have just sent a copy of this to your agent and your attorney."

The contract was for more money than Scott had ever imagined, but that wasn't what mattered.

"As I said before, a good sports story is all about narrative, and everyone loves a comeback. Sign here to be the champion again, Mr. Blackburn."

He didn't think. He just acted.

We're here at the final stage of the Manzanita System division championship with Scott Blackburn. He's been called the last man standing, the final human contender in a sport now dominated by robots and post-humans. How're you doing today, Scott?

It's been a hell of a match, Wendy. The high gravity and fire winds always make shooting Manzanita a real challenge. I'd like to thank my sponsor, Krasnov Multinational, for sending me with quality gear that holds up even in these tough conditions.

Scott, you're currently forty-eighth out of fifty shooters on the board. That's a long way down from your peak showings—

The competition has gotten better.

Yes, exactly. Fans are wondering if this will be the last time you ever compete in Open Class, and if that's the case, could this be the last time that any unaugmented human competes at this level? Is this the end of an era?

Not if I can help it.

MINOR HOCKEY GODS OF BARSTOW STATION

✦ ✦ ✦

by Beth Cato

"You were born to be a player.
You were meant to be here.
This moment is yours."
—Herb Brooks,
U.S. Olympic Hockey Coach, 1980

Beth Cato is the author of The Clockwork Dagger *steampunk fantasy series from Harper Voyager. Her short fiction has appeared in* InterGalactic Medicine Show, Beneath Ceaseless Skies, *and* Daily Science Fiction. *She shares the household with a hockey-loving husband and a numbers-obsessed son, and together they are season ticket holders for the Arizona Coyotes. Her web site is* BethCato.com *and she's on* Twitter @BethCato.

What if you played a sport so long it became part of your identity? What if you'd been playing it alongside a sibling, then one of you decided to quit? Cato's hockey story examines these questions as a brother and sister launch into what could be their last game together.

✧ ✧ ✧

I skated down the corridor to holding bay thirteen, my
gear bag's strap heavy on my shoulder and sticks in my
gloved hand. For the next three hours, I was a goddess,
and for the last time.

The alien Pashi ran Barstow Station. During this time
span every six-day cycle, they locked themselves away for
some kind of holy purification ritual. To them, all species
became incarnations for this three-hour block, though I
wasn't sure what the Pashi actually *did* during their time
as self-proclaimed gods. When humanoids with
specialized tentacle limbs need quiet time, you don't ask
questions. As for us six humans remaining on board, we
devoted our time as so-called deities to one thing: hockey.

I glanced at the commlink on my wrist, willing it to
ding. Willing for us to have a last chance to play against
the Daru Baru. The screen was black, the speaker mute.
I didn't even know if they had gotten my message about
our plight months ago. Ansibles were stupidly unreliable,
though they were even worse out toward Earth.

I skated around a curve in the hall. The entire station
was like a big ice rink. The Pashi's mass of lower tentacles
included blades; they glided everywhere on their icy home
world. The sound of a smacked puck and the clatter of a
stick echoed ahead. Familiar, cozy sounds. I closed my
eyes to slits to meditate amidst the ruckus when I heard a
burst of profanity.

Also familiar, not so cozy.

My twin brother was already there. Most athletes

stretch before workouts; Sal Salazar warmed up with obscenities instead. I clenched the sticks tighter and paused in the archway.

Sal was out in the docking bay we took over during this time of minimal operations. His body was wrapped in the full-body navy blue suits we had to wear against the Pashi-regulated cold. Sal looked three times his normal thickness thanks to the pads layered beneath his suit. Thermo gear alone did nothing to shield us from pucks or body checks.

Sal slammed a puck into the makeshift net on the far side. Trish was out there, too, doing warm-up stretches on the sideline.

"Gloria."

"Hey there!" I turned and almost smacked Kazuo with my sticks. "Sorry."

"So. Last game." His voice sounded husky, even through the helmet. Nicolai and Maurice skated by us with a wave. "Just us humans. As usual."

"Yeah." Frustration tightened my throat as I glanced at the commlink again. There'd been twenty-five of us originally, our full team plus two refs. We'd gone into cryo for the long haul to Daru Baru, certain we were going to wake up to glory and fame. Thirty intelligent races were invited to compete in the Games, showcasing hundreds of sports. The Daru Baru were downright fanatical about athletics.

I'd hoped, maybe, they'd love hockey enough to come to Barstow Station since we couldn't afford the full trip to the Games. Oh well. The Games were over and done. Our time on Barstow was, too.

Sal missed a shot and let loose curses so acidic they probably melted the ice in spots.

Kazuo snorted. "Sounds like your bro sat on a stick again."

"It's a permanent fixture." I skated out onto the bay, frustration and melancholy fueling my strides. Kazuo's skates swished behind me. Sal bum-rushed me, but I pivoted and took a glancing blow off the shoulder instead.

"Hi to you, too!" I called.

Anyone who met Sal first expected me to be just as crazy, someone who'd accept a dare to do an atmospheric jump off the Central Am Space Elevator (security busted him in an off-limits zone) or drink a shot of Nu liqueur (he'd always been curious about how it felt to get his stomach pumped). He was the one who always wanted to bum around in space. Me? I was the reasonable Salazar twin, the girl who told other kids to stay out of contaminated zones, the one who finished college, the one who wanted to study alien races, not challenge them to drinking games. He had begged me to join the Humanity United Roller Hockey team to play against the Daru Baru.

"Hello to Salazar numero dos," called Trish.

I waved with my sticks and started my usual warm-up routine. Big loops around the ice, leg stretches, froggy bends. All the stuff our mom taught us ages ago when she first strapped us into rollerblades. We never had ice, but we heard all the stories about when ice hockey had been a worldwide sport, when electricity had been so abundant that buildings kept permanent ice rinks all year long, even in Los Angeles.

Crazy talk.

We sure never expected to play ice hockey for months while stuck on a frigid alien space station.

A chime rang over the intercom, denoting some new stage in the Pashi's Holy Hours. I teamed with Kazuo and Trish. Sal, Nicolai, and Maurice had white stripes painted around the arms and legs of their thermo suits to set them apart.

I skated to center to face off against Sal. Through the visor, eyes identical to mine stared back at me.

People sometimes asked me if twins can really communicate without speaking. For us, no. Not until we suited up for hockey. Our brains synced in that need for the puck.

"Let's play some goddamned hockey," Maurice said, tapping his stick's blade on the ice.

"It's damned if you say so," called Kazuo. A few of the others laughed.

I cast a final glance at the commlink as I fumbled the puck from my pocket. Last time to play on Barstow, and as a temporary deity, and as a pro.

By the grace of the Pashi faith, we became sweaty, sweltering gods. Deities wrapped in blue crinkling suits, grunting and paying homage to centuries-old idols of Gretzky, Crosby, Malaucap. Our incense, the constant musk of our own bodies and the odd tang of our over-worked thermo gear. Our laments and halleluiahs laced in profanities and hard checks into the shipping barrels that lined the metal walls. There was no bench, no switching out. We took breaks every ten minutes for our communion of water, spouts pressed to the piercing in our suits, then out we went again.

Funny how, here on an alien space station months from home, in a time when we were designated divine, I felt so very *human*, with the full array of emotions.

Angry at being stuck on Barstow Station—nicknamed that by Sal because years ago we'd been stranded overnight in the god-awful desert ghost town of Barstow, California.

Sad—grieving—to end my career like this. Years of practice. Didn't even make it to Daru Baru.

I should be happier at this point. We hadn't needed to travel en masse to go home, so our other teammates had already shipped out. The six of us were finally leaving after Holy Hours. I'd go to sleep tonight, wake up in six months, on Earth.

Soon I'd have a class of kids I could gross out with stories of how it felt to awaken from cryo. I wanted to teach, and yet . . .

My lungs burned and my muscles seared as my Pashimade skates shoved me forward. Sal's heavy breathing, his presence, chased me. We countered each other so damn well; nothing felt so good as busting through our stalemate. I slapped the puck into the goal—a small shipping crate—and cheered. Sal whooped, too, even as he bumped me in the shoulder.

Right now, hockey was my happiness. Not thoughts of Earth.

After an hour, we'd normally stop. This time, in unspoken consensus, we played on. Slower. Clumsier. I was reminded of the pick-up games the two of us played as kids, when we continued for hours and hours. Mom often joined us as part goalie, part coach. Her parents had migrated from Canada, driven south from the Maritimes as the coastline flooded. Hockey was in our blood.

Play slowed as another conversation started.

"It's going to be awesome to just wear hockey gear again, none of these thermo layers," said Trish.

"Yes. To move freely." Maurice stretched. "We'll need to get together again, when there is money for us to meet."

Sal snorted. "In that case, see you again in ten years."

I played in the American West Coast League with Sal, but the rest of the team was scattered around the world. We had a lot in common, though. Long weekend road trips. Trading out drivers, sleeping in back seats that reeked with months of compounded body funk. Playing in makeshift rinks in old warehouses with tractors or freight along back walls. Bartering labor for ration cards or food or gas to make it home. The glamorous lives of roller-hockey pros.

Once we were back, sure, I'd do pick-up games every so often, but no more weekends away, no more playing to empty bleachers. I'd planned for this trip to be a grand end to my career since Sal talked me into joining the team, but I still hadn't confessed that to anyone, certainly not my brother.

"Hey, at least we'll have stories to tell," said Trish.

"Not about the Daru Baru," added Sal. Ever the buzz kill.

I felt their gazes on my commlink as I skated by. I couldn't help but look at it, too. Still dark. Still quiet.

I also had the main docking bay page me every few weeks, just to make sure the unit worked. Eight months here, and no one had pinged it, not even from Earth. Freaking antique ansibles. We still didn't know exactly what happened to our team funds. As far as we could figure, our sponsors absconded with the money after we were underway. We were lucky—ha!—to wake up on Pashi station, really. Sure, the bulk of the station was set to a cozy 10 degrees Fahrenheit to mimic their home world, but they were willing to provide us jobs, rent a room block set to 70 degrees, and enable us to slowly save up funds for our tickets home.

Better than a swift kick out the airlock, that's for sure.

I scooped the puck and made a run for the far side. Maurice moved to block, but the puck zinged between his legs and into the crate. Score: 38 to 36.

"What day job you think you go for, Sal?" asked Nicolai, his English thickened by a Ukrainian accent.

"Dunno." We faced off again. "Not worried about it. I'll go with the flow."

I slapped the puck so hard it left a new dent in a barrel.

An odd trilling sound almost caused me to trip forward in surprise. I glanced down. The commlink blinked red.

"Oh my God." I scraped to a halt.

"You gotta be kidding me." Sal stopped beside me, gawking at my wrist as if a tarantula had landed on me. "We barely have an hour before the Pashi want this bay back and—"

"I know," I snapped.

"Could be Earth?" said Kazuo.

I tapped the screen as the rest of the team gathered around.

"Hola hola!" The high-pitched voice of my Zarash crew

boss carried over the device, clear as if he stood next to me. "Your Daru Baru landed. They coming to you. Capiche?" The guy had an annoying fascination with Earth's diverse languages.

"You're sure?"

"Yes yes! No one else dock but them. They got them trees and clothes and already had blades on."

"Sticks," I corrected him absently. "Thanks." The screen blinked off.

I stared at everyone. Everyone stared at me. A fuse lit in my nerves, giddiness causing me to bounce on my skates. "This is it! This is what we've been waiting for! Kazuo, your goalie gear—"

"It's in the locker up the hall, I was going to stow it after our game. Damn! Nic, come give a hand for a quick change."

The Daru Baru. Here. The main hangar was a ten-minute walk away. In my letter, I'd invited them to play and said the Holy Hours were the only time it could work, but this was cutting it so damn close.

The air within my suit felt thinner, my gear lighter. The team split up, chattering. Only Sal remained with me. His face was cast in shadow, but I knew by the tilt of his head that he was giving something serious thought. A noteworthy event.

"The Daru Baru take their sports seriously. That's why they hosted the Games, right? So they could play everyone?"

"Yes. Athleticism is the highest virtue, the body as a temple, all that."

"Damn." He shook his head as he glided backward. "We're so screwed."

"Don't say that!"

"When we left Earth, we were good, primed. But look at us here. Six left. In these suits. On blades, not wheels—"

"We always wanted ice, like in the stories, like before the wars—"

"Well, we got ice." He extended his arms as if to embrace the frigid arena. "We've also lived on Pashi food for months. We've all lost weight, muscle. We've only gotten to practice once every six days for a few hours. Gloria, *we're going to lose*." He tapped his stick on the ice as he turned away, but he couldn't disguise the quiver in his voice.

"Don't give up already!"

"Give up? Hell no. I'll play, it's just—I never expected it to be easy, but I knew we'd win. Hockey belongs to Earth, to us. In my head I saw it—I saw it like the Stanley Cup finals. Stupid, I know."

For an instant, I remembered him as a little kid. Mom sewed us jerseys, 20th-century—style, SALAZAR in bold letters across the shoulders. He was Salazar 01. I was 02. Sal, with all the enthusiasm of his six years, said he was going to wear that sweater when he won the Stanley Cup.

Me, already Miss Know-It-All, told him the Cup didn't exist anymore. It melted down with the rest of Edmonton.

He had sobbed his heart out and refused to play hockey with me for weeks. Only time in our lives that ever happened.

"Not stupid at all, Sal. This—this game still means something. Everything. We'll have burned up a year of our lives just in travel time. This *is* our Stanley Cup game."

"For no audience, with only six of us playing."

"Like back home. Like when we were kids." I looked at the quiet commlink again. "It's why I wore this every day, just in case some word came through."

"You're acting like this is your final game ever or something." Sal started to laugh. Something must have shown on my face, because he froze. "God. It is. Gloria Salazar. You're planning to quit."

He realized this now, of all times. I braced myself. "I want to teach, to learn, not spend my Sunday nights grading schoolwork by flashlight in the van."

"But you love hockey." His voice sounded small.

"I do." I refused to cry. Not here, not now. "But I need to grow up."

"Unlike me."

"That's not what I said."

Sal brought a hand to his helmet as if he could rub his face. "Sure. Yeah. So, last game. Big drama. Intergalactic stakes. Hope it turns out well for you." He skated away. I stared after him, fists balled.

"Cold, cold! God, it's cold!" Kazuo skated by me, shaking out his arms. His blue suit was even thicker now due to the swift change to goalie pads.

"You didn't lose any vital body parts, did you?" I called, keeping my voice light.

"The parts I need for hockey are all good."

"Don't think you'll feel that way when you're back on Earth," I said. Loud echoes carried down the hallway behind me. Skates. Lots of them.

By God, they were really here. The Daru Baru wore bronze thermo suits, hockey sticks in hand. By their height and bipedal nature, they could pass for human.

I glided forward, the rest of my team gathered behind me. One of the Daru Baru advanced. Behind the visor, the vivid yellow of her skin reminded me of sunflower petals. Her eyes were fully black, nose two slits, her lips wide.

"You are Dearest Gloria Salazar, team captain?" she asked with a tip of her head.

Her English speech surprised me—her accent was vaguely Swedish. "You must be Dearest Vanfen." I bowed my head in turn. I'd forwarded her play manuals and hundreds of hours of video after we submitted roller hockey as a Games sport.

"We were aggrieved at your inability to compete in Daru Baru. The sport of roller hockey has become our life's blood, and so we have sought you here among the Pashi."

The phrase "life's blood" caught me. That meant they really had gone hardcore, essentially converted to roller hockey as a religion. I'd hoped they would love it, but . . . wow.

"Dearest, where are your other teammates?" Vanfen continued, looking around. "This rink is not regulation size."

"It was most prudent for our teammates to return to Earth as we could afford it and as ships were available. There are only six of us left. You're correct that the rink isn't regulation size, but we have had to make do, Dearest." I barely remembered to add the proper diminutive.

A long, thin tongue lashed out to trace her lips. From my reading, I knew this was a sign of agitation. Her neck gills were probably fluttering, too. Damn, I wished I could fully gauge her appearance, get to know her. Daru Baru was a world of like size, oxygen content, and climate to Earth. We could comfortably socialize in our human quarters, if we had time. "Make do. As with these . . . blades. Like Pashi feet."

The Daru Baru tended to be very literal in their interpretation of a sport's rules. Variations were like schisms in a church. "On Earth, we used to wear shoe-blades like this for a popular international version of hockey, back before the wars and the rise of the sea. It was far, far more popular than roller hockey has ever been. Now most humans don't live where ice like this is found, and it expends too much energy to generate such large amounts of ice indoors."

Vanfen's tongue withdrew. Apparently, I had placated her. "This 'making do' is a return to an old tradition, dearest?"

Tears welled in my eyes as I nodded. Hockey, as it was meant to be played on Earth, but here we were in the boonies on the far side of the sun. I wanted to tell her more about that old style hockey. I wanted to tell her about Pyotr Baranovsky and Gordie Howe and Catherine DuBois.

"There's not much play time left," Sal said in a low voice.

"Dearest," I said. "The Holy Hours end soon, and the Pashi will need this hangar again. I need to tell you of other adaptations before we play." I sped through our modified rules for holding bay 13. Vanfen pared down her team to six; we didn't have anyone on the bench, so they wouldn't play with reserves, either. If the cut players were disappointed, it didn't show. Two Daru Baru refs patrolled the ice.

We assembled. I positioned myself for a face off against Vanfen. Another tone rang over the intercom as part of the private Pashi holy ritual that we'd never see. It reminded me of what this time was, what I was right now.

My stick on the ice, an alien before me, I knew I was a goddess of hockey.

My existence was a slick rink, a hand-carved puck, and the chaotic symphony of clattering sticks and hissing skates. I snared the puck and passed it to Trish, and she bounced it to Nicolai. He dumped it into their end.

Vanfen collected it along their boards—storage barrels—but Maurice clung to her like static, pinning her. The goal was some fifteen feet to the left. I moved in and swiped the puck. Sal was open. I passed the puck and made a beeline for the goal. Sal sent the puck back to me, deflecting it off my stick and through the goalie's five hole. Score!

Human whoops erupted all around me. My teammates granted me quick fist-bumps and smacks to the shoulder and we gathered for another face-off. This time the Daru Baru won and passed it off to their left wing. My God, they were fast, but not flawless. Their stick-handling needed practice and the refs didn't seem to know just where to be. I had the sense that they memorized the vids I sent, and this new setting had shuffled the dynamics.

Action moved to our end of the ice, where Kazuo hunkered in the crease, waiting. Vanfen was on me now, her height equal, her reflexes faster. She seemed to anticipate my every effort to move around her—it was reminiscent of playing against my brother. All the data flashed through my mind again, about how Daru Baru biologically adapted to their chosen sport, about our current condition as pessimistically assessed by Sal.

Kazuo blocked the puck. It pinged off the boards just feet away. I angled my stick but Vanfen was there. Then Sal. He collided with her, his stick up.

The sound of a whistle took me off guard. I spun to stare at a ref as he made the stretched arm motion for high sticking.

"We programmed the appropriate sound of the whistle, so it would not be lost even in this thermo gear," said Vanfen.

"I—thank you for your thoughtfulness," I said, then turned on my brother, escorting him to the sideline. "Two minutes in, and you get a penalty?"

He gripped my arm. "Why do you really want to stop playing?"

That took me off guard. "I . . . something more to life. Deeper meaning, I guess." I squinted at him. "Did you just high-stick Vanfen so you could ask me that?"

"Like I need an excuse to high-stick anyone."

There wasn't any more time to chat. I skated back to the right side of our goal and motioned for Maurice to take the face-off.

The Daru Baru scored a minute later. Sal tore back onto the ice. Play resumed. Moments later, a Daru Baru player was penalized after catching Trish across the hands with her stick, but we weren't able to take advantage of it.

I held back a little to study the Daru Baru. Even

layered in pads and gear, they moved with the grace of old time figure skaters out of a vid. Sinuous. Beautiful. Not perfect, sure, but damn good and so *fast*. No breaths rasped through their vents. The first period ticked by, and they didn't appear tired at all.

We weren't faring as well. We'd played through almost two hours before the Daru Baru arrived, and it showed. That giddy adrenaline rush faded. Maurice leaned forward, pushing himself to skate. Trish kept leaning onto her thighs for breathers. Kazuo's reflexes slowed. My heavy breaths roared in my helmet. Sweat stung my eyes like acid. My heartbeat ticked in my ears. My lungs burned, my calves throbbed.

I skated. I skated hard. I was a goddess.

Sal matched me, stride for stride. Through the visor, the dark skin around his eyes was ruddy and wet.

We called the game at two periods. All of us were hockey gods right now, but some gods are mightier than others.

Final score: 8 to 5. Victory to Daru Baru.

I leaned on my legs, trying to absorb the reality but only feeling hollow. We lost, and yet . . . The Daru Baru, in their bronze suits, formed a line to high-five each other. They were chattering and cheering.

They'd been willing to come out into the boonies of deep space, just for this. They loved hockey. I grinned and tasted salt through my cracked lips. We might have lost, but this was a hell of a way to end the trip, end everything.

I shook hands with the Daru Baru, Earth-style, and directed them down to our corridor. We had twenty minutes until Holy Hours were up. Enough time to chat with the Daru Baru for a few, dry shower, and get to the hangar to go earthbound.

Sal worked his way over to me. "You played the best damn game I've ever seen you play."

"I'm still dropping the full time team when we get home," I whispered.

"You'll regret it."

"I'm not making you stop, you know. It's okay for you to keep on playing."

He sighed, shoulders slumped, and skated ahead.

Once we were in the human-friendly climate of our corridor, both sides stripped off their headgear. The smell—well, our suits had wicked a lot, but there was an oddly sweet garlicky odor that I guessed was an indicator that the Daru Baru had worked up a sweat, too.

I approached Venfen. "Dearest, I am glad you arrived when you did. Our transport to Earth leaves in a little over an hour." Around us, humans and Daru Baru mingled and chatted.

I could barely see Vanfen's neck gills flutter above her collar. "We were surely blessed. In claiming hockey as our life's blood, we have all vowed to make a pilgrimage to your world, but we cannot do so now, not with a fertile season approaching. We must return to Daru Baru within hours as well."

"How long is the journey home in one of your ships?" Daru Baru tech was a lot better than most.

"Three months, by human account of time, dearest."

A long way to come for forty minutes of game time. Not that she seemed to mind.

"Dearest," I said, "Whenever you do make it to Earth,

keep in mind that hockey isn't what it used to be. The past few generations, it's all been about survival, about bringing up our population again and resettling to avoid radiation and high water. I'm returning home to teach more than to play hockey." It was easier to say that aloud to a stranger than to my brother or the rest of my team.

Vanfen's furred ears tilted forward. "Teach hockey?"

"Ah, no, that's not what I meant. Academics, mainly. To children. Maybe a little hockey, too."

She settled back in disappointment. "Oh. To be a devoted teacher of sport, that is the highest of callings, and one for which you seem greatly qualified." She made a sinuous hand motion. It took me a second to interpret it as a symbol of higher respect than "dearest."

My mind raced. "I do know a lot about the sport. It's in the life's blood of my family, going way back." Sal stepped alongside me.

"Select athletes from the Games have stayed as teachers among us." Vanfen made the gesture again. "Would such a role interest you?"

"Yes." No hesitation.

"Do you have a cold stasis apparatus for your kind?"

"A cryo berth? Yes. It's in the hangar, ready to be loaded."

Vanfen's face gleamed with excitement. "My pardon. I must confer with my sisters." She turned away and emitted a slight trill. The conversations around us abruptly ceased and the Daru Baru clustered together in a metallic-suited mob.

"Gloria?" Sal whispered, paragraphs of questions in the word.

"Sal, I think I might be getting an offer for a new teaching position."

"You, going to Daru Baru by yourself." To my surprise, he grinned and nodded. Our teammates gathered around us.

"Sal, you're the spontaneous one. You're the one I would have expected to do this," I said.

"No. Me, coach? Never. *You* want to teach. You want to learn. You would have gone back to Earth and kept looking at the stars. Plus, this means you'll keep playing hockey."

"Not with you," I said softly.

"Hell, I'll make do. Like you said, this is our life's blood."

"He's right," added Trish. "This is your lucky day. Do it. Besides, they want to make a pilgrimage to Earth, so you can eventually hitch a quicker ride home and even play tour guide." Maurice and Nicolai nodded, grinning.

"You'll be Earth's ambassador of hockey," said Kazuo.

Vanfen turned toward me, smiling. The other Daru Baru tittered and whispered as they reached for their helmets.

"Not an ambassador, or even a coach," I said. "I think to them, it's more like being a priest. A priestess."

"Kind of a demotion after being a goddess on Barstow," said Sal. He gripped me in a sweaty hug. Tears stung my eyes as I let go.

"I'll make do," I said, and bowed to Vanfen.

POMPOMS AND CIRCUMSTANCE

✧ ✧ ✧

by Esther M. Friesner

"There may be people that have
more talent than you, but theres no excuse
for anyone to work harder than you do."
—Derek Jeter,
New York Yankees

Nebula Award winner **Esther M. Friesner** *is the author of over 40 novels and almost 200 short stories. Educated at Vassar College and Yale University, where she received a Ph.D., she is also a poet, a playwright, and the editor of several anthologies. The best known of these is the Chicks in Chainmail series that she created and edits for Baen Books. The sixth book,* Chicks and Balances, *appeared in July 2015.* Deception's Pawn, *the latest title in her popular Princesses of Myth series of Young Adult novels from Random House, was published in April 2015.*

Esther is married, a mother of two, grandmother of one, harbors cats, and lives in Connecticut.

Apparently, cheerleading has hidden dangers besides

broken nails and wounded pride. You'll see for yourself in Esther's humorous tale.

KayT scowled. The Snarg was staring at her pompoms. She was used to this sort of unwanted attention from male Terrans, but having a Snarg—even a female—do it made her feel uneasy, vulnerable, and contributed to a hostile workplace environment. On the plus side, for a pert blond cheerleader like her, it was the stuff of which highly profitable lawsuits and a subsequent career as a PPSW (Permanent Professional Sitcom Walk-on) were made.

Or at least that *would* have been the case had she still been back home in Orange Glory, Florida ("The Navel Capital of the Citrus Belt") instead of here, tucked away in one of the countless practice halls dotting the site of the forthcoming Galactic Games.

"Ew, is that . . . *thing* looking at *me*?" KayT's colleague BeBe wrinkled her tiny nose in distaste. Her revulsion might have sounded a bit more sincere if she hadn't accompanied it with a fetching toss of her raven hair. As always, little BeBe was posing for the surveillance equipment. Reportage of the actual competitions was the teensiest tusk-tip of the interstellar media mammoth covering the sprawling event. The ladies, gentlemen and what-you-will of the press had set up their recording gear *everywhere* as they swarmed over the body of the Games like starving mosquitoes on a bloated water buffalo.

KayT pursed her lips. *Again, BeBe?* she thought. *We're supposed to be focused on our routines, not cruising for instant celebrity. If you screw up practice and someone gets hurt, where will we be?*

She knew the answer to that. It involved the Snargs and it wasn't pretty. Nothing *could* be pretty if it concerned those horrible aliens. She leveled a bitter stare at her teammate. *And BeBe's not the only one. The other girls are almost as bad, but at least they're subtle publici-sluts. BeBe wouldn't know "subtle" if it filled her boob implants with helium. Ugh, just look at her preening! Desperate for face time, the transparent little snot-on-a-stick.*

"Katie?" As though wizard-summoned, the squad's Games-assigned interpreter was abruptly *there*. If the head cheerleader had been one to relish life's little ironies, she might have gleaned some amusement from the fact that the interpreter *was* a transparent little snot-on-a-stick, or at least resembled such a thing thanks to the thick layer of slime covering her entire body. As it was, the only reaction that this abrupt mucusoid apparition evoked from KayT and BeBe was a brace of shrill squeals. The rest of the cheerleading squad and the scattering of visitors in the bleachers stared. More than a few snickered.

"Ohmahgod, Buffy, how many times have I told you not to sneak up on me like that?" KayT yelled at the creature.

"No, no, Katie, I am not Buffy. I am B'*fai*," came the patient reply.

"Yeah, well, I'm not Katie, I'm Kay-*Tee*," was the sharp riposte.

The interpreter cringed, which made her look like a

grape becoming a raisin on Fast Forward. "My deepest apologies. On my homeworld, Zisplin, it's very important to speak the names of others properly."

"Whatever." KayT didn't care about anything so trivial as cultural differences, but she did know that there were times to *pretend* she gave a rat's ass. The whole squad learned *that* lesson barely a week ago, at orientation.

That was when all the Snarg-related trouble started. The memory raised goosebumps on KayT's immaculately exfoliated skin. The Terran girls arrived expecting a quick infodump accompanied by a breakfast buffet and hopefully the distribution of Welcome to the Galactic Games goodie bags. Instead they'd been herded into a stale-smelling room furnished with two rows of uncomfortable chairs, a lectern, and lighting that did no favors to anyone's complexion, unless you wanted to count the Snargs.

Ah yes, the Snargs. It was KayT's first close encounter with those beings. Three were present. At first she failed to see them because of the awful lighting but also because the Snargs had snubbed the chairs in favor of crouching on the floor behind the lectern.

Whoa, that is the weirdest place for futons I've ever seen, KayT idly mused. *And why do they all look like an elephant barfed on*—? The penny dropped. *Wait, they're alive? Gah! They* are *alive! Gross and alive! And gross! Really, really gr*—

That was when one of the Galactic Games officials accidentally bumped into the Snarg closest to the lectern. The affronted alien leaped up, armored underbelly gleaming. Its face presented a jaw-dropping array of fangs and bony outgrowths, including a triple set of horns on the brow. Foam dribbled from its snarling maw and a sharp, noxious odor pierced the air. The sounds it made were like a blender trying to puree a double load of shrews and turtles.

"Oh, good," said B'fai from her place next to KayT. "She's not mad. She just wants an apology."

"That's a *she*?" KayT whispered.

"They are *all* females at the Games, KayTEE," the Zisplin translator said, this time taking care to pronounce her charge's name properly. "The males have no time for such frivolities. They consider their energies better spent in laying waste the galaxy."

"Like, the whole galaxy and stuff? Omahgod, and they still let them into the Games? Ew."

A burbling noise from B'fai might have been the Zisplin equivalent of a dismissive tsk-tsk. Or it could have been a burp. It was hard to tell. "Not exactly. Male Snargs fight abroad, female Snargs rule from home, maintain diplomatic relations, and keep the males from ruining profitable trade agreements. An endless offworld war is to their advantage. It keeps the males from coming home permanently, burrowing into the government bureaucracy and doing *real* damage."

"But—but all those innocent worlds that they're, you know, laying waste—!"

Again the burble. "Do not fear. The males only attack two worlds in turn, Nizko and Porvex, both uninhabited except for *k'splairs*."

"K'what?"

"Pardon. That is the Snarg term for extremely realistic and expendable androids. The males slaughter them, declare victory on Nizko, come home for a big parade and breeding time. Meanwhile the females secretly send rebuilding teams to Porvex, give the place a new name, restock it with *k'splairs*, and send the males off to conquer it. Again. This goes on for centuries, sending the males back and forth between the two battlefield planets. They are always transported on stasis ships, asleep and with much emergency beer in case they wake. They never catch on."

KayT nodded. "Jocks." An afterthought struck her: "Um, how secret is all this if you know about it?"

B'fai's translucent exterior rippled and her color brightened. It was probably the Zisplin way of nonverbally expressing *Wow, you're not as stupid as I thought.* "The Snarg females have let it be known that they don't care how many offworlders are privy to their ways. However, at the least hint that someone has upended the legumes, they will see to it that the next target of the Snarg legions is neither Nizko nor Porvex but—"

"—but the blabbermouth's homeworld," KayT concluded, a spot-on comment so insightful that it almost caused B'fai to go incandescent while shivering herself to *Yowza!* on the Richter scale.

While B'fai was bringing KayT up to speed, the stumblefooted Games rep was busy tendering a long, eloquent apology to the inadvertently trodden-upon Snarg. B'fai translated both the apology and the Snarg's gracious acceptance. A smattering of polite applause rose from the audience to acknowledge this display of mutual courtesy.

Then the Snarg ate the Galactic Games rep, red shirt and all. Insane panicky hijinks ensued.

"I thought you said she wasn't mad!" KayT shrieked at B'fai as the two of them were swept towards the exit in a wave of fear-maddened cheerleaders.

"She was not. That's why she requested an apology."

"But he apologized!"

"Indeed. And that is why she took pains to kill him *before* devouring him. Nor will she use any part of his body for a souvenir, nor as part of the Sigguna rituals."

KayT only half-heard the Zisplin translator's explanation of Sigguna—a traditional Snarg form of entertainment for their young, rather like a Punch and Judy show staged with entrails. She was feverishly planning her escape from the Games.

She soon learned that the option of fleeing back to Orange Glory was so far off the table that the figurative family dog had already gobbled it down, horked it up, and rolled in it.

"Sorry, girls," said one of Terra's own G.G. reps. "I know you've all applied for immediate return trips, but it's just not possible. When you signed on to showcase cheerleading at its finest you agreed to stay for the duration of the Games."

"But I want to go hooooome!" BeBe wailed, managing to look completely devastated yet fabulous at the same time.

"We all do," KayT said firmly. She felt like yowling even louder than BeBe and the rest of the squad, but as team captain she had to be the grownup. With great pompoms came great responsibility. "No one told us about the Snargs. I mean, Buffy did—"

"B'fai!" came the monitory call from the always-nearby Zisplin.

"See, that's exactly the sort of stuff that's got us all scared, you know? I mean, you were there, right? You saw what happened even after the Games rep said sorry, okay? I mean, he was all, like, *I didn't mean to trip on you, my bad, I'm* sooooo *embarrassed* and the Snarg was all, like, *OM nom nom nom*! I mean, ohmahgahd, what happens if *we* bump into them? Because we're not going to be able to do the Pyramid of Victory if we lose even one of our base girls, and that's our best move *ever*, you know? So you might as well let us go home, right?"

Battered weary by KayT's eloquence, the Games rep sighed. "I told you, you *can't* go home until you fulfill your commitment. Not unless you can reimburse our hosts for the cost of bringing you here, and then you'll have to pay for your own return passage. Let's see, that would come to—" He named a figure that left the whole cheerleading squad looking like a flash mob recreating Munch's *The Scream*.

The Terran rep was not heartless, merely a bureaucrat—a fine distinction, true. The girls' distress moved him. "I'll tell you what," he said in soothing tones. "Why don't I arrange to keep you girls and the Snargs as far away from one another as possible until after you've given your performance?" He beamed, expecting heartfelt gratitude, and he got it, KayT style:

"Whatever."

That *whatever* turned out to be more thanks than the Terran rep deserved. Unlike the Snargs, his offer lacked teeth. This became evident the next morning when KayT learned that not only would she *not* be kept away from the Snargs, but in fact—

"—one of them's going to be *on the squad*?" KayT's fists clenched so tightly that she bent the handles of her second-best set of pompoms. "Are you, like, *mental*?"

The Terran rep shrugged. "I'm helpless. The Snargs attended your orientation because one of them saw your squad listed on the Games roster and asked what sport you played. Zisplin translators tried to explain the purpose of cheerleading, but unfortunately—"

"I don't like where this is going," KayT said grimly. "Make it go somewhere else."

"—unfortunately even the best translators can't control how their words will be interpreted. The Snargs are highly competitive. When they learned about cheerleading, they decided it doesn't just *encourage* athletes, it provides a— a sort of charm that actually enhances their chances of winning. They have rather strong, culturally ingrained attitudes towards what we might call magic. And that's why they want one of their own included on your squad, as a conduit for any of that, uh, cheerleading woo-woo."

"No," said KayT. "Absolutely, positively N-O, no, no way, no chance, no—"

"I understand," the rep replied. "That's an acceptable reaction."

"Good, because—"

"Now *you* tell it to the Snargs."

Here followed much loud, enraged, terrified, and futile back-and-forth during which KayT was not just made to embrace the inevitable, but press-ganged into a forced marriage. What choice did she have? She could stand by her refusal, but once the Snargs learned about it, she wouldn't be standing for long.

Which was how she found herself (and her pompoms) the cynosure of a glittering pair of Snarg eyes in the practice hall that morning.

"Kay-*Tee*?" A soft touch from B'fai brought the cheerleading captain back to the matter at hand. "Kay-*Tee*, we should not keep Azhil waiting. That might be considered an offense, and you know how the Snargs—"

"I know, I know!" KayT steeled herself and strode across the practice hall to where her unwelcome new teammate waited.

"Good luck, Captain!" BeBe called out over badly smothered giggles.

"Good luck," my butt, KayT thought. *You're just praying I make a mistake and get killed so you can take over. The captain always gets more face time and you know it. Well, you're not getting mine!*

KayT forced herself to stand at arm's length from the Snarg. It was much too close for her liking, but she endured it.

B'fai gave her another nudge. "Greet her," the Zisplin whispered.

She nodded, though her mouth felt like she'd been gargling with ashes. "Um, so hi?" she queried/said. "I'm, like, really happy to welcome you to our team, okay? My name's KayT and we're going to show a lot of spirit at the Games together because we're all on, you know, the same team, right?" She finished with a big smile, though she kept it tight-lipped just in case Snargs saw bared teeth as an invitation to commence mayhem.

A few seconds passed in silence. KayT's fingers curled as she braced for the Snarg's response and prayed that whatever it was, it wouldn't leave a scar. Throughout this grueling time she maintained eye contact with the alien to such a degree that she began to see her own reflection clearly in the creature's corneas.

Ohmahgod, I have got to tweeze my eyebrows! I mean, if I survive.

A guttural sound from the Snarg brought KayT out of her trance. To her amazement, instead of incomprehensible growls, the alien spoke English:

"I greet you, KayT, and offer the blood-bond of student to master. I am Azhil, daughter of Na and an unknown disposable sire. To you I submit myself for guidance without hesitation or threat. Teach me, I beg. As proof of my complete surrender, behold how I have abased myself by learning your inferior tongue!"

"Uh, yeah, that was fast," KayT muttered in an aside to B'fai. She recalled her own shortcomings in Spanish 101 and the smoking crater it left in her grade point average.

"Female Snargs are consummate merchants," the Zisplin replied softly. "They pick up languages with frightening ease, the better to drive a bargain. If they did not disdain further interaction with foreign cultures, they would be formidable competition for my people."

"See me now before you, O my mentor!" the Snarg continued. "Accept me as the vessel of your inner *nishah*—the great force that empowers you—so that together we may hasten the day that I pay you the ultimate honor a student can bestow upon her teacher! I am yours to create, yours to destroy, and yours to command." With that, the horriffic alien threw herself face down at KayT's feet.

"Um, cool?" KayT said, perplexed. She gave B'fai a *Now what?* look.

"Tell her to get up," the translator whispered, then amended: "*Order* her."

"For real? How rude! I mean, when we're training is one thing, but—?"

"She has declared herself your underling," B'fai said with unusual intensity. "She has shown you the supreme honor of learning your language. You must reinforce your higher status at once."

"Why?"

"So that you may live a while longer. The Snarg are a rigidly ranked society. They never kill their superiors."

KayT turned sharply from the translator and planted her feet a hairsbreadth from the Snarg's head. Either B'fai was correct and she'd have to step up or else the Zisplin had pulled that *Come down hard on the scary homicidal lizard-rhino-futon-thing* stuff out of her jelly-covered butt, in which case KayT would be going home soon, as a parcel. Either way, she couldn't live with the suspense. Stress made her binge.

"On your feet, Azhil!" she snapped. The Snarg obeyed instantly, eyes shining with devotion, and made no move to reduce the cheerleader to gut pudding. That was encouraging. "Listen up: you're on *my* team now! We're the best and we're going to *stay* that way, so you better not let me down. Are you going to do everything I tell you, no questions asked?"

"Yes, revered KayT," Azhil replied. "Your words just

now have given me at least six reasons to destroy you, and yet see how I am not doing that."

"And don't start! So who's my new cheerleader?"

"I am!" the Snarg cried happily.

"Who's your capt—I mean, master?"

"You are!"

"And who's going to spend a whole lotta time on the bench watching the rest of us actually do the cheers, so no one gets hurt and junk?"

Azhil hesitated. "Bench?"

"Did I *ask* for an echo?" KayT was getting into the spirit of bossing the Snarg around. "Now say it! Who's ready to warm the *hell* out of that bench? Who is? Who?"

"*I* am!" Azhil's roar of complete commitment shook the walls. "I am *ready!*"

"*Okay!*"

There was a good deal of whining when KayT introduced Azhil to the squad. The other girls regarded the Snarg with enough fear and loathing for any number of Hunter Thompson jokes. The only time they manage to smile at Azhil was when the media thronged their practice hall, avid to cover the story of Team Spirit Meets Pants-Wetting Terror. The amount of face time the cheerleaders got, as individuals and as a group, mollified them. KayT's assurance that Azhil was well and truly under control—*her* control—also helped.

"We've got, like, this very special relationship going on and—Shut *up*, BeBe! What are you, nine years old? Get your mind out of the gutter for, like, two seconds. So anyway, nobody worry: I'm only going to let Azhil march in with us for the opening routine, then I'm sending her straight to the bench. She won't mind. She thinks cheerleading's, like, magic, but I told her that she doesn't have to *do* anything for the magic to work; just *be* on the squad. It's a *nishah* thing." Several huh/what? reactions from the other cheerleaders later, KayT added: "It's kind of like karma or *mana* or, um, whatever. Deal with it. Now come on, our X-Out basket isn't going to toss itself. Let's go!"

KayT's little pep talk did the trick, and things went well for the rest of practice. Azhil sat placidly on the bench, an attentive observer. KayT fought the urge to toss the Snarg a cookie for being a Good Girl and settled for asking Azhil to sit with her at dinner. It went well. Azhil had countless questions about cheerleading and KayT was happy to share her knowledge. Their tête-à-tête also attracted the notice of a prowling pack of reporters, which in turn drew BeBe and the rest of the squad like moths to a flamethrower. By lights-out, Azhil was *this* close to clinching the title of Miss Congeniality, with a fair chance of going on to become Homecoming Queen.

The next day, things in the practice hall did a definite somersault. Sara-Jenn, one of the squad's strongest bases, showed up with one foot in a cast. "I got thirsty in the middle of the night so I stuck a cred in the soda machine out in the hall and it didn't work so I kicked it," she said by way of explanation.

"What soda machine?" KayT felt the cold sweat of dread leap into mortal combat with her antiperspirant.

"The one in the hall by my room."

"Sara-Jenn, I've got the room next to yours. There is no soda machine there."

"Yeah, I know, it turned out to be some guy from this planet where they're part robot or whatever. And they don't like being kicked."

"*Or* getting creds shoved into their—wherever,"Be Be opined.

"No, he was okay with that," Sara-Jenn said. "We're going out later. He's buying me dinner to apologize for how he overreacted when I kicked him. It's all good."

"No, it is *not*," KayT said grimly. "Without you, we can't do any of our pyramid formations. And we can't do some of the really awesome basket toss maneuvers either. If we scratch those, it puts half our material in the garbage. We might as well be doing rhythmic gymnastics. Jeez, Sara-Jenn, I could kill you!"

"Oooooh, may I watch and be enlightened, O my mentor?" Azhil popped up at KayT's elbow like a carnivorous jack-in-the-box. "Surely you have many intriguing methods of destroying those who have offended you by their unholy lust for carbonated beverages. Permit me to take notes and enhance my own humble repertoire of death-dealing. Pleeeeeease?"

Azhil did not take it well when KayT explained the concept *figure of speech*. (She had to do so loudly, to make herself heard over Sara-Jenn's shrieks.)

"I have spoken foolishly before my mentor," said the crestfallen Snarg. "I am abashed and dishonored. Let me redeem myself by doing you some small service, else I must give up my own life to atone for this shame."

KayT made haste to prevent Azhil taking such extreme

measures. *If she kills herself, they'll just send in another and I'll have to housebreak it all over again. Better the Snarg you know . . .*

"Hey, no big, be cool. Look, why don't you help out by taking Sara-Jenn's places for a run-through of the Junior Pyramid of Good Sportsmanship? Just give it a try and we'll call it even, okay? So what you do is—"

"With respect and overwhelming joy, my master, I have witnessed the Junior Pyramid of Good Sportsmanship repeatedly. I *know* what to do." Azhil grinned in an unnerving manner. "Behold!" And with that, the Snarg took it upon herself to bark the *go* signal for the formation.

The whole squad sprang into action. A well-trained cheerleader is a marvelous amalgam of creativity, grace, and stamina, but sometimes sheer reflex kicks in and sends her flying into her routine at the drop of a *Ready? Okay!* from just about anyone. Before the girls realized it, they had executed a perfect Junior Pyramid of Good Sportsmanship with Azhil earning double brownie points for (A) executing Sara-Jenn's base role impeccably and (B) not executing anyone else in the process. It was not the squad's automatic participation but the Snarg's display of cheerleading talent that left KayT dumbstruck.

Her open-mouthed gawp slowly transformed into a Cheshire cat smile. She had been vouchsafed a vision of the Terran cheerleading squad's future. It was fanged, dangerous, and butt-ugly, but ohmahgahd, was it ever going to bring them all some *mad* vid face time!

"You like it?" KayT held up the mirror so Azhil could get a good look at the results of her ministrations. The head cheerleader didn't know it, but she had just made galactic history, being the first person to give a Snarg a makeover and live to tell the tale.

Azhil cocked her head, contemplating the effects of lipstick, blush and eyeshadow on her leathery complexion. "I respect you as my teacher," she replied evenly. "Thus I must say I am pleased."

"Oh, come on, you can be honest," KayT said, stowing her cosmetics. The two of them were in her sleeping quarters, one of the few places off-limits to the media. "If you don't like it, that's okay. My makeup looks best on blonds and you're a—well, you're a sort of a beige-green. Don't wear it if you don't want to."

The Snarg hesitated. "I may remove it without fear of repercussions? This ritual of using make-*up* for making *over*—what else does it make? Does it promote our readiness and our ongoing potential for being okay? Is it meant to enhance my *nishah*? If so, I will retain it, no matter how humiliating."

"Ohmahgahd, no way! It's just for fun." KayT laughed. "If wearing too much skanky-looking makeup added anything to your *nishah*, BeBe would be up to her saggy granny-panties in the stuff."

A mischievous idea sparked in KayT's brain. Ever since the Snarg's gift for cheerleading revealed itself, she'd relaxed in Azhil's company. She was even comfortable without the safety net of B'fai's presence. KayT now felt certain that she *understood* her new teammate. This confidence now tempted her to her second heretofore unheard-of action of the day, namely offering the Snarg a joke:

"It's not like it's your pompoms, right?" she asked archly.

"My pompoms?" Azhil was perplexed. "But I do not have any. My place in the routines does not call for me to brandish them."

"Well, you should have some anyway," KayT went on, doing a brilliant job of deadpan delivery. "Everyone knows they're, like, a cheerleader's number one *nishah* magnet. Total rabbit's foot and four-leaf clover territory!"

"I do not understand—"

"Good luck charms," KayT explained with a straight face. "Very powerful." She wiggled her fingers and made an *Oooooh!* face. "*Magic.* Which is why I'm going to give you my very own second-best set to use when we march in for the opening ceremonies, okay?"

The Snarg lowered her eyes. "My revered mentor, I thank you, but I must refuse. You have done more for me than I dared hope. You have taught me the mystic words, gestures, and splits that will bring glory to my people. You have aided me in defying the laws of physics so that I might execute a faultless cartwheel. You have *believed* in me! My honor forbids me to receive such largesse from you. Rather, I beg that you will let me repay my debt with the greatest gift a student can bestow upon her master."

"Gift?" KayT's ears perked up. She liked gifts. "No, for real, you don't have to do that, I take a size three in most stuff and I only wear gold jewelry. Also my birthstone is sapphire, but—"

Her litany of loot was interrupted by an insistent knocking at the door. "Open," KayT said, but when she saw that her uninvited caller was BeBe, she wished there was a *slam the door in that dumb bimbo's stupid face* command. Failing that, she slapped on a smile radiant with insincerity and exclaimed, "BeBe! What's up?"

BeBe countered with an equally artificial look of concern. "Oh, KayT, are you all right? No one's seen you for *ages* and we were all *so* worried! There's all these reporters in the practice hall, and God knows why but they keep *asking* for you!"

"But you were there, right? Wasn't that enough for them?" KayT clucked her tongue. "They should appreciate you *so* much more than they do, you poor thing."

"Oh, I don't mind," BeBe replied. "I mean, you know what that's like. The only reason they want to see *you* is because of Azhil. She's the real draw. I'd rather be valued for my *own* accomplishments."

"And both of them bought and paid for, too," said KayT, staring meaningfully at BeBe's bosom.

BeBe's laugh could have cut glass. "Wow, you are *so* cute when you're trying to be funny! Keep trying. But for real, the reporters are waiting and one of the Games reps said, 'If what's-her-name and Azhil aren't here in two minutes, we're going to have to get a different captain for the cheerleading team. One who *deserves* the face time!'"

"Someone like you, I suppose?" KayT raised one now-satisfactorily-plucked eyebrow.

"I never said that, but we both know I'd show a lot more gratitude for all this publicity than you do."

"It'd be the first time you ever got down on your knees to give *thanks*."

Oddly enough, BeBe didn't fire off a return shot.

Instead she sighed. "Okay, good one. You win. So are you coming or what?"

Either her rival's admission of defeat made KayT feel magnanimous or else the three large colas she'd drunk while giving Azhil that makeover were having their effect. For whichever reason, she declared: "Why don't you and Azhil go ahead? Get yourself some vid-ops with her and tell everyone I'll be there in a sec'."

The Snarg looked doubtful. "Shall I unmake the makeover makeup before I go, my master?"

"Why not leave it on? It'll get you two a *lot* of media attention, and that'll make BeBe happy, won't it, sweetie?"

BeBe smiled.

A lot can happen in a "sec'."

"No *way*!" KayT shouted at the Games rep who had just spoken the unspeakable. "You can't fire me! I'm the captain! I *came* here as the captain and I am *staying* the captain and if anyone *does* have the authority to say I'm not the captain, it's—"

"Them," the rep replied. He nodded at the assembled cheerleading squad who had grouped themselves in a photogenic array to one side of the practice hall. "*They* did it. They only asked me to break the news to you in case, um . . ." He faltered and dabbed nervous sweat from his brow.

"In case you reacted in a physically violent manner and caused injury to the person or persons who delivered the message," B'fai piped up from behind the Games rep. "Your teammates are deeply committed to avoiding occurrences that might cause them to suffer facial scarring."

"Wow, B'fai, I didn't know you spoke fluent *coward*," KayT snarled. She whirled to confront her teammates. "Why are you doing this? I'm a good captain! What the *fig jam*?!" Even in her fury, she remained aware of the cameras gobbling up her every word and move. She was not about to lose viewer sympathy by being a potty-mouth.

Sara-Jenn hobbled forward on her crutches. "It's not our fault, KayT," she said. "We didn't have a choice. Azhil said that if you stayed in charge, she was going to quit the team."

The dethroned captain blinked, pole-axed by this news. "Azhil—?" She scanned the ranks of her squad in vain for a glimpse of the Snarg.

"She's not here," BeBe said, trying to keep a heavy note of glee out of her voice and failing spectacularly. "She was really upset. I told her she could leave."

"*You* told her," KayT's words were as hostile as the look of betrayal in her eyes. "Of course you did. Because you're the captain—you're her *master* now, am I right?"

"Only because she asked me to take over from you. Azhil trusts me—" BeBe's freshly glossed lips lifted at the corners in the smuggest of smiles. "—the way she *used* to trust you."

"How did you do it, BeBe?" KayT's gaze narrowed as if she were calibrating an optic death-ray. "What did you say to her, you backstabbing little weasel?"

"Who, me? All I did was tell her the truth." BeBe fluttered her eyelashes. "I explained that when someone gives you a makeover, it's more than just dabbing on a bunch of cheap cosmetics: It *really* makes you over. You're a whole new you, reborn and fresh and innocent . . . and free of all your pesky old *nishah* because it drains *right into the hands of whoever made you over!*" She smirked straight into KayT's livid face. "Unless you get a really *good* friend with the power and the cotton balls to strip off all that *nishah*-sucking gunk before it takes effect." She struck a coy pose and concluded: "That would be me."

The Games rep grabbed KayT by the shoulders and yanked her back before she could high-kick BeBe's teeth down her throat. The reporters went into a feeding frenzy that did not abate until BeBe fled, leaving her frustrated rival sobbing on the practice hall floor.

There were only so many angles from which to cover the breaking news story "Cute Cheerleader Cries a Lot!" Eventually the media minions trickled away, most likely in search of exclusive interviews with the new captain. The Games rep went with them as soon as he determined that KayT's spirit was too broken for her to be a threat to the rest of the squad. The other girls remained, as did B'fai. The Zisplin translator did her best to recreate traditional Terran gestures of comfort, but her attempts at *there, there* back-patting left KayT feeling less assuaged than aspic'ed.

"Okay, enough," she said, shrugging free of B'fai's ministrations. She got back on her feet and glowered at her teammates. "What are *you* looking at?"

Once again it fell to Sara-Jenn to be the squad's voice. She took a deep breath and spoke rapidly: "Um, we want to let you know we're sorry this happened and we want you to understand we had to do what we did and we want to swear we're really on your side and we want all of us to still be friends and we want—"

KayT cut her off with a sharply upraised hand before the poor girl ran out of air. "I *know* what you want: My word that I won't quit the squad, am I right?"

The other cheerleaders looked sheepish but nodded. KayT allowed herself a cynical smile. "I thought so. Because without me, we won't have enough girls for the big routines. Well, don't worry, I'm staying; *some* of us know the meaning of team loyalty. See you at practice, losers." Head high, she marched back to her room where she spent four minutes drawing a crude caricature of BeBe on her pillow and the following half hour doing horrors to it that were not lawful to be named.

The air was thick with flecks of shredded foam rubber when a knock at the door put pause to KayT's self-prescribed therapy session. She spit out a wad of pillowcase. "If it's someone I *don't* want to kill, come in!"

The door slid open. Azhil stood on the threshhold. "Please do not want to kill me," the Snarg said. "Otherwise I will have to kill you and then we will be too shorthanded to perform the Pyramid of Victory."

KayT rolled her eyes. "I was *kidding*." One look at the Snarg's bewildered face made her add: "Oh. You don't get 'kidding,' do you? Whatever. So why are you here? Aren't you afraid I'll throw a loaded powder puff in your face and slurp up all your om-nom-nommy *nishah*, like BeBe said?"

Azhil looked more and more confused. "The only threat to one's *nishah* comes from our superiors. Since you are not my master now, you are harmless."

KayT toyed with the idea of making a smartypants reply along the lines of *Don't bet on that*, then wisely jettisoned the impulse. Her former immunity as Azhil's mentor was gone. If she wanted to see Orange Glory again, she'd have to keep things amicable around the alien.

Fortunately, years on the cheerleading circuit had given her excellent survival skills. She'd learned as early as seventh grade that no matter how many decent people ran the competitions, there was still the occasional letch-lizard who could give B'fai lessons on How to Be a Total Slime. If KayT could flutter and giggle her way out of the clutches of such bottom-feeders, she could maintain good (i.e. unslaughtered) relations with Azhil until the end of the Games.

Smiling as though/because her life depended on it, she cheerfully said, "Well, even if I'm not your teacher any more, I'm still your teammate. So, what's up?"

The Snarg turned away in an almost human expression of awkwardness. "O my former master, when I was still your student, you offered me a gift I could not then accept."

"I did? What—?" Enlightenment struck. "Oh, right! My second-best set of pompoms." KayT's fake smile softened with genuine amusement at the thought of Azhil armed with the most emblematic of cheerleading accessories. "Sure, you can have them, but why is it okay now?"

Azhil seemed startled by the question. "You do not know? If the master *gives* and the student passively *receives* a gift it is the same as declaring that the master was not skilled or competent enough to teach the student how to *take*. I would never have dishonored you in such a terrible manner! But as I am not your student now—"

"I'll get the pompoms." After a brief session of rooting through her belongings, KayT produced a large blue drawstring gear bag. "Here you go," she said, handing it over. "I bent the handles a little, back when I first heard we'd have to include—Er, never mind, long story. Anyway, they're still good. Shake them proud."

Reverently, Azhil took the rumpled gold-and-black pompoms out of the sack. Holding one aloft and resting the other at her right hip, she declaimed, "I am ready. It is okay. What do I want? To thank KayT! When do I want to do that? Now! And behold, I have accomplished that! Twos, fours, sixes, threes! Death to all my enemies! Hey, hey, ho, ho, crush the skull of every foe! Hold that tiger! It is an excellent source of protein! Raw, raw, ra—!"

"Ohmahgahd, Azhil, *stop*!" KayT knew she was risking her life by disrupting the Snarg's sis-boom-bombing run, but if she had to hold back her laughter any longer, she was going to die in the inevitable gut-busting explosion. "I mean, you've got to save some spirit for the team, right?"

"Indeed, you are right. I value your wisdom even though you are no longer my mentor." Azhil stuffed the pompoms back into their bag and gave KayT a sorrowful look. "But I wish you still were. It is not the same team without you as our captain. I should have had more courage. I should not have let BeBe's words affright me. I should have left your makeover in place and let you keep my *nishah*. I am ashamed."

The Snarg's simple honesty touched KayT's heart. "Awww, don't say that, okay? You're all about the *nishah*, right? The way BeBe's all about the face time, the vid-op-hungry little harpy. Not that I'm bitter. I'm kind of glad she got me booted. Sometimes captains have to watch from the sidelines instead of being a part of what cheerleading's really all about: Getting out there and showing your spirit! Thanks, Azhil. You know what? I like you. You could crunch my bones like carrot sticks and you scare the pi—the pony rides out of me, but aside from that, I really do like you."

The Snarg's lips parted in a display of gum and fang that was her equivalent of a shy smile. "I like you too, KayT. I am glad we remain teammates. I only regret that I will not be able to honor you with the accomplished student's supreme gift to her mentor, as I once intended. Although BeBe is my master now, she never taught me a fraction of what you did."

"Don't sweat it, sweetie; I flunked fractions. Just give the whatever-it-is to BeBe. I'll be happy imagining it's cheap, the wrong color, and three sizes too small." Before Azhil could respond, a muted but clear series of chimes sounded in the room. "Whoops, five-minute warning!" KayT exclaimed. "And if I know BeBe, she'll have my head if I'm late. Let's scamper!" She rushed for the practice hall with Azhil lumbering after.

On the day of their long-anticipated Opening Ceremonies performance, the Terran cheerleaders were waiting for their cue to enter the main arena when they were blindsided by a BeBe-launched bombshell: "Okay, cool newsflash, girls. Azhil and I are gonna be adding a little something extra to the performance, so we've gotta go get ready for our special entrance. You'll love it, pinky swear! See you on the floor." And with that, she grabbed the Snarg by the wrist and raced back up the passageway, leaving her team agape and unable to utter so much as a single *What the fig jam?!* over her announcement.

"Did she say they're *adding* something to the show?" one of the girls demanded once she recovered the use of her voice. "Like, a major surprise *two seconds* before we're supposed to go on?"

"I know, right?" another chimed in. "After she said our moves have to be crazy perfect and if we add so much as one unchoreographed *blink*, she'll shave our heads in our sleep and soak our undies with pepper spray!" Mutinous agreement grumbled through the squad. Only KayT held back.

"Oh, grow *up*!" she exclaimed. "I'll bet I know what this is about: It's a Snarg ceremony. Azhil's got to thank BeBe for being her teacher."

"This is true," the Zisplin interpreter averred. "It is a time-honored practice of the Snarg, the culmination of any important student-teacher relationship. The student pays her master the ultimate accolade: She proves that she is no longer the mentor's underling by rising above her and becoming a teacher herself."

"See?" KayT turned to the squad. "Now kwitcherbitchin about one weensy little last-minute change. This is a big deal for Azhil, so let's be happy for her. She's our teammate after all, and in case you forgot, she's going to get us so much media attention the sec' we're on the field together that our *unborn grandchildren* will be booked for talk shows! So what do you say?"

A thunderous, communal *"Okay!"* shook the passageway, and just in time: A red light flashed, a buzzer sounded, and the doors into the arena opened. Filled with enthusiasm, the squad streamed forth, pompoms rustling with anticipation.

It was a splendid display. The myriad of alien spectators crowding the arena didn't know a cartwheel from a cartographer, but now the magic of cheerleading cast its spell over them all. They roared approval to behold ordinary human females transformed from creatures of flesh and blood into the blazing embodiment of pure spirit. They used whatever organs best suited the purpose of rhythmic clapping when exhorted to invoke V-I-C-T-O-R-Y. They agreed loudly that whatever it was that the cheerleaders wanted, they were inarguably right to have it *NOW*.

The audience's approval was wasted on the squad. The spellbinding spirit of Spirit had descended upon them. They had given themselves over to a force so great that it didn't need the pretentiousness of an initial upper case letter to give it validation. Lost in a trance state that only a Nordic berserker could appreciate, KayT and her teammates were unaware of anything except the sheer beauty of performing a cheer flawlessly. Yin and Yang united in the Eternal Yay.

The rapture did not last. As they drew toward the end of their introductory numbers, a faint malaise began to creep over the squad. KayT sensed her own euphoria giving way and promptly identified the reason: *Ohmahgahd, it's almost time for us to form the Pyramid of Victory, but where's Azhil? We can't do it without her! What are we going to—?*

A roar of joy burst from one specific section of the arena. It came from the Snarg delegation, conspicuous and easily identifiable by the number of empty seats surrounding them. Their triumphant clamor blared forth to hail Azhil's arrival, for here she came, loping onto the field, pompom tote bag swinging. Amazingly, one of the Snargs now began to send up a shrill, spine-chilling wail so piercing that it overpowered even the loudest supportive bellow. Azhil yanked one gold and black pompom from her bag and waved it vigorously at the yowler.

As a seasoned cheerleader, KayT had no trouble leaping to the obvious conclusion: *Wow, I guess all parents cry at graduations. This must be the whole teacher-student ceremony thing, but . . . now where's BeBe? No way she'd miss being the center of attention.*

Then Azhil pulled out the other pompom.

It didn't match its mate. It was considerably heavier and more unwieldy. It wasn't gold and black any more than the Snarg's formerly blue gear bag was still all blue, not blue and red and perceptibly sticky. When Azhil flourished it, it . . . leaked.

All in all, a fine illustration of how high the student had risen above the teacher. Any nitpicker could quibble over report cards and performance evaluations, but you couldn't argue with decapitation. Not for long.

In the calm before the screaming, KayT's shattered sanity had time for one last lucid observation: BeBe was finally getting her face time.

THE OLYMPIAN

✦ ✦ ✦

by Mike Resnick

"I always felt that my greatest asset was not
my physical ability, it was my mental ability."
—Bruce Jenner,
U.S. Olympic Gold Medalist, Track and Field

*Mike Resnick is, according to Locus, the all-time leading
award winner, living or dead, for short science fiction. He
is the winner of five Hugos from a record 37 nominations,
a Nebula, and other major awards in the United States,
France, Spain, Japan, Croatia, Catalonia, and Poland.
and has been short-listed for major awards in England,
Italy, and Australia. He is the author of 76 novels, over
250 stories, and 3 screenplays, and is the Hugo-nominated
editor of 42 anthologies. His work has been translated into
26 languages. He was the Guest of Honor at the 2012
Worldcon and can be found online as @ResnickMike on
Twitter or at www.mikeresnick.com.*

*This classic tale of a great race first appeared as part of
his novel* Birthright: The Book of Man *in 1982 and later
in a 1984 anthology. This is its first appearance since.*

. . . Like the Pony Express, which earned a place in human history far surpassing the importance of its accomplishments in its eighteen-month lifetime, so did the cult of the Olympians receive an amount of publicity totally out of proportion to its achievements during its brief, twenty-two-month existence. This in no way is meant to denigrate those romantic idols of the early Democracy, for at that time Man needed all the heroes he could get, and certainly no group ever filled that need with the zest and flourish of the Olympians . . .

—*Man: Twelve Millennia of Achievement*

. . . Perhaps worthy of a passing mention are the Olympians, for it is doubtful that any other segment of humanity so accurately mirrored Man's incredible ego, his delight in humiliating other races, and . . .

—*Origin and History of the Sentient Races*, Vol. 8

There were fifty thousand beings in the stadium, and countless billions more watching via video. And every last one of them shared the same goal: to watch him go crashing down to defeat.

"Big moment's coming up!" said Hailey, who slapped life into his legs as he lay, face down, on the rubbing table. "Today's the day we'll show 'em, big fella."

He stared dead ahead, unmoving. "You hope," he said.

"I know," said Hailey. "You're a Man, kid, and Men don't lose. Ready to meet the press yet?"

He nodded.

The door was unlatched, and a flood of reporters, human and nonhuman, pressed about him.

"Still think you're going to take him, Big John?"

He nodded. Olympians were known for their reticence. They had managers to answer questions.

"It's one hundred and thirty degrees out there," said another. "Not much oxygen, either."

He simply stared at the reporter. No question had been asked, so he offered no answer.

"Boys," said Hailey, stepping in front of him, "you know Big John's got to get emotionally up for this, so shoot your questions at me. I'll be happy to answer any of them." He flashed a confident grin at one of the video cameras.

"I didn't know Olympians *had* any emotions," said a Lodin XI reporter sarcastically.

"Sure they do, sure they do," jabbered Hailey. "They're just too professional to show 'em, that's all."

"Mr. Hailey," said a space-suited chlorine-breather, using his T-pack, "just exactly what does Mr. Tinsmith hope to prove by all this?"

"I'm glad you asked that question, sir," said Hailey. "Very glad indeed. It's something I'm sure a lot of your viewers have wondered about. Well, let me put the answer this way: Big John Tinsmith is an Olympian, with all that implies. He took his vows four years ago, swore an oath of total abstinence from sexual congress, alcoholic stimulants, detrimental narcotics, and tobacco. As a member of the cult of the Olympians, his job is identical to that of his brethren: to travel the length and breadth of the galaxy as an ambassador of Man's goodwill and sportsmanship, challenging native races to those physical contests in which they specialize."

"Then why haven't any Olympians challenged a Torqual to a wrestling match?" came a question.

"As I was saying," continued Hailey, "the natives of Emra IV pride themselves on their fleetness of foot. Foot racing is their highest form of physical sport, and so—"

"It wouldn't have to do with the fact that the Torqual are twelve hundred pounds of solid muscle, would it?" persisted the questioner.

"Well, we hadn't wanted to make it public, but Sherif Ibn ben Iskad has challenged Torqual to put up its champion for a match next month."

"Sherif Iskad!" whooped a human reporter. "Now, that *is* news! Iskad's never lost, has he?"

"No Olympian has," said Hailey. "And now that that's settled, I'll get back to the subject. Big John Tinsmith will be running against the very finest that Emra IV has to offer, and I guarantee you're going to see . . ."

On and on Hailey droned, answering those questions that appealed to him, adroitly ducking those that he didn't care for.

Finally, fifteen minutes before post time, he cleared the room again and turned to Tinsmith.

"How do you feel, kid?"

"Fine," said Tinsmith, who hadn't moved a muscle.

"Herb!" snapped Hailey. "Lock and bolt the door. No one comes in for ten minutes."

The trainer's assistant secured the door, and Hailey pulled out a small leather bag from beneath the rubbing table. He opened it, pulled out a number of syringes, and began going over the labels on a score or more of small bottles.

"Adrenalin," he announced, shooting a massive dose into Tinsmith's arm. "Terrain looked a little rough, too. Better have a little phenylbutazone." One dose was inserted into each calf. "Something to make you breathe the air a little easier . . . here, this'll ease the heat a bit . . . yep, that's about it. Getting sharp?"

Tinsmith moved for the first time, sitting up on the edge of the table, his long, lean legs dangling a few inches above the polished floor. He took two deep breaths, exhaled them slowly, and nodded.

"Good," said Hailey. "Personally, I was against this race. I think it's a little soon for you yet. But Olympians can't say no, so we stalled as long as we could and then agreed to it." Tinsmith lowered himself to the floor, knelt down, and began tightening his shoes. "Now, this guy's fast, make no bones about it," said Hailey. "Damned fast. He'll knock off the first mile in under three minutes, which means you'll be so far back you probably won't be able to see him. But the Emrans are short on staying power. Figure he'll get the second mile in three and a half, the third in three and three-quarters. Save your kick until then. It's four miles and eighty yards. If you run like you trained, you ought to pull even with him a good quarter mile from the finish."

Hailey chuckled. "Won't that be something, though! Have that bastard pull out by hundreds of yards and then nip him at the wire just when every goddamn alien from here to the Rim thinks an Olympian has finally gone and got himself beat. Sheer beauty, I call it!"

"Ready," said Tinsmith, turning to the door.

"Just remember, kid," said Hailey. "No Olympian has ever lost. You represent the race of Man. All of its prestige rides on your shoulders. The first time one of you gets beat, that's the day the Olympians disband."

"I know," said Tinsmith tonelessly.

Hailey opened the door. "Want me to go with you? Give you a little company till you reach the track?"

"Olympians walk alone," said Tinsmith, and went out the door.

He strode through a long, narrow, winding passageway, and a few minutes later reached the floor of the massive stadium. The air was hot, oppressive. He took a deep breath, decided that the shot was working, and walked out to where the throng in the stands could see him.

They jeered.

Showing and feeling no emotion, looking neither right nor left, he walked to where his opponent was awaiting him. The Emran was humanoid in type. He stood about five feet tall, and had huge, powerful legs. The thighs, especially, were knotted with muscle, and the feet, though splayed, looked extremely efficient. His skin was red-bronze, and both body and head were totally without hair. Tinsmith glanced at the Emran's chest: It seemed to have no greater lung capacity than his own. Next his gaze went to the Emran's nose and mouth. The former was large, the latter small, with a prominent chin. That meant there'd be no gasping for air through his mouth during the final mile; if he got tired, he'd stay that way. Satisfied, and without a look at any other part of the Emran nor any gesture of greeting, he stood at the starting line, arms folded, eyes straight ahead.

One of the officials walked over and offered him a modified T-pack, for it was well known that Olympians spoke no language not native to their home worlds. He shook his head, and the official shrugged and walked away.

Another Emran began speaking through a microphone, and the loudspeaker system produced a series of tinny echoes from all across the stadium. There were rabid cheers, and Tinsmith knew they had announced the name of the homeworld champion. A moment later came the jeers, as he heard his own name hideously mispronounced.

Then the course of the race was mapped—thrice around the massive stadium on a rocky track—and finally the ground rules were read.

A coin was flipped for the inside position. Tinsmith disdained to call it, but the Emran did, and lost. Tinsmith walked over to his place on the starting line.

As he stood there, crouching, awaiting the start of the race, he glanced over at the Emran and studied him briefly. He was humanoid enough so that Tinsmith could see the awful tension and concentration painted vividly on his already-sweating face.

And why not? He was carrying a pretty big load on his shoulders, too. He was the fleetest speedster of a race of speedsters. The Emran, aware of Tinsmith's gaze, looked at him and worked his mouth into what passed for a smile. Tinsmith stared coldly back at him, expressionless.

He had nothing against this being, nor any of his past opponents, just as Iskad had nothing against all the beings he had destroyed with his muscle, just as the brilliant

Kobernykov had nothing against the hundreds of beings he had defeated at the gamesboards. He didn't want to cause this opponent the shame of defeat before this vast audience of his peers.

But Olympians had no choice but to win. If any Olympian, anywhere, lost, the myth they were building about Man's invincibility would be shattered, and they would be just one more race of talented competitors on the gamefields of the galaxy. And that, he knew, was unacceptable. More than that, it was unthinkable.

It was not for the adulation of Man that the Olympians competed.

That was a side benefit, and an occasionally bothersome one. They lived only to hear the jeers of the other races when they stepped onto the field, a little less vocal at each successive event, and to hear them diminish throughout a contest until there was a respectful silence, perhaps mixed with awe, at the conclusion. The awe was not for the individual Olympian, but the race he represented, which was as it should be.

There was no time for further reflection, for the race began and the Emran sprinted out to a quick lead. Tinsmith tried briefly to keep up with him, then fell into stride, his long, lean legs eating up the ground with an effortless pace. For the first quarter mile he breathed through his nostrils, testing the efficacy of the stimulants; then, satisfied, he resumed his normal method of breathing, one gulp of air to every three strides.

Far ahead of him the Emran was increasing his lead, pulling out by first two hundred, then three hundred yards. The Olympian paid no attention to him. Hailey had told him what the Emran could and couldn't do, and he knew his own capabilities.

If Hailey's information was right, he'd be pulling up to the Emran in about eleven minutes. And if Hailey was wrong . . .

He shook his head. Hailey was never wrong.

The crowd was cheering, screaming the name of its champion, and across the galaxy 500 billion viewers watched as the Olympian fell so far behind that the video picture couldn't accommodate both runners. And every single one of them, Tinsmith knew, human and nonhuman alike, was asking himself the same question: Could this be the day? Could this be the day that an Olympian would finally lose? Everyone but Hailey, who sat quietly in his box, stopwatch in hand, nodding his head. The kid was going well, was obeying orders to a T. The first half in 1:49, the mile in 3:40. He picked up his binoculars, saw that his charge was showing no signs of strain or fatigue, and leaned back, content.

At the end of the second mile the Emran's lead had not diminished, and even the handful of humans in the stadium sensed an impending upset. But then, slowly, inexorably, Tinsmith began closing the gap. After three miles, he was once again only two hundred yards behind, and as they turned up the backstretch for the final time, he had narrowed the Emran's advantage to one hundred and fifty yards.

And there the margin stayed, as first the Emran and then, more than twenty seconds later, Tinsmith hit the far turn. The Olympian peered ahead through the dust after the flying bronzed figure ahead of him.

Something was wrong! The Emran should be coming back to him by now, should be feeling the strain of that torrid early pace on those heavy, burly legs, should be shorter of stride and breath.

But he wasn't. His legs were still eating up the ground, still keeping that margin between them.

Tinsmith knew then that he couldn't wait any longer, that the homestretch was too late, that his body, already beginning to feel the strain, would have to respond right now. There would be no breather for him, no tired opponent to pass at his leisure, if he was to attain the anonymity of victory, the knowledge that he was just another addition to an immense list of triumphs, rather than the last Olympian.

He spurted forward, spurred on more by fear than desire. His legs ached, the soles of his feet burned, his breath came in short, painful gasps.

Into the homestretch he raced, his body screaming for relief, his mind trying to blot out the agony. Now he was within seventy yards of the Emran, now fifty. The Emran heard the yells of the crowd, knew the Olympian was making a run at him, and forced his own tortured legs to maintain the pace.

On and on the two raced, each carrying a world on his shoulders. Tinsmith was still eating into the Emran's margin, but he was running out of racetrack. He looked up, his vision blurred, and willing the spots away from his eyes he focused on the finish wire. It hung across the track, a mere two hundred yards distant.

He was thirty yards farther from it than the Emran.

He was going to lose. He knew it, felt in every

throbbing muscle, every bone-shattering stride. When they spoke of the Olympians in future years, on worlds not yet discovered, *he* would be the one they'd name. The one who Lost.

"No!" he screamed. *"No! Not me!"*

His pace increased. He was not running after the Emran any longer, he was running from every human, living or yet to be born, in the galaxy.

"NO!"

He was still screaming when he crossed the finish line five yards ahead of his opponent.

He wanted to collapse, to let his abused body melt and become one with the dirt and the stone on the floor of the stadium.

But he couldn't. Not yet, not until he was back in the dressing room.

He was vaguely aware of one of Hailey's assistants breaking through the cordon of police and officials racing up to support him, but he brushed him away with a sweep of his long, sweat-soaked arm. Someone else came up with a jug of water.

Later he'd take it, later he'd pour quarts and gallons into his dry, rasping throat. But not now. Not in front of *them*.

The fire in his lungs was beginning to diminish, to be replaced by a dull, throbbing ache. Suddenly he remembered the cameras.

He swallowed once, then drew himself up to his full height. He glanced calmly, disdainfully, at the throng of reporters, then turned and began the slow, painful trek to the dressing room.

Hailey moved as if to accompany him, then stopped. Another of Hailey's aides began to walk after him, but the trainer grabbed his arm and held him back. Hailey understood.

Olympians walked alone.

PETRA AND THE BLUE GOO

✧ ✧ ✧

By Kristine Kathryn Rusch

"If you can't outplay them, outwork them."
—Ben Hogan,
Professional Golfer,
Nine Time Major Professional Champion

Kristine Kathryn Rusch has won awards in every genre for her work. She has several pen names, including Kris Nelscott for mystery and Kristine Grayson for romance. She's currently writing two different science fiction series, The Retrieval Artist and the space opera Diving series. WMG Publishing is releasing her entire backlist. She's also editing the anthology series Fiction River. For more on her work, go to kristinekathrynrusch.com.

This story examines books and libraries, things dear to readers, and their role in a very unusual scavenger hunt.

They squooshed. That's what Petra first thought when she heard them approach. They squooshed.

241

Worse, they left not-so-little blobs of wet blue goo wherever they went.

Petra stood behind the desk at the Nuovo Italiano Rare Books Library and thanked every god she'd ever heard about that the actual books were behind clear walls. Because these creatures had no respect for anything.

She folded her hands together so that she wouldn't hit the security button below the desk. She'd hit it too many times in the early days of her career here, and she'd become known as Petra the Panicker. Quintavas, one of the guards, even called her Pee-Pee, and winked whenever he did it, as if she appreciated the joke as much as he did.

Maybe she was folding her hands together so she didn't have to call him.

The Bathybobles bounced their way past security, holding their gold passes in their cilia. The gold was striking against their bright blue bodies, which made her think of nothing more than ugly pulsing balloons with hair stuck randomly to the exterior.

She tried not to shudder as she watched them bobble inside. That bright blue splotchy trail they left smelled of rotting fish tacos, and made her think of the night she had gotten the job, when she and her then-boyfriend celebrated at a campus food cart, and followed everything with tequila.

She hadn't had fish tacos or tequila since.

The Bathybobles did not speak any human languages. In fact, they did not speak in the way that humans understood speech. Instead, a pale little balloon floated about the group and then broke into pieces, spelling:

We Have Come For Our Book.

The fifth group today. Damn the organizers and their lack of specificity.

The first four times, she'd been polite. But the idea of these squooshy damp things near her precious books made her want to heave. (Okay, to be fair, it was the stench that made her want to heave. But the sentiment remained the same.)

"No, you haven't come for your book," she said, not caring that she sounded both annoyed and rude. She had no idea if Bathybobles could even hear, and she doubted they understood tone.

We Need A Book.

"Read your—" she almost said "damn" and caught herself just in time. "—instructions. You're not entitled to a book. You need some kind of image of yourself—" *Yourselves?* she wondered, and that sent her down the thicket of nouns, proper nouns, and aliens.

If the Chair of the Museum Headquarters had wanted her to deal with aliens, then that chair should have trained her in alien communications. But nooooo, she'd been promised a humans-only job, in a humans-only environment, in the humans-only section of Nuovo Italiano's Roma Principa.

She wasn't supposed to interact with aliens if she didn't want to.

Well, she didn't want to, and yet here she was, staring at the fifth group of them today.

They were all looking at her expectantly, with beady black eyes that popped up along the front of their balloony selves. A dozen beady black eyes each.

Oh, these creatures gave her the creeps, worse than the last ones had.

"You need some kind of image of yourselves with a book," she said as firmly as she could. "That's all we can provide here. If you want to *purchase* a book, then you can go to Delia's Old Earth Treasures, which is six neighborhoods from here, in Antique Village. I can give you a map—"

No Map! the broken-up pale bubble read. *Book!*

Oh, great. Their translation program was weak. Who the hell designed this stuff anyway?

She leaned over the desk, raised her voice, and spoke slowly. "I am not authorized to give you a book. I am only—"

Not Give. We Buy.

"Not here," she said. "This is a library. We don't sell anything."

Yes. The stupid balloon was forming to read. *Library. Book Home Base. We understand.*

"You don't understand," she said, raising her voice even more. Then she realized what she was doing. She was yelling at smelly things that had no ears.

Good job, Petra. Very mature.

But she didn't know what to do. She obviously didn't speak Bathyboble either.

"We. Do. *Not*. Sell. Books," she said, deciding to keep it simple.

The stupid translation balloon thing formed a question mark. Well, that, at least, was clear.

"Go. To. Delia's Old Earth Treasures," she said, just as slowly. "They. Sell. Books."

Not here? the balloon read.

"Not here," she said.

Then there was hissing and burbling. The Bathybobles piled on top of each other, forming some kind of blob. Their cilia merged into hairy tentacles. Two tentacles gripped the desk, pulling it back. Two more reached for her.

She managed to push the security button before she got swept up in a mound of cold blue goo.

Rotted fish tacos really didn't come close to describing the smell. Maybe gigantic mounds of rotted fish combined with gallons of cat urine and an undercoating of stale beer came closer. But not much closer.

Petra had never smelled anything like it, and she had never smelled anything like it *on her*, and the only thing that kept her from vomiting was the feeling that she was already covered in vomit—and not her vomit either. Cold vomit, collected from the back of some restaurant that had given all of its patrons food poisoning.

She shook her hands, trying to get the blue goo off them, and then realized it was hopeless. *She* was hopeless. And the white linen dress—*historical* white linen dress that vaguely suggested something one of her heroines, Jane Austen, would wear—was completely and forever ruined.

Petra had donned that dress early in the morning, when she had thought the promotion that the library had signed up for would be decorous, and she needed to be part of that decoration.

She considered wearing something that suggested

Earth's New York of the 1930s, where the scavenger hunt rose in popularity among the wealthy. An homage, she thought, to the current scavenger hunt, which had been designed to serve as adventure travel and local promotion.

Of course, it had evolved beyond that—various wealthy alien groups trying to outdo one another by winning the hunt the fastest—but she had never imagined this.

She had imagined herself, leading scores of new tourists through the displays, explaining how, even though books and reading had gone digital five centuries before, collectors still liked the feel of actual paper books, so much that when those collectors first traveled into space, they used up some of their weight allowance to bring a beloved *physical* book.

So many beloved physical books made it into space that the Nuovo Italiano Rare Books Library was actually a branch of rare books libraries all over the human-inhabited system. And each branch, each and every one, had at least one book by Jane Austen.

Only a handful of other authors writing in English could claim that distinction—and only a few of that subset, a very few, were women.

Oh, Petra had imagined her little talk, and then maybe a promotion because her clear love of the written (emphasis on *written*) word would make her invaluable to the library, and her boss would realize what a treasure he had in her, and she would become the head librarian, someone allowed not only to touch the books, but to actually read one without a guard in place to make sure she didn't rip a page out of the book or try to slip it into a pocket.

On some level, she had known that the dream wouldn't become reality, but she hadn't expected it to explode in a geeble of blue goo as Bathybobles ran roughshod over her library.

She wanted to cry.

Instead, she wiped goo out of her eyes as Quintavas the security guard touched the edge of the overturned desk as though it might burn him.

"Where'd they go?" he asked her.

She looked at him incredulously. "Follow the trail," she said, and somehow did not add *you idiot*. "And hurry."

Suddenly, alarms went off throughout the section. She closed her eyes to gather herself, and instead, her eyelids stuck together. She wiped her hands on her dress, then wished she hadn't. All she could do was shake off her hands, and then shove her fingers in her eyes, ignoring the sting, and hoping that nothing bad was happening to her eyeballs.

When she finally got her eyes open, she saw Quintavas slowly picking his way around the bright blue slime trail.

"Oh, for God's sake," she said and pushed past him, deliberately bumping into him along the way.

"Hey!" he said.

"They're getting that crap on the books," she said, "and if the books are ruined, you'll lose your job!"

Somehow, that didn't galvanize him into action. Maybe he thought the books were already ruined. Maybe he didn't like the job.

She didn't care. She loved her job (except on days like today) so she sprinted down what was usually one of her favorite corridors in the entire building.

It was built of real wood from Earth, and if she had given the tourists their imaginary tour, she would have pointed out each type of grain, and which wood was made from extinct trees, and maybe even mentioned how difficult it was to import those woods to this place.

Instead, she could see the slime eating away at the wood's surface, and as she ran, she thanked her lucky stars that she hadn't been the one who suggested the scavenger hunt to promote the library. In fact, she had argued against it.

You like the quiet a bit too much, Ms. Relling, her boss had said. *We need a bit of excitement around here.*

Well, they had excitement, in spades, as the wealthy set in Old New York used to say. The alarms were screeching, and she was running (running!) and that made her breathe in the occasional drop of goo, stinging her tongue and hoping to hell that the goo wasn't peeling the enamel off her teeth the way it peeled the varnish off the floors.

She reached the first T intersection where the main corridor branched into two before a wall of floor-to-ceiling books encased in a clear box that protected them against the light.

And apparently, against Bathyboble tentacles, since goo dripped off the display.

She paused for only a moment, trying to decide which way to go. The screeching alarm seemed to come from everywhere and nowhere, so she couldn't use that as a way of determining where the Bathybobles were and what they had done.

She had to go by the layers of goo. And there was more goo heading off to the right than there was to the left.

She glanced over her shoulder. No Quintavas. He was probably still daintily picking his way past the goo trail, trying to keep his stupid shoes pristine.

Normally, she would hope that the other security guards would hurry to the crisis, but she'd never been in the library during a crisis, and Quintavas's behavior made her doubt the initiative of his colleagues.

So she stopped long enough to do something that was completely forbidden for someone of her level: she broke a tiny seal on one of the walls, activating emergency protocols. Now, the security guards in the facility had to respond, as did the guards within thirty minutes of the library.

Anyone who failed would lose their jobs.

On any other day, she would have felt guilty about putting their jobs at risk, but today, she didn't care. She wasn't going to be able to stop the Bathybobles alone.

She rounded the corner, and saw a long bulging line of blue pressed up against a wall display. It took her a moment to realize that all of the Bathybobles had become one long Bathyboble, which was trying to squeeze itself (themselves?) into the cracks between the floor and the protective covering.

Tentacles were forming, and heading for the bookshelves.

If the blue goo destroyed wood floors, it would definitely destroy books—which were, after all, made of wood.

"Stop!" she screeched.

They didn't. The tentacles waved, blue and out of control.

"*Stop!*" she screeched again.

They couldn't hear her. Dear God, she had forgotten that. They probably weren't taking time to read their translation program either.

She had to get their attention.

"*Stop!*" she screeched one final time. "You're violating your participation agreement! If you touch those books, you'll forfeit!"

The tentacles froze as if a hard frost had hit the shelves.

What? the stupid little word bubble appeared over the thick blue line.

"You heard me," she said, although she knew that technically wasn't true. They hadn't heard anything at all. "If you touch those books, you'll forfeit, and you'll never be able to participate in a sanctioned scavenger hunt again."

She had no idea if that was true, but by God, she'd make it true if she had to fight the league to her dying breath.

(Which might be Real Soon Now, considering the way her lungs felt after she'd swallowed even more blue goo.)

You cannot make us forfeit, the pale blue bubble read. *We are district champions.*

"I wouldn't make you forfeit. Any violation of the rules automatically disqualifies you," she said. Or, at least, she prayed it was so, because if it wasn't, she had no leverage at all.

Where were those stupid security guys?

The tentacles waved, and her breath caught, forcing her to inhale even more goo. She cleared her throat so she wouldn't cough.

And then the tentacles slid out of the cracks and back into the long line of blueness. The blueness separated into its various blobs and bounced toward her.

She resisted the urge to kick them.

We need a book! the stupid bubble read.

"No," she said. "You need an image of you with a book, and we can get that from our security feeds."

The bubble's message remained the same, and she was about to repeat herself when the message reformed.

Acceptable.

She let out a tiny *huh* of satisfaction. Two birds, one little image. A sign that the Bathybobles had found the book for their scavenger hunt, and a sign that the stupid creatures nearly destroyed thousand-year-old artifacts.

Then she realized that she had killed three birds here. She would have definitive proof for her boss that scavenger hunts involving non-humans were a stupid idea to promote a library in the human section of a human neighborhood of a primarily human city.

She almost told the Bathybobles to stay put, but she doubted they would.

She looked around. No security guards yet. And the alarm sounded far away.

She peered at the clear wall in front of the books. Technically, that wall had not been breached.

The alarm was coming from another part of the library. Oh, joy.

She corraled the Bathybobles and led them outside the library. She told them if they didn't wait on the sanctioned floor material that could absorb their slime (and yes, she said slime, and yes, it felt good), then she would personally disqualify them.

The Bathybobles vibrated, sending a hum through the area. It took her a moment to realize that her words actually scared them, and that was the Bathyboble equivalent of shaking in fear.

Before she went back inside the library, she stopped in the public restroom and washed off as much goo as she possibly could. Her dress (which was fortunately not dissolving—apparently linen was not composed of wood fiber) was plastered against her body, but there was nothing she could do about that.

She squeezed out the linen so it wouldn't drip, rinsed off her hair and face, and took off her ruined shoes. She rinsed off her legs and feet, then walked barefoot back to the library, carefully avoiding the trail of blue goo she and the Bathybobles had left.

As she stepped back inside, the alarm shut off mid-thrum. A group of Aenrosids huddled near the desk, shifting from foot to foot to foot to foot in unison, as if they were practicing some kind of dance. She had no idea that square four-footed creatures could be so coordinated.

Excuse me, one of them said, **but can you point us to the Librarian?**

"I'm the librarian," she snapped, "and I'm dealing with an emergency. You stand still. If you so much as move a muscle, I swear, I will break you into little pieces."

Then she stomped off, not even berating herself for her unprofessional behavior.

She could just hear them. *Where are the books? We need a book. We'll buy a book. What's a book, by the way?*

She wanted to punch something. She wondered, if she punched a Bathyboble, would it squoosh or explode?

She kinda hoped she would find out.

She stomped back to the security room, expecting to find the lazy guards sitting on their butts and laughing at her predicament. Instead, she found the room full of Hairy Maglefesians. She had no idea how they even got in.

They were the size of small dogs. They had probably snuck in when she wasn't looking. She'd heard that Hairy Maglefesians practiced the art of stealth: she just hadn't believed it until now.

She didn't see any of the guards. The Hairy Maglefesians looked at her as if she were going to kill them with long and slow torture.

She was tempted.

As she reached for the comm, the door opened, and Quintavas pushed a young human male into the room. He had a collector's bag, perfectly designed to handle the most fragile items.

"Look what I found on the way to the goo fest," Quintavas said. "The son of one of our sponsors."

The young man raised his hands and said to Petra, "I didn't do anything. Please, help me before this man ruins my reputation."

The young man's fingers glimmered in the light. Petra did something she wouldn't have done two hours before.

She slapped her palm against his.

His skin exploded in light and color.

Bastard.

"If you didn't do anything," she said, "why do you have a collector's bag and protective skin seal?"

Only people who handled fragile collectables even knew what that stuff was.

"I—I never come to the library without them," he said.

"I'm sure that's probably true," Petra said. "It makes theft of valuable artifacts so much easier."

The Hairy Maglefesians chuffed behind her.

"We're not stealing anything," one of them said to her.

"Oh, I know," she said. "You're participating in the scavenger hunt."

"Yes!" it said, its tail wagging. "All we need is a book."

She sighed in exasperation. "All you need is an image of you *with* a book."

"Actually, no," the young man said. "They need a book. It's in the rules."

Her gaze met his. "Give me a copy of the rules," she said.

He called the rules up on a small device, and she realized he could give her anything he wanted to.

"No." She whirled, and spoke to the Hairy Maglefesians. "You give me the rules. And the map."

One of the Maglefesians handed her a device that felt like someone had drooled on it.

She understood the map, but she couldn't read the words, if indeed the scratchings on the screen were words.

She extended the device back to its owner. "Call up the English version, would you?"

The Maglefesian tapped the device with its wet nose. She felt her gorge move again, and she swallowed hard.

If this day ended without vomit, she would be very, very happy.

The English version of the rules came up, in six-point

type, sixty-five pages long. But she'd read more complicated documents in her day, and it didn't take her long to find the pertinent section.

The young man was indeed right. Participants had to have the physical artifacts.

Then she leaned over security's internal systems, and found the documents that her boss had agreed to. She had been right too: Images only. Participants were not allowed to touch any physical objects.

She looked at the young man. All of this was designed to protect someone from accusations of theft.

"Quintavas, get your colleagues and shut the library down. No one comes in or goes out."

"You can't—"

She raised her eyebrows at him—the Librarian Glare of Death—and, bless him, he got the message.

"Yes, of course. Yes."

And he backed out of the security room.

"It stinks in here, you know," the young man said. "I have to leave. I have allergies."

She was the one who smelled bad. (Although she knew that Hairy Maglefesians weren't exactly the most sweetly scented creatures either.)

"Too damn bad," she said. "You're staying with me. And you'll be here as long as it takes."

"As long as it takes to what?" he asked.

She raised her head, and looked down her nose at him. "As long as it takes to figure out why you people wanted to destroy my library."

They didn't want to destroy it. They simply wanted one

of the most expensive items in the collection, a first-edition *Harry Potter and the Philosopher's Stone* from late twentieth-century Earth. On the open market, that book could raise enough money to fund a small country—or a spectacular library.

All in all, sixteen different groups reached the library before the authorities stopped the scavenger hunt and forced everyone to return the items—and/or pay for damages.

The Bathyboble paid the most, at least to the library itself, although Petra believed that when the suits and countersuits were done, the amount the Bathybobles paid would pale in comparison to the fines and fees the organizers of the hunt would pay.

After all, they were claiming a simple proofing error in the regulations was to blame. And that would probably have worked, if the error wasn't repeated in all languages—and if the founder's son hadn't been caught with a collector's bag and skin seals.

Petra followed the proceedings, partly because she had to testify several times and partly because she was feeling vindictive. She couldn't get a new dress to replace that linen one—she couldn't afford it. Not even with her promotion.

She now ran the library. Her boss, who wanted the scavenger hunt to come to the library as a promotional tool, had been fired, and so had his boss and his boss's boss.

Petra didn't have the qualifications to rise higher in the library food chain—yet—and she wasn't sure she wanted to when the time came.

She loved being among the books.

She could touch them now without guards watching her, and better yet, she could read the books whenever she wanted.

It only took her three months to get enough nerve to read the *Harry Potter* book that started all of this. Her hands shook the entire time.

The archaic language made her struggle. The references to things she did not understand, like drills and cupboards and traffic jams, slowed her down. But she worked her way through it all without using an Archaic English translation guide, and felt as accomplished as she had when she caught the Bathybobles.

Oh, hell. She felt more accomplished.

Because books stayed with you forever. Deeds remained only if they were recorded in story and song— and even then, such accomplishments were hard to understand without their proper context.

She didn't want to give anyone the context, although she had. Nor did she want to revisit that day, although the smell of a fish taco always made her slightly faint.

That, and a glance at the front desk.

She didn't ever want to work the front desk again.

She simply couldn't be polite any more.

People came here wanting to gawk at her books. And she would do everything she could to prevent it.

Even if it meant telling her story, and thinking about slime, rotted fish tacos, and displaying her ruined dress.

Even if it meant a bit of notoriety.

A good librarian did what she could do to protect her books.

And Petra was a very good librarian indeed.

GREEN MOSS RIVER

by David Farland

"You can motivate by fear,
and you can motivate by reward.
But both those methods are only temporary.
The only lasting thing is self-motivation."
—Homer Rice,
Former Head Coach, Cincinnatti Bengals

David Farland is a New York Times *bestselling author
with over fifty novel-length works to his credit. His latest
novel,* Nightingale, *won the International Book Award for
Best Young Adult Novel, the Next Gen Award, the Global
E-Book Award, and the Hollywood Book Festival Award
for Best Novel of the Year. Dave is currently finishing the
last book in his popular* Runelords *series, and there will
be no sequels.*

*In our second story involving shooting, Farland examines
an unusual hunting contest from the perspectives of both
hunters and prey.*

Lailas switched her wispy tail as she watched the hunters

leave their ship. They shouted and celebrated, eager for the hunt. They poured its ramp, more of them than she could begin to count, like the baby fish expelled from their mothers in Green Moss River.

Hidden under a strangleroot tree's sheltering boughs, she flared her silver-velvet nostrils, sucked in their scents. *Too many of them to sort. So many different hunters.*

But no jalwraiths this time. She shook her mane in relief, remembering creatures as tall as trees, scaly and dank and smelling of swamp, which had pursued the does last year. Claws as long as her head had flipped the does off their feet and gutted them with a single stroke.

None this time. Now the hunters lumbered across the grazing field, gathering into clumps like small herds, while the fading lights of the twin suns dimmed for the night. Only as darkness deepened to red did her questing eyes settle on a figure that separated itself from the mob. It stood alone, two-legged and upright, wearing a jointed shell like the little rock-crawlers that scuttled underfoot on bare hillsides.

The creature strode under the Gate of the Purple Moon, a stone arch that rose high over its head, and pulled out his weapons.

Human, she realized. She studied him, and stamped a three-toed front foot. She had heard of humans. This one brandished a weapon and raised it ceremoniously.

Ancient memories demanded that she rise to its challenge. She crept forward to study him, heart hammering with fear, the hide twitching on her flanks.

Love had driven her here, love for a herd leader. There was only one way to win the right to mate with him, unite as one. She would have to outrace death this night.

Show no fear, she thought, and swiveled her triangular ears forward as she now raced toward her adversary, leaping over fallen trees and pools of fetid water.

Kember Hafen squinted through the reddening light at the boiling, bloated gas giant that filled most of the sky. He sniffed at the air, surprised at the lack of odor. "Atmosphere check," he requested of his biolink, and perused the ethereal chart instantly projected before his right eye.

Ratios of methane and sulfur proved consistent with Earth's atmospheric mix, but oxygen edged slightly higher. He quirked his remaining eyebrow under his half-helmet. *That could give me an advantage.*

From where he stood, in a grassy meadow with forest and craggy mountains beyond, the gas giant's third moon, Malebour, appeared placid.

Kember knew better. As a veteran of Earth's Expeditionary Space Marines, he'd spent too much time on too many rocks that had seemed harmless from a distance. Up close and personal, they had chewed men up and spit out their remains. He'd lost both legs and a chunk from his face, his left eye and ear, on a world with pastoral vistas and skies as blue as Earth's.

Still, the posting on Mercenaries InterGalactica had caught his attention. The ad had been straightforward: Hunters wanted to kill harmless aliens for Galactic Games, payment of one thousand galactic garos per head.

The hologram accompanying the ad showed an animal

called a panapy. It could have passed for some kind of Earth gazelle, complete with twisting white horns, except for its size, like a small horse. Kember had noted the broad forehead like a horse's, with surprisingly intelligent eyes, and the hindquarters, well-muscled for leaping. It had a silver-white hide with a wispy bluish-white mane and tail, and a silver-blue muzzle that ended with several finger-like lips.

Killing bugs? Hell, I've done plenty of that. He'd snorted. In the Corps, all aliens were called "bugs." *This looks more like a big-game hunt. But with that kind of pay, I could bag four or five and afford to retire. Wonder how they taste?*

Kember had queried the universal knowledge base via his biolink. Panapies rated Level 3 on the intelligence scale, he'd learned, three slots below him. Marginally sentient and pre-technical. Barbarians with hides and horns, in other words.

Kind of tough to develop technology when you lack opposable thumbs, he'd smirked.

But they lacked more. Their prefrontal lobes were too small. Poor planners. In other words, panapies seemed to be a species with no future, but to make up for it, they had evolved an expanded *progonikal* cortex, a portion of their brain which stored genetic memories essential to the species' survival. Earth's biologists wanted panapy brains for study, in hopes of learning to create something with the same function for humans. *That explains payment by the head.*

He wondered at that. It seemed that the panapies were doomed to repeat the same mistakes, one generation after another.

Kember swept his gaze across the landing zone. The light reflecting from the gas giant cast an odd, rusty hue over the shallow valley and his fellow hunters. A few hundred of them, he estimated, studying the crowd.

They were trundling off to their own stations. Easing away from the crowds, he spotted some h'rikathi from Dath, leggy and yellow-eyed and wearing only their own streaky, tan pelts; and trologs from Suroomo, with legs like tree trunks, two-toed feet, and hides like rhinos.

Kember scowled at a flashback—trologs racing away from battle in terror. *One of those trologs blinks at me the wrong way and I'll be hunting more than panapies.* They had been unreliable allies in the war with the chewanda. *With friends like that . . .*

He recognized a dozen other species, and spotted some he'd never seen before. But no other humans. *Fine with me. I don't have any more use for humans than I do trologs.*

The rusty light darkened to a bloody twilight with the moon's rotation. Kember checked the power charge on his plasma rifle, the canteens snapped into his plate body-armor, the extra power cells and marker beacons clipped to his tactical vest. He switched his cybernetic left eye to IR night-vision with a thought.

A few yards away, the other hunters' voices lowered to tense murmurs. But the sensation of being watched, too familiar after twelve years in combat zones, came from behind. Kember shifted just enough to stare over his shoulder.

The human turned. Half of his face seemed to be covered with a shell, like his body, but Lailas saw the hard, straight line of his mouth and his soulless, distant stare. Danger spilled off his bulky shoulders and roiled the air about him.

She shuddered. *This killer is more deadly than a jalwraith*. Trotting near, she lowered her head until her muzzle almost touched her hooves. *You are Death. I bow to you*.

Two more panapies joined Lailas, her sisters. She smelled their fear as they also bowed.

The human looked down at Lailas and its mouth moved oddly, a grim smile forming. It showed its teeth and spoke. A translator on its shoulder broadcast, "You're all dead meat."

Good, Lailas thought as her heart began to race with excitement. As a foal she had often been told that "There is no greater thrill than to be hunted," and she needed a hunter like this to prove her worth. *Merciless, seasoned, a killer*.

She reared on her hind feet, pawed the air, and uttered her own challenge, "Come for me, Lord Death. Prove my worth."

In night-vision mode, the panapies' body heat glowed pale gold, apparitions upon the fields. The leader pivoted and leapt away toward the tangled black roots of trees, bounding high, then landing, seeming almost to fly.

Damn, they're fast.

Its two fellows whirled and followed in formation— ghostly specters. Their beauty smote Kember. They floated over the land silently, leaping and falling like his childhood dreams of unicorns.

Idiot creatures must have a death wish. I've got my first targets of the night.

He raised his plasma rifle to fire, and the creatures suddenly veered, as if some sixth sense warned of the danger—instantly they swept under the trees.

Kember gave chase, racing over plains covered in lush alien grasses, leaping a brook, sidestepping some rocks. A small mink-like creature ducked into the grass.

With the tech in his legs, he covered 600 yards in twelve seconds, until he stood at the edge of the trees, black boles rising up from tangles of raised roots, creating a bizarre serpentine jungle.

Like common willows with their drooping boughs, but with broader, feathery leaves of palest red. *It could pass for a gazebo in some tropical garden.*

Eyeing the spot where the gazelle-creatures had entered, Kember resisted the urge to curl his finger into the rifle's trigger well.

Behind him, a wedge-shaped aircar slid in above the muttering mob of hunters and came to a hover with a steady thrum of engines. Kember couldn't see its occupants, but the voice that emanated from unseen speakers clearly wasn't human.

"Welcome, sportsmen, to the annual Wild Hunt," the voice reverberated. "You may utilize the hours of darkness to kill as many panapies as you can. By doing so, you do them the favor of culling their herds. Only the females that survive this hunt will be allowed to mate, and they are eager to start.

"Your hunt starts here, and it is a thirty-mile course. You may fell them anywhere along the route until they enter the Green Moss River. You may not pursue them or launch missiles of any kind across the water. Fly-eyes will be deployed to guarantee your adherence to this rule and beam images to sports fans across the galaxy.

"You must plant your beacon on the carcass of any panapy you kill in order to locate it once the hunt has ended. You may not set off until the starting gun fires. Good luck to all!"

That's all? No regulations against hunting other hunters? Kember's scarred lip curled. *Just give me an excuse, trologs. Any excuse will be sufficient. . . .*

Lailas and her sisters rounded up in the glade with the rest of the does that would race. She saw nervousness in flicking ears and switching tails. Felt tension quiver through her own body.

Fathe, her fleet-footed sister, and Tevethal the clever drew up to her. Lailas gave them her impression of the human with the hard eyes and empty stare, and the mass of other hunters.

"They will have to chase us through the strangleroot trees," Tevethal said slyly. "That will stop many of them and give us more time."

Lailas shivered. *It will take more than strangleroots to stop the one with hard eyes. And if he falls, he's only one of . . . countless.*

"We should stay with the herd," Tevethal counseled. "In the middle of it, where our coats will mix with the others' and make us harder to pick out. Fathe, you must not run out in front, and Lailas, you must not fall behind. That's where it's easiest to catch you."

Lailas hoped Tevethal was right. *Tevethal has always been the smart one, the one who figures things out. And Fathe is perhaps the fastest in the herd. She will be able to outrun hunters when she needs to. But I'm small, I'm the runt of our litter. What can I do? How can I help us survive this night?*

By the time they reached mating age, panapy does far outnumbered bucks. So to strengthen the herd, before mating season, females who had come of age had to race. They had to run from Grass Valley to Green Moss River, the whole way in one night.

In the time long ago, does only faced local terrors along the route. Packs of screaming biters, hump-shouldered and hairy, that leaped on them from cliffs and tore out their throats. Mud-wallowers in the swamps, that caught slender legs in crushing jaws and pulled them down to drown. Swaying fire fronds at the edges of creeks that stung if one brushed against them, causing paralysis and a slow death.

Now hunters from other worlds had joined the slaughter.

The does who survived, who crossed the river before dawn, earned the right to mate.

The weak, the stupid, the slow—they earned death.

Lailas trembled, dreading the race. Then she thought of the buck with whom she had bonded. Strong Haloro, with his flowing mane and horns like spears. Haloro, who had chosen her over her sisters, so that they had bonded with other males. *I'm not strong and smart*, she thought, *but I will do this for you, Haloro. You will not be left waiting on the bank, like last year, when jalwraiths killed too many does.*

A sharp crack boomed through the snarled forest, like a bolt of lightning, shattering the taut stillness. Lailas jumped. Heads and ears went up, and someone uttered a cry.

"The hunt begins!" said Tevethal. "Stay in the herd, stay close to me, Lailas, and run straight to the east."

With a leap, Lailas and her sisters began to flee.

A canister launched from the game master's aircar with a boom. It burst in the air, shooting fly-eyes in all directions. NE 4923 whizzed free of the cluster and arced wide. Swift movement below caught its sensors, and it followed.

A split-second scan confirmed the identity of its subject. "Kember Hafen from Earth," the internal recorder began. "First human ever to join the hunt. As the starting gun fires, Hafen appears to have spotted his prey. . . ."

At the bang of the starting gun, Kember whirled, rifle in the ready position. Thunder rumbled underfoot as the mob of hunters behind him charged. Closest to the trees, he used his rifle's barrel to prod aside sagging branches.

On his second step, something whipped around his titanium right leg, ankle to groin. Its tug dragged him to the ground. Another whistling cord lashed his torso, pinning his arms to his body. He cursed.

Around him, bellows, screams, and roars from hunters split the night. He heard thrashing, grunts, strangled gasps.

Kember laughed aloud, a "Huh!" of bitter recognition,

not mirth. *Sounds like my fellow hunters are being culled, too.*

"Activate arm saws!" he panted.

Slender double blades rose, humming, from sheath ridges in his armor, down the outsides of his arms. He felt their buzz, smelled scorching wood. The squeezing bonds slackened, twitched, and fell away.

He drew a deep breath and leapt to his feet. "Retract arm saws, activate right thigh and calf saws."

Armor saws had saved him a few times during his career, from trapping nets, cables, and once a tentacle thicker than his arm. The remembered odor of it burning almost made him gag again. He'd insisted on the same tools for his prosthetics.

Resisting the reflex to scramble up, which would probably trigger another attack, he searched the ground for snares. *What the hell grabbed me?*

His cybernetic eye picked out a root network, reaching across the topsoil like a woody spider's web. Two sawn-off tendrils, oozing sap-like blood, confirmed his suspicion. Setting the plasma rifle on low, he pulled the trigger.

Fire erupted in a stream some sixty feet long. He upped the power a notch and seared the whole root mass to stinking, steaming ash.

He continued to sweep the ground with plasma bursts as he advanced, leaving behind the gurgles and thrashing of dying hunters, and sending up billows of vapor. The wet heat made him sweat; and the sweat ran itching down his sides. His own smell mingled with the scent of rotting vegetation, so thick he could almost taste it.

Clouds of tiny black butterflies began to flee the heat, swarming like starlings on Earth, taking strange paths among the trees.

His prosthetic legs carried him with longer, swifter strides than his real legs could have. His enhanced lungs pulled in oxygen without effort. But he didn't have the forest to himself.

Shapes of other hunters who'd escaped the roots lurked around him, glowing as brightly as their game. Some crashed heedless through branches and undergrowth, some cleared their way with vibro-blades or machetes.

In minutes his IR vision glimpsed pale shapes bounding ahead between the trees. A mass of them, brighter with their combined heat than the creatures he'd seen at the landing zone. Kember charged forward.

Lailas glanced back. Herd mates surged all around her, necks outstretched, eyes white-rimmed, some with mouths open. They pressed her from behind and on both sides. She leaned into Tevethal a little as she ran.

Behind them, the crushing and snapping sounds of breaking trees grew louder, closer. Spouts of blue-white flame flowed along the earth like lightning turned to water. Lailas's heart clenched in panic at the thought of fire nipping at her tail.

A herd mate's cry from behind, then another and another, flicked her ears around. She gasped, a cry waiting in her own throat. *They've been killed.*

"Don't look back!" Tevethal urged. "Focus ahead. Look at me, look at me, and think of Haloro waiting for you."

Lailas swallowed, and pressed once more into her sister's side. "Don't leave me, Tevethal!"

Two lengths in front, Fathe and the herd leaders darted left and right through the trees, weaving and springing. Lailas panted, mouth open, as she followed. The forest floor slanted up and her lunges came with greater effort. Her chest had already begun to burn.

"It's the crest!" someone ahead called over her shoulder. Lailas didn't know who, she saw only flying tails through the misty gloom.

"Burrowers' mounds!" warned someone else.

Fewer trees, mostly wind-wrenched, leafless ones, grew on the other side of the ridge. The great, orange face of the giant planet cast just enough light to distinguish lumpy, scattered heaps of soil between them.

Coming upon the first hillock, Lailas sucked in a breath and gathered herself. *Let me leap far enough! Don't let me fall through!* Breath caught, she launched herself after Tevethal, straining to reach out with her forelegs.

Front hooves met solid ground. She released a whoof of relief and collected herself for the next leap.

New death cries rose on the breeze behind her. Through the tail of one eye she glimpsed blue-white fire arc across the sky, saw a silhouetted herd mate crumple as the fire struck. Fear made her breath ragged, left her legs weak.

"Tevethal!" she called. "I keep hearing the cries. My legs are too weak to keep jumping. I'm so scared. Don't leave me!"

"I'm here," Tevethal said. "Turn your ears forward and listen to me. Go around the burrows if you can't jump them. I won't leave you."

❖   ❖   ❖

NE 4923 cruised after its target, a couple of yards behind and somewhat higher than the man's head. "The human Hafen is burning his way through the strangleroot trees," it recorded. "He is skilled at firing on the move, and has already made two kills. He raises his plasma rifle again . . ."

Kember swung the rifle to lead one of the bounding gazelle-things. The plasma burst caught it in the air, struck its midsection, and reduced it to a momentary fireball. He followed the trail of smoke, white against the night, to the crumpled heap of charred flesh and bones.

A thudding footfall wrenched him around. Something bulky and smelly loomed over him. "Mine!" Kember yelled, leveling his rifle. The hulking shape lurched away, giving him a wide berth. *Trolog, or something else?*

It didn't matter. He yanked a beacon off his vest, and wrinkled his nose at the burned odor as he crouched. *Not much left. But as long as the brain's still intact. . . .* He drove the beacon's spike through the carcass's blackened ribcage.

Ahead of him, the trees thinned, revealing a hill's crest. He raced to it. From the top he viewed a long, gradual slope down to an expanse of shallow water. The herd had spread out, and stragglers cast hot, bright blots on the cool turf. *Two or three more easy shots before I make it down to the water.*

Before him, the planet-lit hillside appeared broken, as if enormous moles had burrowed and kicked up mounds around their holes. Kember watched the trailing panapies, almost in range, leap over hummocks with increasing effort. Watched two buckle at the ends of other hunters' crimson tracers. Thin wails reached him a few seconds later. Their death cries were strange, he thought. They were long ululating wails, a trumpeting animal noise, but similar to the cries of Arabic women when they mourned.

Hurdling a mound in his path, he lined up his next shot. As he squeezed the trigger, the earth opened beneath him.

He pitched forward, tucked his head to take the fall as a roll, but found himself falling much further than imagined.

He landed hard on his back, half winded, as a shower of moist soil and pebbles swelled to a torrent. Must have fallen forty feet.

Kember Hafen found himself at the bottom of a shaft, something like a well. Without his armor, the fall alone would have killed him.

Seizing his rifle and spitting out mud, he shoved himself to his feet. Ducked clear of the landslide and peered up. *Damn, I could've been buried! But there's more than one way to get out of a hole.*

Slinging his rifle onto his back, he began to climb, slipping and falling, sliding soil under his feet.

"Earthling Kember Hafen has encountered another obstacle on his hunt," recorded NE 4923 as it circled the pit. Its multi-mode lens zoomed in for images of the human working his way out. Its tiny go-lights caught him in an insubstantial beam of white. The whine of its miniature propulsion system cut through the clack and buzz of nocturnal insects. "While he does not appear to be injured, this surely will delay his making another kill."

The steady whine caught Kember's attention. *No biologic sounds like that; they all have some kind of variation or pulse. That's a techy bug.* He paused at his task, scanned the orange-tinted dark.

His IR vision lit up the fly-eye, a bright orb the size of an eyeball with faint running lights.

He knew that this was a race, that the panapies that he hunted had wanted this in order to cull the herd, but he suddenly felt outraged.

He remembered Dev, a friend of his youth, bleeding out on some godforsaken rock whose name he had forgotten, eyes and ears and nose flowing red after a chewnadan's sonic missile took him out.

"Don't leave me," Dev had cried, his voice hollow.

Dev was reaching up, blindly trying to grasp Kember's hand, his whole body wracked by spasms.

But the enemy had been advancing, and there wasn't any saving a man whose guts had been ground to sausage.

"Sorry, bud," Kember had had to say as he stood and ran away, dodging the incoming.

Dev had died that day, but something inside of Kember had died a little, too. After twelve years of that shit, he'd died a lot.

Killing isn't a game, he thought.

Bracing himself on his settling ramp, he pulled his rifle around, took careful aim. A brilliant burst left the scent of fried electronics on the humid air.

As he emerged from the pit, he studied the hillside

below for more tell-tale upheavals. "Terrain survey," he requested of his cybernetic eye. Dark patches showed cool gaps beneath the thin surface.

The herd of panapies, noticeably thinner now, still bounded down the gradual decline. Two miles ahead, he gauged. Dimming patches of IR return marked dead ones scattered and cooling on the slope. Many of the remaining hunters had passed him by, too, driving the herd toward the water.

He grimaced at the scent rising from it. *The last remnant of an ancient lake. It smells like swamp.* He recalled the giant leeches on Pergoth III, large enough to suck the blood from a man in three seconds. *God, I hate swamps.*

Kember took a long pull from his canteen, ejected his rifle's spent power cell and slapped in a fresh one, before he started again. He glanced at the readout on his GPS. Twenty-three miles lay behind him, but he suspected that the toughest leg of the hunt remained.

Lailas had never feared water. The scent of it, lifting on a listless breeze, eased her distress. She saw Fathe still loping ahead, pushing forward as weariness began to weigh on the leaders, and Lailas felt an urge to join her.

As if sensing her mood, Tevethal said, "Stay close," and then called, "Fathe, drop back! Stay with us."

Fathe's playful eye glittered as she glanced at her sisters over her flying tail. "We're almost there!"

Hours had passed. Death was on the wind.

The great planet's orange light glinted on the water's rippled surface. Lailas's nose twitched at its sour scent.

This is mucky water. I'm so thirsty, but it's no good for drinking. She sagged against Tevethal's flank. *I want to stop, I'm so tired, but I can still hear the cries, and the herd is so much smaller now. If I stop, the hunters will shoot me, too.*

Reeds and grasses poked through mud and lapping water in swaying tufts. They rattled on lazy breaths of heavy air as if calling to the racing does.

"Don't slow down when we reach the water," Tevethal said. "Leap out as far as you can. There are mud-wallowers at the water's edge, with big teeth."

"I can't leap anymore!" Lailas cried. "I'm too tired, I'm too weak." Her muscles had turned to pain, and she could move them no more. She felt exhausted, her mind whirling. She was ready to die.

"Do it," Tevethal said. "Do it for Haloro."

Below, a few of the leaders hesitated at the lapping shore, paced back and forth. As they watched, something huge and mud-colored erupted in a burst of spray, seized the nearest doe in its gaping maw, and vanished with a towering splash. In the next heartbeat, red tracers arced out of the woods and crumpled two more of the herd.

"No!" Lailas cried, and stopped.

"Hurry! We must run!" Tevethal urged.

"I can't. I'm too scared. Tevethal, don't leave me!"

"Run!" Tevethal replied. She seized Lailas's mane in her finger-lips and pulled.

All my strength, all I have left, Lailas thought as her feet touched the gravelly shore. She bunched her muscles and thrust herself off the bank.

❖   ❖   ❖

Ambling down the slope, Kember watched the hunters ahead of him racing to the swamp's bank. Waiting. None of them, even the pair of trologs slouching at the water's edge, seemed inclined to shoot panapies as they half swam, half slogged through algae-slimed mud. They were sitting ducks, but Kember had no desire to shoot one; he'd have to haul it to shore to claim it.

It amused him, watching the gazelle-things struggle. What drove them? Did they know the hunt hadn't ended? That all but maybe the fastest would be picked off as they dragged themselves out of the swamp?

If they weren't swallowed by its denizens first.

A query to the universal knowledge base via his biolink called the swamp-dwellers wahkameks, primitive reptilians that apparently had never finished evolving from eels to alligators.

Chuckling in his throat, Kember toggled the translator button in his half-helmet, said, "Panapy," and nudged the projection volume to maximum.

The human's voice seemed to boom from the sky, as if from the baleful gas giant itself. Lailas froze, ears high on alert, her wide eyes searching the sky.

"Why do you run?" the voice demanded. "Most of your herd has been killed. The rest of you will die when you come out of the water. What's the purpose of it? Do none of you have a will to survive? Do your lives have no value to you?"

I want to survive! Lailas thought. *I want to meet Haloro at Green Moss River. I want to live with my sisters, and raise our young together.*

"Death waits for you to come out of the water," said the voice. "We are prepared to finish this. We are Death."

For the first time since the boom of the starting gun, Lailas felt angry, a surge of defiance and determination. *I bowed to you last evening, Death,* she thought, *but I was wrong to do it. You are not what I thought. You only mock our ways.*

She pushed forward, hooves sinking into mud, and almost passed Tevethal.

Sure enough, a shot flared across the swamp as the first panapy jumped onto the far bank, slime streaming down its legs. It dropped, and splashed into the water, legs flailing.

Kember quickened his pace. Rifle aimed at the water, alert for stirrings beneath the surface, he strode in. The hunters who remained followed.

The bowl that had sloped so gradually behind them rose in a steep wall before them, with only a narrow pass to the river valley beyond. Once he reached the pass, it would be like shooting fish in a barrel. It was a perfect spot to take down the rest of the herd.

If I push it, Kember thought, *I can get a dozen more kills before the last of the herd makes it to the boundary river.*

"Terrain map," he requested of his cybernetic eye, and saw through the billowing silt where rocks and tangled weeds and other debris lay.

More tracers lit the night, more panapies crumpled on the far bank. A thrashing began, water flying and spraying, when a hunter Kember hadn't paid much attention to before crouched to drag his kill clear, only to be seized along with it by the largest wahkamek he'd seen yet.

"Dumbass," he muttered, and took aim as another panapy sprang lightly onto the bank.

The blue-white flash struck Fathe broadside with a force that blew her off her feet before it slammed her to the soil. Smoke twisted from the blackened crater that had been her ribcage.

"No!" Lailas screamed. "Fathe, no!"

For the first time, Tevethal's firm voice lost its composure. "Don't look, Lailas. You've got to run." And she shoved herself between Lailas and the sprawled body. "Go. Just keep going."

Crimson tracers lanced between their horns. Lailas ducked her head, leaned against Tevethal, and ran.

Kember squinted up the slope ahead as he slogged through hip-deep slime. Not as high and not as sheer as he'd thought at a distance. The gas giant's dull glow cast the pass into brown shadow.

It's only two miles. It was what they'd called a "kill box" back in combat, *but if the bugs get through, they're home free.*

The image Kember had summoned from the knowledge base stood clearly in his mind. The pass opened onto a broad riverbank, sufficiently forested to provide cover.

I've got to cut the bugs off somehow so we can finish this. They're fair game until they hit the river.

He could climb over the hill, he realized. He'd scaled steeper cliffs on Dadaqir, without lines. He'd do some quick reconnaissance from the top, figure out a course of action.

Clambering onto the bank, he paused only long enough to plant his beacon on the panapy with the smoking chest cavity. He had one beacon left. Considering how well he could retire with the pay from eight kills, he slung his rifle onto his back and started up the cliff's face.

The thud of the panapies' hoof-like toes clattering into the narrow canyon below echoed up to him as he climbed. He gritted his teeth, seized the next handhold, hauled himself higher. *Really smart, Kember, taking the long way when you're in a hurry.*

His prosthetic legs, pistons and gears, never tired. He clawed, pulled, and pushed himself up faster than should have been possible. Bellying onto the ragged crest, he didn't waste time catching his breath. He scrambled across deep-shadowed rock, half jogging, until he peered down into the canyon.

IR vision highlighted cold, racing water, a warm belt of trees, and dozens of bright, hot gazelle-creatures gathering along the far bank. With the canyon walls as a sound chamber, his cybernetic ear picked out eager snorts and brays through the river's tumbling roar. *The welcoming committee. Not much left to welcome. Not by the time we're done.*

The first racing panapies crested the pass. As if endowed with new strength, their weary gallops burst into dead runs, bounding and floating like a waterfall. They charged down toward the river.

Kember pointed the plasma rifle down, and waited for one second more. . . .

With Green Moss River's scent filling their extended nostrils, Lailas and Tevethal plunged forward. For the first time in their journey, Tevethal left Lailas behind. But it didn't matter now.

Tevethal was drawing ahead, a full stride toward the grove's protective cover, when the monstrous voice boomed from above once more.

"And so it ends, victory for the chosen few." The human's voice carried mockery, cold as the eyes of the human to whom Lailas had bowed. "The fastest, the smartest, the bravest are left. The weak have been culled.

"The best live to breed and produce more young," it roared, "which will one day race to their deaths. Your cycle of life. Your cycle of death. It ends now. I am Death!"

The trees, dried by the constant canyon winds, suddenly exploded around them into flame.

The human was shooting into the trees—blocking their path!

For a heartbeat, Lailas glimpsed her sister wreathed in blinding fire. And then she heard her scream.

Nothing terrified Lailas more than fire. Not mud-wallowers, not even the human with soulless eyes. She froze before the towers of flame. "Tevethal! Tevethal, come out!"

The translator worked both ways. Kember hadn't known that. Shrill voices that he knew belonged to the gazelle-creatures filled his helmet's earphones. He stared into the canyon, lit by a couple hundred torches of blazing oak-like trees.

"Tevethal!" he heard. "Come back to me!"

"I can't! I'm too scared! Lailas, don't leave me!"

He could see one panapy in the midst of the blackening trees, not pinned, not trapped, but petrified. Glowing debris rained down on it.

The smaller one called Lailas paced just outside, apparently terrified, too. "This way, Tevethal!" it called. "I can see you. Turn around and come to me."

"I can't, I can't! I'm too scared!"

Tevethal's mane caught fire, then its tail. It reared and plunged and screamed, but seemed unable to move forward or back.

Then the one called Lailas lowered its head and lunged in.

"Idiot!" Kember said through clenched teeth. "Do you want to burn, too?"

"I'm coming, Tevethal!" cried Lailas. "Close your eyes, don't look at it. I won't leave you." The smaller animal pressed close to its paralyzed companion, took the other's smoldering mane in its finger-lips, and pulled.

Tevethal followed, staggering, swaying, nearly dead on her feet. Once clear of the conflagration, she collapsed, falling onto her side.

Even from his perch on the clifftop Kember knew that she was burned badly, knew she was dying.

Easy money. He raised his plasma rifle, thinking to finish it, but didn't pull the trigger . . . yet. He didn't have a clear shot. Lailas was in the way.

"Go!" he spat at the small one. "Get to the river!"

If she heard his bellow over the roar of the fire, she gave no sign. She planted herself in front of her fallen companion, and through her snorting and head-tossing he heard, "Stay away! Stay back! I won't leave my sister."

Stupid bug. There was still a path ahead for her, if she hurried.

Kember shifted his gaze. The last hunters were cresting the hill. Most froze in shock before the blazing conflagration. Smoke trailed up the hill like a black serpent, winding through the canyon, flames leapt from trees, an inferno.

But one trolog raised its long gun.

"You just gave me an excuse," Kember growled, swinging his plasma rile. He aimed and squeezed the trigger. "That's for her, and this," he nailed a second trolog too, "is for me."

He hesitated for a moment, thinking of the panapies.

This isn't a dead-end species, he told himself, astonished by the realization. The herd instinct was strong in them—the desire to help others above self, to give in to compassion instead of fear. *None of that "Every man for himself" bullshit.*

Kember stood slowly and shouted through the storm of rising smoke and ash, "Life is not just for the strongest or smartest. I am Death, but you, Lailas, have proven yourself most worthy to live."

The panapy whirled and looked toward him, then used her muzzle to push her sister to her feet.

Together they limped through the flames into Green Moss River.

THE ON-DECK CIRCLE
✧ ✧ ✧
by Gene Wolfe

"My motto was always to keep swinging. Whether
I was in a slump or feeling badly or having trouble off
the field, the only thing to do was keep swinging."
—Hank Aaron,
MLB Hall of Famer, Milwaukee Braves

*Gene Wolfe is a SFWA Grandmaster and speculative
fiction writer noted for his dense, allusive prose as well as
the strong influence of his Catholic faith. He is a
prolific short story writer and novelist and has won many
science fiction and fantasy literary awards, including
multiple Nebula, Locus, and World Fantasy Awards. He
is most famous for* The Book of the New Sun *(four
volumes, 1980–83). In 1998,* Locus *ranked it third-best
fantasy novel before 1990—*The Lord of the
Rings *and* The Hobbit *were first and second—based on
a poll of subscribers that considered it and several other
series. On a side note, he helped invent Pringles, which
continue to be eaten during many a sporting event around
the world.*

This story first appeared in Postscript's *Autumn 2006*

issue. This is its first anthology appearance. Imagine baseball . . . played on speed boats.

Standing near the on-deck circle with the rest, Scooter Scarlata, late of the Pirates, watched the ball come in—a ball with roaring engines and blazing blue lights. A ball that was, in fact, a big speedboat.

"Fast ball." The tall man standing next to him spoke in the portentous tones of the self-anointed expert.

Scooter nodded absently. The fastball was almost straight up, its creamy white wake more visible than its blue aura from where they stood. "I hate night games," he muttered.

The player in the on-deck circle lisped, "Don't you thee?" She was a blonde in a capacious pink halter and white shorts. "Ith got to be at night, Thcooter, for live TV. We're in prime time."

"We could play somewheres else." He had played winter ball in Japan in . . . ? The year had slipped quietly away. Forty-five, maybe. Or forty-four. Could have been forty-three.

"Fog's closing in," the expert said.

"I hate fog, too," Scooter told him. He had played in fog. Nobody hit except by dumb luck. Nobody caught a fly either, except by dumb luck. Pop-ups plopping out of a dirty-yellow cloud so close you could almost touch it.

"Tho we've got to have the gameth—" the blonde in the pink halter began. Then the ball raced into the brilliant, plate-shaped sea created by spotlights below the surface. The player in the batting box flung his bat at it, failing by twenty feet to lead the flying blue boat sufficiently. Everyone sighed. To his surprise, Scooter discovered that he had sighed, too. "Stupid game," he muttered.

"STRIKE THREE!" boomed the speakers of the huge screen forward. "NUMBER SIXTY-SIX, LISA LOCKLIN, WILL BE OUR NEXT BATTER!" Obediently, the blonde jiggled away.

"Scarlata?" It was an assistant director, the tall one who wore polo shirts.

Scooter turned to him. "She's got as much chance as a pigeon with a peanut shell out there."

"Get in the circle, Scarlata." The assistant director was looking toward the pitcher's mound, where the stately *M.S. Charlotte Amalie* readied the next pitch while rolling ever so slightly on a column of rising water. After a moment he added, "She's window dressing—big blue eyes and tits. You can't have a hit show without sex."

"The World Series—"

"That's different. This was the top-rated show last season. Did you know that?"

People had said the same thing at least twenty times; Scooter said nothing.

"This year the ratings have slipped. Do you know why?"

Scooter watched the blonde's bat fall short by fifty feet and waited for the speakers to announce strike one before he said, "Yeah."

"There isn't a team in the league that's getting enough hits," the assistant director continued gamely. "That's why we've enlisted the help of people like you, Scarlata. Famous baseball players." His pause lent his next words weight. "That's why we're paying you the money we are. You're going to get a hit."

"I'll try," Scooter said.

"*No.*" The assistant director's voice sounded as firm as the voices of assistant directors ever get. "Let me say it again. You. Are. Going. To. Get. A. Hit. The first pitch will be a slider, not too fast. Understand?"

Scooter nodded.

"If you miss it—and you won't, I know you won't—the next will be a change-up."

Scooter nodded again.

"I'm going to let you choose the third. I'll have plenty of time to set it up, so what would you like?"

Scooter spat over the rail. "I guess you never saw me play."

"You were before my time." The assistant director sounded happy about it. "What would you like?"

"Fastball, in on the hands."

The assistant director looked dubious. "A fastball? Are you sure?"

"Hell, yes!"

"Okay, I'll tell them. Have you met Jack Keech?"

Scooter shook his head, but the expert who had told him the fog was closing in said, "We've been chatting."

"Good. Jack's our boat man. He's worked on all the balls and raced speedboats."

Keech said, "I'm the ball boy, in other words."

Scooter nodded. "I got it."

"After you get your hit, you take the wheel so we can

show you there. Then you get out of the way and let Jack do it."

"I'm a singles hitter." Scooter spat at the rail, wishing it had been in the assistant director's face. "That's what I been hearing all my life. Just a singles hitter. In forty-six—"

"We need a home run," the assistant director put in.

Scooter ignored him. "I hit for the cycle. That's a single, a double, a triple, and a homer, all in one game. You ever go to Cooperstown?"

"STRIKE TWO!" blared the loudspeakers.

"I have," Keech said.

"You see me there? My picture? My number?"

Keech shook his head. "Maybe. I don't remember."

"You didn't, 'cause I'm not in there. To get in, you gotta be a slugger. You gotta hit lotsa homers. Nothin' else matters, see? Four gold gloves? Don't matter!"

"We understand," the assistant director said. "Now, for God's sake, shut up and listen. We have to have a home run from you. Not a single, not a double, not a triple. A home run. And the last thing in the world we need is for your hit to be caught in the infield. You know the rules."

Scooter shrugged. "Sure. And I know this cruise boat's no burner."

Keech said, "Ship, Scooter. This is a cruise ship."

Scooter wanted to spit again. "Not a fast one, it ain't."

"You're correct," the assistant director told him, "It isn't. If you're caught in the infield, the *Sunrise* will be out. Out automatically, under the rules. If you're caught in the outfield—well, it won't take them long to get their team on the ball. The *Sunrise* might easily be thrown out at first.

Even if it isn't, we don't need a single. We've got to have a home run. It means the ball has to touch land—"

Keech put in, "Over the fence, Scooter."

"Correct. Without being caught. It can beach, or tie up at a pier. That doesn't matter. As soon as a single member of your team steps ashore, that's a—

The loudspeakers blared, "STRIKE THREE."

"Put on your earphones, Jack," the assistant director whispered.

"YOU KNOW HIM FROM THE WHITE SOX, THE BRAVES, AND THE WORLD CHAMPION PITTSBURGH PIRATES! OUR NEXT BATTER WILL BE ONE OF BASEBALL'S LEGENDARY SHORTSTOPS. I MEAN NONE OTHER THAN OLD NUMBER EIGHTEEN HIMSELF! NONE OTHER THAN THE GREAT SCOOTER SCARLATA!

The bat was papier-mâché, but surprisingly heavy at the head where the firework was. Scooter took a few practice swings for the TV cameras, as he had been told he must, feeling his shoulder muscles loosen with every swing. What would the first pitch be? A slider?

Then it was time to walk the narrow gangplank (with nearly invisible black nylon railings) away from the ship's side and into the eternally nodding batter's box twenty-five feet on the wrong side of the rail. A light flashed overhead as soon as his foot crossed the line, a signal to the *Charlotte Amalie* that she might launch the ball when ready.

"One thing for sure," Scooter muttered to himself, "I'm not gonna get hit by no pitch."

For a moment he rested the bat at his feet. Then the

ball was on the way, blue lights blazing, coming fast but not too fast. He threw as it faded toward the edge and off the bright plate, his bat vanishing in the shining water a yard or more in front of the ball's prow and a yard or two short.

Someone passed him a new bat.

There was a wait that seemed interminable until the next pitch. At last, the glowing blue boat rushed at him like a fastball—only to slow at the final moment. He threw, and the frantically waving arms of the team aboard the ball knocked his bat to one side and into the water.

Strike two.

A solemn bat boy bought a new bat, reminding Scooter that the assistant director's boat expert had called himself the ball boy. Smiling grimly, Scooter gripped the new bat and took a few more practice swings.

The fastball was practically standing on end by the time it crossed the plate. It swerved in "on the hands" as promised, and he had only to toss the bat in front of its streaking hull.

For a split second, ball and bat seemed frozen in time: his bat a scant yard above the golden water of the plate, the dark hull framed in blue about to strike it.

Then the bat exploded with a bright, harmless flash and an impressive bang, showering ball and plate with glittering confetti.

Behind him, the loudspeakers went crazy, hysterical in their synthetic excitement. Behind him, his teammates were cheering, or diving, or jumping from the rail into the warm Caribbean. The batter's box had no nylon rope railing. He had not swum or dived for years before being picked for this; but there had been three days of frantic practice before he boarded the *Sunrise*, and practice every day in the big salt-water pool on the Lido Deck while he and his team waited for the game to start.

The ball boy held out a life vest. Scooter stuck his arms into it, and the boy pulled its straps tight and tied them expertly. Kicking off his shoes, Scooter stepped to the edge of the batter's box and made a creditable dive, knowing that some two hundred million watched.

He saw the boat's soft blue aura as soon as his head broke water. It was moving toward him—not fast. In a moment more, the expert he had spoken to on deck was pulling him out of the water. "Grab on, Scooter!" Like everyone else on board, he was dripping wet.

"I been picked up by a ball a lot," Scooter remarked, pushing his hair away from his eyes. "Only this's the only time it happened after I got a hit."

"Right. Take the wheel. We've only a got a couple more seconds before the end of the break."

Scooter did.

"Pulling it toward you will speed us up, but don't try it too fast. Get the feel. Push it forward to slow down. Way forward will reverse the engines, so don't. I'll take it as soon as the camera's off us. Get into position."

Scooter did, half sitting in the tiny seat behind the wheel, both hands on the rim.

"Great." There was a long pause. "Now go."

He jerked the wheel back, and a woman shrieked. The blue lights blazed again, and the whole boat shuddered and leaped as if flung forward by an explosion. In a moment more, the bow had risen so high that he could see only by peering around it.

"I told you not to do that!" the expert shouted.

Scooter scarcely heard him. He had discovered a small screen to his left. In it, the *Island Princess*, the *Palm Coast*, and the rest of infield were closing in.

"Expectin' a dribbler, were ya?" Scooter grinned and headed for the third base line, still holding the wheel all the way back and glorying in the deafening clamor of the engines.

"Okay! I'll take it now!" The expert beside him put a hand on the wheel.

Scooter knocked it away.

"I can do it! You can't!" There was so much wind noise, so great a thunder from the engines, that the expert could scarcely make himself heard.

The *Island Princess* had been playing third wide; now she was churning water to get on the line. At shortstop, the *Palm Coast* had almost stopped moving altogether. Scooter chuckled.

"We lost two or three people!" The expert yelled.

"They got jackets! Umpire'll pick 'em up!"

The blonde who had struck out was at his left elbow. Saying something he could not hear, she linked an arm through his. Her pink halter looked black in the boat's blue light. It was soaked, and clung like paint.

"Ever see a hit split short and third?" Scooter shouted to her. "Watch this!"

An overhead view in the small TV screen showed a dozen men hurriedly readying a glove on the *Island Princess*'s big foredeck.

Scooter edged over the wheel until their boiling wake diverged from the base line, then edged it over a quarter turn more. "They're gonna be scared they'll run into each other! Watch!"

The blonde's reply was inaudible, but she smiled warmly and tightened her grip on his arm.

"I never hit lots of homers! Only this's the first hit I could steer!"

The boat expert rushed him, shoving him aside and clawing at the wheel. Scooter's knee caught his groin a split second before Scooter's fist landed a hard, hooking left just below his chin. Grabbing the expert's headphones as he went down, Scooter tossed them over his shoulder into the boiling wake.

"There're gonna thmash uth!" Terrified, the blonde made herself heard.

"Naw!" Scooter shook his head. "They don't wanna hit."

As lofty as beetling cliffs, the sharp prows of the cruise ships were closing on them—already nearly closed—when Scooter steered between them. A second later he heard the grinding crash of their collision, too loud for even his roaring engines to drown out.

The blonde was pointing ahead and shouting.

"Sure! I see him! That's *Martinique*, left field."

The expert was standing again. "You moron! We're going right to her!"

"You bet we are!" Scooter grinned. "Ain't no ball so hard to catch as one coming straight at you fast."

It was perhaps thirty tense seconds later when the *Martinique* fired her glove, silver rockets spreading a wide and gleaming net. They raced beneath it, and most of the team turned to watch it fall into the sea.

The white line of breakers appeared long before the rocks—long, in this case, being seven seconds at least. In those seven seconds, the expert made one last desperate attempt to take the wheel, before they hit. And failed.

A home run! He had hit a home run! What did the Hall of Fame matter now? Yet he would be in the Hall of Fame. He would be there because he would have to be there. He would have to be there because every visitor would want to know where he was.

It seemed to him then that the water was sinking below him. Eight or ten stories down, though wisps of fog, he could see three teammates stumbling ashore—see himself, still wearing the orange life vest the bat boy had strapped on him, rolling in the surf. See his body, and hear the cheers that shook the stadium.

Higher, until the circle of the horizon was visible on every side. Had he not waited in circles like this before?

Far away, where the dark sky met a darker sea, they were coming for him. Coming, and they shone, filled with a white radiance brighter than their spotless uniforms. They were coming, and he knew them—he, who had studied their photographs so often: Ernie Banks and Pee Wee Reese.

Both waved, and the cheers were louder than ever, cheering that felt as if it would never end.

STRESS CRACKS

✧ ✧ ✧

by Anthony R. Cardno

"Make each day your masterpiece."
—John Wooden,
Revered UCLA Men's Basketball Coach
and Former Player,
Indianapolis Kautskys

Anthony R. Cardno's first published work was a "hero history" of Marvel Comics' The Invaders *for the late, lamented* Amazing Heroes. *His short stories have appeared in* Willard & Maple, Sybil, Space Battles: Full Throttle Space Tales Volume 6, Beyond The Sun, OOMPH: A Little Super Goes A Long Way *and* Tales of the Shadowmen Volume 10. *In 2014 he edited* The Many Tortures of Anthony Cardno, *in which 22 authors Tuckerized him, to raise money for the American Cancer Society. In addition to a full time job as a corporate trainer, Anthony is a proofreader for* Lightspeed *magazine, writes book reviews, and interviews authors, singers, and other creative types on* www.anthonycardno.com, *where you can also find some of his other short stories. In his spare time, Anthony enjoys making silly cover song videos on*

Youtube. You can find him on Twitter *@talekyn. "Stress Cracks" is his first professional story sale.*

A long favored Olympic event, you've never seen figure skating like this. Here, it is downhill figure skating, and that brings whole new challenges.

Interviews were Cyndric Driscoll's least favorite part of having been named to his home world's team for the Galactic Games. Not because he hated talking to people, but because every interview inevitably and quickly moved from discussion of his downhill figure skating abilities to thinly veiled gossip about his family history. Still, the interviews were part of the deal, especially when you were a front-runner in your sport. Every sports-interested citizen on Earth and on the planets of the Denthen system wanted athlete profiles, personal interest stories, the chance to see whether an athlete was holding up or cracking under the pressure.

As the studio lights came up and the director counted down, Cyndric took one last look at himself in the mirror held by the make-up artist. His own sky-blue eyes gazed back at him, taking in his clean-shaven face, smooth cheekbones and the sweep of light red hair tousled perfectly over his forehead. Vanity wasn't one of his faults; the make-up artists had done a great job covering up the skin blemishes that came with half of his heritage.

And then the mirror was gone, the director was

counting down to "one" on his fingers, and the interviewer was talking to the camera.

"Good day, everyone. I'm Brad Cooney, broadcasting from the Galactic Games media center on Tarasque." He swiveled in his chair to face a new camera, a smile on his face. "Cyndric Driscoll doesn't need to win a gold medal this week in downhill figure skating in order to be famous," Cooney intoned. Cyndric schooled the wince out of his face before it appeared. "His family name takes care of that. Driscoll is the great-grandson of the first man from Earth to travel to the Denthen system. One of his grandfathers is the first child born of a relationship between an Earth man and a Tarasquen woman; another grandfather is perhaps the most well-known, and most revered, religious leader in the Denthen system, while the third is a deceased hero of the destruction of Refarael. Driscoll's mother is the current leader of Denthen's Gladiators, a system-wide first response team that people on Earth have likened to comic book characters like the Legion of Super-Heroes, a band of talented individuals from different planets. His older sister is the current ambassador from his home world, Tarasque, to Earth." Through all of this, the in-studio monitors showed what the audience was seeing: photos of Cyndric's illustrious family; the resemblance, especially the bright red hair sported by his great-grandfather, one grandfather, and sister, was unmistakable. The interviewer turned to him as Cyndric's own live-in-the-studio face replaced his sister's on the monitors. "Welcome, Cyndric. Thanks for joining us."

"It's a pleasure to be here, Brad," Cyndric smiled, while thinking what a pleasure it was not that the interview was already focusing more on his family than on his athletic prowess.

"Unlike most of your family, you're carving your own path, not in military service, space travel. or politics, but in sports. My first question, although probably not the most important, is . . ." In the pause, Cyndric steeled himself for a question about his family. ". . . How does it feel to be the face of downhill figure skating in two star systems, especially given that the sport was unheard of on Earth even just forty years ago?"

Cyndric hoped the quirk of his eyebrows at the unexpected question didn't show on screen.

"Well, it's still surprising to be referred to that way," he answered quickly, "although I'd be lying if I didn't say it wasn't flattering." This brought a chuckle from Cooney. Cyndric leaned forward in his seat, like he was taking Cooney into his confidence. "But really, I've been doing this all my life. It's hard to grow up at the base of the Draskar Ice Floe and not take up this sport. It's really no different from someone growing up in the Alps on Earth excelling at downhill skiing, or growing up in Colorado and becoming the face of snowboarding." He paused, and then added with a smile, "Then again, maybe the real reason is my hair. I wouldn't be the first young redheaded winter athlete to be called the face of his sport. Especially on Earth."

"No, that's very true," Cooney agreed. He looked down at the note-cards in his hand, a gesture Cyndric was sure was just for effect. "Like the flat-ice figure skating that's been a staple of Earth winter games since their inception, downhill figure skating is divided into two performances:

the long-course and the short course." The monitors cut to footage of Cyndric's long course run from two days previous.

"At the end of the long-course runs," Cooney continued, "commentators were remarking on your slower time and slightly lower artistic/athletic scores. Every skater has the opportunity for two runs down the long course, with the higher of two scores counting." Cooney suddenly had an incisive, challenging gaze the cameras could not dampen. "Given that the slower time and lower scores put you behind leader Jeremy Kowalik going into the short course, why did you choose not to take that second run?"

"A good question, Brad." Cyndric shifted comfortably in his seat again, leaning back to contemplate the wording of his response. "Look, we all have our strengths. And we all know that on the long course, Jeremy is very hard to beat. He just amazes me with the clean artistic line he rides down the ice, no matter the course conditions, and both his time and his scores reflect that. I could waste half a day attempting to move a percentage point or two closer to his long course scores, or I could spend that time practicing for the short course."

"Where, it's been noted repeatedly, you are the favorite."

"Again, I'd be lying if I said that weren't true." Cyndric smiled again. "Jeremy plays to his strengths, I play to mine, and the ice does to us what it will."

"So, in preparation for your short course, can we expect to see the same routine you've done in practice?" The glimmer in Cooney's eyes said he was looking for a scoop about changing plans.

"Pretty much," Cyndric deadpanned. "I mean, why mess with what works, right?" Cooney's glimmer faded a little until Cyndric added, "Then again, there are always course corrections to be made on a natural-formed ice floe like the Draskar. So you never know what you might see." And then he winked at the camera for added effect.

"Well, we look forward to seeing what you'll do. Good luck on the course, Cyndric Driscoll."

"Thanks, Brad. Hopefully, I'll see you back here after the event, with a gold medal around my neck." At that, Cooney nodded and swiveled his chair back to facing the original camera.

"We'll be right back with a profile on Cyndric's top two competitors, both from Earth: Japan's Hideyoshi Soga and current leader Jeremy Kowalik of Canada."

The studio lights dimmed as soon as the cameras cut away to an advertisement. Cyndric shook hands with Cooney, thanked him for a great interview, and headed out to find his coach.

In the hall, he bumped into Jeremy Kowalik. Cyndric was tall for a Tarasquen, thanks to the human blood mixed in. Brown-haired, brown-eyed Jeremy towered over him by several inches. They hugged in greeting, this process of being in overlapping interviews a familiar habit by now.

"Solid interview," his closest competitor nodded. "Thanks for the nice words."

"Credit where credit is due, my friend. There's no one I'd rather lose to," Cyndric grinned. "*If* I lose, that is."

"Jerk," Jeremy punched him in the arm. "Good questions Cooney asked, though, yeah?"

"Definitely. Felt nice not to field questions about my ancestors for once. That certainly doesn't happen often."

"I'm glad Cooney knows what's important. One less stress for you to deal with . . . before . . ." Jeremy's voice trailed off as his eyes drifted from Cyndric's face to a point over his head.

Cyndric knew there was a viewscreen there and was afraid to turn around. "What is it?"

"Cyn, man. Your grandfather."

"Which one?" Cyndric closed his eyes, rubbed them with his thumb and forefinger.

"The religious leader. What's his title? The Dakot?"

"Yeah." Cyndric shook his head. "What's he done now?"

"Apparently, he's coming to watch our event."

That night's sleep was not easy to achieve. Cyndric lay in bed under heavy blankets, his mind refusing to slow down. He understood that the athlete village was traditionally a rowdy place; he'd participated in some of that rowdiness on previous nights, and probably would have on this night as well if not for the news of the Dakot's attendance at the downhill figure skating final. Jeremy had asked him to share dinner, but Cyndric had begged off for a rain-date after their event was over. He hoped the man's obvious disappointment wasn't going to turn to disinterest, but it wasn't concern over his intentions nor the general sound level of the Village as a whole that kept Cyndric awake long after he should have been dreaming.

It was the question of why, of every possible event, his grandfather was coming to the final that kept his mind active. The Dakot had never broken tradition before to support a family member's private endeavors; it was a point of pride and a source of consternation for the family that the Dakot did not play favorites or let family matters distract him from being . . . well, him. By rights, his grandfather's next public appearance should have been at the Closing Ceremonies a week hence. So why tomorrow? And why Cyndric's event and not one of the dozen others spanning the entire day?

Tired of tossing under the covers, Cyndric got up and paced to the small refrigerator in his room. He pulled out a bottle and tried to concentrate only on the feel of the cold water in his mouth and throat. It didn't help slow his mind.

He didn't want to be cynical about his grandfather's motives, but the act was so out-of-character he couldn't help questioning. Then again, Cyndric's grandfather had never been the most traditional of Dakots. There was the possibility that he honestly just wanted to stand at the side of grandfather Calden, the man he'd spent his life with, and watch their grandson win a gold medal in competition with athletes from both home worlds. Cyndric hoped that was it.

Even with that hope, he needed to take unusual measures to get any restful sleep. Sleep aids in drug form were forbidden, and Cyndric knew his limits with alcohol would not result in restful sleep or a clear head in the morning. He placed the unfinished bottle of water in the refrigerator and padded back to bed. He'd never been particularly good at meditating but knew that it was his only hope for not arriving at the Ice Floe muddled. And so he began the deep breathing and mind-clearing exercises he'd been taught by the very same grandfather whose uncharacteristic actions were keeping him awake in the first place.

Even with the prep room's viewscreen volume down to almost silent, Cyndric knew what the announcing team was saying.

"The three front-runners for today's medal are Canadian Jeremy Kowalik, Japan's Hideyoshi Soga, and the hometown boy representing Tarasque, Cyndric Driscoll. If Driscoll's name sounds more like an Earth name than you'd expect, viewers will recall that Cyndric is the great-grandson of pioneering Earthman Rory Driscoll."

Cyndric turned away from the screen so that even lip-reading was not an option. All the reporters were talking about again was his family history. He knew the announcer would segue from great-grandpa Rory to his grandfathers and mother and sister, and not one word of his ability on the ice would be mentioned unless it was to point out that, as half-human, a Driscoll gold medal would be a win for both systems. Any focus on Cyndric himself that might have been gained from the interview with Brad Cooney had been lost in a matter of minutes, and the media storm had not abated since.

From the prep-room windows, Cyndric could see the priority viewing boxes where the Dakot and other dignitaries were seated to view the most of each athlete's run down the Ice Floe. Once he was in the starting gate, his view of them would be cut off until he was passing in front of them, at which point he'd be too preoccupied to pay them any attention. So it would almost be like his grandfather wasn't present at all. He could only hope.

His turn on the ice floe was coming up. Despite being the frontrunner by a narrow margin, Jeremy had drawn the straw to go first in this final group of five. Cyndric was in the middle of the pack and Soga last. His coach had wanted to appeal the order but Cyndric had talked him down. Third was a comfortable spot to be in: he'd know what was necessary to beat Kowalik but not have the pressure of being the final run down the course. He could complete his run and then whatever would be would be, and he would try to not spend the time after his run figuring out what his grandfather was up to with this public appearance.

A light tap on his shoulder from his coach brought Cyndric's attention back around to the viewscreen. The image had cut away from the announcing pair to a triumphant Jeremy Kowalik at the bottom of the run, hugging his manager as his time and scores flashed across the bottom of the screen.

Kowalik had made it through the course in just shy of three Earth minutes, a new record for the course in particular and the event in general. His artistic scores for jumps and choreography were not quite high enough to guarantee first place, but there was precious little wiggle room for Cyndric to squeeze by him, and even less for Soga. The second competitor in this grouping, a F'ren athlete who was lighter on his paws than his bulk might infer, had no shot at gold but could easily place fourth or take the bronze if the ice took a bad turn for Cyndric or

Soga or both. The viewscreen cut to the F'ren in the starting box; Cyndric turned away to finish gearing up and begin his mental preparations.

beep
First deep breath.
beep
Release.
beep
Second deep breath.
beep
Release.
beep
Third deep breath.
BRRONNNNKKKK

He releases the third breath as he propels himself out of the box, pushing off with his toe-pick and out with both arms, his left leg extended directly before him as his right leg lifts in the opposite direction. He feels the perfection of the split as he sails over the ice; part of him exults at a grand start. He is in the moment, as all athletes must be, so he won't consciously register that exultation until later.

He closes the split sharply and makes first contact with the ice floe less than a second later, both blades hitting the ice in unison as required, with a bare minimum of reaction from his thighs or upper body. He brings his left leg up behind and lowers his torso so they form a smooth line parallel to the ice, and then he rides that position, with dramatic arm choreography, through three small ice swells. His right leg stretches and contracts to accommodate the varying height of the swells while his upper body and left leg stay at the same height, an artistic move that looks to spectators like he's collapsing in on himself.

As he clears the third swell he feels a slight grab against his blade and lifts his toes just a fraction to avoid digging into the crack he's found. That small grab will slow his time infinitesimally, but he avoids any larger slowdown or reduction in points by waiting to bring his left leg down until he is past the marker.

The next stretch of ice before him is deceptively smooth, the course placed here to allow the skaters to build up speed towards the next jump. He leans into it and propels himself with short running steps on his toe-picks, a comical artistic choice he had to fight his coach to include when most of his competitors used/took longer strides through this section. The shorter steps run the risk of finding the flaws in the ice longer strides might glide right over but they also propel him faster towards the first launch.

Seconds before hitting the two-foot ice swell that will lead into his first big jump, he turns on his left blade and reverses the direction he's facing. Skating backwards down the ice now, the short steps are replaced with a long glide up onto the launch. At the top, he jams his right foot down onto the ice and twists his torso, bringing his arms in tight. Clear of the launch his ankles come together as well, entering the first of his intended five rotations. He more senses than sees a quarter-sized chunk of ice fly up from the swell he has just left and is sure he'll be deducted points for kicking up too much ice on his launch. He is momentarily distracted by the arc of the ice chunk, which does not go where his internal compass says it should, but puts it out of his mind because he's through four of the five rotations and it's time to land this jump.

He sticks the landing single-footed on his inside right edge, jams the left toe-pick into the ice a second later and throws his torso parallel to the ice again so that his legs fly behind and slightly above him in a move called the i'Teroth Helicopter. He manages the planned rotation-and-a-half before he comes down on his right skate again. The Helicopter is usually landed two-footed, but he has perfected his coach's maneuver and knows there will be extra difficulty points awarded, even if the move will never be renamed.

Halfway down the course now, he has another breather stretch. He knows he's near the priority spectator boxes but they don't even register in his periphery as he uses longer strides to propel himself toward the second jump launch.

Something in the air catches the sun in front of him, a glint visible even through his shaded goggles. Ice kicks up from the very bottom of the next launch, a chunk that would go unnoticed by an average hiker but significant for someone riding two thin blades towards a three-foot swell of ice.

He wavers slightly trying to assess if this new divot in the ice is in his path; another moment that reduces his speed. It can't be helped. The divot is definitely on his approach and he knows he has two choices: keep both blades on the ice and separate his feet around the divot, a move beginners use to quickly slow their speed, or go to one blade and skirt the divot, which will not slow him down but will ruin the set-up for his intended jump and cost him artistic points.

Or he can take a real chance and throw in an unscheduled element, an option every skater has but which few risk with a medal on the line.

He makes his last two strides short and skips over the divot with enough height for the cameras to catch that he's jumping over something unexpected. This brings both feet together at the base of the swell, which would kill his momentum if he were going to skate up it. Instead, he digs both toe-picks in and tucks his torso forward as he launches into the air.

He manages two perfect tucked forward somersaults, hands on his ankles, directly over the top of the swell. The ice after the swell drops away, giving him enough air to come out of the second somersault with both legs extended as though he were diving feet-first into water. He lets his back arch gracefully behind, arms extended below and behind his head before coming forward and above, leading his head and torso up so that as his blades touch the ice, he is already positioned to tuck into the sprint towards the third and final launch.

His improvisation is already forgotten as he lunges towards the six-foot swell in measured strides setting up for the final jump. He ignores the burning in his calves and thighs, rotates sharply to approach the swell backwards once again. He drops his right toe-pick just past the apex of the swell, almost too late to do any good but exactly where he'd intended. Catching the lower, shadowed, harder face of the ice propels him over the ten-

foot drop in perfect spinning form. He windmills two distinct finger-to-toe splits before landing one-footed on his forward blade and follows it with a half-rotation and another toe-pick into a single back flip.

The finish line is in sight and the rest of the run is about artistry and speed. The skaters are not allowed a straight sprint to the line, so he executes a series of sweeping S-glides with attendant arm choreography; alternating left and right single-footed glides that will not slow him down but which are graceful and open to the cameras.

He comes across the finish line firmly on his right blade, left leg behind and arms open wide to the receiving crowd. Even with his helmet on he can hear the roars as he arcs into a slowdown that brings him toward the fence where his manager awaits.

He is considering adding a little tight spin for his fans when something large barrels into him, catching him across the chest and dragging him down to the ice.

Cyndric's entire body shook with the triple impact of ass, shoulders, and helmet hitting the flat ice just beyond the finish line, but it was the full weight of a body landing on top of him that drove the wind from his lungs. He thought his vision had gone bad from the collision until he felt hands on his goggles.

"Get. *Off!*" He pushed up against the weight of the body on him and it obligingly rolled to his left. Before attempting to sit up, he ripped his goggles from his eyes and down past his chin. He saw a mild form of chaos around him: bodies running past, people shouting.

"Are you all right?" The voice to his left was familiar

but Cyndric couldn't place it for a moment, other than that it belonged to the body that had just rolled off of him. He sat upright and turned toward it.

Jeremy lay next to him. A grimace creased his lips but somehow did not diminish the sparkle Cyndric always saw in his eyes.

"Other than not understanding why you just knocked me on my ass, I think so." Cyndric hoped his voice conveyed the right amount of "what-the-hell?"

"Good." Jeremy smiled thinly. "Because the bullet that hit me probably would have killed you."

"I . . . what?" Cyndric looked Jeremy over from head to foot, almost missing the trickle of blood staining the ice near the other athlete's hip. "How bad . . . ?" Cyndric started to ask, only to be interrupted.

"Thank Denthen!" Cyndric's manager exhaled, reaching down to pull Cyndric to his feet. "Mister Kowalik, are you . . . ?"

"Grazed, that's all." Jeremy answered, with obvious discomfort. "I'll live."

"Thank Denthen, indeed," Cyndric was not surprised at how relieved he felt at that news. "Although I owe you more thanks than that, it seems. Could one of you please tell me what just happened?"

"Not here." His manager's relieved smile fell to a thin line. "I've been ordered to escort you both off of the ice immediately." Before Cyndric could interrupt, he added, "Explanations inside. I promise."

They were ushered into the Dakot's presence a little while later: Cyndric, Jeremy, and Cyndric's manager along with his coach who had come speeding down the mountain in a flyer as soon as he'd seen the murder attempt on screen. Most of Cyndric's family were already in the room as well, greeting him with hugs and words of pride and congratulations. Cyndric had known they were coming, mother and younger siblings and his mother's father as well, grandfather Calden, but their presence had been overshadowed by the Dakot's.

Jeremy, still limping, had immediately been ordered into a seat in the corner. As a member of Denthen's Gladiators, Cyndric's mother was trained in field first-aid measures, and fussed over Jeremy not being given medical assistance at the finish line. She cut a gap open in his pants along the path the bullet had taken, and then pulled out a kit and began cleaning and dressing the wound. But Cyndric knew, despite her activity, she would be attending to every word about to be said.

"There were a total of three attempts on your life," Grandfather Calden explained. "Two during your run, which you perhaps didn't notice."

"Didn't notice?" Cyndric laughed. "I may not have known what was happening, but believe me, I noticed ice flying up past my face. Or did you think I threw in that forward tuck somersault move to show off?"

"You have to teach me that move, by the way," Jeremy murmured with a smirk. Cyndric couldn't fight the blush that crept onto his face.

"No, we did not think you were showing off," Calden sighed. "But at least you didn't see the bullets."

"Actual bullets?" Cyndric's eyes went wide, the reality of the danger he'd been in hitting home.

"Rifles, we think, for the two attempts actually during

the run. And of course Mister Kowalik recognized the small handgun the shooter at the finish line used."

"Wait." Jeremy interrupted again. "If they wanted Cyndric dead during his run, why use projectile weapons that would be so imprecise at that distance? An energy weapon would have had better range and been more effective, even if it just melted the ice he was about to skate over and sent him tumbling down the mountain out of control."

"All very true, and very perceptive, Mister Kowalik. I can see why my grandson is drawn to you," the Dakot finally spoke. Cyndric looked at his other grandfather for the first time, attempting not to blush even deeper. It was no secret that like grandfather Calden and the Dakot, who had spent their life together, Cyndric was gay. But how damned perceptive was the man, reading his interest in Jeremy from a few nods and blushes? "The reason, I believe, is that they were attempting to send a message rather than actually commit murder."

"You could have fooled me," Cyndric shook his head. The Dakot ignored him. "What message, and why?"

"As to the first," Grandfather Calden took over the conversation again, "They want the Dakot, and thus all of us, to know that our family is not safe just because of who we are." He paused, and some silent communication passed between him and the Dakot. "As to the second: it is no accident you were targeted today, despite having been in the public eye and unguarded for weeks now in the lead-up to the Games."

It took a moment for the implications of grandfather Calden's words to sink in.

"You knew. You knew this was going to happen. You announced this appearance to draw them out."

"Yes." The Dakot, as was his nature, did not attempt to elaborate or excuse. If the scarred birthmarks on his face were more wrinkled that normal, Cyndric chose to ignore it.

"Never mind how it might impact the most important thing I've done in my life, the one thing that gets me out of my relatives' famous shadows?"

"You will never be out of that shadow, boy. You are a Driscoll."

"Never mind, then, that it could have killed me?"

"You were in no real danger, based on the intelligence we'd gathered. Our plan was to capture the shooters before you could be hurt."

"And how did that work out for you?" Cyndric refused to be placated, and was beginning to understand why this meeting was happening in a windowless security bunker far from cameras. "How many did you catch?"

The Dakot looked away, and grandfather Calden's eyes dropped to the floor.

"The one at the base of the run swallowed a poison capsule immediately after being taken into custody," Calden finally answered. "The other two have disappeared into the mountains."

"That's what I thought." Cyndric turned to his manager. "I suppose the run's been disqualified?"

"Actually, no. You were over the finish line before you hit the ground. Your time counts."

"And?"

"We tied for time," Jeremy answered before the

manager could. "But for artistic/athletic points, that damn forward somersault move put you in the lead. Everyone saw the ice chunk leave that divot none of us thought you'd be able to avoid without losing speed or points. So unless Soga does something miraculous, I've got the silver medal, and you've got the gold." The smile on his face was genuine as he added, "Congratulations."

"Thank you," Cyndric smiled back. "And to you, too." He crossed the room to Jeremy, who was now standing and testing for comfort the field-dressing over his bullet wound. And then he hugged the man who had quite possibly saved his life. He cast a challenging glare at his grandfathers. Calden's face was full of what Cyndric was sure was regret at the way politics had interfered with his defining moment. The Dakot's face was inscrutable as always. Other than congratulating him on an excellent run, Cyndric's mother and siblings had remained silent throughout the meeting, but he could see the anger boiling in his mother's eyes. There would be very sharp words after he was gone. And he found that he didn't care. What mattered to him was the sport, and the sportsmanship.

"I'm sure by now they've fixed the ice near the third swell and cleared Soga for his run." Cyndric clapped Jeremy on the shoulder and turned him towards the door. "Let's go meet him at the finish line and get ready for the medal ceremony."

RUN TO STARLIGHT

✧ ✧ ✧

by George R. R. Martin

"It's not whether you get knocked down;
it's whether you get up."
—Vince Lombardi,
Famed NFL Coach, Washington Redskins,
namesake of the Super Bowl trophy

#1 New York Times Bestselling author **George R. R. Martin** *sold his first story in 1971 and has been writing professionally ever since. Known for his epic fantasy series* A Song of Ice and Fire *from which HBO's* Game of Thrones *series was spawned, he also spent years in Hollywood writing for shows like* Max Headroom, Beauty and The Beast, *and the new* Twilight Zone *as well as writing and producing* Game Of Thrones. *A prolific editor who often partners with Gardner Dozois, Martin also leads the* Wild Cards *series of anthologies and fifteen novels featuring multiple authors working in teams. A multiple Hugo nominee and winner, he was named one of* Time's *most influential people of the year in 2011 and is the only author we know of in this anthology who has been interviewed by* Sports Illustrated. *He is also a huge fan of the New York Jets and Giants.*

This classic football story made its first appearance in Amazing Science Fiction's *December 1974 issue and has been reprinted several times since. I can't think of a better story to represent football here.*

Hill stared dourly at the latest free-fall football results from the Belt as they danced across the face of his desk console, but his mind was elsewhere. For the seventeenth time that week, he was silently cursing the stupidity and shortsightedness of the members of the Starport City Council.

The damn councilmen persisted in cutting the allocation for an artificial gravity grid out of the departmental budget every time Hill put it in. They had the nerve to tell him to stick to "traditional" sports in planning his recreational program for the year.

The old fools had no idea of the way free-fall football was catching on throughout the system, although he'd tried to explain it to them God knows how many times. The Belt sport should be an integral part of any self-respecting recreational program. And, on Earth, that meant you had to have a gravity grid. He'd planned on installing it beneath the stadium, but now—

The door to his office slid open with a soft hum. Hill looked up and frowned, snapping off the console. An agitated Jack De Angelis stepped through.

"What is it now?" Hill snapped.

"Uh, Rog, there's a guy here I think you better talk to,"

De Angelis replied. "He wants to enter a team in the City Football League."

"Registration closed on Tuesday," Hill said. "We've already got twelve teams. No room for any more. And why the hell can't you handle this? You're in charge of the football program."

"This is a special case," De Angelis said.

"Then make an exception and let the team in if you want to," Hill interrupted. "Or don't let them in. It's your program. It's your decision. Must I be bothered with every bit of trivia in this whole damned department?"

"Hey, take it easy, Rog," De Angelis protested. "I don't know what you're so steamed up about. Look, I—hell, I'll show you the problem." He turned and went to the door. "Sir, would you step in here a minute?" he said to someone outside.

Hill started to rise from his seat, but sank slowly back into the chair when the visitor appeared in the doorway.

De Angelis was smiling. "This is Roger Hill, the director of the Starport Department of Recreation," he said smoothly. "Rog, let me introduce Remjhard-nei, the head of the Brish'diri trade mission to Earth."

Hill rose again, and offered his hand numbly to the visitor. The Brish'dir was squat and grotesquely broad. He was a good foot shorter than Hill, who stood six four, but he still gave the impression of dwarfing the director somehow. A hairless, bullet-shaped head was set squarely atop the alien's massive shoulders. His eyes were glittering green marbles sunk in the slick, leathery gray skin. There were no external ears, only small holes on either side of the skull. The mouth was a lipless slash.

Diplomatically ignoring Hill's openmouthed stare, Remjhard bared his teeth in a quick smile and crushed the director's hand in his own. "I am most pleased to meet you, sir," he said in fluent English, his voice a deep bass growl. "I have come to enter a football team in the fine league your city so graciously runs."

Hill gestured for the alien to take a seat, and sat down himself. De Angelis, still smiling at his boss's stricken look, pulled another chair up to the desk for himself.

"Well, I—" Hill began, uncertainly. "This team, is it a—a Brish'diri team?"

Remjhard smiled again. "Yes," he answered. "Your football, it is a fine game. We of the mission have many times watched it being played on the 3-V wallscreens your people were so kind as to install. It has fascinated us. And now some of the half-men of our mission desire to try to play it." He reached slowly into the pocket of the black-and-silver uniform he wore, and pulled out a folded sheet of paper.

"This is a roster of our players," he said, handing it to Hill. "I believe the newsfax said such a list is required to enter your league."

Hill took the paper and glanced down at it uncertainly. It was a list of some fifteen Brish'diri names, neatly spelled out. Everything seemed to be in order, but still—

"You'll forgive me, I hope," Hill said, "but I'm somewhat unfamiliar with the expressions of your people. You said—*half-men*? Do you mean children?"

Remjhard nodded, a quick inclination of his bulletlike head. "Yes. Male children, the sons of mission personnel. All are aged either eight or nine Earth seasons."

Hill silently sighed with relief. "I'm afraid it's out of the question, then," he said. "Mr. De Angelis said you were interested in the City League, but that league is for boys aged eighteen and up. Occasionally we'll admit a younger boy with exceptional talent and experience, but never anyone this young." He paused briefly. "We do have several leagues for younger boys, but they've already begun play. It's much too late to add another team at this point."

"Pardon, Director Hill, but I think you misunderstand," Remjhard said. "A Brish'diri male is fully mature at fourteen Earth years. In our culture, such a person is regarded as a full adult. A nine-year-old Brish'dir is roughly equivalent to an eighteen-year-old Terran male in terms of physical and intellectual development. That is why our half-men wish to register for this league and not one of the others, you see."

"He's correct, Rog," De Angelis said. "I've read a little about the Brish'diri, and I'm sure of it. In terms of maturity, these youngsters are eligible for the City League."

Hill threw De Angelis a withering glance. If there was one thing he didn't need at the moment, it was a Brish'diri football team in one of his leagues, and Remjhard was arguing convincingly enough without Jack's help.

"Well, all right," Hill said. "Your team may well be of age, but there are still problems. The Rec Department sports program is for local residents only. We simply don't have room to accommodate everyone who wants to participate. And your home planet is, as I understand, several hundred light-years beyond the Starport city limits." He smiled.

"True," Remjhard said. "But our trade mission has been in Starport for six years. An ideal location due to your city's proximity to Grissom Interstellar Spaceport, from which most of the Brish'diri traders operate while on Earth. All of the current members of the mission have been here for two Earth years, at least. We are Starport residents, Director Hill. I fail to understand how the location of Brishun enters into the matter at hand."

Hill squirmed uncomfortably in his seat, and glared at De Angelis, who was grinning. "Yes, you're probably right again," he said. "But I'm still afraid we won't be able to help you. Our junior leagues are touch football, but the City League, as you might know, is tackle. It can get quite rough at times. State safety regulations require the use of special equipment. To make sure no one is injured seriously. I'm sure you understand. And the Brish'diri . . . "

He groped for words, anxious not to offend. "The— uh—physical construction of the Brish'diri is so different from the Terran that our equipment couldn't possibly fit. Chances of injury would be too great, and the department would be liable. No. I'm sure it couldn't be allowed. Too much risk."

"We would provide special protective equipment," Remjhard said quietly. "We would never risk our own offspring if we did not feel it was safe."

Hill started to say something, stopped, and looked to De Angelis for help. He had run out of good reasons why the Brish'diri couldn't enter the league.

Jack smiled. "One problem remains, however," he said, coming to the director's rescue. "A bureaucratic snag, but a difficult one. Registration for the league closed on

Tuesday. We've already had to turn away several teams, and if we make an exception in your case, well—" De Angelis shrugged. "Trouble. Complaints. I'm sorry, but we must apply the same rule to all."

Remjhard rose slowly from his seat, and picked up the roster from where it lay on the desk. "Of course," he said gravely. "All must follow the regulations. Perhaps next year we will be on time." He made a formal half-bow to Hill, turned, and walked from the office.

When he was sure the Brish'dir was out of earshot, Hill gave a heartfelt sigh and swiveled to face De Angelis. "That was close," he said. "Christ, a Baldy football team. Half the people in this town lost sons in the Brish'diri War, and they still hate them. I can imagine the complaints." Hill frowned. "And you! Why couldn't you just get rid of him right away instead of putting me through that?"

De Angelis grinned. "Too much fun to pass up," he said. "I wondered if you'd figure out the right way to discourage him. The Brish'diri have an almost religious respect for laws, rules, and regulations. They wouldn't think of doing anything that would force someone to break a rule. In their culture, that's just as bad as breaking a rule yourself."

Hill nodded. "I would have remembered that myself if I hadn't been so paralyzed at the thought of a Brish'diri team in one of our leagues," he said limply. "And now that that's over with, I want to talk to you about that gravity grid. Do you think there's any way we could rent one instead of buying it outright? The Council might go for that. And I was thinking . . ."

❖   ❖   ❖

A little over three hours later, Hill was signing some equipment requisitions when the office door slid open to admit a brawny, dark-haired man in a nondescript gray suit.

"Yes?" the director said, a trifle impatiently. "Can I help you?"

The dark-haired man flashed a government ID as he took a seat. "Maybe you can. But you certainly haven't so far, I'll tell you that much. My name's Tomkins. Mac Tomkins. I'm from the Federal E. T. Relations Board."

Hill groaned. "I suppose it's about that Brish'diri mess this morning," he said, shaking his head in resignation.

"Yes," Tomkins cut in at once. "We understand that the Brish'diri wanted to register some of their youngsters for a local football league. You forbade it on a technicality. We want to know why."

"Why?" said Hill incredulously, staring at the government man. "Why? For God's sakes, the Brish'diri War was only over seven years ago. Half of those boys on our football teams had brothers killed by the Bulletbrains. Now you want me to tell them to play football with the subhuman monsters of seven years back? They'd run me out of town."

Tomkins grimaced, and looked around the room. "Can that door be locked?" he asked, pointing to the door he had come in by.

"Of course," Hill replied, puzzled.

"Lock it then," Tomkins said. Hill adjusted the appropriate control on his desk.

"What I'm going to tell you should not go beyond this room," Tomkins began.

Hill cut him off with a snort. "Oh, come now, Mr. Tomkins. I may be only a small-time sports official, but I'm not stupid. You're hardly about to impart some galaxy-shattering top secret to a man you met a few seconds ago."

Tomkins smiled. "True. The information's not secret, but it is a little ticklish. We would prefer that every Joe in the street doesn't know about it."

"All right, I'll buy that for now. Now what's this all about? I'm sorry if I've got no patience with subtlety, but the most difficult problem I've handled in the last year was the protest in the championship game in the Class B Soccer League. Diplomacy just isn't my forte."

"I'll be brief," Tomkins said. "We—E. T. Relations, that is—we want you to admit the Brish'diri team into your football league."

"You realize the furor it would cause?" Hill asked.

"We have some idea. In spite of that, we want them admitted."

"Why, may I ask?"

"Because of the furor if they aren't admitted." Tomkins paused to stare at Hill for a second, then apparently reached a decision of some sort and continued. "The Earth-Brishun War was a ghastly, bloody deadlock, although our propaganda men insist on pretending it was a great victory. No sane man on either side wants it resumed. But not everyone is sane."

The agent frowned in distaste. "There are elements among us who regard the Brish'diri—or the Bulletbrains, or Baldies, or whatever you want to call them—as monsters, even now, seven years after the killing has ended."

"And you think a Brish'diri football team would help to overcome the leftover hate?" Hill interrupted.

"Partially. But that's not the important part. You see, there is also an element among the Brish'diri that regards humans as subhuman-vermin to be wiped from the galaxy. They are a very virile, competitive race. Their whole culture stresses combat. The dissident element I mentioned will seize on your refusal to admit a Brish'diri team as a sign of fear, an admission of human inferiority. They'll use it to agitate for a resumption of the war. We don't want to risk giving them a propaganda victory like that. Relations are too strained as it is."

"But the Brish'dir I spoke to—" Hill objected. "I explained it all to him. A rule. Surely their respect for law—"

"Remjhard-nei is a leader of the Brish'diri peace faction. He personally will defend your position. But he and his son were disappointed by the refusal. They will talk. They already have been talking. And that means that eventually the war faction will get hold of the story and turn it against us."

"I see. But what can I do at this point? I've already told Remjhard that registration closed Tuesday. If I understand correctly, his own morality would never permit him to take advantage of an exception now."

Tomkins nodded. "True. You can't make an exception. Just change the rule. Let in all the teams you refused. Expand the league."

Hill shook his head, wincing. "But our budget—it couldn't take it. We'd have more games. We'd need more time, more referees, more equipment."

Tomkins dismissed the problem with a wave of his hand. "The government is already buying the Brish'diri special football uniforms. We'd be happy to cover all your extra costs. You'd get a better recreational program for all concerned."

Hill still looked doubtful. "Well . . . "

"Moreover," Tomkins said, "we might be able to arrange a government grant or two to bolster other improvements in your program. Now how about it?"

Hill's eyes sparkled with sudden interest. "A grant? How big a grant? Could you swing a gravity grid?"

"No problem," said Tomkins. A slow grin spread across his face.

Hill returned the grin. "Then, mister, Starport's got itself a Brish'diri football team. But oh, are they going to scream!" He flicked on the desk intercom. "Get Jack De Angelis in here," he ordered. "I've got a little surprise for him."

The sky above Starport Municipal Stadium was bleak and dreary on a windy Saturday morning a week later, but Hill didn't mind it at all. The stadium force bubble kept out the thin, wet drizzle that had soaked him to the bones on the way to the game, and the weather fitted his mood beautifully.

Normally, Hill was far too busy to attend any of his department's sporting events. Normally *everyone* was too busy to attend the department's sporting events. The Rec Department leagues got fairly good coverage in the local newspaper, but they seldom drew many spectators. The record was something like four hundred people for a championship game a few years ago.

Or rather, that *was* the record, Hill reminded himself. No more. The stadium was packed today, in spite of the hour, the rain, and everything else. Municipal Stadium was never packed except for the traditional Thanksgiving Day football game between Starport High and its archrival, Grissom City Prep. But today it was packed.

Hill knew why. It had been drilled into him the hard way after he had made the damn-fool decision to let the Brish'diri into the league. The whole city was up in arms. Six local teams had withdrawn from the City League rather than play with the "inhuman monsters." The office switchboard had been flooded with calls daily, the vast majority of them angry denunciations of Hill. A city council member had called for his resignation.

And that, Hill reflected glumly, was probably what it would come to in the end. The local newspaper, which had always been hard-line conservative on foreign affairs, was backing the drive to force Hill out of office. One of its editorials had reminded him gleefully that Starport Municipal Stadium was dedicated to those who had given their lives in the Brish'diri War, and had screamed about "desecration." Meanwhile, on its sports pages, the paper had taken to calling the Brish'diri team "the Baldy Eagles."

Hill squirmed uncomfortably in his seat on the fifty-yard line, and prayed silently that the game would begin. He could feel the angry stares on the back of his neck, and he had the uneasy impression that he was going to be hit with a rock any second now.

Across the field, he could see the camera installation of one of the big 3-V networks. All five of them were here, of course; the game had gotten planetwide publicity. The newsfax wires had also sent reporters, although they had seemed a little confused about what kind of a story this was. One had sent a political reporter, the other a sportswriter.

Out on the stadium's artificial grass, the human team was running through a few plays and warming up. Their bright-red uniforms were emblazoned with Ken's Computer Repair in white lettering, and they wore matching white helmets. They looked pretty good, Hill decided from watching them practice, although they were far from championship caliber. Still, against a team that had never played football before, they should mop up.

De Angelis, wearing a pained expression and a ref's striped shirt, was out on the field talking to his officials. Hill was taking no chances with bad calls in this game. He'd made sure the department's best men were on hand to officiate.

Tomkins was also there, sitting in the stands a few sections away from Hill. But the Brish'diri were not. Remjhard wanted to attend, but E. T. Relations, on Hill's advice, had told him to stay at the mission. Instead, the game was being piped to him over closed circuit 3-V.

Hill suddenly straightened in his seat. The Brish'diri team, which called itself the Kosg-Anjehn after a flying carnivore native to Brishun, had arrived, and the players were walking slowly out onto the field.

There was a brief instant of silence, and then someone in the crowd started booing. Others picked it up. Then others. The stadium was filled with the boos. Although, Hill noted with relief, not everyone was joining in. Maybe there were some people who saw things his way.

The Brish'diri ignored the catcalls. Or seemed to, at any rate. Hill had never seen an angry Brish'dir, and was unsure how one would go about showing his anger.

The Kosg-Anjehn wore tight-fitting black uniforms, with odd-looking elongated silver helmets to cover their bullet-shaped heads. They looked like no football team Hill had ever seen. Only a handful of them stood over five feet, but they were all as squat and broad as a tackle for the Packers. Their arms and legs were thick and stumpy, but rippled with muscles that bulged in the wrong places. The helmeted heads, however, gave an impression of frailty, like eggshells ready to shatter at the slightest impact.

Two of the Brish'diri detached themselves from the group and walked over to De Angelis. Evidently they felt they didn't need a warm-up, and wanted to start immediately. De Angelis talked to them for an instant, then turned and beckoned to the captain of the human team.

"How do you think it'll go?"

Hill turned. It was Tomkins. The E. T. agent had struggled through the crowd to his side.

"Hard to say," the director replied. "The Brish'diri have never really played football before, so the odds are they'll lose. Being from a heavy-gravity planet, they'll be stronger than the humans, so that might give them an edge. But they're also a lot slower, from what I hear."

"I'll have to root them home," Tomkins said with a smile. "Bolster the cause of interstellar relations and all that."

Hill scowled. "You root them home if you like. I'm pulling for the humans. Thanks to you, I'm in enough trouble already. If they catch me rooting for the Brish'diri they'll tear me to shreds."

He turned his attention back to the field. The Computermen had won the toss, and elected to receive. One of the taller Brish'diri was going back to kick off.

"Tuhgayh-dei," Tomkins provided helpfully. "The son of the mission's chief linguist." Hill nodded.

Tuhgayh-dei ran forward with a ponderous, lumbering gallop, nearly stopped when he finally reached the football, and slammed his foot into it awkwardly but hard. The ball landed in the upper tier of the stands, and a murmur went through the crowd.

"Pretty good," Tomkins said. "Don't you think?"

"Too good," replied Hill. He did not elaborate.

The humans took the ball on their twenty. The Computermen went into a huddle, broke it with a loud clap, and ran to their positions. A ragged cheer went up from the stands.

The humans went down into the three-point stance. Their Brish'diri opponents did not. The alien linemen just stood there, hands dangling at their sides, crouching a little.

"They don't know much about football," Hill said. "But after that kickoff, I wonder if they have to."

The ball was snapped, and the quarterback for Ken's Computer Repair, a rangy ex-high-school star named Sullivan, faded back to pass. The Brish'diri rushed forward in a crude blitz, and crashed into the human linemen.

An instant later, Sullivan was lying face down in the grass, buried under three Brish'diri. The aliens had blown through the offensive line as if it didn't exist.

That made it second-and-fifteen. The humans huddled again, came out to another cheer, not quite so loud as the first one. The ball was snapped. Sullivan handed off to a beefy fullback, who crashed straight ahead.

One of the Brish'diri brought him down before he went half a yard. It was a clumsy tackle, around the shoulders. But the force of the contact knocked the fullback several yards in the wrong direction.

When the humans broke from their huddle for the third time the cheer could scarcely be heard. Again Sullivan tried to pass. Again the Brish'diri blasted through the line en masse. Again Sullivan went down for a loss.

Hill groaned. "This looks worse every minute," he said.

Tomkins didn't agree. "I don't think so. They're doing fine. What difference does it make who wins?"

Hill didn't bother to answer that.

There was no cheering when the humans came out in punt formation. Once more the Brish'diri put on a strong rush, but the punter got the ball away before they reached him.

It was a good, deep kick. The Kosg-Anjehn took over on their own twenty-five yard line. Marhdain-nei, Remjhard's son, was the Brish'diri quarterback. On the first play from scrimmage, he handed off to a halfback, a runt built like a tank.

The Brish'diri blockers flattened their human opponents almost effortlessly, and the runt plowed through the gaping hole, ran over two would-be tacklers, and burst into the clear. He was horribly slow, however, and the defenders finally brought him down from behind after a modest thirty-yard gain. But it took three people to stop him.

On the next play, Marhdain tried to pass. He got excellent protection, but his receivers, trudging along at top speed, had defensemen all over them. And the ball, when thrown, went sizzling over the heads of Brish'diri and humans alike.

Marhdain returned to the ground again after that, and handed off to a runt halfback once more. This time he tried to sweep around end, but was hauled to the ground after a gain of only five yards by a quartet of human tacklers.

That made it third-and-five. Marhdain kept to the ground. He gave the ball to his other halfback, and the brawny Brish'dir smashed up the middle. He was a little bit faster than the runt. When he got in the clear, only one man managed to catch him from behind. And one wasn't enough. The alien shrugged off the tackle and lumbered on across the goal line.

The extra point try went under the crossbar instead of over it. But it still nearly killed the poor guy in the stands who tried to catch the ball.

Tomkins was grinning. Hill shook his head in disgust. "This isn't the way it's supposed to go," he said. "They'll kill us if the Brish'diri win."

The kickoff went out of the stadium entirely this time. On the first play from the twenty, a Brish'diri lineman roared through the line and hit Sullivan just as he was handing off. Sullivan fumbled.

Another Brish'dir picked up the loose ball and carried it into the end zone while most of the humans were still lying on the ground.

"My God," said Hill, feeling a bit numb. "They're too

strong. They're too damn strong. The humans can't cope with their strength. Can't stop them."

"Cheer up," said Tomkins. "It can't get much worse for your side."

But it did. It got a lot worse.

On offense, the Brish'diri were well-nigh unstoppable. Their runners were all short on speed, but made up for it with muscle. On play after play, they smashed straight up the middle behind a wall of blockers, flicking tacklers aside like bothersome insects.

And then Marhdain began to hit on his passes. Short passes, of course. The Brish'diri lacked the speed to cover much ground. But they could outjump any human, and they snared pass after pass in the air. There was no need to worry about interceptions. The humans simply couldn't hang on to Marhdain's smoking pitches.

On defense, things were every bit as bad. The Computermen couldn't run against the Brish'diri line. And Sullivan seldom had time to complete a pass, for the alien rushers were unstoppable. The few passes he did hit on went for touchdowns; no Brish'diri could catch a human from behind. But those were few and far between.

When Hill fled the stadium in despair at the half, the score was Kosg-Anjehn 37, Ken's Computer Repair 7.

The final score was 57 to 14. The Brish'diri had emptied their bench in the second half.

Hill didn't have the courage to attend the next Brish'diri game later in the week. But nearly everyone else in the city showed up to see if the Kosg-Anjehn could do it again.

They did. In fact, they did even better. They beat Anderson's Drugs by a lopsided 61 to 9 score.

After the Brish'diri won their third contest, 43 to 17, the huge crowds began tapering off. The Starport Municipal Stadium was only three-quarters full when the Kosg-Anjehn rolled over the Stardusters, 38 to 0, and a mere handful showed up on a rainy Thursday afternoon to see the aliens punish the United Veterans Association 51 to 6. And no one came after that.

For Hill, the Brish'diri win over the UVA-sponsored team was the final straw. The local paper made a heyday out of that, going on and on about the "ironic injustice" of having the UVA slaughtered by the Brish'diri in a stadium dedicated to the dead veterans of the Brish'diri War. And Hill, of course, was the main villain in the piece.

The phone calls had finally let up by that point. But the mail had been flowing into his office steadily, and most of it was not very comforting. The harassed Rec director got a few letters of commendation and support, but the bulk of the flood speculated crudely about his ancestry or threatened his life and property.

Two more city councilmen had come out publicly in favor of Hill's dismissal after the Brish'diri defeated UVA. Several others on the council were wavering, while Hill's supporters, who backed him strongly in private, were afraid to say anything for the record. The municipal elections were simply too close, and none were willing to risk their political skins.

And of course the assistant director of recreation, next in line for Hill's job, had wasted no time in saying *he* would certainly never have done such an unpatriotic thing.

With disaster piling upon disaster, it was only natural that Hill reacted with something less than enthusiasm when he walked into his office a few days after the fifth Kosg-Anjehn victory and found Tomkins sitting at his desk waiting for him.

"And what in the hell do you want now?" Hill roared at the E. T. Relations man.

Tomkins looked slightly abashed, and got up from the director's chair. He had been watching the latest free-fall football results on the desk console while waiting for Hill to arrive.

"I've got to talk to you," Tomkins said. "We've got a problem."

"We've got lots of problems," Hill replied. He strode angrily to his desk, sat down, flicked off the console, and pulled a sheaf of papers from a drawer.

"This is the latest of them," he continued, waving the papers at Tomkins. "One of the kids broke his leg in the Starduster game. It happens all the time. Football's a rough game. You can't do anything to prevent it. On a normal case, the department would send a letter of apology to the parents, our insurance would pay for it, and everything would be forgotten.

"But not in this case. Oh, no. This injury was inflicted while the kid was playing against the Brish'diri. So his parents are charging negligence on our part and suing the city. So our insurance company refuses to pay up. It claims the policy doesn't cover damage by inhuman, superstrong, alien monsters. Bah! How's that for a problem, Mr. Tomkins? Plenty more where that came from."

Tomkins frowned. "Very unfortunate. But my problem

is a lot more serious than that." Hill started to interrupt, but the E. T. Relations man waved him down. "No, please, hear me out. This is very important."

He looked around for a seat, grabbed the nearest chair, and pulled it up to the desk. "Our plans have backfired badly," he began. "There has been a serious miscalculation—our fault entirely, I'm afraid. E. T. Relations failed to consider all the ramifications of this Brish'diri football team."

Hill fixed him with an iron stare. "What's wrong now?"

"Well," Tomkins said awkwardly, "we knew that refusal to admit the Kosg-Anjehn into your league would be a sign of human weakness and fear to the Brish'diri war faction. But once you admitted them, we thought the problem was solved.

"It wasn't. We went wrong when we assumed that winning or losing would make no difference to the Brish'diri. To us, it was just a game. Didn't matter who won. After all, Brish'diri and Terrans would be getting to know each other, competing harmlessly on even terms. Nothing but good could come from it, we felt."

"So?" Hill interrupted. "Get to the point."

Tomkins shook his head sadly. "The point is, we didn't know the Brish'diri would win so *big*. And so *regularly*." He paused. "We—uh—we got a transmission late last night from one of our men on Brishun. It seems the Brish'diri war faction is using the one-sided football scores as propaganda to prove the racial inferiority of humans. They seem to be getting a lot of mileage out of it."

Hill winced. "So it was all for nothing. So I've subjected

myself to all this abuse and endangered my career for absolutely nothing. Great! That was all I needed, I tell you."

"We still might be able to salvage something," Tomkins said. "That's why I came to see you. If you can arrange it for the Brish'diri to *lose*, it would knock holes in that superiority yarn and make the war faction look like fools. It would discredit them for quite a while."

"And just how am I supposed to arrange for them to lose, as you so nicely put it? What do you think I'm running here anyway, professional wrestling?"

Tomkins just shrugged lamely. "I was hoping you'd have some ideas," he said.

Hill leaned forward, and flicked on his intercom. "Is Jack out there?" he asked. "Good. Send him in."

The lanky sports official appeared less than a minute later. "You're on top of this City football mess," Hill said. "What's the chances the Kosg-Anjehn will lose?"

De Angelis looked puzzled. "Not all that good, offhand," he replied. "They've got a damn fine team."

He reached into his back pocket and pulled out a notebook. "Let me check their schedule," he continued, thumbing through the pages. He stopped when he found the place.

"Well, the league's got a round-robin schedule, as you know. Every team plays every other team once, best record is champion. Now the Brish'diri are currently five to zero, and they've beaten a few of the better teams. We've got ten teams left in the league, so they've got four games left to play. Only, two of those are with the weakest teams in the league, and the third opponent is only mediocre."

"And the fourth?" Hill said hopefully.

"That's your only chance. An outfit sponsored by a local tavern, the Blastoff Inn. Good team. Fast, strong. Plenty of talent. They're also five to zero, and should give the Brish'diri some trouble." De Angelis frowned. "But, to be frank, I've seen both teams, and I'd still pick the Brish'diri. That ground game of theirs is just too much." He snapped the notebook shut and pocketed it again.

"Would a close game be good enough?" Hill said, turning to Tomkins again.

The E. T. Relations man shook his head. "No. They have to be beaten. If they lose, the whole season's meaningless. Proves nothing but that the two races can compete on roughly equal terms. But if they win, it looks like they're invincible, and our stature in Brish'diri eyes takes a nose dive."

"Then they'll have to lose, I guess," Hill said. His gaze shifted back to De Angelis. "Jack, you and me are going to have to do some hard thinking about how the Kosg-Anjehn can be beaten. And then we're going to call up the manager of the Blastoff Inn team and give him a few tips. You have any ideas?"

De Angelis scratched his head thoughtfully. "Well—" he began. "Maybe we—"

During the weeks that followed, De Angelis met with the Blastoff Inn coach regularly to discuss plans and strategy, and supervised a few practice sessions. Hill, meanwhile, was fighting desperately to keep his job, and jotting down ideas on how to beat the Brish'diri during every spare moment

Untouched by the furor, the Kosg-Anjehn won its sixth game handily, 40 to 7, and then rolled to devastating victories over the circuit's two cellar-dwellers. The margins were 73 to 0 and 62 to 7. That gave them an unblemished 8 to 0 ledger, with one game left to play.

But the Blastoff Inn team was also winning regularly, although never as decisively. It too would enter the last game of the season undefeated.

The local news heralded the showdown with a sports-section streamer on the day before the game. The lead opened, "The stakes will be high for the entire human race tomorrow at Municipal Stadium, when Blastoff Inn meets the Brish'diri Baldy Eagles for the championship of the Department of Recreation City Football League."

The reporter who wrote the story never dreamed how close to the truth he actually was.

The crowds returned to the stadium for the championship game, although they fell far short of a packed house. The local reporter was there too. But the 3-V networks and the newsfax wires were long gone. The novelty of the story had worn off quickly.

Hill arrived late, just before game time, and joined Tomkins on the fifty-yard line. The E. T. agent seemed to have cheered up somewhat. "Our guys looked pretty good during the warm-up," he told the director. "I think we've got a chance."

His enthusiasm was not catching, however. "Blastoff Inn might have a chance, but I sure don't," Hill said glumly. "The city council is meeting tonight to consider a motion for calling for my dismissal. I have a strong suspicion that it's going to pass, no matter who wins this afternoon."

"Hmmmm," said Tomkins, for want of anything better to say. "Just ignore the old fools. Look, the game's starting."

Hill muttered something under his breath and turned his attention back to the field. The Brish'diri had lost the toss once more, and the kickoff had once again soared out of the stadium. It was first-and-ten for Blastoff Inn on its own twenty.

And at that point the script suddenly changed.

The humans lined up for their first play of the game but with a difference. Instead of playing immediately in back of the center, the Blastoff quarterback was several yards deep, in a shotgun formation.

The idea, Hill recalled, was to take maximum advantage of human speed, and mount a strong passing offense. Running against the Brish'diri was all but impossible, he and De Angelis had concluded after careful consideration. That meant an aerial attack, and the only way to provide that was to give the Blastoff quarterback time to pass. Ergo, the shotgun formation.

The hike from center was dead on target and the Blastoff receivers shot off downfield, easily outpacing the ponderous Brish'diri defensemen. As usual, the Kosg-Anjehn crashed through the line en masse, but they had covered only half the distance to the quarterback before he got off the pass.

It was a long bomb, a psychological gambit to shake up the Brish'diri by scoring on the first play of the game. Unfortunately, the pass was slightly overthrown.

Hill swore.

It was now second-and-ten. Again the humans lined up

in a shotgun offense, and again the Blastoff quarterback got off the pass in time. It was a short, quick pitch to the sideline, complete for a nine-yard gain. The crowd cheered lustily.

Hill wasn't sure what the Brish'diri would expect on third-and-one. But whatever it was, they didn't get it. With the aliens still slightly off balance, Blastoff went for the bomb again.

This time it was complete. All alone in the open, the fleet human receiver snagged the pass neatly and went all the way in for the score. The Brish'diri never laid a hand on him.

The crowd sat in stunned silence for a moment when the pass was caught. Then, when it became clear that there was no way to prevent the score, the cheering began, and peaked slowly to an ear-splitting roar. The stadium rose to its feet as one, screaming wildly.

For the first time all season, the Kosg-Anjehn trailed. A picture-perfect place kick made the score 7 to 0 in favor of Blastoff Inn.

Tomkins was on his feet, cheering loudly. Hill, who had remained seated, regarded him dourly. "Sit down," he said. "The game's not over yet."

The Brish'diri soon underlined that point. No sooner did they take over the ball than they came pounding back upfield, smashing into the line again and again. The humans alternated between a dozen different defensive formations. None of them seemed to do any good. The Brish'diri steamroller ground ahead inexorably.

The touchdown was an anticlimax. Luckily, however, the extra point try failed. Tuhgayh-dei lost a lot of footballs, but he had still not developed a knack for putting his kicks between the crossbars.

The Blastoff offense took the field again. They looked determined.

The first play from scrimmage was a short pass over the middle, complete for fifteen yards. Next came a tricky double pass. Complete for twelve yards.

On the following play, the Blastoff fullback tried to go up the middle. He got creamed for a five-yard loss.

"If they stop our passing, we're dead," Hill said to Tomkins, without taking his eyes off the field.

Luckily, the Blastoff quarterback quickly gave up on the idea of establishing a running game. A prompt return to the air gave the humans another first down. Three plays later, they scored. Again the crowd roared.

Trailing now 14 to 6, the Brish'diri once more began to pound their way upfield. But the humans, elated by their lead, were a little tougher now. Reading the Brish'diri offense with confident precision, the defensemen began gang-tackling the alien runners.

The Kosg-Anjehn drive slowed down, then stalled. They were forced to surrender the ball near the fifty-yard line.

Tomkins started pounding Hill on the back. "You did it," he said. "We stopped them on offense too. We're going to win."

"Take it easy," Hill replied. "That was a fluke. Several of our men just happened to be in the right place at the right time. It's happened before. No one ever said the Brish'diri scored every time they got the ball. Only most of the time."

Back on the field, the Blastoff passing attack was still humming smoothly. A few accurate throws put the humans on the Kosg-Anjehn's thirty.

And then the aliens changed formations. They took several men off the rush, and put them on pass defense. They started double-teaming the Blastoff receivers. Except it wasn't normal double-teaming. The second defender was playing far back of the line of scrimmage. By the time the human had outrun the first Brish'dir, the second would be right on top of him.

"I was afraid of something like this," Hill said. "We're not the only ones who can react to circumstances."

The Blastoff quarterback ignored the shift in the alien defense, and stuck to his aerial game plan. But his first pass from the thirty, dead on target, was batted away by a Brish'dir defender who happened to be right on top of the play.

The same thing happened on second down. That made it third-and-ten. The humans called time out. There was a hurried conference on the sidelines.

When action resumed, the Blastoff offense abandoned the shotgun formation. Without the awesome Brish'diri blitz to worry about, the quarterback was relatively safe in his usual position.

There was a quick snap, and the quarterback got rid of the ball equally quickly, an instant before a charging Brish'dir bore him to the ground. The halfback who got the handoff streaked to the left in an end run.

The other Brish'diri defenders lumbered towards him en masse to seal shut the sideline. But just as he reached the sideline, still behind the line of scrimmage, the

Blastoff halfback handed off to a teammate streaking right.

A wide grin spread across Hill's face. A reverse!

The Brish'diri were painfully slow to change directions. The human swept around right end with ridiculous ease and shot upfield, surrounded by blockers. The remaining Brish'diri closed in. One or two were taken out by team blocks. The rest found it impossible to lay their hands on the swift, darting runner. Dodging this way and that, he wove a path neatly between them and loped into the end zone.

Once more the stadium rose to its feet. This time Hill stood up too.

Tomkins was beaming again. "Ha!" he said. "I thought you were the one who said we couldn't run against them."

"Normally we can't," the director replied. "There's no way to run over or through them, so runs up the middle are out. End runs are better, but if they're in their formal formation, that too is a dreary prospect. There is no way a human runner can get past a wall of charging Brish'diri.

"However, when they spread out like they just did, they give us an open field to work with. We can't go over or through them, no, but we sure as hell can go *between* them when they're scattered all over the field. And Blastoff Inn has several excellent open-field runners."

The crowd interrupted him with another roar to herald a successful extra-point conversion. It was now 21 to 6.

The game was far from over, however. The human defense was not nearly as successful on the next series of downs. Instead of relying exclusively on the running game,

Marhdain-nei kept his opponents guessing with some of his patented short, hard pop passes.

To put on a more effective rush, the Blastoff defense spread out at wide intervals. The offensive line thus opened up, and several humans managed to fake out slower Brish'diri blockers and get past them to the quarterback. Marhdain was even thrown for a loss once.

But the Blastoff success was short-lived. Marhdain adjusted quickly. The widely spread human defense, highly effective against the pass, was a total failure against the run. The humans were too far apart to gang-tackle. And there was no way short of mass assault to stop a Brish'dir in full stride.

After that there was no stopping the Kosg-Anjehn, as Marhdain alternated between the pass and the run according to the human defensive formation. The aliens marched upfield quickly for their second touchdown.

This time, even the extra point was on target.

The Brish'diri score had taken some of the steam out of the crowd, but the Blastoff Inn offense showed no signs of being disheartened when they took the field again. With the aliens back in their original blitz defense, the human quarterback fell back on the shotgun once more.

His first pass was overthrown, but the next three in a row were dead on target and moved Blastoff to the Kosg-Anjehn forty. A running play, inserted to break the monotony, ended in a six-yard loss. Then came another incomplete pass. The toss was perfect, but the receiver dropped the ball.

That made it third-and-sixteen, and a tremor of apprehension went through the crowd. Nearly everyone in the stadium realized that the humans had to keep scoring to stay in the game.

The snap from center was quick and clean. The Blastoff quarterback snagged the ball, took a few unhurried steps backward to keep at a safe distance from the oncoming Brish'diri rushers, and tried to pick out a receiver. He scanned the field carefully. Then he reared back and unleashed a bomb.

It looked like another touchdown. The human had his alien defender beaten by a good five yards and was still gaining ground. The pass was a beauty.

But then, as the ball began to spiral downward, the Brish'diri defender stopped suddenly in midstride. Giving up his hopeless chase, he craned his head around to look for the ball, spotted it, braced himself—and jumped.

Brish'diri leg muscles, evolved for the heavy gravity of Brishun, were far more powerful than their human counterparts. Despite their heavier bodies, the Brish'diri could easily outjump any human. But so far they had only taken advantage of that fact to snare Marhdain's pop passes.

But now, as Hill blinked in disbelief, the Kosg-Anjehn defenseman leaped at least five feet into the air to meet the descending ball in midair and knock it aside with a vicious backhand slap.

The stadium moaned.

Forced into a punting situation, Blastoff Inn suddenly seemed to go limp. The punter fumbled the snap from center, and kicked the ball away when he tried to pick it up. The Brish'dir who picked it up got twenty yards before he was brought down.

The human defense this time put up only token resistance as Marhdain led his team downfield on a series of short passes and devastating runs.

It took the Brish'diri exactly six plays to narrow the gap to 21 to 19. Luckily, Tuhgayh missed another extra point.

There was a loud cheer when the Blastoff offense took the field again. But right from the first play after the kickoff, it was obvious that something had gone out of them.

The human quarterback, who had been giving a brilliant performance, suddenly became erratic. To add to his problems, the Brish'diri were suddenly jumping all over the field.

The alien kangaroo-pass defense had several severe limitations. It demanded precise timing and excellent reflexes on the part of the jumpers, neither of which was a Brish'diri forte. But it was a disconcerting tactic that the Blastoff quarterback had never come up against before. He didn't know quite how to cope with it.

The humans drove to their own forty, bogged down, and were forced to punt. The Kosg-Anjehn promptly marched the ball back the other way and scored. For the first time in the game, they led.

The next Blastoff drive was a bit more successful, and reached the Brish'diri twenty before it ground to a halt. The humans salvaged the situation with a field goal.

The Kosg-Anjehn rolled up another score, driving over the goal line just seconds before the half ended.

The score stood at 31 to 24 in favor of the Brish'diri.

And there was no secret about the way the tide was running.

✦ ✦ ✦

It had grown very quiet in the stands.

Tomkins, wearing a worried expression, turned to Hill with a sigh. "Well, maybe we'll make a comeback in the second half. We're only down seven. That's not so bad."

"Maybe," Hill said doubtfully. "But I don't think so. They've got all the momentum. I hate to say so, but I think we're going to get run out of the stadium in the second half."

Tomkins frowned. "I certainly hope not. I'd hate to see what the Brish'diri war faction would do with a really lopsided score. Why, they'd—" He stopped, suddenly aware that Hill wasn't paying the slightest bit of attention. The director's eyes had wandered back to the field.

"Look," Hill said, pointing. "By the gate. Do you see what I see?"

"It looks like a car from the trade mission," the E. T. agent said, squinting to make it out.

"And who's that getting out?"

Tomkins hesitated. "Remjhard-nei," he said at last.

The Brish'dir climbed smoothly from the low-slung black vehicle, walked a short distance across the stadium grass, and vanished through the door leading to one of the dressing rooms.

"What's he doing here?" Hill asked. "Wasn't he supposed to stay away from the games?"

Tomkins scratched his head uneasily. "Well, that's what we advised. Especially at first, when hostility was at its highest. But he's not a *prisoner*, you know. There's no way we could force him to stay away from the games if he wants to attend."

Hill was frowning. "Why should he take your advice all season and suddenly disregard it now?"

Tomkins shrugged. "Maybe he wanted to see his son win a championship."

"Maybe. But I don't think so. There's something funny going on here."

By the time the second half was ready to begin, Hill was feeling even more apprehensive. The Kosg-Anjehn had taken the field a few minutes earlier, but Remjhard had not reappeared. He was still down in the alien locker room.

Moreover, there was something subtly different about the Brish'diri as they lined up to receive the kickoff. Nothing drastic. Nothing obvious. But somehow the atmosphere was changed. The aliens appeared more carefree, more relaxed. Almost as if they had stopped taking their opponents seriously.

Hill could sense the difference. He'd seen other teams with the same sort of attitude before, in dozens of other contests. It was the attitude of a team that already knows how the game is going to come out. The attitude of a team that knows it is sure to win—or doomed to lose.

The kickoff was poor and wobbly. A squat Brish'dir took it near the thirty and headed upfield. Two Blastoff tacklers met him at the thirty-five.

He fumbled.

The crowd roared. For a second the ball rolled loose on the stadium grass. A dozen hands reached for it, knocking it this way and that. Finally, a brawny Blastoff lineman landed squarely on top of it and trapped it beneath him.

And suddenly the game turned around again.

"I don't believe it," Hill said. "That was it. The break we needed. After that touchdown pass was knocked aside, our team just lost heart. But now, after this, look at them. We're back in this game."

The Blastoff offense raced onto the field, broke the huddle with an enthusiastic shout, and lined up. It was first-and-ten from the Brish'diri twenty-eight.

The first pass was deflected off a bounding Brish'dir. The second, however, went for a touchdown.

The score was tied.

The Kosg-Anjehn held on to the kickoff this time. They put the ball in play near the twenty-five.

Marhdain opened the series of downs with a pass. No one, human or Brish'dir, was within ten yards of where it came down. The next play was a run. But the Kosg-Anjehn halfback hesitated oddly after he took the handoff. Given time to react, four humans smashed into him at the line of scrimmage. Marhdain went back to the air. The pass was incomplete again.

The Brish'diri were forced to punt.

Up in the stands, Tomkins was laughing wildly. He began slapping Hill on the back again. "Look at that! Not even a first down. We held them. And you said they were going to run us out of the stadium."

A strange half-smile danced across the director's face. "Ummm," he said. "So I did." The smile faded.

It was a good, solid punt, but Blastoff's deep man fielded it superbly and ran it back to the fifty. From there, it took only seven plays for the human quarterback, suddenly looking cool and confident again, to put the ball in the end zone.

Bouncing Brish'diri had evidently ceased to disturb him. He simply threw the ball through spots where they did not happen to be bouncing.

This time the humans missed the extra point. But no one cared. The score was 37 to 31. Blastoff Inn was ahead again.

And they were ahead to stay. No sooner had the Kosg-Anjehn taken over again than Marhdain threw an interception. It was the first interception he had thrown all season.

Naturally, it was run back for a touchdown.

After that, the Brish'diri seemed to revive a little. They drove three quarters of the way down the field, but then they bogged down as soon as they got within the shadow of the goal posts. On fourth-and-one from the twelve-yard line, the top Brish'diri runner slipped and fell behind the line of scrimmage.

Blastoff took over. And scored.

From then on, it was more of the same.

The final score was 56 to 31. The wrong team had been run out of the stadium.

Tomkins, of course, was in ecstasy. "We did it. I knew we could do it. This is perfect, just perfect. We humiliated them. The war faction will be totally discredited now. They'll never be able to stand up under the ridicule." He grinned and slapped Hill soundly on the back once again.

Hill winced under the blow, and eyed the E. T. man dourly. "There's something funny going on here. If the Brish'diri had played all season the way they played in the second half, they never would have gotten this far.

Something happened in that locker room during half-time."

Nothing could dent Tomkins' grin, however. "No, no," he said. "It was the fumble. That was what did it. It demoralized them, and they fell apart. They just clutched, that's all. It happens all the time."

"Not to teams this good it doesn't," Hill replied. But Tomkins wasn't around to hear. The E. T. agent had turned abruptly and was weaving his way through the crowd, shouting something about being right back.

Hill frowned and turned back to the field. The stadium was emptying quickly. The Rec director stood there for a second, still looking puzzled. Then suddenly he vaulted the low fence around the field, and set off across the grass.

He walked briskly across the stadium and down into the visitors' locker room. The Brish'diri were changing clothes in sullen silence, and filing out of the room slowly to the airbus that would carry them back to the trade mission.

Remjhard-nei was sitting in a corner of the room.

The Brish'dir greeted him with a slight nod. "Director Hill. Did you enjoy the game? It was a pity our half-men failed in their final test. But they still performed creditably, do you not think?"

Hill ignored the question. "Don't give me the bit about failing, Remjhard. I'm not as stupid as I look. Maybe no one else in the stadium realized what was going on out there this afternoon, but I did. You didn't lose that game. You threw it. Deliberately. And I want to know why!"

Remjhard stared at Hill for a long minute. Then, very slowly, he rose from the bench on which he was seated.

His face was blank and expressionless, but his eyes glittered in the dim light.

Hill suddenly realized that they were alone in the locker room. Then he remembered the awesome Brish'diri strength, and took a hasty step backwards away from the alien.

"You realize," Remjhard said gravely, "that it is a grave insult to accuse a Brish'dir of dishonorable conduct?"

The emissary took another careful look around the locker room to make sure the two of them were alone. Then he took another step towards Hill.

And broke into a wide smile when the director, edging backwards, almost tripped over a locker.

"But, of course, there is no question of dishonor here," the alien continued. "Honor is too big for a half-man's play. And, to be sure, in the rules that you furnished us, there was no provisions requiring participants to—" He paused. "—to play at their best, shall we say?"

Hill, untangling himself from the locker, sputtered. "But there are unwritten rules, traditions. This sort of thing simply is not sporting."

Remjhard was still smiling. "To a Brish'dir, there is nothing as meaningless as an unwritten rule. It is a contradiction in terms, as you say."

"But why?" said Hill. "That's what I can't understand. Everyone keeps telling me that your culture is virile, competitive, proud. Why should you throw the game? Why should you make yourself look bad? Why?"

Remjhard made an odd gurgling noise. Had he been a human, Hill would have thought he was choking. Instead, he assumed he was laughing.

"Humans amuse me," the Brish'dir said at last. "You attach a few catch phrases to a culture, and you think you understand it. And, if something disagrees with your picture, you are shocked.

"I am sorry, Director Hill. Cultures are not that simple. They are very complex mechanisms. A word like 'pride' does not describe everything about the Brish'diri.

"Oh, we are proud. Yes. And competitive. Yes. But we are also intelligent. And our values are flexible enough to adjust to the situation at hand."

Remjhard paused again, and looked Hill over carefully. Then he decided to continue. "This football of yours is a fine game, Director Hill. I told you that once before. I mean it. It is very enjoyable, a good exercise of mind and body.

"But it is only a game. Competing in games is important, of course. But there are larger competitions. More important ones. And I am intelligent enough to know which one gets our first priority.

"I received word from Brishun this afternoon about the use to which the Kosg-Anjehn victories were being put. Your friend from Extraterrestrial Relations must have told you that I rank among the leaders of the Brish'diri Peace Party. I would not be here on Earth otherwise. None of our opponents is willing to work with humans, whom they consider animals.

"Naturally I came at once to the stadium and informed our half-men that they must lose. And they, of course, complied. They too realize that some competitions are more important than others.

"For in losing, we have won. Our opponents on

Brishun will not survive this humiliation. In the next Great Choosing many will turn against them. And I, and others at the mission, will profit. And the Brish'diri will profit.

"Yes, Director Hill," Remjhard concluded, still smiling. "We are a competitive race. But competition for control of a world takes precedence over a football game."

Hill was smiling himself by now. Then he began to laugh. "Of course," he said. "And when I think of the ways we pounded our heads out to think of strategies to beat you. When all we had to do was tell you what was going on." He laughed again.

Remjhard was about to add something when suddenly the locker-room door swung open and Tomkins stalked in. The E. T. agent was still beaming.

"Thought I'd find you here, Hill," he began. "Still trying to investigate those conspiracy theories of yours, eh?" He chuckled and winked at Remjhard.

"Not really," Hill replied. "It was a harebrained theory. Obviously it was the fumble that did it."

"Of course," Tomkins said. "Glad to hear it. Anyway, I've got good news for you."

"Oh? What's that? That the world is saved? Fine. But I'm still out of a job come tonight."

"Not at all," Tomkins replied. "That's what my call was about. We've got a job for you. We want you to join E. T. Relations."

Hill looked dubious. "Come, now," he said. "Me an E. T. agent? I don't know the first thing about it. I'm a small-time local bureaucrat and sports official. How am I supposed to fit into E. T. Relations?"

"As a sports director," Tomkins replied. "Ever since

this Brish'diri thing broke, we've been getting dozens of requests from other alien trade missions and diplomatic stations on Earth. They all want a crack at it too. So, to promote goodwill and all that, we're going to set up a program. And we want you to run it. At double your present salary, of course."

Hill thought about the difficulties of running a sports program for two dozen wildly different types of extraterrestrials.

Then he thought about the money he'd get for doing it.

Then he thought about the Starport City Council.

"Sounds like a fine idea," he said. "But tell me. That gravity grid you were going to give to Starport—is that transferable too?"

"Of course," Tomkins said.

"Then I accept." He glanced over at Remjhard. "Although I may live to regret it when I see what the Brish'diri can do on a basketball court."

MARS COURT RULES

✧ ✧ ✧

by Brad R. Torgersen

"I've failed over and over and over again in my life.
And that is why I succeed."
—Michael Jordan,
NBA Player, Chicago Bulls

Brad R. Torgersen was a 2012 nominee for the Campbell, Hugo, and Nebula awards, and is a past winner of both the Writers of the Future award, and Analog magazine's AnLab readers' choice award. His first novel, The Chaplain's War, *released from Baen in 2014. He also has two bestselling short fiction collections out from Wordfire Press. A frequent contributor to* Analog, *Brad has collaborated with Hugo and Nebula award winner Mike Resnick, is currently collaborating with Hugo winner and bestseller Larry Niven, and has several works pending publication including his second novel from Baen and short fiction in Larry Correia's* New York Times *Bestselling Monster Hunter universe. His web site is www.bradrtorgersen.com.*

In this story, a young boy discovers a talent for basketball in a colony on Mars playing by Mars Court rules.

The basket and backboard were over three meters off the gym floor.

JayDee Watson stared up at the net, which hung limply from the painted orange steel rim.

"It's not exactly the rec center back in Cleveland, is it?" said an adult's voice from over JayDee's left shoulder. The boy turned and looked at his aunt, who'd been showing him around the installation exercise facilities. If Mars had been impressive during the ride down from orbit, for the first time since leaving Earth, JayDee experienced the fluttering sensation of intimidation in his stomach.

He frowned, and tried to keep his fear from showing.

"I didn't realize they play it differently here," he said, with as much manly bravado as any fourteen-year-old can muster.

Aunt Catha chuckled. Which only got on JayDee's nerves.

"Everything's different here," she said. "Including the sports. You should try skiing the polar caps some time. If we can ever hitch a ride on one of those expeditions."

"How come the basket has to be so high?" JayDee asked.

"Mars has less than half of Earth's gravity," Aunt Catha answered. "A boy your size can easily dunk it. To say nothing of a grownup. Heck, *I* can dunk it like a pro. And I don't even play. So they changed the layout. Made the game challenging again. Wider and longer courts. Higher baskets, with larger backboards, because you'll be shooting from farther away. And the hoop is larger too. Which reminds me. Here, take this, and walk out to the top of the key. Try to make a free-throw. See what happens."

JayDee took the ball in his hands—larger than a usual junior ball, but not by much, and bright blue instead of orange—and walked across the painted portion of the court beneath the basket. Only his steps were more like lazy rabbit hops. A motion he still wasn't used to, even after a full week on-planet.

Assuming the position—at the line dividing the circle atop the painted zone—JayDee unconsciously threw the ball down one-handed for a couple of customary pre-shot bounces.

The blue sphere popped back up and through JayDee's fumbling hands, going very high into the air of the inflatable dome that covered the entirety of the court, and much else of the gym as well. JayDee cussed mildly under his breath, and waited for the ball to come back to him. It hit the skin of his outstretched palms much more gently than a basketball on Earth would have. Just one more odd difference about this place that JayDee was going to have to get used to.

Whistles and laughter sounded from the other side of the court, where a cluster of boys—full Martian blood, by the fluid looks of their movements and their superhumanly tall frames—were loping about, dropping shots through their own basket; using long, luxurious arcs.

JayDee felt his cheeks go bright red.

"Maybe this is a bad idea," he said to Aunt Catha.

Her expression darkened as she stared at the other

boys, who quieted down and returned to minding their own business. Then she looked back down at her nephew.

"Your older sister told me you were city league material, back home. She thought it might even be your ticket to a good secondary school, if the law didn't get you first. Or have you forgotten the reason why you got sent to live with me in the first place? Cleveland is still a city that devours guys like you. Up here, with me, maybe you can turn things around."

"I don't need another lecture," JayDee said defensively. "And I certainly don't need you trying to be my moms, the way Toti always thought she had to be."

Aunt Catha's eyes softened a bit, while JayDee glared up at her face.

"You're right, you don't need me to be your mother. If my sister were still around to take care of you, maybe none of this would have happened. But she isn't. The rest of us in the family have had to chip in where we can. And I am sorry there isn't much more for you here on Mars than a spare bed, three meals a day, and no juvenile officers waiting to haul you back before the judge. Think about *that* before you go running your mouth again, understand?"

Now it was JayDee's eyes who softened. He dropped his gaze.

"Sorry," he mumbled.

"Speak up," Catha ordered.

"I said I'm sorry, okay? I'm sorry. I'm sorry Toti kicked me out, I'm sorry you had to pay for me to come all the way out here—"

"Nope," Catha said.

"What?" JayDee replied.

"Nobody in our family paid. The Mars Immigration Project footed the bill. I showed them your test scores from school. And some footage Toti sent me, of your playing. I wrote a letter to the MIP telling them I thought you might make good first-generation colonist material. They agreed. But you'll have to earn your keep. Every child on the planet has lots of classwork. And you're already expected for the junior high team try-outs next week."

"Next week?" JayDee blustered. "I can't even dribble in this sh—"

He stopped, as Aunt Catha raised an eyebrow.

"—stuff," he finished.

"The lower gravity makes it that hard, huh?" Aunt Catha asked.

"Yeah. It'll be like learning to play all over again, for the good it's going to do me in one week. I wish you hadn't made any promises to anyone about the kind of player I'm supposed to be."

"No promises," Aunt Catha said. "Just an appointment for the first practice. You won't be the only Earth kid there, you know. There will be others."

"How many Mars kids?" JayDee demanded.

"Who knows? Lots, I guess. But you've got time to get ready."

JayDee rolled the blue ball in his hands, feeling the surface with the experienced tips of his fingers. His instinct was to bounce the ball again, before trying to make his shot. But having just seen the previous results, he nervously eyed the too-far-and-too-high hoop, then lifted his wrist, cocked his hand to his ear, and launched the ball one-armed.

The shot sailed clear up and over the backboard.

Which elicited more whistles and laughter from the opposite end of the court.

JayDee's face remained bright red.

"Screw this," he said sullenly. "Can we just go home?"

"Sure," Aunt Catha said. "But only if you promise to come back after dinner.

The court was empty this time. Save for the presence of a single, extremely tall girl. JayDee had a tough time estimating her age: she was wire-thin, had light skin and black hair cut short. She seemed to neither notice nor care about JayDee as he strolled onto the court—again, lazy bunny hops—before setting himself up at the top of the painted rectangle directly in front of the same hoop he'd missed so spectacularly that afternoon. The sun was on the horizon, so the translucent dome was going dark, and the overhead lamps had been turned on. The court glowed with artificial light. Not all that different from the rec center back in Cleveland.

JayDee spun the blue ball in his hands, hating the fact that the confidence he'd earned on Earth was deserting him here.

"Okay, let's do this," he said under his breath.

JayDee dribbled, and the ball went high again, practically squirting out of his hands. He had to chase after it this time, bumbling-and-fumbling as every running step sent him vaulting into the air. After what seemed like an embarrassing eternity, he got the ball back under control and returned to the top of the painted rectangle: an almost clownishly large space, in this oversized exaggeration of the game he had once thought himself quite good at.

JayDee dribbled again, this time gently pushing the ball to the court. It sprang back up at him, but he successfully caught it in two hands.

Another dribble, and another two-handed catch. Which wasn't going to work during a game, that much was certain. JayDee was so used to the ball rebounding exactly up into his palm—in precisely the expected fashion—that having to actually put his eyes on the ball was a monumental distraction. But he didn't dare look away while the results of each dribble were still difficult to gauge. Muscle memory reflexes, which had been honed on hard asphalt, were suddenly untrustworthy on Mars. It was like learning to ride a bicycle after a brain injury. JayDee could remember having been very quick and skilled on the court, but none of that mattered now, because his every decision had unintended consequences for which his brain wasn't yet rewired.

JayDee cussed. There was no way he'd be ready in a week. He was going to have to start all over again. He tried to simply walk with the ball and dribble at the same time. And wound up chasing it as it caromed off of his foot and ultimately settled into one of the corners at the opposite end of the court, where the very-tall girl was practicing layups—with far more grace and finesse than JayDee could imagine himself being able to muster, under the circumstances.

Flustered and embarrassed, JayDee took his ball, and

decided he'd had enough punishment for one night. The revolving door would take him back into the corridors of the installation where Aunt Catha worked and lived. He'd fulfilled the letter of his obligation to her. He didn't feel like humbling himself any further than he had to, for one day.

"It's about the physics," the girl said loudly to JayDee's back.

He paused at the revolving door, his hand clenched on one of the door's bars.

"What?" JayDee said over his shoulder.

"Earth people always have to learn the same lessons," the girl said. "On Earth, it takes a certain amount of force to put the ball onto the court, and have it pop back up into your hand. Here? The same force gets you over twice as much of a bounce. Because there's less than half the gravity pulling the ball back down again. Same for when you run. Or shoot."

JayDee's hand remained gripped on the bar.

"I guess that's good for you then, isn't it?" JayDee said, a bit more sarcastically than he intended.

"Good for me?" the girl said. "Yah, maybe. Look. I get it if you're mad. I probably would be too in your shoes. You're not the first guy from Earth who's come in here, made a fool out of himself, and quit. Just remember what I said: it's about the physics. If you start thinking about the numbers behind what you're doing—how the numbers are more than doubled, or over halved, depending on how you look at it—that might help. And if you want someone to practice with . . . I usually come in here at night after dinner, too. When the court's mostly empty."

JayDee was silent, his brow furrowed.

"Thanks," was all he finally managed to say, and none too happily.

The revolving door spun quickly with his hasty exit.

The next day, JayDee went to school for the first time, but feigned a stomachache and was sent back to Aunt Catha's quarters after lunch. Some people got a funny sort of space sickness while adjusting to Mars' lower gravity. It was JayDee's ideal excuse to duck out and seek some alone time.

Aunt Catha glowered at him as he lay on his bunk, his arms behind his head and his eyes staring directly up at the unpainted metal of the compartment's ceiling.

"Feelin' sorry for yourself ain't gonna change nothin'," Aunt Catha said, her drawl—softened by years in school, then the corporate sector—coming out.

"I'll be fine," JayDee protested. "I just need an afternoon to rest and think."

"Well," Aunt Catha said, "that may be. But consider this. There's no rule that says you have to stay here. And I won't be able to stop them if they decide you're not fit to be a first-generation colonist. Whether I am family or not, if they think you can't cut it, they will send you back. Mars doesn't have the resources for people who aren't motivated to be here and contribute. Do you understand how hard *I* had to work to come to Mars? This was my dream, going back to before I was even *your* age. And while I'd hate to see you blow it, I can't make you want to be successful either. So you can go back to Earth, and you can go back to the street if you like those options. I'm sure the judge won't be surprised to see you. Though I doubt Toti will be there to speak up for you this time."

The hatch to the compartment slammed shut before JayDee could get another word in. Aunt Catha's disappointment in him was palpable.

JayDee let her unhappiness seep across his soul for the rest of the afternoon, at which point he fell asleep. And did not awaken until clear into the following morning, when Aunt Catha poked her head back in and roused him for school.

The toilet situation on Mars wasn't too difficult to figure out, though the flushing needed a suction assist. The shower was like climbing into a gigantic water balloon—because the droplets and spray would go all over in the Mars gravity, if not kept properly contained. Like the toilet, the shower's drain had a suction assist. And so did the sink's drain as well.

Breakfast was hearty: eggs, toast, cereal, and juice, all of it shipped from Earth, and none of it tasting particularly fresh. Though—having missed dinner the night before—JayDee happily wolfed it all down and asked for seconds, before rushing off to make the first bell.

Class was class, though the classrooms were much smaller, more intimate, and the students seemed to literally be from all over the Solar System. Many were obviously Mars-born, with the customary tall spines and long, spidery arms. Some were like JayDee: Earth dwarves, with lots of muscle, but not much stature in comparison to the Mars natives. JayDee didn't like the way some of the Mars kids looked at him, but then, that had been par for the course in Cleveland too. He was not the kind of person to deliberately invite confrontation. He'd seen two cousins wind up dead that way, with gunshots. And though violence of that sort was practically unheard of on Mars, for JayDee, old instincts died hard.

Lunch time found him quietly eating alone: another plate of processed food, shipped from Earth. Though he did get to have a Mars-grown apple, which was surprisingly sweet and crunchy.

Before lunch was over, JayDee got stopped in the hall by the same girl who'd been practicing layups on the court two nights prior.

"Didn't see you for practice," she said, looking down at him.

"Huh?" JayDee replied.

"I thought you'd be back the next night, but you never showed. So, you decided it's not worth the effort?"

JayDee felt his cheeks grow hot again.

"I haven't decided anything yet," he said, and brushed past her, so as not to be late to the next period.

"Come out and give it another try!" she said to the back of his head as he moved quickly away.

He didn't pay much attention to class, for the rest of the day. Thoughts of that super-high rim and backboard kept clouding his mind. If even a half-hearted free-throw could send the ball way over the top, he'd have to dial back big time on the force of his extension. To say nothing about dribbling, which now bothered JayDee tremendously. But he wasn't going to let some girl see him be a coward. If she was serious about practicing with him, he was serious about showing her that he was no fool when it came to his favorite game.

Using his installation-issue mobile device, JayDee texted Aunt Catha that he was going to the court directly after school, to get a jump on his practice.

Unfortunately, the same group of Martian boys who'd seen him two days prior were there again. And this time, without Aunt Catha in tow, it was obvious they weren't going to leave JayDee alone.

This too was not entirely unfamiliar. JayDee had walked onto any number of courts in his neighborhood, and been stared down by the bigger, older guys who liked to consider the court their personal property. Speed and skill had usually made the difference, either because JayDee could prove he was an asset to any pick-up team who'd have him, or because he could outrun the tougher boys who were determined to make JayDee pay for his temerity.

But on Mars, there weren't many back alleys or side streets down which to disappear. When the Martian boys crowded around JayDee and began to taunt him, the revolving door that lead back to safety suddenly seemed a million kilometers away.

"Runt thinks he can come in here and share the floor with us," one boy said.

"Earth attitude," said another. "Thinks he already owns the place."

There were five of them, and they surrounded JayDee as he stood on the line at the top of the key, preparing to engage in however many free-throws it took to get the hang of the reduced Mars gravity. Only JayDee's new enemies were so tall and imposing, they practically blotted out the afternoon light that filtered through the dome.

"It's a big court," JayDee said. "Plenty of room for everybody."

"None of us gave you permission to speak," said the first Martian boy. "Let's just get something clear. We don't want or need you Earth runts. This isn't your planet. It's *our* planet."

"I don't see your names on it," JayDee shot back, keeping his head down, and his hands on the ball, which was held tightly at chest level. *This* aspect certainly hadn't changed. The back-and-forth. The taunting and clever ripostes. Sometimes, a group would respect you if you could be snappy with comebacks. But the vibe with these Martians wasn't like it was in Cleveland. There was more to the hatred in these boys' eyes than merely disliking an intruder on their court. For them, JayDee represented something different. Something threatening, at a basic level.

He suddenly remembered Aunt Catha's warning when she'd greeted him coming off the ramp at the spaceport.

Mars-born people aren't like you and me. While we can go back to Earth if we want, most of them won't fare as well, after leaving Mars. Being born in the weaker gravity means their bodies aren't adapted to Earth. Most Martians—going to Earth for the first time—quickly discover that they hate the work it takes just to live normally. There's a lot of resentment as a result. Be careful that you pay attention to it, if ever a Martian gets up in your face.

JayDee also remembered the girl's advice about numbers.

For a fourteen-year-old, JayDee's legs, arms, and torso

were lean, but lined with hard muscle. Five-to-one in Cleveland would have been near-lethal odds. But five-to-one on Mars?

When one of the taller boys shoved JayDee, he said, "Don't touch me."

The hoots and derision were loud and boisterous.

Another shove, and JayDee warned them again.

The third shove was all the permission he needed. JayDee cocked the ball with full force, launching it into the face of his assailant. The Martian's head and neck snapped back, a stream of blood flying from the older, taller boy's nose.

After that, it was a blur of legs and fists. The Martians were not as weak as JayDee might have hoped, but then, a kid from Cleveland didn't get to be JayDee's age without learning a thing or two about fighting. Two of the taller boys got thrown bodily away from the brawl, thanks to one of JayDee's fists in a stomach, and one of JayDee's shins to a groin. The two boys who'd not yet been touched wrapped their freakishly long arms around JayDee's body and then they pinned him to the court, almost like he'd been tied with ropes.

Unable to break free, JayDee showered cuss words at them as the boy with the bloody nose came back, and began ramming his foot into JayDee's side. Not hard enough to crack a rib, but plenty hard to knock the air out of JayDee's lungs, and hurt him like hell.

The look on the bloodied boy's face was murderous.

Just then, a whistle began blaring, and suddenly the Martian boys were being pulled off of JayDee by Martian and Earth-born adults alike.

JayDee was unceremoniously delivered to Aunt Catha's door, his hand clamped over his side where the kicks had left deep bruising.

"Couldn't make it one week without getting into trouble," Aunt Catha said, disgusted.

"It wasn't my fault," JayDee said as she eased him into a seat at the dinner table, and pulled off his shirt. Though his skin was even darker than hers, the blue-black blotches on his ribcage worried her. Especially when he winced as she gently probed with her fingertips.

"Martian boys?" Catha said, as she applied a frozen bag of veggies to the bruising, and put JayDee's hand over it so as to keep the bag in place.

"Yup," JayDee replied.

"I was afraid this might happen," Aunt Catha said. "I should have told you to wait until I could come out and keep an eye on you. If I'd been there, maybe this wouldn't have happened."

"It's all right, Aunt Catha," Jaydee said. "Just me and the locals having to sort out a little business. No different from back home. They were just longer and taller than I'm used to, that's all."

Aunt Catha crouched down and stared at her nephew, eye to eye.

"The other adults and I will have to do some sorting-out of our own now," she said. "I think you broke the nose on one of the sons of somebody I work with. That father isn't going to be too happy when he learns what transpired, and at the hands of whom. Just promise me one thing?"

"What's that?" JayDee asked.

"That you did it in self-defense *only*."

"I swear to God, Aunt Catha, they started it first. I gave them two solid warnings to back off. And they didn't stop. I'm not sure what else I was supposed to do."

Aunt Catha merely nodded her head, and told him to keep the frozen veggies applied.

Dinner was a quiet, solemn affair, after which JayDee put on a fresh pair of shorts and a T-shirt, and began lacing up his court shoes again.

"Are you crazy?" Aunt Catha said. "Do you want to get whupped twice in one day?"

"Someone promised to meet me if I showed up tonight," JayDee said.

"Who?" Aunt Catha asked, her head cocked to one side—in suspicion.

"I don't know her name," JayDee said. "But she was there before, and had the court to herself. She said she'd help me practice. And, so far, she's the only friend that I've got on this planet."

"Does she have a name?" Aunt Catha said.

"I will ask her," JayDee said, and then he was bounding out of Aunt Catha's compartment before she could think of a reason sufficient to keep him.

"Heard about what happened today," the tall Martian girl said as she met JayDee at the revolving door. The overhead lamps had just been switched on, and were not yet warmed up, so the court was dark with the onset of twilight. A couple of portholes on the far side showed a clear view to the horizon. JayDee hopped over to take a look, while the tall Martian girl followed.

"I hope nobody got hurt too bad," JayDee told her as he looked out at the vast, desert-like barrenness of the Martian surface. Boot prints and rover tracks ran every which way, through the rust-colored soil. The briefing movie JayDee had sat through on the ride down said that they were bringing in comets and letting them burn up in the Martian atmosphere. Someday, maybe many hundreds of years in the future, there would be enough nitrogen and oxygen outside for people to walk on Mars' surface without suits. Until then, the slight thickening of the atmosphere during even the few decades humans had lived on the surface made sunsets a spectacular sight.

"The ones who did get hurt thoroughly had it coming," the girl said. "I know them all. Bullies. Which is why you won't ever find me trying to come in here and practice after class. Too many jerks trying to prove something."

"Aren't I intruding, then?" JayDee asked her, turning to stare up at her face. Like most teenaged girls, she was still in transition from child to woman. But there were hints of true adult beauty in the way her cheeks were becoming more pronounced.

"Yes," the girl said. "But for the boy who broke Fitzer McGibbon's nose, I'll happily make an accommodation."

JayDee sighed.

"I didn't want to fight," he said.

"Fitzer is an ass," the girl said. "First-rate. His dad's an ass too. Maybe Fitzer won't be so quick to push people around anymore, now that somebody finally taught him a lesson."

JayDee took no comfort in her words. Sometimes, bloodying an enemy just meant the enemy came back meaner and harder the next time. And there would be no friends or uncles or cousins to help JayDee if this Fitzer character and his cronies decided that it was JayDee who really needed to be taught a lesson.

The girl? She wouldn't be a reliable ally, if what she said was true. She was already avoiding the boys who'd ganged up on JayDee.

Screw it, JayDee hadn't come to discuss street strategy. He'd come to ask her for help on the court.

"I'm JayDee Watson," he finally said, turning to the girl and offering his hand. She took it—her fingers long and strong—and they shook.

"Balikaya Novorostok," she said. "But most people just call me Bal. My family lives in a compartment cluster on the other side of the ring."

"What's it like to spend your whole life indoors?" JayDee asked, returning his stare to the dimming horizon. If he'd not known better, he'd have thought you could walk outside—only needing to tighten the collar on your jacket. The air didn't *look* poisonous, nor well below freezing. Certainly you couldn't tell by putting a hand on the soft, flexible inner layer of the gym dome. Most of the newer, larger structures were being built with domes: multi-layered, insulated tents that inflated the moment you put even a little bit of air into them—because the pressure outside was just a tiny fraction of Earth's normal air pressure at sea level.

"What was it like for you on Earth?" Bal responded.

"What do you mean?" JayDee said.

"Well, *duh*," Bal said, teasing. "You didn't know any different until you came here, right?"

"I guess so," JayDee said, conceding the point.

"I mean, I get outside in a suit from time to time," Bal said. "And I hope to live to see the day when we can all go outside and not worry if a suit is necessary. But Mars is my home, and my family has lived and worked at this particular installation my whole life."

"There are other colonies around the Solar System," JayDee said. "You could move to one of them."

"Maybe I will, eventually," she said.

And then the overhead lights finally popped up to full brightness.

JayDee had to squint for a few seconds until his eyes adjusted.

"Okay, enough wasting time," Bal said. "Do you want to be good enough to beat guys like Fitzer in a fair game?"

"Back on Earth, I'd be good enough now," JayDee said, a bit defensively.

"Right, I get it, but you're not *wired* to beat Martians at Mars Court Rules basketball yet. Is that your goal?"

"It is," JayDee said.

"Good, because I'm one of the best on the girls' team at our school. We took the installation pennant two years in a row, and went to the globals each time."

"Globals?" JayDee said, somewhat incredulous.

"All secondary schools compete to send teams to the Mars global championships. That's where the interplanetary colleges have scouts to scope for scholarship material. If you want to set yourself up for a career on this planet, that's a good way to do it. But first, you have to prove you have what it takes at the local level. Are you ready for me to show you how?"

JayDee realized that probably nothing would make him ready. Not for how Mars gravity had turned his skills all catawampus. But Bal seemed to be his best chance at finding the handle again.

"Let's do it," JayDee said.

And off they went.

Bal drilled JayDee for over two hours. Stuff so basic, it was almost humiliating to have to work at that rudimentary level. But as the minutes went by—dribbling, bounce-passing, set shots, jump shots, the works—JayDee began to forget about his embarrassment and become fascinated by the fact that he was a pint-size goliath in this reduced gravity. Even normal moves had exaggerated effects. The key to keeping control of the ball on Mars lay in applying a very soft hand to every touch.

At the end of the session, JayDee could get a ball through the hoop on almost a fourth of his shots. Not bad. But not great, compared with what he was used to back on Earth, where he prided himself on being fifty percent. Especially when driving to the basket, which he'd considered to be his strongest suit, but which now proved to be maddeningly difficult because his Earth-trained reflexes always took over at the last second, and his shots banged wildly off the floor, off the backboard, or both.

"Rome was not built in a day," Bal said, breathing heavily as they walked toward the revolving dome door.

"What's Rome?" JayDee asked seriously.

The disbelieving look on Bal's face told JayDee he'd best do some hasty research on the installation library net, so that he didn't look like even more of an idiot by the next time they practiced.

✦ ✧ ✦

"Long night," Aunt Catha said when JayDee got in the door, and began heading immediately for the shower.

"Needed it," JayDee said, before throwing himself into the lavatory and buttoning the door shut. The rinse was near-scalding, and necessary; both for sore muscles which hadn't worked this hard in weeks, and to soothe the ache out of his side where Fitzer had kicked him. Practicing had been extra tough because of the pain bruised ribs had caused, but JayDee had gritted his way through it. There wouldn't be time to let himself heal up fully before the try-outs came. And while he might not be fully acclimated to Mars by the time he had to show his worth to the coaches, he was determined to prove to Bal—at least— that he wasn't the kind of guy who shied away from a challenge.

So, for three more days straight, JayDee and Bal met every night for two hours each evening. By the time the third and final night had elapsed, they were doing one-on-one scrimmaging, which Bal proved to be remarkably canny at. Bal was a fighter, and she ran JayDee hard. Up and down the huge oversized Martian court. Forcing him to work his lungs and his legs in the reduced-pressure, enriched-oxygen artificial atmosphere. Making him learn to anticipate the need for slow-braking at either end of the floor. And preparing him for the fact that pump-faking was even more of an art on Mars than it was on Earth.

"Everybody jumps high here," Bal said, as they stood at mid-court, gulping down fruity electrolyte fluid. "The key to getting a clear shot is to get your defender to jump *just* enough, and too soon. Then you get maybe two or three seconds of clear space in which to plant your feet and launch the ball. Until you have more time to train your jumper, set shots are your best bet."

To which JayDee grudgingly agreed. His jumpers were still wildly off the mark. It would be months before he was fully used to reining in his reflexes—and putting a properly soft arc on the ball while elevated that far off the floor. It was still disconcerting enough being able to jump higher than he was tall, without even really putting a lot of effort into it. Trying to just hit the backboard while two meters off the court, and many multiples away from the rim, was a feat. So, grandpa set shots it would be. At least for the tryouts.

JayDee and Bal wrapped up their night with some simple shuttle drills, then went to stand by the portholes as they cooled off. The exterior lamps of the installation showed the non-stop construction activity going on at the new expansion site not too far from the dome. Robot crawlers loaded with beams and deflated domes and other prefabricated equipment drove round the clock, while workers—driving tractors, manipulators, and other equipment—put the pieces together in a display of remarkably efficient chaos.

Every once in a while, another ship from orbit would drop down rear-first on a cone of braking fire. The landing field was always bustling with ships coming and going.

"Aunt Catha says we're both lucky to be here," JayDee said, sucking at his bottle and feeling the cool lemon-lime drink slide down his throat.

"Lots of Earth-born think that," Bal replied.

"Aunt Catha said we're making history."

"My parents say the same thing, too. They were born on Earth, you know."

JayDee blinked. He'd never stopped to consider that probably none of the parents of the Martians Bal's age had been born on Mars. Humans hadn't been living on the small, red planet long enough for there to be *old* Martians. He also suddenly realized for the first time that if he stayed long enough, that maybe he'd marry a girl and have kids here too. And then his sons or daughters might be the tall, wisp-thin Martians—like Fitzer, and Bal, and the many others JayDee saw at school every day.

For an instant, JayDee's fourteen-year-old libido contemplated the idea of being intimate with a Martian girl—so tall, so different, and yet, not *that* different.

He watched Bal out of the corner of his eye, then shook his head.

Cart, JayDee thought, *about a kilometer before the horse.*

"Tomorrow I rest," JayDee declared, quickly getting his mind off his previous musing. "I'll make sure to eat and get plenty of fluid, but I'll let myself have the rebound time. Before tryouts. Speaking of which, are you going to be there?"

"I have to be," Bal said. "Every season, even if you've been on the team before, boys or girls, you have to go through the formality of tryouts. Some people let themselves get out of practice or out of shape between seasons. They don't do it any differently on Earth, do they?"

"Nope," JayDee said. "Same old, same old."

They stared out into the darkness—at the robots, and the men and women in suits—in silence.

Then Bal said, "Fitzer and the others will be there, too."

JayDee considered this new fact for a moment, and said, "Good."

For two school days, JayDee kept his thoughts to himself. Classwork was more technical than anything he'd had to do at school on Earth, but JayDee's aunt had been right about one thing: when he had to, JayDee could calculate with the best of them. He therefore spent a lot of time getting caught up on his homework assignments, and let his body recover after the series of intense workouts Bal had treated him to.

When tryouts finally arrived, the area surrounding the domed-over court was packed with adults and kids alike, both Earth-born and Martian. Folding chairs had been run up the line at half court, and men and women with computer pads sat facing to either basket, where boys drilled on one side, and girls drilled on the other. Aunt Catha came, as did many other parents, and she gave her nephew a smile. She also noticed JayDee eyeing Bal, as Bal raced up and down her side of the court, working hard to show her skills.

"Is that the one?" Aunt Catha said just before JayDee stripped off his sweats and prepared to go out onto the court. He accepted his trial number from one of the adults sitting in the chairs.

"Who, Bal?" He said. "Yeah, she's the one."

"Looks like she's pretty good," Aunt Catha remarked.

"Better than good," JayDee admitted. "Back home, I think she'd give even some of the guys a run for their money. I don't think I've ever had to practice with so much focus in all my life. She didn't just push me, Aunt Catha, she drove me to the edge."

"That's what a good woman *ought* to do, JayDee, you hear?" Aunt Catha said.

He somehow felt her words had a double meaning, but then the whistle was sounding, and JayDee hurried out onto the court where the other boys his age were huddled around one of the coaches—who stood in the center, and had a whistle around his neck.

"I hope you Earth guys are ready for this," the coach said. "In case you haven't figured it out yet, playing in this gravity isn't like playing back on Earth. So you'd best have prepared yourselves in advance, or you're going to get taken off the floor very fast and told to prepare for next season. It's nothing personal. We just don't have time for you to do remedial work before the actual schedule gets underway. Does everyone understand?"

JayDee said that he did, along with all the others.

Then the coach clapped his hands, and the boys all went to work.

Very quickly, it became apparent—among the so-called Earth runts—who had logged the time to get ready, and who hadn't. Several of JayDee's peers got yanked inside of ten minutes, and were taken out of the gym with red faces and heads hanging low.

JayDee was instantly glad to have had the time he spent with Bal. He didn't embarrass himself, and was able to keep up through shuttle drills as well as shooting drills. Having had almost 48 hours of repose, JayDee found that his touch—while approaching the basket—had softened enough so that his layups weren't nearly as comical as they'd been in the days prior. He got enough shots through the hoop that he didn't cringe, though he still wondered if the people observing from the chairs were going to mark his name off—before he'd even had a chance to show his worth in a scrimmage.

Which was when things got real.

Older boys—who'd been sent on a water and rest break—came out to play with JayDee and his age group. They were mixed and divided, with an appropriate number of older and younger players assigned to each scrimmage team, as well as a fair split, Earth-born to Martians. They'd work the contest half-court fashion, since the girls owned the other end. The scrimmage team opposite JayDee's had Fitzer in its ranks. The older boy's nose was cottoned up and kept safely behind a transparent strap-on mask.

Fitzer's eyes drilled holes in JayDee's head as they prepared for the whistle that would announce the beginning of the scrimmage.

First team to twenty-five points would be declared the winner.

Players were positioned for size, so that JayDee ended up matched at shooting guard against another Earth-born. They eyed each other somewhat nervously, but when the whistle sounded, they were off. With only half the court to play in, there wasn't as much long-distance hopping as had been necessary during the practices with Bal, but JayDee found himself hard-pressed to keep up with his new twin, because the older boy had clearly acclimated fully to the Mars gravity, whereas JayDee was still green.

Twice in two possessions, JayDee got schooled off the dribble, and trailed his opponent to the basket where the blue ball sailed up, kissed the backboard, and dropped through the net.

In his younger years, JayDee would have let such small defeats rattle him. But he'd played in far too many pick-up games and organized community events to let the small stuff get to him now. Basketball was a game of swings. Individual successes or failures did not matter nearly as much as how you reacted to the swing. If the opponent racked up a few quick buckets, you either doubled down on defense and closed the gap, or your morale crumbled and the other team ran away with it.

For JayDee, in this case, there was only doubling down.

Four possessions later, with the other team sitting at eight points and JayDee's sitting at just two, he managed to get a hand into one of the overly-long passing lanes. He picked off the ball as it moved between opponents, then JayDee was driving for the basket as best as he could— still somewhat unsettled by the hippity-hop maneuvering dictated by Mars's gravity.

Fitzer loomed in JayDee's path, just outside the paint. The older boy's eyes looked as murderous as they had the day he kicked JayDee in the ribs. Back on Earth, JayDee would have considered going for the contested shot. Now? He wasn't so sure.

JayDee spied one of his own teammates out of the corner of his eye. The Martian boy had set up in the corner, just outside the three-point line—which seemed impossibly far away to JayDee's Earth-trained sensibilities. Smiling to himself, JayDee ran right up into

Fitzer's towering arms, and cleverly dumped the ball off to the boy in the corner, who caught it smoothly and lifted for a slow-motion shot that hung for an Earthly eternity, before finally dropping through the center of the net.

JayDee, meanwhile, got hammered back to the floor. The wind gushed from his chest, and he felt his healing ribs complain badly.

A whistle sounded.

"Hard foul!" one of the coaches—acting as a referee— shouted. "The basket counts, but Player Forty-Nine gets a technical free throw."

JayDee felt himself lifted from the floor under the arms of his teammates, both Earth-born and Martian alike. Suddenly, a wave of emotion passed through his body. He'd been playing as if everyone around him was a potential foe—people to whom he had to prove himself. But as he felt the strength of the boys to either side of him, and he heard their words of encouragement, a bolt of energy shot up from the pit of his stomach and glowed in the center of his chest.

Stepping gingerly to the line, and nursing his hurting ribs, JayDee saw Aunt Catha out of the corner of his eye. Her expression was concerned, but also firm. He turned his head to make full eye contact with her, and she nodded at him, before mouthing the words:

You can do it, JayDee.

He set up at the line, still remembering the high, useless shot he'd lobbed—the first time he'd attempted a free throw here. He'd gotten a bit better since then, but his instincts were still wobbling between Earth and Mars. Back home, he'd been a seventy-percenter. Now? With so little time on Mars to prepare? He figured he was lucky to be at thirty.

But now was as good a time as any to see if he could up the percentage, even by one data point.

The dribble at the line was a good one. JayDee repeated it three times, glad to feel the ball respond to his deliberately gentle touch, just as it would have responded back on Earth. Then JayDee puffed out his cheeks, and gazed up at the rim. His arm cocked back, hand to his ear, and he completed the motion just as he had a thousand times before—but with a fraction of the effort.

The ball floated up, over, and drifted down to hit the front of the rim. It bounced off, hit the back board, then the front of the rim again, then the back board once more, before kicking off the steel heal at the rim's rear edge and dropping to the court.

JayDee grimaced. He'd not gotten the shooter's bounce on that one. But his team clapped their hands anyway as they regrouped and prepared to keep playing.

"Not bad for a new Earth kid," one of the adults in the folding chairs remarked, loud enough for JayDee to overhear.

He felt the center of his chest begin to glow again, and as the scrimmage continued—even with two more deliberately hard fouls on Fitzer's part—JayDee realized that he was going to earn a place on the team. It wasn't Cleveland. But it was still *his* game. And by the time the scrimmage was over he'd racked up three more assists, another steal, and managed a pump-fake shot that sent Fitzer practically crashing into the people seated in the chairs. All while JayDee lined up with his feet planted firmly, hoisted his shot, and made the two-point bucket.

Which was ultimately not enough to defeat the other scrimmage team, but at that stage it didn't matter. A scrimmage was a scrimmage. Not a championship match. All JayDee cared about were the slaps on his butt from Earth-born and Martians alike, as the coaches whistled for everyone to take a ten-minute break: bathrooms and water, before resuming the afternoon's assessment drills.

While refilling his bottle at the fountain, JayDee discovered Bal refilling her bottle right next to him.

"How are you making out?" Bal asked.

"I think I've done what needed doing," JayDee said. "Thanks to you."

Bal smiled at him, her eyes sparkling.

"If ever we're back on Earth," she said, "you remember to do me the return favor, okay?"

"Deal," JayDee said, grinning.

Then they split, and JayDee returned to the drills.

LAST SHOT, FIRST SHOT

✧ ✧ ✧

by Dean Wesley Smith

"You miss 100 percent of the shots you don't take."
—Wayne Gretzky,
NHL Player, Los Angeles Kings

Considered one of the most prolific writers working in modern fiction, USA Today *bestselling writer,* **Dean Wesley Smith** *published far over a hundred novels in forty years, and hundreds and hundreds of short stories across many genres.*

At the moment he produces novels in four major series, including the time travel Thunder Mountain *novels set in the old west, the galaxy-spanning* Seeders Universe *series, the urban fantasy* Ghost of a Chance *series, and the superhero series starring* Poker Boy.

His monthly magazine called Smith's Monthly, *consisting of only his own fiction, premiered in October 2013 and has not missed an issue yet, with over 60,000 words per issue, including a new and original novel every month.*

Before becoming a fiction writer, Dean was a PGA professional golfer, and before that, he was part of the early years of hotdogging, which became freestyle skiing. He also spent a number of years as a full-time professional poker player, which ESPN considers a sport.

For more information about Dean's books and ongoing projects, please visit his web site at www.deanwesleysmith.com.

Dean digs into his past life to give us a story about a one-of-a-kind golf game between players from two leagues with competing sets of rules.

Van Lifting took slow easy swings with a five iron to loosen up his shoulder and back muscles. At forty-five, warming up was critical every time. Over the decades, he had built up his muscles to be perfect to get top club-head speed on demand. But those muscles, as he got older, tore and got damaged easily. Now, a large part of every day was spent just staying loose and moving in fear of injury.

Around the wide, fake-grass practice area, he knew the media cameras recorded his every motion from twenty different hidden angles. He knew, without a doubt, he was being watched by millions on Earth and even more millions in the thousands of domes on moons and planets around the system.

To many golf fans on Earth, with this trip he had become a traitor by just playing in this tournament. And to almost all of those around the rest of the system, he was the enemy, the invader from the strict rules of the Royal and Ancient Golf Club, the rules that governed all golf play on the planet, but did not recognize golf as it was played off Earth.

He didn't feel like either role. He had just wanted the challenge.

He had wanted to do something new.

And in the old traditional game of golf on Earth, there was very little new that he hadn't already accomplished. Mostly he just sat around and dreaded the five years before they would want him to play the Seniors Tour.

The area of this Earth moon dome named Tyco had artificial gravity sat at standard Earth 1, so it didn't feel any different at all than warming up for a tournament back on Earth.

But everything around him looked different. And it was different in all respects. The artificial turf he stood on was a bright green, not like anything found in nature.

Overhead, the dome structure towered into the dark moon night, slowly curving inward and seeming to vanish in the distance, the entire thing an intricate balance of dark black supports and clear panels.

He had no idea why anyone lived on the Moon, or in any dome for that matter, but he did appreciate the beauty. The towering buildings in the center of the city under the dome were shining examples of modern architecture that seemed to aim at the dome over them like old-style rockets.

And the very size of the city had surprised him as well. Larger than the Chicago metropolitan area, over two million people lived in this dome alone, more than now lived anymore in the old city of Chicago.

And the Tyco Dome wasn't even close to the biggest dome on the Moon, let alone in comparison to the massive domes on Mars.

Twenty times more people now lived off Earth than on Earth anymore. That number had been hard to imagine until he came to Tyco and saw this place.

Everything inside seemed to be polished and kept up, while on Earth many of the old courses had clubhouses built hundreds of years before and in desperate need of repair.

Around him, the huge practice area was big enough to hold a hundred golfers, as it had done earlier in the week. Now, only he and one other golfer were getting ready, spread a respectable distance apart.

Bach Runningdeer, a young professional from Bear Dome on Mars, was Van's last opponent.

Runningdeer was the top player off Earth in this new form of golf. He stood six feet tall, had a thin waist and wide shoulders, and hands that seemed almost too big to hold a regular golf club.

Runningdeer's face had the clear-skin look of never having experienced weather. And as the news feeds and sports magazines said, he was also stylishly handsome and still single. Van would have to take their word for the handsome part.

Van was still, even at his age, the top player in the old form of golf played only on Earth. Van was also six feet tall, had slightly graying hair, broad shoulders and a stomach that now seemed far thicker than it should be. He had small hands, a problem he had always dealt with in his game, and the skin of his face, arms, and neck was weather-beaten and wrinkled beyond his years.

And now, because Van and Runningdeer had both won every match up to this point, it all came down to this one contest, a clash of the traditional in golf and the future of golf, as the game spread out over the Solar System and eventually out beyond the system.

This match was a perfect media storm.

Van's or Runningdeer's managers and promotional people could not have set this up any better. Major tournament, two top players from the two different forms of golf going head-to-head on the last day.

Van did a few bends with the club tucked against his back, then went back to swinging slowly, keeping a simple rhythm, letting the muscles loosen before he tried an actual practice shot.

Over the last week of playing against some of the best in the Greater System (as everything off Earth was called), Van had come to appreciate the new form of golf course as well, a form despised and outlawed by the ruling body of the Royal and Ancient Golf Club.

But what did they know? They guarded the old game on Earth like an overprotective father, while out in space, out on the planets and moons, golf took root in a different form, a form still trying to find its balance.

Similar, but yet very different.

Similar enough that Van's skills had gotten him here to the final match, but different enough to challenge his bored feelings.

He had heard so much about this new form, had read the passionate debates, had listened to so many other professionals disparage the players who lived in domes and had no idea what it was like to walk after a tee shot, or try to escape from a sand trap.

But no one on Earth could imagine trying to hit a shot

through a force shield into no atmosphere, low gravity, and have it land where the player wanted the ball to land.

No wind or atmospheric drag to slow the ball, no way to hook or slice the ball, just exact calculations of speed of the ball, trajectory of the ball, and the gravity of the moon or planet being played on.

It took a precision of control at club and ball impact that was only dreamed about on Earth.

So Van had decided to play in the Shepard Open in the Tyco Dome. The tournament was named after Alan Shepard, an early explorer of the Moon who used a six iron to hit three golf balls and be the first person to hit a golf shot anywhere but on Earth.

That had been the start of golf in the Greater System.

And by Van announcing his decision to play off-planet, he had turned this event into the biggest major golf tournament in the system.

Period.

A clash between old and new, between traditional Earth golf and Greater System golf.

For the first time in years, he felt a thrill again, a challenge.

For decades, he had been the best golfer on the planet, winning far more than he lost. The challenge, the thrill had slowly vanished, replaced with only expectations that he'd always win.

He had hefted so many trophies, they just accumulated dust in his basement, stacked on shelves to be sold off when he died. He had no wife, no kids to give them to. No one to really care if he won or lost besides his managers and coaches, and they only cared because of the money.

He had been too busy over the years focusing on being the best golfer on Earth; he had forgotten to be a human.

But now, here, standing on the Moon in artificial gravity on artificial green turf, the thrill, the excitement was back.

The challenge.

And the fear.

The fear had set in six months before, right after he announced he would play in this tournament. He had ordered and had installed in a giant warehouse the football-field-sized putting green that was used in all Greater System courses.

An exact replica, actually. Under the artificial turf, undulations could rise or fall depending on the hole being played. Before each hole being played, the players could see how the green was set, where the hole was placed, to know which area of the green was best to hit toward.

So the same green was used for all eighteen holes. Just all the hills and valleys and breaks were reset for each hole.

Greater System players were deadly putters from two hundred feet and beyond, seldom three-putting. But on Earth, he was known for his accurate short game, his ability to pitch a ball to within inches of a hole.

So he had perfected that on these big artificial greens, since no rule in the Greater Systems prohibited getting the ball in the air even though he was on the putting surface.

The first time he had done that, his opponent had called for a ruling, which Van won, of course. So the headlines on Earth were that he had brought old golf to the Greater Systems and shown them a thing or two. The headlines in the Greater Systems sports commentaries was less favorable, to say the least.

Van hadn't cared. He had won his match and moved on to the next elimination round.

On the way to the Tyco Dome, he had come to appreciate the great distances the Greater System Tour players traveled. Even going what seemed like a short distance from Earth to the Moon just took too long for his tastes.

He had thought the four-hour elevator ride into orbit was long, but then the nineteen-hour shuttle flight to Tyco Dome had gone on forever. Even going first class completely, that was a long way to travel for a golf tournament.

Runningdeer had come in from his home on Mars for this tournament, a five-day flight. That was crazy as far as Van was concerned.

Back on Earth, Van's private suborbital got him to any tournament in just hours from his home. He liked it that way.

There was no way he would take the five-day trip to Mars. This was his limit.

Now, today, he needed to prove he was also the best player in the entire Solar System.

One hour later, Van and Runningdeer shook hands on the elevated tee area and wished each other good luck. Van had a hunch that in different circumstances, he would like Runningdeer.

The first hole measured about forty-two miles long and was a pretty standard par four on the Moon. The distance was also measured in kilometers, but Van only paid attention to the miles and yards. That was his training.

Van, as the visitor from Earth, was awarded first on the tee. He knew maybe billions of people would watch his every move now.

Van could feel the challenge.

And the fear, as he slowly swung a few more practice swings with his driver.

The fear almost made him feel alive again. And after all the years, he couldn't begin to describe how great that felt. He had completely forgotten what being challenged felt like.

And he liked it, wanted more of this, no matter what happened today.

Van stepped to the teeing area. What looked like a standard golf ball sat there on a tee, exactly the height he liked for his driver, waiting for him.

The ball was made of a material that would compress just as a regular golf ball did, not explode when it hit a sudden vacuum. Yet once the ball had finished its flight, it would deteriorate quickly into moon dust when the harsh rays of the Sun hit it in a few days. That way none of the balls would need to be picked up.

Directly in front of the tee was the harsh gray Moon surface. The first time he had stepped on this tee a week before, all he could do was stare out at the Moon landscape and the close horizon. Now, after a week, he had gotten mostly used to it, but he was still stunned by the beauty of the stark grayness.

Electronic lines along the screen showed clearly an out-of-bounds. Van knew that only a force field separated him and Runningdeer from the vacuum of the Moon's surface.

Beyond that invisible force field, the gravity was one-sixth that of Earth, and there was no atmosphere to slow the ball down. Only the speed of the ball and its trajectory mattered.

Clearing his mind, Van let his training take over and sent the ball through the force field and into the Moon's night sky.

On both sides of the force field, a screen tracked the ball's flight. He had pushed the ball slightly to the right, but was in no danger of it crossing an out-of-bounds line.

In orbit above the range, tracking satellites showed every detail of the ball's flight, right down to the moment it touched the Lunar surface.

The screens on both sides of the force field relayed both the height of the shot and the distance it was traveling. Finally, the Moon's gravity took hold and brought the ball down, just over thirty miles from the dome.

He was exactly thirteen miles, three hundred and six yards from the pin.

"Nice drive," Runningdeer said as he stepped to the tee.

Usually Van paid little attention to the swings of the other golfers he played with in any tournament. But for this first drive, he watched the effortless and controlled movement of Runningdeer, and with a sharp click the ball headed out into the void.

The drive came down almost exactly one mile behind Van's ball. But Van knew that was part of the beauty of the Greater System players. They hit each drive a prescribed distance, or at least as close as they could. So each second shot could also be inside a certain range.

Runningdeer was farthest from the hole, so he went next.

That was a standard rule of golf. Van had been surprised just how many of the Rules of Golf of the Royal and Ancient were used in the Greater System.

A ball appeared on the iron mat in front of the force field, and Runningdeer took what looked like a seven iron from his bag, studied the distance on the screen he had remaining to the green for a moment, then with a smooth motion sent the second ball out over the Moon's surface.

The computers would track if his distance was accurate or not, and if he managed to land the ball where the green would be, as if the green were out there on the surface.

If Runningdeer got the distance correct, another ball would appear at the right spot on the massive putting green behind them where his ball hit on the surface of the Moon, and from there, it was regular golf to the hole.

If Runningdeer got the distance or accuracy wrong, he would have to hit another shot onto the green, just as on Earth when a player missed a green.

Van had missed a number of greens in his first matches and discovered that a short shot was difficult to control in the Moon's one-sixth gravity. Very difficult.

Both Van and Runningdeer watched the screen for a moment, then when it became clear that Runningdeer's shot would land on the large green, they both turned.

After a few moments, a ball appeared about fifty paces from the pin.

"Nice shot," Van said to Runningdeer, who nodded.

Van then allowed himself a few moments to study the exact distance he had to the pin, then took an eight iron and sent the ball through the force screen and out into the vacuum over the Moon's surface.

Again, when it became apparent on the big tracking screens that his shot would come down on the massive green, he and Runningdeer both turned toward the huge expanse of artificial putting surface.

Van's ball appeared about a hundred paces from the pin, and behind a large lump in the green.

Runningdeer took a putter from his bag, and Van took a putter and two different wedges from his bag, and they walked side by side, stride by stride, toward the big green.

Since Van was farthest from the hole, he went first. He had decided on a high loft shot over the large mound in the green that he planned to have bounce near the hole, spin, and stop.

He executed it perfectly, leaving the ball only inches from the cup. He could imagine that in front of a gallery on Earth, that would have had the throngs cheering. But in this large chamber, it was only Runningdeer and Van. The crowds were all watching from their own screens.

"Nice shot. Pick it up," Runningdeer said, giving Van the next shot. That was allowed in match play in the Greater Systems, just as it was on Earth.

Then Runningdeer rolled his first putt up to within inches of the cup as well. For a moment, Van had thought he might have made it.

Van gave the next shot to Runningdeer and they started back to the tee box for the second hole, tied.

Van had no doubt he was in the match of his life.

And from the intense look on Runningdeer's face, he felt the same way.

Seventeen holes later, after Van rimmed out a forty-foot putt for the win, Van and Runningdeer were still tied.

For one hole Van had been up, then Runningdeer had won two straight holes to go back ahead, then Van had won the fourteenth hole to send the match back into a tie.

"Well," Van said to Runningdeer as they walked once again toward the tee box, "at least we are giving the viewing audience a real show."

Runningdeer laughed. "That we are. And no matter how this ends up, it has been an honor playing this match with you."

"I feel the same," Van said. "The game of golf is in good hands with players like you taking the lead."

Runningdeer glanced at Van, clearly surprised.

"Just do one thing for yourself and the future," Van said.

"What's that?" Runningdeer asked.

"Have a family to travel this road with you."

Runningdeer looked sort of stunned at Van. Van just smiled as they reached the tee.

"Just trust me on that one," Van said. "From an old guy without a family. Now we got three holes left. Sudden death."

"Three holes," Runningdeer said, reaching out his hand to shake Van's hand. "Good luck."

Van laughed and shook Runningdeer's hand as well. "On Earth we need the luck because the ball bounces and runs and goes against trees and into sand traps. Here I just need good math."

"Then good math," Runningdeer said, laughing.

"Thanks," Van said, smiling back at the man he was coming to like and admire. "Same to you."

On the first sudden death hole, Runningdeer missed a forty-foot putt that would have won the tournament for him.

On the second sudden death hole, Van almost chipped in, a shot that would have won the tournament for him.

On the third sudden death hole, Runningdeer rolled in a thirty-foot putt to keep the entire match tied.

That was it. They were co-champions.

"Nerves of steel," Van said, shaking Runningdeer's hand.

"Had my knees locked so I wouldn't fall down," Runningdeer said, laughing. "I'm just thankful it went in."

"Actually," Van said. "So am I. A tie is the best way for this to end."

"Thank you," Runningdeer said.

With that, the two of them turned to head over the big green to the door that led into the press area. The match between the old world of golf and the new world of golf had ended in a tie.

And in all the hundreds and hundreds of tournaments Van had won, that felt like the best victory ever. He had officially passed the torch to the next generation of golfers.

Runningdeer would carry it well.

And Van would return home and use his influence and a bunch of his money to convince the Royal and Ancient

Golf Club to accept the new way of playing golf and include it in the game he loved.

Granted, it wasn't exactly the same. It didn't have the wind and the rain and the bad bounces.

But it also had precision and timing and planning and strategy, many of the things he loved about this wonderful game that he had made his life.

And maybe in a few years, he'd organize a bunch of his old friends to go with him on a seniors match play tour of the Greater System. He had a hunch some of the old-timers like him might just be able to teach those Greater Systems players a thing or two about a short game.

And maybe, just maybe, he could get with Runningdeer and get the Greater Systems to make the greens a little smaller and add in rough and sand traps around the greens. That would bring some extra Earth-like touches into the Great Systems game as well.

As Van and Runningdeer walked into the large room filled with applauding press people from both Earth and the Greater System, Van felt challenged by the future again.

He was no longer bored, no longer tired.

He felt like he had just played in his first tournament again. And that was wonderful.

THE GREAT IGNORANT RACE

✧ ✧ ✧

by Robert Reed

"There are only two options regarding
commitment. You're either IN or you're OUT.
There is no such thing as life in-between."
—Pat Riley,
Three Time NBA Coach of The Year

*Robert Reed is the author of more than 250 published
stories and a respectable pile of novels. "A Billion Eves"
won the Hugo in 2007. His most recent works include the
well-received* The Memory of Sky, *a collection of three
Great Ship novels published in one titanic volume. Another
Hugo nominated novella,* Truth, *is being made into an
independent movie called* Prisoner X. *Reed has a small but
steady capacity working in the game* Destiny, *created by
the good people at Bungie. The author lives in Lincoln,
Nebraska with his wife and daughter.*

*Reed is also known as an active and successful runner,
but here he gives us an extreme sporting event similar to*

a mix between perhaps Survivor and the Amazing Race—
where every athlete starts in the nude.

Nudity must be important, what with everyone being bare-footed, bare-bottomed naked. Only nobody on the team can offer explanations for why. Or for that matter, why any odd detail matters, including the central mystery: How come each one of them has suddenly come awake, finding himself and herself unclothed in a strange place, and not a hint of panic showing in the bright morning air.

Yet despite the unknowns, certain things are understood.

Each one of them is part of a larger group. "We are the human team," they whisper. Sing. Shout. The declaration stirs warm, wonderful emotions. Nobody can say what the word "human" means, and not one of them thinks of asking why they speak the same language. Which happens to be a new language, nameless and contrived and utterly nonhistoric—a tongue invented yesterday, woven out of random human sounds and devised for this elaborate competition.

They are the human team, and every player begins at the same point: Naked and ignorant.

But not stupid.

And not scared or tentative or willing to blame the gods for this unexplained, possibly treacherous situation.

Common sense is on display. One pragmatic job is counting the faces standing around them. Then each small group sends scouts through the forest, out of the glades and along the shoreline, navigating by landmarks and returning before too long. People just like them are everywhere, except with different faces and bodies and such. Everyone is a player. Each of them carries zero memory about yesterday, yet they share the wherewithal to take a census and go exploring. The rich local fruits and sweet nuts are gathered up by every free hand. The scouts also carry back quite a lot of practical knowledge about the lay of the land, particularly where the water begins and how this is an island in the middle of powerful river, and the middle of their island seems to be "that way." And with a line to follow, each group sets out for the center.

The sun is still short of noon when the full team assembles, standing in close ranks on a brilliant hilltop.

A thorough census is taken.

The great race is well underway.

Nine thousand nine hundred and fifty-seven players stand beneath an alien sun. Humans are allowed ten thousand players. Which nobody knows. There are reasons why their population falls just short of ten thousand, but when you play you can't know about being late for shuttles or sick or personal disasters. All that matters is where you are now. What matters next is making the full count, and by noon the new language and wiped minds can move to the next critical issues.

The landscape is extraordinarily rich, and that includes food and spring water as well as several tame fires that fascinate everyone.

A leader. That's what is necessary. Each original group picks one representative, and the representatives pick three candidates from their ranks, decisions based on the qualities found in most human leaders: Is this a face and voice that I would happily follow? Those three potential bosses stand on different knobs of ground, talking in turn, and with everything at stake, hands are raised. Hands are counted. Then the new team captain makes a few broad declarations while underscoring what needs to be done next. Except of course everything that's obvious to her is obvious to the others, and on their own initiative people are acquiring the rudimentary tools to survive the unknown night.

Fire.

Different people working with empty heads and the native blazes invent the world's first campfires.

Every player is smart, without question. But only certain players are exceptionally gifted.

A man and woman study their group's little campfire. Flying sparks intrigue them. Certain native rocks make sparks when struck together. Tinder ignites with a little urging, and that's how fire can be conjured out of sweat and aiming eyes and good quick hands.

And those two people are deemed special. Their opinions hold more weight than most. They also invent another blessing, or at least they take the credit. But something so natural as sex can't be invented. Not ever. And by morning, most of the human team is taking part in activities as natural as breath and as binding as a thousand promises.

The second day proves colder, and bare feet are getting cut too easily. That's why shoes and other clothes are devised from the wrong materials and then better materials. And after three or four days, when everybody is comfortably dressed, a tiny portion of this new society is dedicated to putting themselves into the best-looking clothes possible.

Fashion is a deeply human trait.

Just like sex and teamwork. And having your team beat all of the other teams to the finish line. That's as fundamental as anything.

The island is a narrow slice of rich ground surrounded by relentless and very deep water. And after six days of close observation it's determined that the river rises every night, and not just a little bit, and its level never shows any tendency to drop back down again.

The true nature of rivers isn't known or knowable. Nobody sits in their woven clothes, wet sandals to the flames, guessing how glaciers are being intentionally melted upstream. And nobody dares imagine an even greater body of water called "the sea" waiting downhill. What people know is what they see. The ground under them is finite and precious, and there's less ground today than yesterday. Presumably there will be much less in a thousand days. The deep river is working to drown them. Water is cruel, and they know this because a few explorers waded out too far and got swept away. Only one of them managed to float and kick his way home again, and after coughing out cold river water, he explained what it feels like to be dragged under by the amoral current, to feel your life being stolen away.

Nobody wants to die.

And the island is dying.

Plainly, the solution is to leave. Which isn't as

ridiculous as it would have sounded on the first day or two. They can see land on the evening side of their world. The ground wears the same color as their ground, except it stands taller when the air is clear, and it's even easier to see with eyes closed, contemplating a future with roaring river water rising around every foot.

But the river isn't just a single complication. No, it is many. Downstream from the island, and not very far downstream, the roaring current bends and drops hard for as far as the sharpest eyes can see. A fabulous amount of energy is expended inside the tumbling fluids. Even at the upstream end of the island, people hear the endless thunder of the waterfalls. On the sixth morning, the two famous geniuses are talking and having sex, and in the middle of everything they decide on an experiment. A large raft is built and pushed off the shoreline. Everyone watches the current take hold of that unmanned explorer, leading it straight into the falls where it tips and shatters, drowning every hypothetical passenger, limp bodies torn apart by the fearsome waves.

The geniuses curse.

That's another natural component of the species. Humans like to throw out words about dung and such.

Nine thousand, nine hundred people gather on the hilltop again.

Their leader finds a moment of quiet before calling out. She begins by telling those who can hear her to repeat her words to those in the back. Then, with a voice full of authority, she confesses that she doesn't know what to do. She has zero talent for building fires or weaving grass or dreaming up new ways to carve wood and stone into useful forms. But she knows who is excellent at that kind of work. Everybody else. And with that, she reminds her people about the wonders accomplished already, and she promises that her little nation could come up with ten different solutions for saving everybody, and save them long before the river drowns the human world.

But ten solutions seems like rather too many, to her thinking.

"Five teams led by the smartest people," she demands. "Each team comes up with its best solution, and we meet again and decide which two solutions are best."

"Why five and two?" someone shouts.

It's an obvious question. The truth is that she gave those numbers no thought. Except that they sounded good.

She needs something better than that.

A perfectly poised response.

"Five fingers in one hand to lay the beginnings," she says. "And then two arms to do the heavy labor.

"That is our best hope for survival," she promises.

Reputations are human. Political social and legal power are human. Inertia is a human flaw, except when something good must happen again and again, and then inertia becomes tradition and everyone benefits.

Because it seems reasonable, the boss puts the flame-cultivators in charge of their own team.

Four other duos are given equal powers.

Couples. Always couples. Because with six days of experience, that seems best. And each pair are allowed to pick only fifty helpers to work with their fresh-born project.

Why so few?

"Because we don't want too many voices talking at once," says the boss. "And because the rest of us will be working hard, hard, hard. Stocking food. Gathering raw materials. Once the projects begin, we'll need everything ready, and everything has to be on hand. Plus meals for everybody, since we'll be busy, busy, busy creating whatever we need."

Fifty helpers are selected by quirky, often arbitrary processes.

Each group led by romantic duos.

People with long memories would have anticipated the trouble. These romances are days old, fragile and gland-inspired. Two of the top couples soon fall to pieces, including the gay men who seemed so totally enamored with each other. But emotional stresses don't hurt too badly, particularly for them. Calculations are made in the head and gut. Elaborate drawings cover the faces of a nearby cliff. What seems like the most ludicrous suggestion became a seductive if still unlikely scheme. Not a raft this time, but something more elegant and elaborate. A new word is invented. Using the new language, the words for "tree" and "empty" and "shove like hell" are strung together.

"Boat," the word means.

As a proof of concept, one dead tree is hacked until its center is removed, and the more pointed end is dubbed the bow. Then ten volunteers launch the new craft from the island's upper end, using paddles of various designs, each wielded with uneven talent. But the group leaders are on board—one in the bow, the other as far from his ex-lover as possible—and some observers remark that all it takes to move the craft is two young men and their curses and a good deal of shared rage.

Out they go and back they come. But not without troubles. Steering proves more difficult than the body-length models had promised. Yet they get back to the island before they are past the island, and by nightfall they are given status as one of the two successes.

The second winner proves harder to come by.

One group advocates for a floating platform, and inspired by the boat example, they vow to build the platform from the island's upper end, pushing sideways to the current with a series of rafts tied in a chain, fiber ropes anchored to heavy stones dropped along the route. Unfortunately their proof of concept goes badly and they lose all credibility. And "unfortunate" is the truth, since that scheme is workable with a few easy fixes and the human team would have reached salvation three days earlier. Which might or might not mean something in the final tally.

The third group comes up with an unworkable but intriguing plan: Crews of workers will dig up ground and stones on the island's dawn side, building a sturdy peninsula aimed at the setting sun.

"We don't mean to reach the next world," says their spokesman. "We just want to cut the distance, giving another team an easier goal."

That plan is thankfully scrapped.

The fourth group takes the personality of their leaders: Creative and quick to point out what nobody is supposed to notice. "We aren't in real danger," they argue. "Our island has been here as long as we can recall, and probably quite a bit longer. And the river has never swallowed the land. So if you want to keep busy and feel useful, maybe we can take mud and rock from every shoreline and pile it on the hilltop. As a final shelter. But we don't think there's any reason to do that, and so we don't plan to do even that."

That group is dismissed by a visibly furious leader. But being a stubborn lot, they ended up presenting a considerable problem, giving laggards excuses to sit and do nothing while everyone around them works hard.

Humans don't often agree with each other, and sometimes it seems that multiple natures exist inside the same head.

And a little too often, even the brightest humans can be simple.

The fifth group is led by the lovers who conjured flame, and flame will have to play a hand in their answer. That is an early, unspoken given, except for certain voices who are subsequently and very rudely dismissed.

Fire is an answer too perfect to ignore.

The island's wettest ground nourishes a nondescript tree—a species barely older than the language spoken by humanity. The tree produces a rich rubbery sap that can be spread in sheets and dried in a day, creating a fabric too smelly and ugly to wear. But the latex is tight to the air and indifferent to heat and sunshine, and it proves agreeable when sheets are sewn together to create one huge bladder covered with rope. Then the rope ends are tied to a platform built from lightweight wood, and the platform is dressed in thin sheets of laboriously hammered copper, better to hold the buoyant fires. And when time comes for a demonstration, the first balloon in any memory seems remarkable. If the flight is less than successful . . . well, the winds are more treacherous in the evening. Morning winds are steady, always blowing away from the new sun, and those are the same winds that will guide the flotilla across the angry water, off to a realm beyond flood and other dangers.

The boat team has its doubts, but they're fighting with one another more than outsiders, leaving the practical questions to a few underlings who don't have the authority to say much of anything.

And the boss makes her choice.

The fire-builders got first hand with resources, and it stays that way almost until the end.

The two are dubbed the "copper wonders." For the pretty fire-resistant platforms built on the first one hundred balloons.

Then the copper grows scarce.

Four, maybe five people can ride one balloon. With luck and perfect winds. Which isn't enough, and everybody endures that moment when they know it isn't enough. But the copper wonders have a gift for convincing voices and confident body language. They talk about new designs made with abundant materials. They draw pictures of enormous balloons, each as big as any hill, and while the river rises higher every night, they manage to build hopes before breakfast, and they draw more pictures, and every person in those drawings wears a hearty big smile.

✦ ✦ ✦

Humans cooperate. Many intelligent species are cooperative, but the humans on the island don't know about anyone else. Nobody is measuring themselves against unknown aliens scattered across distant and identical islands. Cooperation is born out of a sense of identity. What matters to each is how he or she is doing compared to the neighbors. The nine-thousand-plus person team is divided and subdivided, creating a thousand little teams. Each tiny team is focused on its purpose and each feels certain about its importance. Cooperation is often born out of competition, and no team wants to work badly or accomplish nothing. Every individual has a job and wants to master that job. That is the key to success on the island. Prove you can do better than anybody else at one vital task. There stands the human spirit, tall and prideful and fundamentally ignorant.

Humans believe in pride. They can kill over small mistakes involving pride, although thankfully every island brawl ends before there is a murder. Humans also are motivated by simple, bracing imagery. Every player enjoys the same fantasy: The other nine-thousand-plus standing close, pounding hands together to honor him or her. That's the island's version of applause. Human beings are hands meant to tinker when they aren't applauding their betters, and their minds were meant to tinker, and when stakes are high, those minds and hands can be tireless.

That's how boats get built and floated.

Balloons are woven and heated, rising up to the ends of heavy ropes. Most of the players drill with the newest oars, and they conjure hot fires inside the new, much more efficient copper baskets. And inside their heads, each practices the celebrations to come when they stand on the other world—a mysterious place that is going to save them and has to be wondrous because it was their salvation.

Yet for all the passion, doubters exist. A few dozen voices insist on laughing at the majority, arguing that they should ignore the river and trust in their own immortality. Certainly not a large number believe this, no. But it may well be that the doubters are blessings. Humans are motivated by quite a lot, but more than anything they adore the common enemy, and after investing all those days into inventing boats and balloons, the resident skeptics serve as binding agents for the majority.

"Screw them," the nine thousand-plus said to one another. "Work hard and leave the crap standing here, and we'll be free."

In the end, every group proves its value.

Boat builders build the fleet.

Doubters rally the rest.

Earthmovers invent wheelbarrows and the world's best shovels, and using both, construct a small upstream harbor where still water allows each boat to be tested before being safely stowed.

And when boat builders can't find enough worthy trees, bridge builders use their skills to weave good-enough boats out of foliage and knots. Which proves to be a lot faster technique than carving green wood, and suddenly a Launch Day is in sight.

Which leaves the balloon builders to contribute. But every big promise and every little lie adds to the pressures.

The people riding those picture balloons are smiling, but the humans in charge of the project stopped smiling long ago. Latex proves leakier than expected, and subject to tears, and fires have to be very hot to provide adequate lift. Several apparently sound balloons split open and crash—though nobody outside the central group knows about the disasters because those tests are being done at night, while everyone else sleeps.

Would the humans try to ride the balloons regardless?

There is the drama. Huge eager audiences on a thousand star systems are watching the competition. Everything hinges upon who is your favorite. If you love humans, you want the boats to launch. If you favor any other species, which is likely, nine thousand people riding the hot air seems like a wonderful blunder. Nobody will die. Bodies might fall into the river. But in that water, swimming just out of sight, are ten million robot doctors, and everybody can drop and nothing will be hurt, save for the good name of a small species.

In the end, it is the fire-builders, the copper wonders, who decide the human fate.

Ninety-nine days into the race, and the boss is visiting the site where balloons are stitched together and ropes are attached, and then flown for the benefit of anyone who wants to be reassured. The final balloons are elegant and efficient wonders. Copper ovens sporting long chimneys reach far into the bladders, and every balloon practically leaps into the gray-blue alien sky. The boss watches the show. She listens to numbers and projections for future numbers. The two fire-builders usually flank her during the demonstrations. Not today. The man is on her shoulder while the woman is behind them, conspicuously saying nothing.

Silence means that the conversation has gaps.

Being a talkative sort, the boss mentions something that she's noticed several times before. "Your balloons always look the same," she says, pointing at the eight swollen bladders dangling at the ends of taut lines. "Not the same as each other, no. But the same as the eight did yesterday."

She doesn't know what she has noticed. In the boss's mind, this is evidence that eight production lines are each following their own distinct plans. And the man beside her is guessing that and prepared to say as much.

But then his partner breaks down. Why then and why her are fascinating questions. The far-flung audience has watched the duo for quite a while, and the only surprise is how long it has taken the lady to declare that she has had enough. Too many lies spoken with an infectious voice, and her mate isn't sleeping with her anymore, too. And maybe the worst of it is that she burned her hand last night, fighting a fire in the woods where another one of the new balloons secretly dropped from the heavens.

"We can't make the deadlines," she announces abruptly.

Her ex-mate turns to glare at her.

The boss asks, "What is this? What are you saying?"

Looking at his only superior, the man says, "It's nothing."

Then he looks at his ex-mate, and again, with a harsher tone, he says, "It is nothing. Just some little troubles."

"It is something," she replies.

He starts to talk again. He is ready to describe new

patches that will make every balloon secure. But then his voice fails. Maybe he is too tired for a verbal battle now. Or maybe he isn't far from his ex-mate's point of view: Too many lies and too many burned hands pursuing a dream that is no more than that. A dream.

"What are you telling me?" asks the boss.

The man can't lie, but he can't talk either. It's the woman who confesses everything, saying, "There aren't enough balloons and we can't trust the balloons we have, and I wouldn't ride one to save my life. Because swimming is better than falling from the sky with fire and a useless sack of hot air."

There.

The truth lies exposed, and precious.

But then the confessor makes a fresh, unexpected promise. "But let us cut up the balloons we've built. We can work through today and all night and raise the skins on poles that I've already designed.

"Sails."

"I want to build sails for our boats.

"Catch the wind, sails can. And help us with the paddling."

Every race begins long before the starting line. There is the training, difficult and full of failure. But even before training, there is the history of the species that belongs to the race. Humans are defined by thousands of previous generations, and it's the blood and muscle and instincts of those ancestors who helped build that fleet of long boats. It is habit. It is genetics. And it is arguably about the best result that humans could have hoped for: On the hundredth morning, as the nameless sun breaks over what passes for the eastern horizon, nearly ten thousand humans climb into boats and leave together.

Even the doubters ride along.

Because for no clear reason, that is deeply important to each of them—an implanted reflex that nobody questions.

The boat ride is longer than expected. Bodies and minds trained for one level of misery find themselves aching worse than expected, and the island still feels close. But at least they picked the best course. Upstream. They paddle furiously, shoving the boats against the current. Only the slightest bend to the west is allowed, and then the terrible sprint that puts them into smoother water, closer to the next shoreline, and they turn as one fleet, only eight boats capsizing before the midway point, only forty cold bodies clinging to luckier, better boats.

More capsize when the sails deploy. That's part of the learning process. But then the latex grabs the rising breezes and every dry person paddles like mad. With several hundred people in the water, the fleet makes it to the far shore, bows into the muck, and that's the moment when memory began to return.

That is the golden moment when they finally recall what they are and everything that is at stake.

Standing united on the shoreline, most are grinning and many are singing, and shared among all is the intoxicating sense of accomplishment. Not for a final position in any race, no. But here is the sense of doing what few believed possible, and ignorant of the long odds, doing the impossible utterly well.

EDITOR'S BIOGRAPHY

Bryan Thomas Schmidt is an author and Hugo-nominated editor of adult and children's science fiction and fantasy novels and anthologies. His debut novel, *The Worker Prince*, received Honorable Mention on Barnes & Noble's Year's Best Science Fiction Releases of 2011, and was followed by two sequels. His short fiction has been published in magazines and anthologies and includes tie-in fiction in The X-Files, Predator and Decipher's WARS series. As editor, his anthologies include *Infinite Stars and Predator: If It Bleeds* (Titan, 2017), *Joe Ledger: Unstoppable* with Jonathan Maberry (St. Martin's, 2017), *The Monster Hunter Files* with Larry Correia (Baen, 2017), *Little Green Men—Attack!* with Robin Wayne Bailey (Baen, 2017), *Decision Points* (WordFire Press, 2016), *Mission: Tomorrow* (Baen, 2015), *Shattered Shields* (Baen, 2014), *Beyond The Sun* (Fairwood, 2013), *Raygun Chronicles* (Every Day Publishing, 2013) and *Space Battles* (Flying Pen Press, 2012) with five more forthcoming from Baen Books and Edge Science Fiction and Fantasy, amongst others in 2016 and beyond. He hosted *Science Fiction and Fantasy Writer's Chat* on *Twitter* under the hashtag #sffwrtcht and is a frequent guest and panelist at WorldCons and other conventions. His web site is *www.bryanthomasschmidt.net* and his *Twitter* handle is @BryanThomasS.

ACKNOWLEDGEMENTS

✧ ✧ ✧

Thanks to all the writers for trusting me with their work, even those whose work doesn't appear in these pages. All of their contributions helped shape this anthology into the book it is—one I'm very proud of. It is especially a privilege to work with such legends I am a fan of on these projects.

This book came about thanks to a *Twitter* conversation with David Rozansky, Jaleta Clegg, and several others about science fiction sports stories and how fun it would be to do an anthology on the topic. So thanks to them for giving me the genesis of the idea that became this book.

Thanks as always to Toni Weisskopf, Tony Daniel, and the Baen Family for giving me yet another opportunity.

Thanks to Toni, Karina Fabien, Gardner Dozois, Ken Keller, and Alex Shvartsman for story recommendations.

To my parents, Ramon and Glenda, and my editing partner and best friend, Valerie Hatfield, for support, encouragement, and understanding.

To Louie and Amelie, my babies, for unconditional love and snuggling.

And to God for making me a Creator in His image and opening doors for me to create.

Ryk E. Spoor
Best-Selling Author of Science Fiction and Fantasy Adventure

"Space opera in the grand old tradition ... but with modern sensibilities and awareness of current speculations in cutting edge physics." —Fantasy Book Critic

Paradigms Lost
When an informant shows up dead on his doorstep, Jason Wood is plunged into a world far stranger than he ever imagined.
Paradigms Lost * 978-1-4767-3693-8 * $15.00

Boundary Series (with Eric Flint)
A paleontologist uncovers an inexplicable fossil that will lead her on an adventure to Mars and beyond.
Boundary * 978-1-4165-5525-4 * $7.99
Threshold * 978-1-4516-3777-9 * $7.99
Portal * 978-1-4767-3642-6 * $7.99
Castaway Planet * 978-1-4767-8027-6 * $25.00

Grand Central Arena Series
In the vast, physics-defying Arena, the outcomes can mean the difference between life and death.
Grand Central Arena * 978-1-4391-3355-2 * $7.99
Spheres of Influence * 978-1-4767-3709-6 * $7.99

Balanced Sword Series
A highborn young woman must avenge her family's death and bring order to a world overrun by evil forces determined to destroy her.
Phoenix Rising * 978-1-4767-3613-6 * $7.99
Phoenix in Shadow * 978-1-4767-8037-5 * $15.00

"Fast and entertaining action and a world that has the feel of Asimov's Foundation series."—Sarah A. Hoyt, author of the Darkship saga

| 1636: The Kremlin Games | HC: 978-1-4516-3776-2 ◆ $25.00 |
| (with Gorg Huff & Paula Goodlett) | PB: 978-1-4516-3890-5 ◆ $7.99 |

| 1636: The Devil's Opera | HC: 978-1-4516-3928-5 ◆ $25.00 |
| (with David Carrico) | PB: 978-1-4767-3700-3 ◆ $7.99 |

| 1636: Commander Cantrell in the West Indies | |
| (with Charles E. Gannon) | 978-1-4767-8060-3 ◆ $8.99 |

1636: The Viennese Waltz	
(with Gorg Huff & Paula Goodlett)	HC: 978-1-4767-3687-7 ◆ $25.00
	PB: 978-1-4767-8101-3 ◆ $7.99

RING OF FIRE ANTHOLOGIES
Edited by Eric Flint

Ring of Fire	978-1-4165-0908-0 ◆ $7.99
Ring of Fire II	HC: 978-1-4165-7387-6 ◆ $25.00
	PB: 978-1-4165-9144-3 ◆ $7.99
Ring of Fire III	HC: 978-1-4391-3448-1 ◆ $25.00
	PB: 978-1-4516-3827-1 ◆ $7.99
Grantville Gazette	978-0-7434-8860-0 ◆ $7.99
Grantville Gazette II	978-1-4165-5510-0◆ $7.99
Grantville Gazette III	HC: 978-1-4165-0941-7 ◆ $25.00
	PB: 978-1-41655565-0 ◆ $7.99
Grantville Gazette IV	HC:978-1-41655554-4 ◆ $25.00
	PB: 978-1-4391-3311-8 ◆ $7.99
Grantville Gazette V	HC: 978-1-4391-3279-1 ◆ $25.00
	PB: 978-1-4391-3422-1 ◆ $7.99
Grantville Gazette VI	HC: 978-1-4516-3768-7 ◆ $25.00
	PB: 978-1-4516-3853-0 ◆ $7.99
Grantville Gazette VII	HC: 978-1-4767-8029-0 ◆ $25.00
	PB: 978-1-4767-8139-6 ◆ $7.99

MORE . . .
ERIC FLINT

THE CROWN OF SLAVES SERIES with David Weber

Crown of Slaves   978-0-7434-9899-9 ◆ $7.99

Torch of Freedom   HC: 978-1-4391-3305-7 ◆ $26.00
                                     PB: 978-1-4391-3408-5 ◆ $8.99

Cauldron of Ghosts   HC: 978-1-4767-3633-4 ◆ $25.00
                                 TPB: 978-1476780382 ◆ $15.00

THE JOE'S WORLD SERIES

The Philosophical Strangler   978-0-7434-3541-3 ◆ $7.99

Forward the Mage   978-0-7434-7146-6 ◆ $7.99
(with Richard Roach)

THE HEIRS OF ALEXANDRIA SERIES

The Shadow of the Lion   978-0-7434-7147-3 ◆ $7.99
(with Mercedes Lackey & Dave Freer)

This Rough Magic   978-0-7434-9909-5 ◆ $7.99
(with Mercedes Lackey & Dave Freer)

Much Fall of Blood   HC: 978-1-4391-3351-4 ◆ $27.00
(with Mercedes Lackey & Dave Freer)   PB: 978-1-4391-3416-0 ◆ $7.99

Burdens of the Dead   HC: 978-1-4516-3874-5 ◆ $25.00
(with Mercedes Lackey & Dave Freer)   PB: 978-1-4767-3668-6 ◆ $7.99

The Wizard of Karres   978-1-4165-0926-4 ◆ $7.99
(with Mercedes Lackey & Dave Freer)

The Sorceress of Karres   HC: 978-1-4391-3307-1 ◆ $24.00
(with Dave Freer)   PB: 978-1-4391-3446-7 ◆ $7.99

The Best of Jim Baen's Universe   1-4165-5558-7 ◆ $7.99

MORE . . .
ERIC FLINT

Mission of Honor hc • 978-1-4391-3361-3 • $27.00
pb • 978-1-4391-3451-1 • $7.99

The unstoppable juggernaut of the mighty Solarian League is on a collision course with Manticore. But if everything Honor Harrington loves is going down to destruction, it won't be going alone.

A Rising Thunder hc • 978-1-4516-3806-6 • $26.00
trade pb • 978-1-4516-3871-4 • $15.00
pb • 978-1-4767-3612-9 • $7.99

Shadow of Freedom hc • 978-1-4516-3869-1 • $25.00
trade pb • 978-1-4767-3628-0 • $15.00
pb • 978-1-4767-8048-1 • $7.99

The survival of Manticore is at stake as Honor must battle not only the powerful Solarian League, but also the secret puppetmasters who plan to pick up all the pieces after galactic civilization is shattered.

HONORVERSE VOLUMES:

Crown of Slaves (with Eric Flint)   pb • 0-7434-9899-2 • $7.99
Torch of Freedom (with Eric Flint)   hc • 1-4391-3305-0 • $26.00
pb • 978-1-4391-3408-5 • $8.99
Cauldron of Ghosts (with Eric Flint)
hc • 978-1-4767-3633-4 • $25.00
pb • 978-1-4767-8100-6 • $8.99

Sent on a mission to keep Erewhon from breaking with Manticore, the Star Kingdom's most able agent and the Queen's niece may not even be able to escape with their lives. . .

House of Steel (with Bu9)   hc • 978-1-4516-3875-2 • $25.00
trade pb • 978-1-4516-3893-6 • $15.00
pb • 978-1-4767-3643-3 • $7.99

The Shadow of Saganami   hc • 0-7434-8852-0 • $26.00
pb • 1-4165-0929-1 • $7.99

THE DAHAK SERIES:

Mutineers' Moon   pb • 0-671-72085-6 • $7.99
The Armageddon Inheritance   pb • 0-671-72197-6 • $7.99
Heirs of Empire   pb • 0-671-87707-0 • $7.99
Empire from the Ashes   tpb • 1-4165-0993-X • $16.00
Contains *Mutineers' Moon, The Armageddon Inheritance*
and *Heirs of Empire* in one volume.

THE BAHZELL SAGA:

Oath of Swords   trade pb • 1-4165-2086-4 • $15.00
     pb • 0-671-87642-2 • $7.99
The War God's Own   hc • 0-671-87873-5 • $22.00
     pb • 0-671-57792-1 • $7.99
Wind Rider's Oath   hc • 0-7434-8821-0 • $26.00
     pb • 1-4165-0895-3 • $7.99
War Maid's Choice   hc • 978-1-4516-3835-6 • $26.00
     pb • 978-1-4516-3901-8 • $7.99
The Sword of the South   hc • 978-1-4767-8085-6 • $26.00
Bahzell Bahnakson of the hradani is no knight in shin-
ing armor and doesn't want to deal with anybody else's
problems, let alone the War God's. The War God thinks
otherwise.

BOLO VOLUMES:

Bolo!   hc • 0-7434-9872-0 • $25.00
     Keith Laumer's popular saga of the Bolos continues.

Old Soldiers   pb • 1-4165-2104-6 • $7.99
A new Bolo novel.

OTHER NOVELS:

The Excalibur Alternative   hc • 0-671-31860-8 • $21.00
     pb • 0-7434-3584-2 • $7.99
An English knight and an alien dragon join forces to over-
throw the alien slavers who captured them. Set in the
world of David Drake's *Ranks of Bronze*.